THE BOOKWOMAN'S LAST FLING

A CLIFF JANEWAY NOVEL

JOHN DUNNING

THORNDIKE PRESS

An imprint of Thomson Gale, a part of The Thomson Corporation

THOMSON

™

GALE

Detroit • New York • San Francisco • New Haven, Conn. • Waterville, Maine • London • Munich

THOMSON

GALE

™

LARGE PRINT
MYS
DUN

LIBRARY OF CONGRESS CATALOGING-IN-PUBLICATION DATA

Dunning, John, 1942–
    The bookwoman's last fling : a Cliff Janeway novel / by John Dunning.
        p. cm.
    "Thorndike Press large print basic" — T.p. verso.
    ISBN 0-7862-8793-4 (alk. paper)
    1. Janeway, Cliff (Fictitious character) — Fiction. 2. Booksellers and book-selling — Fiction. 3. Antiquarian booksellers — Fiction. 4. Ex-police offic-ers — Fiction. 5. Horse trainers — Crimes against — Fiction. 6. Book col-lectors — Fiction. 7. Idaho — Fiction. I. Title.
    PS9554.U494B67 2006
    813'.54 — dc22   2006012665

Published in 2006 in arrangement with Scribner, an imprint of Simon & Schuster, Inc.

Printed in the United States of America on permanent paper
10 9 8 7 6 5 4 3 2 1

This is for Helen,
for all the reasons there are.
Love and hugs forever,
from the room far below.

ACKNOWLEDGMENTS

Thanks again to Susanne Kirk, who watched over the manuscript, edited it, and kept my stuff straight: who, more than that, pulled Janeway and me out of her slush pile years ago.

To Susan Moldow, who runs the Scribner ship and keeps us all heading north.

To Sarah Knight, who provided great wiseguy yin and yang.

To Phyllis Westberg, my agent since the world began.

To old pals Wick Downing and Pat McGuire for good cheer and wise counsel.

And to the racetracker pals of my youth. To Fred Bates, who rubbed 'em. To Jon Kunitake, who rode 'em. And to Bob Tessier, the drummer guy from Boston. We had a happy shedrow together, forty years ago. Where are they now?

1

The morning was angry but I was cool. The rain rolled in from the west like a harbinger of some vast evil brewing but I had the man's money in my bank account, it was mine, he couldn't get it back unless I went nuts and decided to give it to him, and that made me cool. I had followed his orders almost to the letter, varying them just enough to satisfy my own persnickety nature. Long before the first faint light broke through the black clouds, I got up, dressed, got out of my motel room, and drove out toward the edge of town.

I found the all-night diner without a hitch; parked at the side and sat in my cold car with the motor idling. I was early. I had been told to come at five o'clock, no more or less, but I tend to ignore advice like that, especially when it comes with an attitude. I waited ten minutes and the appointed hour came and went. I could sense his presence off to my left beyond the parking lot: If I looked hard at that patch of darkness I could make out the vaguest shape of a car or truck, a vehicle of some kind in a small grove of trees. At five-oh-five by the clock in my car I got out and went inside. The waiter took my order, a slam-bang something with eggs and pancakes: enough cholesterol to power the whole state of Idaho. I consoled myself. I seldom eat like that anymore unless I am on the road, and apparently I am one of the lucky ones: I have great genes and my so-called good cholesterol readings are always sensational. No matter how much fat I eat, my system burns it. To my knowledge, no one in my family tree has ever died of a heart attack, which only means that I have a fine opportunity to be the first one.

The waiter tried to make the cook understand what I wanted through a serious language barrier. The cook looked illegal as hell: he spoke a kind of Spanglish through the window and the waiter struggled with that. I sat through two cups of coffee and no one came out of the lot beyond parking. My breakfast was surprisingly tasty and hot; I ate it slowly and looked up occasionally for some sign of life in the parking lot. When I looked at my watch again, it was five-thirty. The man was half an hour late.

I stretched out my legs and waited some more. If he didn't come at all it was truly his loss. I had five thousand of his American big ones and that usually guaranteed good faith. I could buy a fairly nice book with that. It was my rock-bottom minimum these days, the least it took for a stranger like him to get me off my dead ass in Denver and on the road to some distant locale. I got the money up front for just such contingencies as this one: a client with guff to match my own. That's one thing people had said about Harold Ray Geiger in all the newspaper accounts I had read of his life and death. He was abrupt, and so was the guy who had called me.

Geiger's man was also mysterious, enigmatic to a fault. He had sent me a cashier's check, so I still didn't know his full name. "My name is Willis," he had said on the phone. "I am Mr. Geiger's representative in Idaho." Normally I wouldn't touch a job like this: I certainly wouldn't leave home and make such a drive without knowing certain salient details. What had sold me on the case were the books. Geiger had died last month with a vast library of great first editions, the estate had a problem with them, and that was partly what I did now. I seldom did appraisal work: I found that boring and there were others who could do it faster and at least as well. There can be huge differences between honest appraisers and I tend to be too condition-conscious for people who, for reasons of their own, want their appraisals high. But I would help recover stolen books, I would try to unravel a delicate book mystery, I would do things, and not always for money, that got me out in the sunshine, away from my bookstore in Denver and into another man's world. It all depended on the man, and the voice on the phone seemed to belong to a five-grand kind of guy.

Six o'clock came and went. I rolled with it, prepared to sit here half the morning. The man deserved no less than that for five thousand dollars.

At some point I saw the truck move out of the shadows and bump its way into the parking lot. It was one of those big bastards with wheels half the size of Rhode Island. The sky was still quite dark and the rain drummed relentlessly on the roof of the truck. I could see his knuckles gripping the wheel — nothing of his face yet, just that white-knuckle grip beyond the glass. I knew he had a clear look at me through the windshield, and at one point I smiled at him and tried to look pleasant. But I had a come-if-you-want-to, don't-if-you-don't attitude of my own. The ball was in his court.

Eventually he must have realized this, for I saw the unmistakable signs of life. A light went on in the truck and a man in a hat and dark glasses materialized. He climbed down and came inside.

"You Janeway?"

I recognized his voice from that cryptic phone call a week ago. I said, "Yep. And you would perhaps be representing the estate of Mr. Harold Ray Geiger?"

"I'm Willis. I was Mr. Geiger's right-hand man for more than thirty years."

He sat in the booth and sent up a signal for coffee. He didn't offer his hand and I didn't try to take it. There was another moment when I might have taken it by force, but then he had moved both hands into his lap and I figured groping around between his legs might cast us both in a bad light. From the kitchen the Mexican cook was watching us.

The mystery man sat sipping his coffee.

"Do you have a first name, Mr. Willis?"

"Yes, I have a first name." He said this with dripping sarcasm, a tone you use with a moron if you are that kind of guy. Already I didn't like him; we were off to a bad start.

11

"Should I try to guess it? You look like somebody named Clyde, or maybe Junior."

I said this in a spirit of lighthearted banter, I hoped, but he bristled. "My first name doesn't matter. I am the man who will either take you out to Mr. Geiger's ranch or leave you to wonder for the rest of your life what this might have been."

Now it was my turn to stifle a laugh.

"Are you making light of this?" I sensed a blink behind his dark shades. "Are you trying to annoy me?"

"Actually, Mr. Willis, I was starting to think it was the other way around."

"You've got a helluva nerve, coming out here with an attitude."

"I wasn't aware I had one."

"Keep it up and you can just climb right back in that car and get the hell out of here."

I stared at him for a long moment. I was suddenly glad I had been paid by cashier's check: his money was now firmly in my bank.

"I want it established right from the start," he said: "You are working for me. You will appraise Mr. Geiger's books and do it ASAP. If it turns out that books are missing and lost forever, I want you to give me a document to that effect, something that will satisfy God, the executor of Mr. Geiger's will, and any other interested party who happens to ask. Is that clear enough?"

"I wasn't told I had to satisfy God as well as all those other people."

"I am not paying you for that kind of wiseass commentary. I was told you are a reliable professional and that's what I want from you. That's all I want."

"Well, let's see if I understand it so far. You want me to look at some books. Supposedly there are some missing titles. I'm to give you a written appraisal and do it on the quickstep. I'm to tell you what's missing based on your assertion that these missing books were ever there in the first place. I'm to do all this in a cheerless environment; I'm not allowed to ever crack a joke or even smile once in a while for comic relief. Twice a day you send a gnome up with bread and water and he hands it to me through the bars. I get to go pee occasionally, as long as I don't abuse this privilege; otherwise it's pucker-up-and-hold-it time. Is that about it?"

"I don't like your attitude."

"We've already established that." I slipped into my Popeye voice. "But I yam what I yam, Mr. Willis. That's what you get for your money, which by the way isn't all that great. And it's looking less great the more we talk."

13

"Then leave," he said in an *I dare you* tone.

I slid out of the booth, picked up the check, and started toward the counter. I sensed his disbelief as I paid the tab and sidled back to the booth to leave the waiter a tip.

"Thanks for the call. Give my regards to Idaho Falls."

I was halfway across the parking lot when I heard the door open. He said my name, just "Janeway," and I stopped and turned politely.

"What are you, crazy? You haven't even heard what this is about."

"Believe me, I would still love to be told."

"Then stop acting so goddam superior."

"It's not an act, Clyde. I don't have any act. This may surprise you, but I have lived all these years without any of Mr. Geiger's money. I've gotten wherever I am with no help at all from you guys, and I'm willing to bet I can go the rest of the way on my own as well. I do appreciate the business, however."

"Wait a minute."

We looked at each other.

"What do you think, I brought you out here just for the hell of it?"

"I have no idea why you do what you do. If you want to talk, let's go. Your five grand has already bought you that privilege."

He stood there for another moment as if, with enough time, he could reclaim some of the high ground he had lost. "You're a slick piece of change, aren't you?"

"Yes, sir, I am. I may not be much of many things, but I am slick. Two things before we go. First take off those glasses, please. I like to see who I'm talking to."

He took them off slowly, and in that act the authority passed all the way from him to me. His eyes were gray, like a timber wolf or a very old man.

"Thank you. Now tell me, please, who you are. Is Willis your first name or last?"

"Last."

"What's your first?"

He stared at me for a long moment. Then he said, "Junior." I swear he did, and that confession made the whole trip worthwhile.

2

I called him Mr. Willis after that. I try to be polite unless people deliberately piss me off, the man was older than me by at least twenty years, and respecting my elders is part of my code. He could have been any age between an old fifty-five and a well-preserved seventy. I parked my car on the street and we drove out of town in his Sherman tank. The city lights fell away and the rain came hard again. I could now see a faint streak of light in the east, but it was still too faint to matter. He drove about ten miles and turned into a dirt road posted KEEP OUT; fenced on both sides with the distinctive wooden slats of a horse ranch.

That was the other thing I knew about Geiger from his obit: In addition to his book collection he had been a horse racing man. But I'd soon found out that I had this chronology backward. In addition to being a lifelong horseman, Geiger had a book collection. Horses were his life and books were now part of it, a combination I found irresistible. I had always been partial to the horse, a nobler, wiser, much gentler, and far more majestic creature than man. I had been an enthusiastic customer at Centennial Race Track in Littleton, just south of Denver, until it closed in 1983. I was one of those daring young kids who got in as soon as the law allowed and maybe a little sooner than that. This was years before my police career began. I had been drawn to the turf by the spectacle, not so much as the lure of fast money. Before I was ten I had read all of Walter Farley's wonderful *Black Stallion* novels, and for a year I pictured myself as an impossible cross between Alec Ramsey and Eddie Arcaro. Of course I could never have been a jockey — I was still a growing boy and already pushing 175 pounds, but at eighteen I could spend entire afternoons watching the races. I talked to the grooms over the rail and I quickly learned their lingo. They were called ginneys, a term going back to old racing days in England, when winning owners tipped their grooms a guinea. Today, I had heard, well-heeled owners passed out bills, not coins, featuring Jackson and Grant, occasionally a Franklin if the winning pot had been good enough. I knew these things, though I had never crossed that magical line between the grandstand and the backside. I knew where the class raced, at Hialeah and Gulfstream in Florida, at Aqueduct, Belmont, and Jamaica in New York, and on the West Coast at Santa Anita and Hollywood Park, among other fabled places. I struggled with algebra but I knew the difference between allowance races and claimers. Claiming races were the guts of almost any racing program. Here a horse's true grit could be calculated, scientifically some said, against others of similar company. In a claiming race, each owner was putting a price on his horse, and the horse could be bought — claimed — by any other owner at the meet who was willing to pay the claiming price. At the same time, the price was a measure of a horse's class. How I loved those hazy, distant Saturdays at Centennial. I was caught up in the majesty of the post parade and the drama of the race, and I didn't care whether I had the two bucks for a bet.

Willis clattered and splashed us along the dirt road for a good quarter-mile. The country here was mostly a gently rolling plain. Occasionally there were trees; I could see them now as the black sky became reluctantly gray; nestled among them were

18

some barns and beyond it all was the house. We turned in among the barns and came up to a small training track. There I got my first look at a man who might have been Geiger in earlier times. He stood at the rail watching an exercise boy work a horse in the slop: a stoop-shouldered figure in silhouette, lonely as hell by the look of him. He wasn't wearing a GEIGER sign on his heavy black slicker; I just figured he was one of the old man's three sons, the way you sometimes figure things out. He glanced over his shoulder as we went past and that's how he took note of us; no wave of the hand, no other movement at all. He wore a hood that showed nothing of his face. He just stood there like some grim reaper in a bad dream; then he turned away as the boy galloped his horse around the track again to complete the mile.

Willis didn't stop and I didn't ask. We didn't exchange any wisdom or wit; he didn't pull up under the big old tree and start showing me pictures of his grandchildren or his prizewinning roses. Sudden camaraderie was not about to break out between us, so my best bet was to keep my mouth shut and not annoy him more than I already had. This I did while he drove along the track and around it, turning up the road to the house, which now loomed before us in the rain. It was an old two-story house, old when Geiger had bought it would be my guess, built here sometime well before the 1920s for another old sodbuster now long dead. None of that mattered now. Willis pulled around to the side and parked under a long overhang. A set of steps went straight up from there. We got out of the car, he gestured at me sullenly, and I went up ahead of him, emerging onto a wide wraparound porch. I stood at the railing looking out at the farm, which was just coming to life in the gray morning. I could see up to the track where the horse was being led back through the gap. The groom held him while the hooded man stood apart, and the boy sat straight in the saddle. On the road he hopped off and they all walked down to the barn where a black man stood waiting with a hot bucket of water. They were a hundred yards away but my eyes were good. The ginney washed the mud off his horse and then skimmed off the water with a scraper. Steam floated off the horse like the bubbling ponds around Old Faithful, but I still couldn't see anything of the hooded man's face. His hood kept him dark and mysterious.

I heard Willis cough behind me. He said,

"You comin'?" and I said yeah sure. His tone remained surly while I tried to keep mine evenly pleasant. I followed him into the house through a side door. He said, "Wait here," and for once I did as I was told. He disappeared along a totally black corridor. A moment later a light came on, far down at the end of the hallway on the other side of the house. He motioned me with his hand and turned into the room. Almost at once I was aware of another light beaming out into the hall, and when I reached it I saw Willis sitting behind an enormous desk. My eyes also took in two dozen horse pictures on the far wall, winner's circle pictures with an oil painting in the center. The centerpiece was a great painting of a magnificent red stallion. The caption said, *Man o' War, 1921.*

"I've got a few chores to do before we talk," Willis said. This was okay. For the moment I was at the man's beck and call; if I computed what he was paying me on a per-hour basis, I would be way ahead of the game for the seeable future. I had never made anything close to this kind of money when I was a cop, so if he wanted me to sit I could sit here all week. At some point I would hear his story, I'd tell him what if anything I could do or try to do for him, and maybe, if the answer was nothing and his demeanor was civilized, I'd consider giving him a chunk of his money back. For the moment I didn't want to drop even a hint of that possibility. Willis asked if I wanted coffee. I didn't; I had had my quota in the restaurant but I said sure, I'd take a cup, I'd be sociable. *Who knows, it might help us break some ice,* I thought. Willis disappeared and I was left to give the room another inspection alone.

The first thing I noticed was, there were no books anywhere.

The second thing, which took me slightly longer to determine, was that Geiger himself appeared in none of the winner's circle pictures. I got up and walked along the wall looking at them.

A winner's circle picture, in addition to being a quality professional photograph, gives some good information in three or four lines. First there is the name of the winning horse. Then it tells the racetrack where the win occurred; then the date, the name of the winning jockey, the horses that ran second and third, the distance, the winner's time, and the names of the owner and trainer. In all of these, H. R. Geiger was named as the owner and trainer, but the only men who had come down to stand with the winning horse and jockey were Willis and the groom. There was no gang of celebrants in any of them and this, maybe, told me a little more about Geiger. Even in cheap claiming races a crowd often assembles around the winning horse. The groom must be there to hold the horse; the jockey, still seated in the saddle, and a whole bunch of people dressed in suits and ties, flowery dresses or plain shirts and jeans, all friends of the winning owner. I had seen winner's circle pictures that had twenty grinning people crowded together as if they personally had pushed the hapless nag the entire six furlongs. But here was a whole wall showing only four faces in each: Willis and the groom, the jockey, and the horse. Willis wore his western attire, boots, the hat, and a string tie tight at his neck. The pictures were in chronological order. The oldest was from April 1962, the most recent from March 1975, about twenty years ago. Geiger's winner in that first shot had been a dark filly named Miss Ginny, who had gone to the post with all four legs wrapped. Willis was a slender young man in those days, he stood almost timidly; the jockey wore a look of authority as if he, not Willis, had been running things; and the groom was a serious black kid who looked straight into the camera. The picture had been taken at Hot Springs, Arkansas: a bright, sunny day from the look of it. The top half of the photo shows the finish line and I could see that Miss Ginny had won handily, beating the place horse by five lengths.

I moved along the wall looking at each individual picture until, at some point, I felt uneasy. I didn't know why then: If I had thought about it at all I might have attributed it to the almost unnatural sameness of the people in the circle. From year to year they never changed places: it was always Willis standing alone on the far left, then a broad gap, then the groom, the horse, and the rider. The jockey was the same skinny white kid for that first half-year; then a series of jocks had replaced him, each riding for the old man for a year, more or less. The ginney was mostly the same black kid; he had been in the first picture and was in the last, with three white kids taking turns with him, holding the horse in the sixties. What was so unusual about that? I finally decided it must be Willis. He wasn't the owner or the trainer; he didn't hold the horse; he had no real purpose in the picture as far as I could see, and yet there he was, standing far apart, staring into the camera with that same eerie way he had. Expressionless — that's how I would describe him. He looked almost like a mannequin, a man with no soul.

"Here's your coffee," he said suddenly from the doorway.

I turned and looked into those vacant gray eyes. His expression never changed: maybe that was part of it. Only when I had irritated him back at the restaurant was it plain just from looking at him that I had. I said thanks and took the mug. Our hands touched briefly before he drew his away. His skin was cold. He wore his western shirt buttoned tight around his neck — not even the string tie to give him a more naturally uptight look. If uptight was what he was trying to project, Junior Willis was doing that. His long sleeves were also buttoned, and the whole picture was of a man who couldn't relax even for a moment. He had not brought any coffee for himself, and as soon as he had delivered mine he left the room again. I drank it to be polite and waited some more. Fifteen minutes passed, marked by no sound other than the ticking of the clock in the corner. I heard footsteps: Someone walked down the porch just past the window. I heard a door close and I figured whoever it was had come inside. There was a momentary murmur, two voices talking in monotone: then an angry shout. "God*dammm*it, doesn't she realize these horses can lose the best part of their racing lives while they screw around with a snag in the will? We've got to get everybody on board and pulling in the same direction here." I heard Junior's voice, lower but still mostly distinct. "Let me warn you about something, Damon. I know she's your sister," and at that moment Damon said, "*Half* sister, goddammit, *half* sister!" There was a pause, then Junior said, "Maybe she's your sister but I know her a helluva lot better than you do, and I'm telling you, you'd better not try any of your loudmouth bullyboy tactics on her. In the first place, she doesn't care whether these horses ever race. In the second place, she won't be moved by money or threats, and in the third place, it's just plain dumb to piss her off. Let me work on her." There was more talk in lower muffled tones, as if they had moved away and were standing across a room or perhaps in the next one. Nothing then for another ten minutes. I looked at the clock and soon I heard footsteps again.

Willis came in alone. Now he looked more annoyed than before. I watch people in situations like that, I am a veritable hub of nerve-endings, I notice changes, and what I

26

knew at the moment was that some kind of change had occurred, no matter how small. A change in the face of an unchangeable man is something you notice. I tried to make it easy on him: I sat at the front of the desk and said, "Just been looking at your pictures," and Willis only nodded. He didn't seem to be focusing well; he was trembling mad. Then, almost thirty seconds later, his eyes did focus on the wall and he said, "So what do they tell you?" I thought there was a clue in that: He was trying a little too hard to find out if I could see my own hand in front of my face. So I looked again and suddenly I saw what I had missed the first time around. Then I had been looking too intently at the action in the winner's circle itself: now I saw a dozen flecks of white behind it as I quickly skimmed the whole gallery. In April 1963 a woman had stood in front of the lower grandstand behind the winner's circle. Her face was clear in that first long-ago shot; I could see that she was decked out in a white dress with a carnation on her lapel. I glanced at the next picture and there she was again, same white dress, fresh carnation, and she stood in the same place behind the circle. Whatever had just happened on that spring day in 1963, she liked it. I didn't point this out immediately. I said, "They tell me you've been with Geiger a long time," and I glanced at the other pictures. The woman was always in the same place behind the action, in that gap between Willis and the horse. For more than ten years, with some notable gaps, she had been there when Geiger had won a race.

"Who's the woman?" I said.

"Mr. Geiger's wife."

"Was there a reason why she never came down in the winner's circle?"

"I'm sure there was. There must have been."

"Am I supposed to guess that as well?"

"Go ahead. I won't be able to tell you if you're right; I never discussed things like that with either of them. But give it a shot if you want to."

"Well, let's see. She was shy. She was humble. She was eccentric or quiet or just superstitious."

"Interesting choice of guesses."

"Which would you pick?"

I didn't think he'd answer that. But after a moment he said, "Maybe all of them."

"Interesting answer."

"She was an interesting lady."

"I take it from the past tense that Mrs. Geiger is no longer with us."

"She died in 1975. She was just forty years old."

"Was this an unexpected illness?"

"You sound suspicious."

"I was a cop for years. Homicide cops are always suspicious when people die."

"It was quite unexpected. She had severe allergies."

"And that's what killed her?"

He nodded. "Mr. Geiger was devastated. They were very close."

"Did he stop racing after that?"

"Not right away. But he didn't put up any pictures after she died."

"He didn't need to. What he's got fills up the wall nicely."

"There are many more in the file. Mr. Geiger won a lot of races. But this represents the best of them . . . the best of her. It covers the whole brief time they were together."

I didn't know whether to find this touching or morbid. She had been dead about twenty years and he seemed to be saying that Geiger had never stopped mourning. I left some open pages in my notebook, where Mrs. Geiger had died, and creased the corners.

"There were some gaps in the continuity," I said. "Here's just one in 1964, then she was back again in 1966, then there are other gaps along the way."

He looked at the 1964 shot. "That's when she was . . . that's when she had Sharon. Her daughter."

He was still uptight: he had trouble saying the word *pregnant,* and he quickly changed the subject. "Lots of people recommended you. Still, I can't help wondering how much of a book expert you are in real life."

"That depends. I know how to tell the front free endpaper from an errata sheet. I know a first edition when I see one. Beyond that it gets fuzzy pretty fast. There comes a point where the best expert is the guy with a good gut . . . the guy who's cautious and on guard . . . who's got the best instincts. The guy who can look at a book he's never seen before and say, 'that knocks my socks off,' and be right almost every time. And the guy who knows how to look it up once his instincts have been, so to speak, aroused."

I told him there are experts on Americana, good solid bookmen who know nothing and don't care about modern lit. "I am a generalist. That means I know a bit about a lot of things and not everything about anything. I have a fair understanding of what makes a book valuable, and I've got a good system for finding out what I myself don't know."

He stared at me.

"Just for the record," I said, "I have never called myself an expert on anything. But I've got good juice. When I see a book I usually know if it's a bad one, just a good one, or maybe a great one. Beyond that we've got to search and find out."

This seemed to please him. "How do you do this searching?"

"I've got a good reference library. And I was on the book fair circuit for most of a year. I saw some great books and I made some great contacts. Specialist dealers, collectors, experts in their fields, guys I can call on if I need them. And a few gals, too."

"How are your experts on kids' books?"

"I know just the man if the books are good enough. The best expert you can get."

Immediately I had thought of Carroll Shaw. Shaw was the curator of the booming collection of juvenile material at the Blakely Library in Northern California. I knew him the way many booksellers and librarians come to know each other, as voices on the telephone. I also knew a high-end specialist in Americana and a librarian who was putting together a collection of incunabula. I had never met any of these men but we had done some good business together, and a mutual trust had formed between us. That year I spent on the book fair circuit was like a postgraduate course in bookselling. I discovered again what I had heard long ago through the grapevine, that a bookman is only as good as his contacts. If I came across a great piece of scarce juvenilia, I knew Shaw would buy it and he wouldn't quibble over the price. Sometimes when I called and he wasn't in, when I was on the road and time was running short, I would buy a piece for him on a blind, at my own risk. Once I spent fifteen thousand on a book I had never seen but I knew well by reputation, I liked it and I was ready to live with it if it went bad. I liked Shaw because he always got me the money with no hassle. I didn't have to hard-sell him a book, I never wasted his time with second-grade stuff, and now he had become one of my valued contacts. I scratched his back; he scratched mine. He was always my first stop when I needed a quick answer to an obscure question on an eighteenth-century kids' book. A ten-minute phone call often saved me ten hours of digging through reference books.

"That's good," Junior said, warming to me, at least for the moment.

I turned again to the wall of pictures. "Mrs. Geiger was a striking woman. Is there a reason for the white dress?"

"She liked it. Isn't that reason enough?"

"Maybe. But this goes beyond liking something, don't you think? Was it some kind of good-luck thing, a superstition of some kind?"

He didn't answer that. After a while I said, "It's almost like a fetish."

I braced for another explosion but he faced this invasion into Mrs. Geiger's character calmly.

"She did believe strongly in luck if that's what you're asking."

"I guess what I'm asking is how relevant all this might be to the real reason I'm here. Look, I'm perfectly willing to shoot the breeze, but if there's a point I'm missing it."

"Mrs. Geiger was the book collector."

"Ah."

"She was a very serious book collector. She spent at least as much money on her books as Mr. Geiger spent on his stable."

"You can buy a lot of books for what one of these horses would cost you."

"Or maybe just one. It's like anything else; it's relative. At least I've learned that much this year. You can buy a cheap horse or a cheap book. Expensive horse, expensive book. She knew what she was doing with books just like Mr. Geiger always knew horses. She was damned good at it. Maybe

33

you think you're good at it but I'd bet serious money that she was better. She was a helluva great bookwoman. She could have been a dealer at the top levels of your profession."

"Why wasn't she?"

"She didn't choose to be. Money didn't matter, so why sell 'em if you don't need to?"

"What kind of stuff did she collect?"

"Kids' books, history, you name it. No popular junk history . . . original documents, early books. If a book had significance she knew what that was, like you were just saying about experts, and she bought it. She never worried about the money, but she knew that a truly rare one would go nowhere but up. Didn't matter what field it was in, she had a feeling for a great book."

"There are people like that. I envy the hell out of 'em."

"There was no one like Candice. Someday somebody will write a book about *her* and her books."

"Sounds like you know a bit about it yourself."

"I know what I could learn in my spare time. I've been reading up on it, trying to make sense of it. But by the time I knew enough to talk to her about it . . ."

I arched my eyes, waiting for the answer.

"By then she had been gone for years," he said.

"So you do know books, is that what you're saying?"

"I've been trying to educate myself, but it's not easy when you're tucked away in Nowhere, Idaho, and you've got nobody to talk to. Like you said, there's a lot to learn, a lot of trial and error, and I've got horses to take care of. I can sometimes tell one edition from another, but I don't know enough to appraise anything. The terminology alone . . . but that's why I need you, isn't it?"

I walked along the wall and looked at the pictures, paying no attention now to the horses or to Willis. Now I looked at her. She was always directly in the center, never more than ten feet behind the circle: apart yet central. Her face was the one ever-changing element. She wasn't beautiful but she sure was striking. She had an unforgettable face. She looked like a lady, then a temptress, then a reveler; she looked thoughtful and regal, mischievous and funny and sad. In one shot she stuck out her tongue impishly, and in the very next one, taken on the same day at Ak-Sar-Ben in Omaha, she looked ready to cry. Geiger had won two races that day.

"She looks drugged in this one," I said.

"She should have been an actress. She'd have been a great one."

"But she didn't do drugs . . ."

"Hell no. Do us all a favor, don't go there again."

"Did she ever do any theater?"

"No. She played all her roles just for him."

I thought we had arrived at an unexpectedly intimate place in our talk. He smiled, the first time I had seen that from him, on the wall or in person, and I felt myself trying to warm toward him in spite of my earlier misgivings. I knew there was more that needed saying but for the moment I wasn't inclined to push him. Then I said, "Tell me about them, Mr. Willis," and I seemed to be pushing him after all.

"What do you want to know?"

"How long did he race after she died?"

"For a while, but there came a time when his heart wasn't in it. He didn't feel the need anymore, and God knows he didn't need the money. But once a year we went to the yearling sales and if he saw one he liked, he bought it."

"And did what with it?"

"Just enjoyed having it, and working with it. Watching it grow and learn, watching it

36

run in the early morning. I don't suppose you'll understand that."

"And he never considered going back to racing?"

"I think he toyed with it. Sometimes he'd say to me, 'I think we'll take this one to Santa Anita this winter,' or, 'Maybe we'll go to Hollywood Park this year.' But he never did. He had been a master with cheap bad-legged horses; that's what he was great at and enjoyed doing. He loved taking a horse nobody thought would run again and bringing it back."

A quiet moment passed. "We've got some classy horses here now," he said. "Not like the old days, when everything had to be patched together. Some damn good studs, some truly fine broodmares . . ."

I thought that might explain the man in the hood working the horse in the rain, but now I had to ask. "Who's the man up at the track?"

"Mr. Geiger's son Damon. He arrived here late last week."

"How was his relationship with his dad?"

"Hasn't had any, not for years. None of them have." He watched me out of the corner of his eye. "Now you'll be wondering what he's doing working the horses."

I nodded. The thought had crossed my mind.

"Go ask him," he said, without any warmth.

"So Damon just shows up and starts giving orders. Have I got it right so far?"

"That's about it."

"Any reason for him to think he can do that?"

Willis shrugged slightly.

"You ever think of stopping him?"

"Damon doesn't stop real easy. He is a blood relative, and I imagine he thinks that makes some kind of difference."

"Does it?" I asked. "Where are the other sons?"

"Cameron's already here. He was sniffing around before Mr. Geiger died. I expect Bax'll be here sometime."

"He didn't come to the funeral?"

"None of 'em came, except Sharon."

"So if and when Bax does get here, then what?"

"Then we'll see. I don't think there's any love lost between any of 'em. But how would I know, I've never had much to do with those three."

"And now the old man's dead and the food fight begins over his estate."

"That's one way to put it."

"What did Mr. Geiger's will say?"

"The farms go to Sharon. I'll eventually get some of the horses. Bax gets some; so does Damon. I guess we'll have to fight over which ones. And there's a sizable cash bequest that's split up among us."

"Split five ways?"

"Four."

I looked at my fingers and counted out five. "Cameron was disinherited," Willis said.

I arched an eyebrow and he said, "That seems clear enough. He's a bad one."

"What about the books?"

"They're part of the estate. Sharon will probably want them. But we'll see."

I wrote some notes. "You mentioned farms, plural."

"There's another one in California."

Then, off the cuff, he said, "It was their private place. Candice died there."

I tried to move him back to the books but he couldn't find the words to get started. At last he said, "Candice . . . Mrs. Geiger . . . collected books all her life. She was a true . . . what's the name for it?"

"Bibliophile," I told him.

"That word makes me cringe. It doesn't sound quite respectable somehow."

"You're thinking of *bibliomaniac*. There's a

difference."

"Explain it to me."

"A bibliophile truly loves books, a bibliomaniac just hoards 'em."

"Why the hell would anybody do that?"

"At its worst it becomes a mental illness. Bibliomaniacs have been known to fill up houses with books they never read. They get their books however and wherever they can. If they have no money . . ."

"They'll steal 'em."

"Many have gone that route. Some have become amazing thieves, able to get major treasures out of libraries all over the country. But they'll also steal from a Goodwill store. Having the book becomes far more important than what the book is."

"They sound like a bunch of goddam crackpots."

I told him about bibliomaniacs, some I had known myself. One Denver man had so many books his foundation had cracked and the house had listed wildly toward the Rockies. The place was crammed with books to the ceilings, every closet was full, he had books piled under his kitchen sink, his floor had buckled, and he didn't have the money to get it fixed. Another fellow had been buried under books when a moderate earthquake hit Southern California.

Cardinals and bishops have stolen books, hoarded them, filling rooms and houses, sheds and outhouses with plunder. Rosenbach, probably the best-known bookman of the twentieth century, tells of men who trekked around the world to get a single book, and Holbrook Jackson in *The Anatomy of Bibliomania* describes a French collector who bought books by the basket, by the yard and acre, filling up rooms and houses, evicting tenants as his book stash grew. Jackson also tells of books bound with human skin, the nipple of the female breast forming a distinct swelling on the cover. Some ghoulish bibliomaniacs have even made headbands out of human hair.

These stories were true but they were lost on Willis. "That wasn't Candice," he said abruptly. "She didn't have time for that. I told you how good she was. She knew more about books than most professional booksellers like you learn in a lifetime. She was remarkable."

"I'll have to take your word for that at the moment. When do I get to see her books? That'll tell us a lot more about Mrs. Geiger than anybody's opinion, won't it?"

He reddened in anger. "What is it with you, Janeway, were you born this impatient?

Haven't I paid you enough to talk to me first?"

I felt justly chastised. "Yes sir, Mr. Willis, you surely have."

He let his eyes roam along the picture gallery, lingering for what seemed a very long time on one shot halfway down the wall. The house was quiet now: No bumps or creaking woodwork, no footsteps walking anywhere within earshot. He looked at me and I thought he might begin then, but again he looked away and the long silence continued. He said to the wall, "It's not easy to make a stranger understand what happened and why when you're not sure why yourself."

"That's okay. Get at it any way you want to."

Willis leaned over his chair and cupped his face in his hands. "Candice . . ." he began, but again he interrupted his thought, letting his hands slip up his face till he almost covered his eyes.

"Silliest goddam thing," he said. "Can't imagine what's wrong with me."

"Take your time."

He took a deep breath. "Maybe if I just explain Candice and the books, it'll be easier."

"However you want to do it. If I have

42

questions later . . ."

He stared at the wall, promising nothing.

"She looks young," I said. "I didn't know Mr. Geiger, but from the little I've heard about him, he would've been quite a bit older."

He nodded.

"Maybe as much as thirty years."

"It happens," he said. "You hear about those May-December romances. It happens."

I knew he was right, I just never understood it. Why would a young woman marry a man old enough to be her father? *It happens:* That would have to explain it, at least for now.

"Candice was thirteen when she started collecting books," he said. "She actually started long before then, but that's when it became her passion. Her life."

He nodded as if she had just spoken to him and approved what he'd said.

"Her father indulged her in everything she did."

They had lots of money, he said.

Lots of money.

"Her father made a vast fortune in aluminum."

Aluminum, tin, and steel.

"Her maiden name was Ritchey."

Suddenly, without another word, I understood a few things. Ritchey Steel ranked just below Kaiser as a key player in the Allied buildup during World War II.

"If Candice wanted a book, suddenly there it was. All she had to do was say so. She was his little girl. Nothing was too good for her."

He bought her lovely things from the Victorian era and earlier, many books with beautiful decorated cloth covers. At first she collected the kids' classics. Joel Chandler Harris. Robert Louis Stevenson. James M. Barrie. Aesop. Tom Thumb. Grimm's fairy tales. Mother Goose and Alice, *Pinocchio* and the *Arabian Nights.*

On and on.

She never lost her love of juveniles. Even later, when her interests broadened into adult literature and history, she was always a sucker for a pristine Hans Christian Andersen or a Red Riding Hood from the early nineteenth century.

"From the beginning she was a perfectionist," Willis said. "At fifteen she'd reject a book if it had a blemish inside or out."

Old Ritchey and his daughter lived in a fantasy world. She never had any friends her own age; it was always Candice and her father. As a birthday present she was given a whole shelf of classics. That was her first real experience with fine first editions, on her fifteenth birthday.

"I learned just last year what he spent on her birthday presents each year. Mr. Geiger had reason to go through her things, papers and mementos they had packed away years ago. You mentioned a dealer named Rosenbach."

"One of the so-called legendary big boys of the old days. Books have in fact been written about his life and times."

"What do you mean 'so-called'? You say that as if you didn't believe it."

"No aspersions on Rosenbach, I'm sure he was great. It's just me. I don't like the word legend. Today every young hot dog is a legend."

"But you wouldn't doubt Mr. Rosenbach's knowledge or integrity."

"Not at all."

"And if someone bought a library of books from Mr. Rosenbach — things like *Uncle Tom's Cabin* and *Moby Dick* and *Huckleberry Finn* — you'd figure that those books would have been what they purported to be."

"I'd be shocked if they weren't."

He nodded. "Mr. Ritchey spent twenty thousand dollars on her birthday that year."

"What year was that?"

"She'd have been fifteen in 1950."

I sighed, deep enough for him to hear. A man could still buy books like that then, at prices that looked positively quaint to us almost half a century later. Twenty grand would go a helluva long way. "That was a nice birthday for a kid," I said.

"Her father believed that great books seldom take a drop in value. So once she had demonstrated her own understanding that she would take care of them, he looked at it as an investment. He was investing his money and at the same time he was making her happy. She was easy to shop for; she never wanted anything else. He bought her books for Christmas or birthdays, or just because he felt like giving her something. All bought from Rosenbach or some dealer of that caliber. You can only imagine what those books would be worth today."

"You could actually figure it out fairly quickly."

"I get the feeling there's an 'if' coming."

"If you had the books to work with. That would make it simple."

But I already knew it wouldn't be that simple and his face confirmed it. He said, "What if you had a list, if you assumed everything was as it should be, if they were all first editions, if you assume original

46

bindings, the condition was fine . . ."

"That's already a lot of assumptions, Mr. Willis."

"If you had a roster from Rosenbach, on his letterhead, with his signature . . ."

"That would all be good. Still, to an appraiser, nothing can substitute for actually seeing them. Feeling them. Smelling them."

"Well, I'm sorry to say you can't."

"Then my assessment would be based on some ideal set of circumstances, wouldn't it?"

"Surely Rosenbach's reputation . . ."

". . . would tell us what they were like when he sold and delivered them."

"I've also told you how meticulously Candice cared for her books."

"That's all fine. But we don't know what might have happened to them since her death."

He nodded grimly as if he had already assumed that. We sat without speaking for a moment; then I said, "I don't think you brought me out here to do a simple book appraisal."

"I would like you to look at the books . . . upstairs in her old room."

I waited patiently for whatever might come next.

"Figure out what's missing," he said.

Okay. If the records were still intact, I could do that. Elementary, Mr. Willis.

Then he said, "Find out who took them."

This was a bit more complicated. It was beginning to look like I would earn my five thousand after all.

"Get them back," he said, "or write me a statement saying why you can't."

Then he said, "Since you were such a hotshot homicide detective, maybe you could put Sharon's mind at ease while you're digging around."

I sat up straight in my chair. "About what?"

"See if you can figure out if Candice was murdered," he said, and the case got murky.

3

We climbed a dark set of stairs and went down a hall to a long room at the end. There had been no more conversation after he dropped his murder bombshell; he stared at me for about fifteen seconds but at the moment I had nothing to add. There would be time later for questions; now the books needed to be seen. I heard a key click in the door and it creaked on old hinges. The room was darker than the stairs. Willis said, "Wait, I'll get us some light," and he disappeared into the inky black. He pulled open a thick drape, turned on several lights, and the room was suddenly brighter than the day. I stopped at the threshold and let my eyes scan the bookshelves for almost a full minute while Willis stood stone still, watching me from across the room. He seemed content to leave me alone and let me discover the room in my own way, and I warmed to him a notch for that. There were perhaps five thousand books on the shelves, but even from a distance I could see that some of the titles were reprints, what we call reading copies in the trade: old books to be sure, but old in itself means nothing. To a casual eye they might look valuable but to a bookseller their wholesale value was no more than ten dollars each.

Now I came into the room and made a slow trek around it, my eyes skimming the spines on each shelf. Occasionally I gestured at a book and Willis nodded his permission to touch it; I took it off the shelf and opened the cover gently to the title page, looked at the copyright page and returned it immediately to its place. So far they were all juveniles and illustrated, mostly very fine first editions with occasional cheap reprints. I took out my notebook and scribbled some words — facts on the left of the rule, impressions on the right. I stopped at half a shelf of Helen Bannerman books — *The Story of Little Black Quibba, Little Black Mingo, Little Black Bobtail,* and others. Most were mid-range first editions but over the top of their market in such beautiful shape as these. They were gorgeous, flawless, perfect books, now nearly one hundred years old, almost sensual in their original bindings.

Willis noticed my interest and said, "Tell me about those."

"They're beautiful. You'd have to go a long way to find any of these titles in such fresh condition. That freshness is the big factor. How many copies like this are available? You said Mr. Ritchey knew that great books seldom fall in value, but I wonder if he really understood the dynamic of what would happen in the future . . . today, for example, in the age of greed. If there are no others in this condition, there might as well be none at all. The value doubles and doubles again, year by year, on a far more impressive scale than any bank would pay you in interest. Forget auction records and price guides — a dealer can ask what he pleases. Mr. Ritchey was right, these kinds of books are among the best investments you can make."

"And there's no question that they're real."

"Oh, they're real, all right . . . except for the most valuable title. Your *Little Black Sambo*'s a Chatto & Windus reprint from the 1930s."

"What does that mean?"

I thought he knew full well what it meant but I told him. "It's a very nice book, Mr. Willis, but it's worth $50, more or less."

"And the original would be what?"

"I'd be guessing."

"Then guess."

"In the same kind of condition, which as I've said you just can't find today, maybe twenty grand. These kids' books were made for kids. They were often flimsily made and treated badly. They just didn't hold up."

He let out a long breath. "Goddammit!" he whispered.

"A real collector with deep pockets might pay two or even three times that," I said. "There's an old cliché in the book trade about the world's best copy. I think almost any bookseller would say that about these books."

"God*damm*it!" He slammed his way down into a chair.

"Sorry," I said.

"What about the ones that are left?"

"Don't hold me to the fire on this; I'd really have to look 'em up. But a ballpark figure for each might be in the thousand-, two-thousand range."

"So he took the right one."

"Looks like it. Which means he knew what he was after."

I moved on. It was the same story on the Frank Baum shelves: Superb, lovely first editions with notable gaps. *The Daring Twins* was here; *The Wonderful Wizard of Oz* was gone, replaced with an early reprint, authentic-looking as hell on the face of it; *The Life and Adventures of Santa Claus* had been replaced with a 1902 later printing, actually worth fair money I thought, until I saw some silverfish damage hidden inside the backboard; *The Flying Girl* was real, in a gorgeous, untouched 1911 dust jacket, but *The Road to Oz* was missing. I made a note that the replacement volume was an early printing, worth $200, I guessed. Near the end of the shelf was a reprint of *The Wizard of Oz* signed by the film cast: Judy Garland, Ray Bolger, Bert Lahr, Frank Morgan, Jack Haley, Margaret Hamilton, and Billie Burke.

"Oh, wow," I said softly.

He leaned forward in tense expectation. "What?"

"Just a helluva nice book. I wonder why whoever he was didn't take this."

"I don't know," he said. "Is it real?"

"I'm wary of signed books, but yeah, it sure looks real."

"Why are you wary?"

"There are too many people today who can sign books and make it look real. But the ink is old and it's from different fountain pens. If she bought this long ago and you have records telling where and when and from whom, we can assume it's real. At least for the moment. And as we say in the trade, these people ain't signing any more of 'em."

"Any ideas?"

"Maybe whoever took these, he wasn't looking for this one."

"I don't understand what you mean by that."

"I don't either. Yet."

My first theory, that the thief knew what he was doing and went after the highest-end stuff, was suddenly in trouble. Why pluck a book like *The Wishing Horse of Oz* when more valuable books were within arm's reach, just as easy to conceal, just as quickly tucked away and gone? Her Disney section had been ravaged: so many wonderful and hugely expensive books, so easily replaceable with good-looking reprints for book-ignorant guys like Willis and Geiger. The value would be in the tens of thousands, hundreds of thousands, I thought, adding the tally mentally and putting in nothing extra for such amenities as signatures. I did find a nice Disney *Pinocchio* under Collodi, signed by Disney with a generous and highly readable full-page inscription. Beside that was a true first edition of the same book, 1883, in Italian: a major rarity if my memory could be trusted. A section away, I found the first British edition of *Alice in Wonderland,* suppressed by the author and virtually unavailable anywhere. I had no reliable idea, but in this exceptional condition I guessed sixty to a hundred grand, maybe twice that. Softly I said "Jesus," and Junior leaned toward me, waiting. "Another good one," I said.

"How good is good?"

I smiled at his choice of words and told him what I thought, adding the usual caveats. He nodded and I moved on. Under Clemens was a pristine *Huckleberry Finn,* signed by the author, but the *Tom Sawyer* was gone, replaced by a reprint from the late 1890s. "Strange for a thief to take one and not the other," I said, but life was strange, and maybe this wasn't so strange after all. Her Joel Chandler Harris stuff looked untouched: all first editions, some signed, all in that wonderful condition. There was a *Song of the South* misfiled, the Grosset & Dunlap edition from 1947, and again it had Disney's signature.

I moved around the room, taking in the obvious high spots: a run of Milne's Pooh books, beginning with the first, *When We Were Very Young,* then *Winnie the Pooh,* and *Now We Are Six,* and *The House At Pooh Corner,* running on and on through the long series, all in dust jackets, *oh my pounding heart, the jackets,* it made my scrotum tingle just to touch them. And the Beatrix Potters! . . . *The Tale of Peter Rabbit* missing with a cheap substitute, but a gorgeous unbelievable signed limited of *The Fairy Caravan* and other first-edition fairy and bunny books were real. I had reached the Arthur Rackhams: more fairies in original drawings and books. *The Compleat Angler* had been replaced, but *A Midsummer Night's Dream* and other signed limiteds had been left. For the moment I did little more than glance at the Tolkiens. I sat on the other chair and Junior and I looked at each other.

"So what're you thinking?"

"Mr. Willis, I have seen a lot of great books, but today I am astonished."

He looked gratified but only for the moment. "Your astonishment is duly noted. The question is, what do we do now?"

"Depends on what you want. I can go around this room and put prices on your books . . . theoretical prices on the ones that are missing, real prices on what's still here. I can do that, but I can't testify to what I haven't seen, and just making the appraisal will take some time. I could be in here for several weeks."

"I don't care about the cost. But I do need it wrapped up soon."

"You made reference to the books being stolen, *maybe*. If you can produce rosters and billings from Rosenbach and others, you might make that case for the insurance company."

"Where else could they go? You think they just sprouted legs and walked out?"

"I'm being cautious."

"I haven't got time for caution."

"Then maybe, sir, with all due respect, you'd better find the time."

I saw instant fury in his eyes but he calmed himself and said nothing.

"They've been in here for what, twenty years?" I said. "Since she died they've been sitting here and it looks like they've been getting picked off one by one. Now you've got 'em under lock and key; you can wait till we see what we think might have happened. Let's try doing it right, see exactly what's missing, and work from there."

"And do what about it?"

"What do you want me to do?"

"Catch the bastard that did this and put him in jail, what do you think?"

"And get the books back."

"Yeah, sure. That goes without saying."

"Nothing goes without saying." *Without writing,* I thought. I had a sudden notion that I'd need everything defined on paper with this guy. A long moment passed.

"Mr. Willis, let me explain something to you. A book thief, unless he's doing his dirty work for some personal motive, usually sells what he steals as quickly as he can. In this case, I've got a hunch that whoever did it knows damn little about books and cares even less. He is taking whatever he takes because he has access and somebody *else* told him what to get."

"How the hell could you possibly know that?"

"I told you, it's just a hunch. But that's how I'd proceed, till I discover something that leads me somewhere else. Whatever happened, we have no idea when the books were lifted — may have been last week, maybe ten years ago."

"Well, it wasn't yesterday. And I'm pretty sure I know who did it."

"Then you don't need me, you need the cops."

"If I could prove it, maybe you'd be right."

"So what you want me to do is get the proof."

Suddenly his thinking seemed to change again. "Sure. But I'll settle for getting the books back. I don't need to make a fuss."

This time the moment stretched into a long minute. I didn't ask him who he suspected, not yet. I didn't tweak him on the subject of Mrs. Geiger's death. All in due time.

"What about the insurance?" I said. "You'll need to have everything documented. Those boys don't just hand out big checks because I tell them to."

He was shaking his head and suddenly I had a sinking feeling. "Don't tell me they weren't insured."

He seethed his answer into the wallboard. Another long minute passed. I could have said a lot of things then, but what was the point? The last thing a dope wants to hear when it's too late is what a dope he's been.

"What's your best guess as to when the thefts occurred?"

"I don't know. Maybe years ago."

"That could be a deep window of opportunity."

"The rooms have been locked for two years. And people haven't been around."

"What people?"

"Nobody. There's been no one living here except Mr. Geiger and me for a long time."

"How long?"

"Since Sharon moved to her own place, seven, eight years ago."

"So before that, anybody who had easy

access to the house could have gone in there."

He nodded, just barely, and I said, "Who might such a list include?"

"Mr. Geiger's three sons."

"What are their names?"

"Cameron, Damon, and Baxter."

I already knew that but now I wrote it all down and raised my eyes in a *go on* motion. "His daughter Sharon," he said reluctantly.

"That's still a small list."

"There were some servants, a cook, some house people, and stable hands. They never lived here, though, and they're gone now too."

"Gone where?"

"Mr. Geiger had me let them go after we realized we might have a problem."

"After you discovered there were books missing."

"Yes."

"No particular reason to suspect them?"

"No. When something like this happens, you hate to look at the people close to you."

"Have you kept tabs on those servants?"

"Sharon hired them."

He looked annoyed as I wrote a long entry in the notebook. "Let's not go there," he said.

"Why not? Is Sharon suddenly off limits?"

"If that's how you want to put it."

"How long did the servants work here before Sharon hired them?"

"You don't hear so well, do you?" he said, and now what had begun on a testy note and seemed to be improving was testy again.

"This really is a simple question, Mr. Willis."

"Suppose I decline to answer it . . . or any other questions along that line?"

"Is that what you're doing?"

This time the silent stalemate extended across one minute and into the next.

"I think I should tell you," I said: "I'm not inclined to take this on, as things stand."

He sneered at me. "Yeah, right. You're not about to walk out on this."

"Try me."

Another minute passed. "I can't work for somebody who wants to dictate how I must do it," I said. "If you know so much about investigation work, do it yourself."

He flushed a bright red and finally said, "All right, what was the question?"

"How long did the house people and stable hands work here before they were fired and Sharon hired them?"

"The older ones, years. I hated to let them go, but . . ."

"Who else might've gotten in there?"

"Some people, just visitors. Some friends of Sharon's, friends of the three sons as well. But that's been long ago, and they were only here for short periods of time. You don't frisk people going in and out of your house."

"Maybe you should have. Who else? Any wives of the brothers?"

"Damon married young, they split almost before the ink was dry. I never met her."

"What about Sharon? She got a husband?"

He shook his head and I studied his face deadpan.

"Of course there's me," he said. "If you want to go that route."

My pen was still, poised on the notebook. "Did Geiger ever give you any reason to believe he suspected you?"

"Would I have the keys to those rooms if he did?"

I had a clever-as-hell answer for that but the moment was awkward enough. Instead I settled for a straight question. "Since you brought it up, what is your standing here?"

I couldn't tell for a moment whether the question had offended him. He said, "I am the man who has paid you to do a job. The executor says I'm to continue running things the way I've always been doing."

"Until the estate is out of probate."

He nodded.

"So as things now stand we've got two angry blood relatives and one more who might show up at any time."

"Afraid you're gonna get arrested?"

"It wouldn't be the strangest thing that's ever happened. I just believe in playing it straight, Mr. Willis, doing things according to Hoyle. If I can."

"You can ask the executor."

"And meanwhile, if Damon or one of the others shows up and demands to get in here . . . ?"

"Leave that to me."

Another awkward moment passed.

"What's wrong now?" he said. "Do you think I took the books?"

"Mr. Willis, I have no idea yet what I think. I barely know you and I haven't seen the others at all. Right now I'm just asking some questions."

I made a few notes and returned to my premise. "Whoever did this didn't do it in a weekend. Those books were carefully removed over time, maybe for years, which points to Geiger's children, maybe the servants . . ."

"And me."

I made a note. "And maybe the friends of the children. Do you have their names?"

"Not handy. Maybe I could come up with

'em. They were horse people. No reason for them to care about books."

"I can think of a million reasons, and none of them have anything to do with a love of literature. You could buy a pretty nice racehorse for what one of these books might bring."

I waited through another silence; then I said, "Would you please get the names?"

"If I can find 'em. If not, you're on your own. I don't know, I haven't seen or heard of them in years."

"Off the top of your head, who do you remember?"

"Sandy Standish. Another horse trainer. Years ago he worked for Mr. Geiger. And there was a fellow the brothers knew . . . what the hell was his name?"

"Don't try so hard, maybe it'll come to you. What about Standish?"

"You don't follow racing much, do you? He wins a lot of races; won a big stakes race at Golden Gate last year with a 40-1 shot."

I wrote down the name *Sandy Standish* in the notebook. "Anybody else?"

"There were some others who hung around. I haven't thought of them in years. Sharon might remember their names."

"Okay then, back to Geiger's sons. Where do they live now?"

"They spend most of their time in California. They are middle-aged and in charge of their own lives."

"What do they do?"

"They are all horsemen."

"Like father, like sons."

"Hardly."

I waited him out. At last he said, "What's eating you now?"

"That disapproval in your voice. It's pretty hard to miss."

"Mr. Geiger was an extraordinary horseman. Not many people, even blood relatives, could come up to his level of excellence."

"What do you think of the sons as people?"

He shrugged: The disapproval was still heavy in the room with us. Again he went into that sullen, moody silence, almost like a murder suspect in the box downtown. If I wanted to get anything I'd have to pry it out of him piece by piece, which might be difficult since he was paying my freight.

"Mr. Willis . . ."

"It doesn't matter what I think," he said shortly. "Mr. Geiger had no relationship with any of them. That shouldn't be so difficult to understand. He hadn't seen them in years."

"So was there some reason for that, or did

he just wake up one morning and decide he didn't like his children?"

"Don't you dare make light of this, Janeway . . ."

"Did Mr. Geiger have a falling-out with his sons?"

"Oh Christ, it was one thing after another. After Mrs. Geiger's death, they became impossible. Cameron in particular turned out . . . wrong. He has a twisted soul."

"And he's a horse trainer?"

He nodded. Then, so softly I barely heard him, he said, "God help any horse that falls into his hands."

"Aren't there rules against abusing horses?"

"You know what they say about rules."

I scribbled some notes. "Where's he at now?"

"He's here in town, living in some cheap flophouse. He comes back here every year or two, always broke, hoping to get his dad to give him some money so he can go racing, probably at some small track till he goes broke again. He's a bush-leaguer."

"Did he ask for money this time?"

"He never got that far. I wasn't about to let him get to Mr. Geiger."

"Did you ever tell Mr. Geiger he was here?"

"Mr. Geiger was sick. And he had made it abundantly clear how he felt about Cameron."

"So the answer to that question is no."

"I took care of Mr. Geiger's affairs. Especially the unpleasant ones."

"The answer then is no."

He looked to be on the verge of a major explosion. "Goddammit, Janeway, I don't like your tone much. And I don't like the implication at all."

"There is no implication, and if I had a tone I apologize. I'm just trying to get a few simple questions answered and so far you aren't helping me much."

"If you think asking offensive questions is part of your job, maybe we should forget about the whole thing and find someone else. Is that what you want?"

I fought back the urge to tell him what I really wanted. *Assume the position, Mr. Willis. Roll this job into a big wad and see how it fits where the sun absolutely does not shine.* I thought but did not say these things. My restraint was little short of heroic, but then he found the words to send our relationship to a new low. "You need to understand something, pal. You are an employee here, you don't have any standing or authority at all, you're a work-for-hire hand, a temporary grunt, and we will get along much better if you remember that."

I sighed. "*Oh,* boy."

"Oh, boy what? Oh, boy what? What does that mean?"

We stared at each other for at least twenty seconds. "Oh, boy *what?*" he said, much louder now. I shook my head and said, "It means oh, boy, it is *such* a thrill to work for a lovable fellow like yourself. Oh, boy, this is so much fun I think I'll have to give you your money back and do it for you free. It means oh, *boy,* Junior, what charm school did you graduate from? Oh, boy is a superlative, meaning wow, terrific, unless it's used sarcastically; then it means your slip is showing, Junior, I've caught you being an asshole again. Can we figure it out from there?"

His hands trembled and I waited while he got control of himself. Softly I said, "This really doesn't look like it's gonna work out, does it?"

"Easy for you to say, you've already been paid. What the hell are the ethics in that?"

But then he began to back out of his rage; I could actually see it leaving him, like the steam rising off one of the horses on a chilly fall morning. The moment passed; he shook his head at the floor and said, "Never mind me. I don't mean what I say."

"Then why do you say it?"

"I'm just pissed over losing those books. Go on, ask your questions."

"So the missing books were first noticed when? A couple of years ago?"

"Yeah," he said sullenly.

"Who first noticed it?"

"I don't remember."

"I'm sorry, you don't *remember*?"

"Goddammit, that's what I said."

"Why'd it take you this long to start an inquiry?"

"Mr. Geiger's decision."

We looked at each other.

"Mr. Geiger had his own way of doing things. Me, I might have done it differently."

"Okay then, back to the brothers," I said. "Cameron's a jerk. What about the other two?"

"Damon races at Santa Anita and Hollywood Park."

"Until he showed up here, you mean."

"Yeah, that's what I meant."

"Hollywood Park, Santa Anita . . . those are pretty classy racetracks."

"He trains for other people. Some of his clients have money, but that doesn't mean he knows anything."

"Sounds like you two don't get along."

"It's a dicey arrangement. That's what we have."

"I couldn't help overhearing you talking out on the porch and in the other room. Sounded really dicey, what I heard of it."

"The man drives me crazy. But for now we've got to work together."

"On what?"

"We both want to take some of these horses racing. Jesus, what's this got to do with anything?"

"That's what I'm trying to find out."

"Look, a racehorse only has a certain amount of time to do whatever he's gonna do. They'll never be three years old again, and one or two of ours would have excellent chances in the three-year-old races at Santa Anita this winter, if we can ever get these people to agree on anything."

"So you're trying to work with Damon." I looked at my notes. "And the other one?"

"Baxter. Crazy as hell, hears voices, talks to the gatepost. I think Bax could have been a decent horseman if he wasn't nutty as a fruitcake. But I hear he gets along. He's been racing at good second-rate tracks . . . Hot Springs . . . Omaha when it was still going . . . Denver in the old days. Now he's trying to make inroads at the big California tracks as well."

"So," I said at last: "Who do you think did this and why?"

"Cameron, of course," he said at once. "He's always been a two-bit buck chaser."

"But you have nothing solid to base that on, right? So far it's just your suspicion."

"If you get to know him you'll understand."

"How did they get along with their mother?"

"If you mean Candice, she was their stepmother. Mr. Geiger was married before, long ago. He had the three boys with her."

"What happened to the first wife?"

"She died years ago."

"Of what?"

"She had an accident. Christ, how can that possibly be important?"

"What kind of accident?"

"Her car rolled over . . . went into a lagoon and she drowned."

I made a lot of notes. He was starting to squirm when I said, "Tell me more about her life and death."

"Tell you *what* for God's sake? Look, this was *years* before Mr. Geiger met Candice."

"Then tell me about Sharon," I said.

"What do you want to know?"

"What's she like? Where does she live?"

"What's she like? Sharon is . . ."

I waited, determined to wait him out if it took all day.

"She looks a lot like her mother," he said at last, as if that told me everything, and I had a short, sharp vision of another young woman who looked a lot like her mother, a fleeting thought of the Rigbys of North Bend. Everything goes around; everything comes around. When I looked up at him, he said, "Put Sharon in that white dress and shoot her picture and you'd swear it was Candice, thirty years ago."

I cleared my head. "What does Sharon do?"

"She has a horse rescue farm."

"What does that mean?"

"She takes in horses that have been treated badly."

"And does what with them?"

"She heals them. She's got the most amazing hands. Healing hands . . . I don't know how else to describe it. I know you think I'm as crazy as Bax now."

"Did I say that?"

"You were thinking it."

"It's not polite to go around telling people what they think, Mr. Willis."

"All I'm saying is, I've seen Sharon heal horses anybody else would give up on."

"Do you like her?"

"That's a strange question. Why wouldn't I like her?"

"Doesn't sound as if you care much for the brothers."

"Sharon is a far different person than those three . . ."

"Those three what?"

"I was about to say something unwise. It doesn't matter whether I like them or not."

"But you do like Sharon."

"Sure. Everybody does."

"How was she with her father?"

He hesitated, just long enough. "So apparently everybody didn't love Sharon," I said.

"You sure read a lot into small things."

"I used to do that for a living. Tell me why I'm wrong."

I didn't speak then for the longest time. I walked around the room again but the room was cold: the room couldn't speak, and even if it could I didn't think it would tell me any more than I was getting from Willis. He said nothing this time and another full minute passed.

"Why am I wrong, Mr. Willis?"

"I was just an employee here. I didn't tell Mr. Geiger what to do."

"But he's gone now. No reason for us not to talk, right? Did he have trouble remembering? . . . comprehending?"

"Occasionally, yes," he admitted, surprising me. "Later in life, especially in the last year. But the next day he'd be fine again. When he was okay, he could remember everything that ever happened to him."

Suddenly I asked, "Why does Sharon think Mrs. Geiger may have been murdered?"

"It was Baxter," he said at once. "That crazy bastard, what can I say about someone like that? We were standing alone in the serving line at her funeral, just him and me, and out of the blue he says, 'Which one of us do you think killed her?' I looked over his shoulder and there was Sharon watching us."

"Did she hear what Baxter said?"

"Sure she did, she was right on top of us. She got white as a ghost, then turned and walked away fast."

"How old was she then?"

"Eleven, I think. How old do you have to be to understand something like that? What she didn't know then was how crazy her damn-fool brother was. Little girls tend to believe that kind of thing, don't they, when it's said by an adult with a straight face?"

"So in addition to finding out about the books, you want me to track down a killer, twenty years later."

"No, I didn't say that."

"I'm sorry, I thought you did say that."

"Listen and get this straight. Your job is to find out about those books."

"Then why bring the question of Candice's death into it?"

"It's gonna come up, that's all. I want you to be ready for it."

"Ready in what way? What does that mean?"

"Ready to deflect it." He tried to wave me off. "Just move past it. I want you to know that it's the raving of a lunatic. If Sharon brings it up . . ."

"Brush it off."

"Exactly. You just pin down those books I'll be happy."

Maybe happiness isn't to be had, I thought. Maybe the books were sold and resold, sold again and again so long ago that there's no trail to be found anywhere. And murder, once it's been put on the table, can't simply be stuffed in a bottle and forgotten. There were still dozens of questions to be asked, but it was time for a different perspective on it.

"Where can I find Sharon?"

"What for?"

"I'll need to talk to her . . . to all of them

at some point."

"Does this mean you're finished with me?"

I shook my head. *Not by a long shot.*

"Mr. Willis?"

"This has nothing to do with Sharon's books. Let's keep focused here."

"Sharon's books?" I blinked. "What books does Sharon have?"

"When Candice died, she left Sharon half her books. Mr. Geiger got the rest."

"Ah," I said. "When were you planning to tell me that, Mr. Willis?"

"It's got nothing to do with the job you're here for."

"It's good to know you think that. But I'd like to see her anyway."

"I don't think so."

I stared him down.

"Screw it, if you've got to, here, take my truck. She lives on thirty acres down the road at the edge of the ranch. I'll wait here till you're done."

I drove down the muddy road and the question I'd had up in Geiger's book room was still with me. Why steal a $700 *Oz* book when a *Pinocchio* worth at least $65,000 could be lifted as easily? What kind of thief would do that?

4

The rain had stopped and the thick clouds in the east were pale orange now. I splashed over the wet road in Willis's truck and soon I saw a grove of trees and a house; beyond that a barn and a fenced field, a small group of paddocks, another barn, and some animals. I saw two tiny goats and three dogs, a pheasant, a flock of chickens, some ducks, a donkey, and perhaps fifteen horses. The number of horses grew as I came closer until I counted eighteen in the big field and another half dozen in individual pens or corrals at the side of the barn. I pulled up at the edge of the house, stopped the truck, and got out. The three dogs, goldens, came running. One barked menacingly but I got down to one knee and he turned to mush, rolling over on his back in the mud, wagging his tail and begging for a belly scratch.

I got up and walked around the house. It looked deserted in the gray morning, but then I heard the unmistakable growl of a tractor. I stood at the edge of the porch and watched as she inched it out of the barn. It was a small tractor with a flatbed loaded three high and four across with bales of hay. I was standing about fifty yards away and she missed me in her concentration. The two goats stood up and pranced on their hind legs, actually danced a jig in front of her tractor. "C'mon, guys, get out of there," she yelled clearly over the motor noise. She jerked forward and they moved aside; the tractor turned into the road and she saw me suddenly and killed the motor.

"Hey." Her voice wasn't challenging but it wasn't overly warm either. She sat forward on the seat, her long-sleeved shirt rolled up to the elbows, a perfect picture of a working farm gal. She was in her early thirties, I guessed; blond, and probably years younger than her half brothers. I stepped out into the yard and said, "I take it you're Sharon," and she nodded slightly, still uncommitted. I told her my name as her eyes took in the truck behind me. "Is Junior here?"

I shook my head and told her he had loaned me the truck. I started across the yard.

"So what's this about?"

"I'd like to talk to you for a while, if you've

got the time."

"How long's a while?"

"Depends on what you say."

"Well, it'll have to be later if it's something deep. I'm getting a late start this morning. These guys are hungry and I should be done by now."

"I think you would call this something reasonably deep."

"Give me a hint."

"It's about your mother and her books."

She sat perfectly still for a moment, as if the words had frozen her there. "Actually I've been expecting someone like you. Could you come back in three hours?"

"I've got a better idea. How about letting me help? Maybe that'll get you done faster."

"Or maybe not. Are you any good at this?"

"I've got a strong back and I follow orders well."

"Those are the good things. What if one of these horses kicks you in the head?"

"That would be my responsibility, wouldn't it?"

"Maybe, maybe not. You must be a Republican."

"I'm not much of anything. I don't tend to join stuff, don't belong to political groups."

"Hope you've got a change of clothes. It

gets messy."

"I can handle that. These clothes are no great shakes and I've got others back at the hotel."

She looked at me more keenly now. "I'm sorry, what did you say your name is?"

"Cliff."

"Okay, Cliff, get up on the back."

I climbed up behind her and we went rocking along a muddy road that skirted the main field. "Watch I don't throw you off," she yelled. "Don't hang on to the bales, you'll pull them off on top of you and break your neck if you fall. Grab on to the back of my shirt if you need to hold something."

Across the field I could see the horses gathering. One whinnied loudly, a cry that carried over the noise of the tractor. "They're hungry," she said. "Hang on."

She banked sharp right and stopped at a gate, gestured for me to open it, and I got down to let her in. She rolled out to the middle of the field, where an old roan stood with his teeth bared and dared anyone to come close. "He's mostly bluff," she said; "still, it's best to watch him till he gets used to you. He can give your arm a nasty bite if you get too close." She stopped the tractor and together we lifted a bale off the flatbed. She cut it open and pulled off another. She asked if I had ever driven a tractor and I told her I could figure it out; she gestured down the hill and said, "Open two more about fifty yards down there."

I could see the residue on the ground from yesterday's drop, and by the time I had the bale off the tractor and cut open she was there, hoisting the second and gesturing me on toward the fence. The bales weighed about sixty pounds each and she handled them as easily as I did. I drove on to the next drop and this was how it went, scattering the hay in half a dozen drops around the field while the horses moved from one place to another. She made no attempt to talk while the work went on. Once we had emptied the flatbed she motioned me to the gate and walked ahead to hold it open. Back to the barn we went, to do it all again. "I'll throw the bales down from the loft," she said. "You stack 'em on the tractor." She climbed a wooden staircase and vanished into the darkness upstairs. A moment later a bale dropped through the chute and bounced heavily on the floor. I heaved it up onto the tractor as the next bale thudded on the floor. We found a rhythm and quickly got the flatbed loaded as the sun broke through the clouds and lit up the earth outside.

There still wasn't much talk and what little there was was all business. "You fill up the water buckets," she said; "I'll take care of these guys over here." She disappeared into the barn and a moment later I saw her doing something inside one of the smaller corrals. It looked like she was tending to a horse with a terribly deformed face; feeding him through some kind of syringe drip while she cradled his head against her breast. We hustled back and forth, passing each other but much too absorbed in the work to do more than make occasional eye contact. "When you're done there, fill up the water buckets along this row. These guys on this side are in quarantine, so don't let the hose touch the buckets."

The buckets were big and this took a while. Then came the small chores. I swept the barn floor while she worked outside, doing whatever she did. At one point she passed the open barn and the sun coming through from the other end lit her up. She turned and glanced my way, really no more than a look before she moved on past the doorway, but in that span of seconds I saw what Willis had seen: a vision of her mother, the woman in white. *Put her in a white dress* . . .

I joined her at the corral near the horse

with the shattered face. "What happened to him?"

"I got him two weeks ago," she said. "Some kids were feeding him cherries, where he was before. One of them tossed a lit cherry bomb into his stall and he tried to eat it. He's lucky he didn't swallow it."

"He doesn't look lucky."

"You should've seen him before I wired his jaw together. He was like something from a freak show."

We walked across the yard to the house, took off our shoes, and left them there on the steps. The back door opened into a kitchen just off the porch and I could see on past, through a hall into what looked like a living room. I saw some books in a bookcase but the curtains were drawn and the light too dim to see what they were. "I'll fix us some breakfast," she said. I had eaten earlier but that was hours ago and I had worked up an appetite. "You make the coffee," she said, "while I go grab a shower." She disappeared into a hallway, leaving me to grope around in the cupboards. I found the beans and the grinder, started the coffee perking, and looked for a place to squat in the cluttered room. The kitchen was well lived-in, as if she spent most of her time here. It had a nook with a table and chairs and papers piled high across one end. She had horse pictures on the walls, but none of racing horses and none of her mother. Maybe that told me something, maybe not. So far she seemed relaxed and easygoing. Except for that fraction of a moment in the barn she hadn't shown any curiosity about what I wanted or why, but her eyes were keenly intelligent and I had a hunch she knew.

For the second time that morning I walked along a wall and looked at horse pictures. But the horses on Geiger's wall were winners; these were losers. They were worth nothing, less than nothing because as long as they lived they continued to consume; they cost money and gave nothing back. At least dead they would be worth whatever the going rate was for horseflesh. That was one way to think.

I looked at a pathetic little pony named Wizard. He stood in a small pen near a barn that I now knew well. I watched this frightened-looking horse as he had appeared on the day his picture was shot, three years ago according to the date on the photograph. He looked like death warmed over. The second picture was Wizard again but except for the name on the photo I'd never have known him. Then he had been defeated by life; now he had put on weight, his coat gleamed, and he was thriving. I couldn't tell where he was but it wasn't here, I could see what looked like tropical trees in the background. Another young woman was hugging his neck and two small boys were taking obvious delight that he was there and theirs and alive.

"That was one sweet horse," Sharon said from the doorway. "He sure didn't deserve what was about to happen to him."

"Which was what?"

"He'd be dog food if we'd been much later. But they don't all turn out like Wizard."

"No automatic happy endings."

"Nope. There are no guarantees, Cliff."

"With horses or people."

"At least people can take care of themselves."

She caught my dubious look and said, "You don't think so?"

"Not always."

"Give me a for instance."

"I'll take a rain check."

"Maybe I'll never see you again after today." She smiled faintly. "Good thing I'm a trusting soul. So don't forget, you owe me a story."

She began stirring around on the stove.

She looked pretty and fresh in the sunlight coming through the window. "Good job out there," she said. "You saved me an hour this morning."

She started an omelet and soon the aroma of food filled the kitchen. I washed my hands at the sink; then I found the silverware and the china. I poured her coffee and asked how she liked it. She said, "Just like it comes," and I pushed a cup gently across the counter. She sipped it and said, "Oh, that's good; you give good coffee, Cliff." Then she sat with the counter between us and said, "So what's this all about?"

I told her. She didn't interrupt, didn't change expressions or the gentle rhythm of her breathing while I spoke. A long silence fell over us; she stared at the wall behind me, but when she did speak, all she said was, "Well, let's eat."

The omelet was superb but the conversation was stilted. At some point I said, "So what's going on in that head of yours?"

"I guess I'm still thinking," she said. "Did Junior really say that, about her being murdered?"

"Apparently Baxter said it, way back when she died. Junior seems to think it's also been bothering you."

"It's one of those things that plants itself

in your mind and won't let go."

"Do you believe it?"

"No," she said decisively. But a few seconds later she said, "I don't know what to believe."

She watched my eyes. "What do you think about Junior?"

"Hard to tell. There are lots of questions to ask him yet."

"But he is a strange old duck, don't you think so?"

I cocked my head and did not say what I was thinking. Yes, Junior was strange. So apparently was the old man he worked for.

"Why did Junior send you over here?"

"He didn't. I was asking questions, and you were a logical question."

"So you're saying you haven't been told anything about me."

"That's why I'm here."

"Well, I don't know what I can possibly tell you that would matter to anyone. Was my mother murdered? That question has always been there, hiding in the weeds. Am I curious? Hell yes, wouldn't you be? Have you found anything at all that indicates she might have had an enemy?"

"I haven't even asked any questions along those lines yet. Your father never mentioned any of this to you?"

"I hadn't spoken to my father in any substantive way in years."

I looked at her incredulously but she turned away and poured us more coffee. "Hey, I couldn't force him to see me."

"Was he . . ."

"What, crazy? Is that what you're asking? How would I know that?"

"Well, cutting off his family doesn't seem normal."

"I don't think anybody's normal today." She twisted her cloth napkin and let it drop on the table. "What are you, a detective?"

"Used to be. I worked in Denver homicide for years."

Her eyes opened wide. "So what do your homicide instincts tell you in this case? Do you know how she died?"

"Junior said she had allergies."

"I got 'em too. Some different, some the same. I'm allergic to corn, certain kinds of fish, sunflower seeds. I'm like my mamma, got to watch what I eat. By the way, how'd Junior find you way out in Colorado?"

"I guess he got a referral from somebody."

"What kind of referral?"

"I'm a book dealer and I used to be a cop. You don't find that combination every day."

"It's about the books," she said at once.

"Some of them are missing."

"And I've got a bunch of them."

I let the moment stretch slightly: then I said, "Damn, I wish every case was this easy."

"Sorry, this is a different bunch. Mine are legitimately mine. In fact, I was the one who first sent up the storm warnings when certain copies turned up missing."

I nodded slowly and watched her eyes. "You want to tell me about that?"

"After I finished college and vet school, about seven years ago, I took my part of Mamma's books and brought 'em here. Then, two years ago, I began searching the book world for books with my mother's bookplate. I had three booksellers looking at once, and whenever they found one I would either trade the dealer for it or buy it outright. On one trade the dealer returned my book and said it was a cheap reprint."

"So you and your dad inherited this fortune in books and neither of you had a clue what they were."

"We had too much money in other areas, we didn't think of the books that way. Neither of us cared much what the books might be worth." She smiled in irony. "We simply didn't care. But I learned quickly after that. I went through my half and weeded out the bad ones. And I've been on a pretty intense hunt for the real ones ever since."

"And when they fired the servants, you took that hard."

"Yes, of course. I felt responsible for what happened to them. If I hadn't told Junior what I had learned, they'd still be working there. I grew up with those people and they work for me now."

I made notes and said nothing for the moment.

"You want to see the books?" she said.

I followed her into the next room. She said, "Keep going, these are all veterinary and horse books," and we went through a hall to a staircase that wound down into a basement. "This was quite a project, waterproofing this room and making it fireproof, I had my house ripped apart for weeks, but it's about as safe now as modern technology can make it." She flipped on lights as we went, and at the bottom we came into a cool book room that stretched across the length of the house. It looked like a vault in a bank. She sat on the stairs and watched me sleepily, and again I walked around a room and looked at books. I worked the room in a fast and superficial way, taking mental note of the genres as they changed. There was a wall of children's and illustrated, containing many of the same titles from the old man's house; there was a section of classics, then the early Americana: approximately equal sections as I went along and took stock. I didn't need to touch them, I could see enough for my immediate purpose, and as before I was amazed at the condition and the vast numbers. At some point I did say, "May I?" and she nodded. I plucked a beautiful copy of *Heidi* and carefully opened it. I was guessing seven grand, maybe twelve for this copy, but what drew my immediate attention was an elaborate color bookplate tightly affixed to the inside front board. The illustration showed an adolescent girl standing naked in a bright garden with her right arm wrapped around a tiger, her left dropped below her navel and hidden by a bush. I opened another book: same bookplate. The material looked like vellum, perhaps paper vellum, which I had heard could be almost as tough as leather. The background was a fleshy pink, the style art deco.

"Is this your mother's bookplate?"

"That's actually my grandfather's doing. He had that designed especially for her, way back when she was just a child. It's got her initials in the illustration if your eyes are keen enough to see."

I looked carefully; couldn't see them.

"It's in the strands of her hair. Very subtle."

Then I did see them. The girl's hair was parted in the middle and hung in equal waves around either side of her neck, flowing over her tiny breasts and hiding the nipples. The letter C was cleverly formed in a few strands on her right; the R was in the hair at her left arm. "Grandpa had a noted French artist make the design. You ever hear of François-Louis Schmied?"

"I believe he did a lot of art deco bookbindings. Illustrated leather covers."

"Today I'm told he's considered a master, but he always had money problems. Grandpa got him to do this for what you'd consider peanuts today. I've got the original art hanging upstairs. When we divvied up the books, I took all those with the bookplates. Maybe that was foolish, I don't know. I just wanted them. You hear such differing opinions about bookplates. What do you think, do they ruin the books?"

I shook my head and smiled sadly.

"Mamma didn't like that painting, but she'd never have told him that. So she put the bookplates into her books all those years and just hated doing it. When Grandpa died she started picking up second copies and gradually replacing her old ones with the bookplates. She'd trade them back to dealers, two or three to one in their favor, to get an unblemished one. Today you see them offered for sale occasionally: Some bookseller will get one, or a small lot will come up for auction, and they never know about the heritage or the girl's name hinted in her hair. They cost a pretty penny anyway now but I always buy them when I hear of one."

"I think you're smart to get them. What you've heard applies to stupid bookplates with balloons and clowns and stuff. I don't know, a purist would argue, but these bookplates enhance them to a whole new dimension. Sell them only if you get tired of having them. Whatever you want for them I'll try to find you somebody with the money who will appreciate them."

I worked my way to the far end, where I found a section of bibliographies and other reference books. I saw a shelf of Rosenbach's old catalogs and a copy of his personal bibliography, *Early American Children's Books*. I opened it and saw an inscription. "To Candace Geiger, bookwoman, from the author, A.S.W. Rosenbach." He had spelled her name wrong, but she probably didn't care. I looked back at Sharon. She was watching me with half-closed eyes as I started across the room on the other side. I stopped and took the two volumes of *Uncle Tom's Cabin* off the shelf. Just for my own information, I said, "Do you know what this is worth?" She peered under the light and said, "Haven't looked at it in a while. I don't know, twenty thousand?"

"Maybe twice that now for this copy. But I am impressed anyway."

"About what?"

"It tells me you're not sitting on a fortune in total ignorance."

"Cliff, I don't mean to brag so don't think badly of me when I say this, but these books are a tiny piece of the fortune I am sitting on. However, since you brought up this ugly question of money, my mother left me half of the Ritchey Steel fortune. That's more money than I'll spend in ten lifetimes. And it's like some monster; if I don't use it, it keeps on growing. I put a lot into other horse rescue operations and I still can't spend it fast enough to deplete it."

"I guess most people would say give it to a real charity if you don't want it yourself; why spend it on a bunch of broken-down old horses when people need it too. But then it would get sucked into some fiscal budget and half of it would go to pay executive salaries."

"*Exactly*," she said. "This way I can control what happens to it."

"Then it's good. You're still young, you can always figure out what else to do with it."

"I'm not that young. But here you are, a man after my own heart. Next thing you'll want to know why I do what I do."

"I'd be fascinated, if you want to tell me."

She cocked her head and looked at me sleepily. "Long ago I read an article about how horses are treated on their way to be butchered. I couldn't believe it so I went to see for myself. I saw firsthand what happens when the killers get them. It's not so much the butchering and the slaughter, I'm talking about real mean-hearted cruelty. I saw horses shoved into pens with broken legs and killed with hammers. I saw them murdered, and if you think that's too strong a word, come with me someday and I'll show you something. Just bring along a strong stomach."

"I think I'll take your word for that."

"I get an enormous satisfaction when I can save a horse from those bastards. But sometimes it's hard to make a stranger understand that."

"Actually it's easy to understand."

"But it's not why you came."

"It's all grist for the mill, Sharon."

"You're a strange guy for a cop. I think Mamma would probably like you. I like to think she would appreciate what I'm doing with the horses, just as I appreciate her books. I enjoy having them here where I can come touch them if I want to. They were hers, after all. Sometimes it seems like they're the last living part of her."

"That's an interesting way of putting it."

"I can be a sentimental fool sometimes. I went through a period a few years ago when I was intensely interested in everything she had done in her life. I looked her books up, I learned about authors and points and values. But then I realized, I'll never be a bookwoman like she was."

"You don't have to be to appreciate books like these."

"Yeah. Someday I may give them all to a library, but I'm not sure of that either. Stupid I guess, to put all this money and effort into a book room and then give them all away."

"You'd have to choose your library well," I said, thinking again of Carroll Shaw at Blakely.

"I don't know this for a fact, but I have a hunch they don't all take equal care of books."

"Trust me, they don't. Be careful, look around, talk to people."

"Meanwhile, if I want to read that Steinbeck I can get a cheap copy and I don't have to worry about spilling coffee on it. And that's a real fear because I'm clumsy, I do spill coffee, and thinking about being careful and not spilling it doesn't stop me from being clumsy and spilling it."

I watched her eyes, which held steady as she talked, as she came closer. She said, "Look, if you've got questions I'll try to answer them, and we might as well start here. My mother left her books to my father and to me, half and half. Except for the bookplates it doesn't matter, they are all what you'd call very fine, there were a lot of second and third copies, especially in the juveniles, and he probably didn't know one from another anyway. One day long ago I told him if he had become so paranoid that he wanted my half he could send a truck over here whenever it was convenient, I said I'd load them up for him, I didn't need his grief. As far as the money goes, he knew what he could do with that, too. I'm glad now he didn't send that truck."

She bobbed her head sleepily and I liked her. She asked if I was finished down here for now, I said sure, for now, and we went upstairs to sit again in the kitchen. She poured more coffee and took a deep sip. "You must think I'm a screwball," she said. "I could hire no end of help, and I do have our old house people, who come in a few days a week to help me. But after a while I crave the solitude, early in the morning when it's just the horses and me. I like that, and I don't really know what other life would give me this kind of peace and satisfaction. If a horse gets sick I make him well. I'm a licensed vet so I can treat what ails them. It's people like my father I can't understand."

"Why would he cut off all ties to his children?"

She thought about it and in a while she shrugged. "Paranoia . . . fear of death . . . a mind that lost ground steadily for twenty years . . . take your pick. After my mother died, what was a mild case of paranoia deepened and became a textbook case. I don't think he ever got over her death."

She looked away at something in the corner of the room; then slowly her eyes returned to mine. "But oh there was a time," she said: "Back when *she* was alive, when they lived for each other and she shared his world; oh, wow, back then he was a powerhouse. That's how I remember them from my childhood. I can only imagine what he was like when they first met. But he never knew what he wanted after she died. By the time I left home he'd become impossible, he trusted nobody but Junior. But all he had to do was reach out to me, not to Junior or anybody else . . ."

"And what would have happened?"

"I'd have gone up there and sat with him, we'd have had us a talk, and I'd hold his hand."

She reached for the last of the coffee and split it between us. Questions lingered but she knew what they were before I asked. "I don't know everything about her youth by any means," she said. "I do know some of the facts of her life, but as to why she was the way she was, or how much that way she really was . . ." She shrugged.

"What does that mean, the way she was?"

"All I can do is tell you how she was raised. She never had what you and I would consider a normal childhood. Her adolescence wasn't normal, and when she became a woman that wasn't normal either. She had no friends her own age; she was never courted as a kid or taken to the homecoming dance. But who am I to talk? I never was either."

"Stupid boys." I shook my head. "That

was their loss."

"Well, thank you. I mean thanks and all but don't get the wrong idea. I haven't led a monastic life here or anything like that; I've had friends, I just don't put marriage and society anywhere near the top of my list of things to do with my life. What about you?"

"I have a friend."

"Back in Denver?"

I nodded.

"What's her name?"

"Erin."

"So what does Erin do?"

"She's a lawyer. We're also partners in the book business."

There was a brief awkward moment, then she got on track again. "I don't know how much of this was actually the fault of the boys she knew. I think it was her, she just wasn't interested. She was her daddy's girl; she moved through an adults' world and was bored silly by kids and kid-games. When her father died she would have been lost if my dad hadn't come back into her life. Then she was safe, she had that father figure again. That's what I think."

"So you're saying he had known her earlier?"

"They had what you'd probably call an explosive first meeting."

"To a stranger like me that seems unlikely. Sounds like their worlds were far apart."

"Her father knew some racing people in New York, and later they met some others on trips out to the Coast. Mostly they were rich owners, in it on a much higher level than HR was. But when it came down to what he knew, he took a backseat to nobody. You could ask anyone there at that time and they'd tell you. H. R. Geiger knew exactly what a horse's leg should look like. He could trot one down the shedrow and tell you what ailed it. And that's how she met him, way back when she was a young woman and her daddy took her to the races on Saturday afternoons. They came west on a trip and someone introduced her to HR in the clubhouse at Santa Anita, and the rest as they say was history. It was the first day of racing that year, the day after Christmas 1954."

"Did she tell you about all this herself?"

"I missed knowing a lot by being a kid — you don't ask questions like that when you're young. She once told me rockets went off in her head, that's all. And apparently it was the same for him. People meet, they ignite something in each other; sometimes it doesn't matter about differences in age. My dad was striking then, very virile and sure of himself. Even her father's money and power didn't inhibit him."

"Still, he didn't just show up on her doorstep with flowers in his hand. Or did he?"

"No, but they did write to each other. I found the letters in her stuff a few years ago. The first one was dated mid-January 1955, three weeks after they'd met. When old Grandpa Ritchey died, HR stepped right in: off one treadmill and onto another, so to speak. They had some happy times; then she died and he never recovered. At some point he began getting senile, and that's one reason I've stayed here. I figured somebody had to keep an eye on him, and that would be me. But hey, he didn't care. In the end I just left him alone and that's what he wanted anyway. I didn't have it in me to put him away, so maybe that was the best thing I could do for him: just leave him alone with Junior."

She shook her head. "What a pair they've made. All these years, just the two of 'em, training their horses for what? Just like they always did, they'd get up in the morning and take 'em to the track, have 'em galloped two or three days and then they'd get worked, then walked for a day. He kept 'em in top shape, don't ask me why, because if old HR ever raced a horse in the last twenty years, I don't know about it." She craned her neck and looked at the clock. "Sorry, I've got to go pick up a horse. If I can tell you anything else, speak now."

"Anything you know that might help me understand Junior better."

"Ha! Lots of luck."

But I could almost see the wheels turning in her head. Suddenly she said, "Did he tell you any details about the will?"

"A little."

"Did he tell you a new will was written after we found the books were missing? This delays everything, the horses, the books, everything."

"But the books don't lose their value with age, like the horses."

"Exactly. Junior's got to satisfy the executor that he's put in a good-faith effort to find and recover them. Now he's charged with doing that. And the old lawyer knew HR for years; he's like a piranha, he trusts none of us and he's taking it as a personal cause to turn over every rock. This could tie up the estate long enough to make the racehorses irrelevant. Unless someone like you comes along and figures something out."

"So now, unless they try to challenge HR's

state of mind . . ."

". . . everything's in limbo, at least for the moment. Tell you what, Cliff, there were some angry old men when that was read. My own thought is, this may have been my father's last real testament. If they want to challenge him on it, they may have to fight me as well."

"So you would wade in as a friend of Junior's."

"Sure. Junior's been with Daddy when the rest of us couldn't get close, so I'm not going to sit on my hands and let Damon and Bax screw him around if that's not what the old man intended. I want to see that HR's final intent is carried out. So if they want a fight, they'll get more than they bargained for."

"Bet you never thought you'd be taking up for Junior."

"Not in this lifetime. He can make it difficult."

"So what happens if the books never are found? Eventually something's got to be done with all that money and property."

"It'll all go to us anyway. At least the three of us."

"Leaving Junior out in the cold."

"That's a possibility. Junior's only covered in the new will if he tries to find the books.

I don't know, I'm not a lawyer. There may be questions that can be raised about HR's mental state."

"So it's in Junior's interest to get me to do a quick assessment of what's missing . . ."

". . . and turn over some rocks, whatever the executor will accept . . ."

". . . tell them the books are impossible to find, and rubber-stamp my report."

This was far more complicated than Junior had said. Candice had traded away some of the books from her childhood, scattering those with the bookplates far and wide and leaving any potential dealer or appraiser with a mountain of difficulty getting them straight.

Slowly her eyes came up to meet mine and again I could see new trouble and doubt there.

"She'd be so easy to kill," she said. "She was born with what killed her. You could kill her with a peanut."

5

I got into the truck and headed back along the road to the farm. I knew I had come to the fish-or-cut-bait point with Junior: I needed some straight talk and the freedom to dig without the threat of a sudden temper tantrum or an ultimatum to do it his way. I wondered how far I could push him as I drove along the road between the two farms and there was no clear answer. As the house came into view through the trees I made the decision to push him hard, to the wall if I had to, and that always means living with the consequences.

He was sitting on the porch with his glasses in his lap when I pulled into the yard. I got out and walked up the steps through a light rain. He didn't move. There was something about the way he watched me, he had a kind of madness in his eyes as if he knew and had been enraged by everything Sharon had told me. I stopped at the top of the steps and we looked at each other.

"So what's goin' on?" he said. "How long's it gonna take you to figure this out?"

"I don't know yet." I glared at him and said, "I'll see if I can wrap it up before lunch."

"Don't you use that smart-ass tone with me. *Answer me!*"

I smiled sadly and shook my head. "That's really a nasty temper you've got, Mr. Willis."

"Never mind my temper. You've done nothing since you got here but impugn my motives with your slick talk. What did Sharon tell you?"

"She explained what the will requires you to do."

"Hell, I could have told you that, but it's not germane to your job. The will's a personal matter, it's got nothing to do with you finding those books. To put it bluntly, it's none of your damn business."

A moment of silence followed.

"I'm paying your freight," he said. "I've got a right to expect accountability."

"You've got a right to expect a result, or my best effort to get you one."

"Well, I can't wait forever. My horses are gettin' older every day." He gestured with his hands. "I would think you could wind this up in a week, tops."

"Surely you realize I can't just sign off on something till I look into it."

"Go ahead, look your ass off."

"And then what?"

"Give me a paper saying what you did, you've either got the books or they're lost."

"Come on, Mr. Willis, I've only been here a few hours, I haven't even talked to Damon or the servants yet, I don't know what Cameron might have done, and there's no telling how long it will take to exhaust all the leads. And every little argument we get into along the way lengthens the process."

"Meaning, you'd like me to butt out."

"Meaning, yes, I need a free hand and I need certain things understood."

"What things?"

"I think it's going to take some time."

"How much time?"

"First we've got to know exactly what's missing. That could take a week or more, and the real job just begins then. If you want these books appraised, that could take weeks. Then I need to find out if the missing books have been bought or sold in the book trade in the last twenty years. Not just these titles, Mr. Willis, these copies. Then we can try to trace them, see where they are now."

He looked at me coldly and I said, "A month would be lucky."

Into his silence, I said, "Could be twice that. Even then we might not know anything definite. We might never know."

"You don't want much, do you?"

"I believe in telling you up front what you're facing. If you don't agree, you don't need me. Many good, competent booksellers can do an appraisal. I can give you some names, people whose opinions have been accepted in court cases."

"Who says this is going to court?"

"Let's just say in case."

"Why can't you just shut up and do what you're told?"

Now I felt my own temper rising. "That's your answer for everything, isn't it? You're the boss, I'm just here to jump up and salute when you bark. Come on, Junior, I don't tell you how to train a horse, it would be presumptuous of me to try."

A long stretch of sullen silence threatened to extend into the afternoon. I waited but he wasn't inclined to elaborate. Softly, I said, "You want me to give you my word I did my best, and in fact I haven't even started yet. You want me to be an expert, but one you could hire over fast food at McDonald's or Burger King. I've got to tell you, that sounds a little suspicious. I don't know the executor of the will, but I wouldn't like it much if I were him."

His face was a mask.

"I think you're a control freak, Junior," I said. "You want control, fine, give me a pitchfork and a pile of muck and you can tell me just how to move it. But you can't control how this goes."

I told him under the circumstances I would not be willing to go into that book room again. I'd want something in writing from the executor acknowledging my right to be there. Now I was going back to the hotel. I'd be here a few days, and if he should have a change of heart I'd be happy to revisit him. I appreciated the offer; I would rethink the money and he might have some kind of refund coming after all. But I promised nothing.

This was at least in part a calculated bluff. In fact, I didn't like Junior much and now I didn't trust him. As a bookman I was intrigued by his case and I still didn't want to lose it, but I let him drive me back to town without another word.

Alone in my hotel room I thought about Harold Ray Geiger and his wife, frozen forever in her dead youth. That's how I saw her, the eternal daddy's girl, even at her death in early middle age.

But now what I had done seemed hasty and half-baked. If it had been a bluff, so far it had backfired. I had learned long ago not to bluff with an empty hand, and it looked like I had learned it again. But you can't work for a man you don't trust. Etch that in stone.

He'll call me, I thought: he'll think it over and back down. One minute I was sure of this, a minute later I was full of doubt. Noon came and I had a light lunch. Back in my room I made a call to Carroll Shaw at the Blakely Library, hoping he could fill in some gaps on Junior and the Geigers and maybe even on Candice. This was a long-shot, but I was in a down time, time perhaps for playing the odds. Carroll got around, he had interviewed many collectors in the field and had written a descriptive bibliography on juvenilia that had become part of every good bookman's reference section. It was a thick doorstop that contained detailed points and gorgeous color facsimile title pages, on books that were truly rare and a few that had long been assumed extinct. Its two-volume slipcased limited edition had sold out immediately, even at $250 a set, and these days when it turned up, at book fairs and in glass cases, the asking price was at least $500.

Carroll was out when I called, but I left word with the woman who answered the phone: If he knew anything at all about the Geigers, especially Candice Geiger née Ritchey, would he please call me back in Idaho Falls?

I sat on my bed and watched part of a boring football game. At three o'clock I did some simple arithmetic on the money Junior had paid me and I decided if he didn't call again I'd refund him two thousand. That would still give me a good payday after expenses, not bad for getting on an airplane and flying home again. But I knew that deal would leave a sour taste in my mouth. I have never liked being paid for doing nothing, and by the time I ordered my second drink in the bar I had decided screw it, I would send back almost four thousand, take the high road out of here and let him cover only my expenses. I didn't like that either. This whole trip was a failure, and that lingered in my mind through the long afternoon and into the gray dusk. Now I told myself I only wanted to be rid of it, but this too was false. Wherever I looked, there they were: If I stared into a dark place I saw Junior peering out of it. I saw Sharon with her horses and the old man on his deathbed with only Junior standing by. In one of my bleaker moments I saw Candice, not the striking young woman behind the winner's circle, but a grinning corpse in an immaculate white dress, standing beside a hooded man, clutching at something under his rain slicker.

At four o'clock I called my bookstore in Denver. Erin had just come in after a long day in her law office on Seventeenth Street. "Just the voice I need to hear for a quick pickup," I said. "How are things in Glocca Morra?"

"Just splendid."

"Is that little brook still leaping there?"

"Oh, please! If you go all the way through that cockamamie song I swear I will scream your eardrum out and fall straight into catatonic arrest. So how's it going on your end of the stick?"

"Not so good. The only good news is, I saw some truly fabulous books this morning. The library of a lifetime."

"I can remember a day when that would have been enough. What's the bad news?"

"I may not be able to help this guy after all. He's very difficult. He wants something I don't think I can do. Probably have to give him his money back if it comes to that."

I told her all about Junior Willis, Sharon, the books, and the horses. She sat quietly on her end while I related both the facts and my impressions of the case. It was a case now, more than a job, less than a full investigation, but still a case. But I had no employer at the moment, and I was floundering in self-doubt.

"You are wallowing in self-doubt," Erin said, six hundred miles away.

"Floundering, perhaps."

"You're splitting hairs, Janeway. Whenever you do that, I know you've been wallowing."

"I needed to talk to a voice of reason and for some goofy reason, yours came to mind."

"You want guidance."

"I would settle for that."

"I'm afraid it's all you'll get from six hundred miles away."

"How'd we do in the store today?"

"Don't ask. It's a good thing one of us has a day job."

"That's the book biz for you. Feast one day, famine the next."

"It's been famine all week. So what can I tell you? Your choices seem to be, come on home, stay there for another day or two and see what happens, or go crawling back to this Junior jerk on your knees, begging his

114

forgiveness."

"I never could sell a begging act. Then they know they've got you by the, ah . . ."

"I should be there instead of you, I wouldn't have to worry about getting squeezed in those particular places. I can be just as tough and I don't wallow afterward."

"If you wanted to fly up here and check old Junior out, I could bill him for both of us."

"You should've gone to law school. You've already got the billing part down pat."

This went on for at least another fifteen minutes, nonsense guaranteed to make me sleep better. "In case you don't know," I said, "I miss the hell out of you."

"I know you do. Same here. You keep in touch. I like to know where you are."

The day's rain had turned to snow and my mood was as cold and dark as the night. I wished I had never heard of Geiger or his wife: I especially wished I had never made the acquaintance of the spooky Mr. Junior Willis. At eight o'clock I went to the first decent-looking restaurant I could find nearby and had dinner, but my troubled mind continued poking through the ashes of Geiger's life and death, and afterward I couldn't remember what I'd had or how it had tasted. I lingered over coffee, thinking now about Sharon. I sensed more trouble than I could imagine, and I didn't like the notion that I was walking out on something extraordinary without having any idea what it really was or more than a glimmer of what it might be.

I got back to the hotel before ten o'clock. As I walked in, the desk clerk said, "Mr. Janeway, there's been a gentleman asking about you."

"What kind of gentleman?"

"Elderly African-American. He waited here for more than an hour."

"He didn't say where he was going?"

"I thought he was still here. Maybe he just stepped out for a minute."

"Well, if he comes back in the next two hours or so, have him call upstairs."

I sat in my room and looked at the telephone. This was it, I thought: this had to be about the Geigers; no one else knew I was here. I read some of the local paper that the hotel had left outside my room that morning and I learned again how small cities have most of the same problems that Denver has. You can't go far enough today to escape murder, rape, global warming, mayhem, and the troubles of fools. I waited and read, but when the phone rang again it wasn't my African-American. Immediately I recognized the deep voice: Carroll Shaw at the Blakely Library.

"Hey, Cliff, we haven't heard from you in a while."

"Way too long. I haven't seen anything lately that's got your name on it."

"If you do, I'm always buying."

"So I take it you got my message about the Geigers."

"Sure did. I wish I could tell you something about it but the word is that stuff's locked away like Fort Knox."

"But you've heard of it."

"Oh hell, yeah. There were rumors in the book trade twenty years ago. A woman in white just shows up suddenly and makes your day; makes your whole year if you've got the right stuff. Book dealers have been talking about her forever. I'm surprised you never heard of her till now."

"You keep forgetting, I got a late start in this. What's the scuttlebutt?"

"Only what I'm sure you already know. Young heiress buys every flawless high spot she can get her hands on, back when you could still pick up stuff like that. Dies young and leaves the books to her daughter. As far as I know, the daughter's still sitting on it, up in Montana or South Dakota, some damn place."

"She's sitting on half of it right here in Idaho. The old man got the other half."

"That I didn't know. Jesus, is he still alive?"

"Was, until last month."

"He must've been close to a hundred."

"He was up in his nineties; eccentric as hell from what I could pick up. He was pretty well-heeled, didn't need money, on the outs with all his kids; God knows what'll happen to the book collection now that he's in the ground. I think they all know now that it's something special, so they won't put it out in the trash. But none of them except the daughter knows how to take care of it."

"If you do get in to see it, I'd be very interested in a report."

"Already seen it, both the daughter's and the old man's. I was out there today."

"That thumping sound you hear is my heart beating overtime."

"Oh, it's great stuff, Carroll. I didn't come close to appraising it; couldn't even examine much of it in the time I had. But what I did see sure made me think of you."

A moment passed. "I'd fly out there just for a look," Carroll said. "No strings attached."

"That might be possible with the daughter's half. I can ask her."

"Please do. What about the rest of it?"

"It's locked up in the old man's house. There may be some squabble over his estate. At the moment it's being watch-dogged by an assistant, fellow named Junior Willis."

"What's in it for him?"

"Some substantial cash and some damn nice racehorses."

"Nothing wrong with racehorses, but you know I'm interested in the books. And you also know we'd pay top dollar, and an extra-good finder's fee for your trouble."

"I know you would. But it may be an ethical problem for me to get that closely involved with the money. I was officially on Willis's payroll . . . still am, till I decide how much of his money to send back."

"Send it all back and let us deal with it then. I don't even want to know how much it is."

"Five thousand big ones."

"Cliff, you're getting deaf in your old age. That's way more information than I need."

"I gotcha. Look, I'll let you know if anything changes."

"Meanwhile ask the daughter when I can come see her. No strings attached."

I said I would, we hung up, and that same

instant the phone rang under my hand. The desk clerk said, "That gentleman's down here to see you, sir."

"Good. Send him up."

I picked up the papers from the bed and splashed some cold water in my face. Two minutes later there was a soft knock at the door.

In that first second as I looked into his face he seemed faintly familiar, but I couldn't put my finger on where or when we might have met. He smiled almost timidly and said his name, "I'm Louis Young, sir," and I shook his hand and invited him in. Whatever this was, I thought again, it had something to do with the Geigers, but I played it cool. "Would you like a drink, Mr. Young?"

He shook his head but his eyes said yes-maybe. I said, "I'm having one." I wasn't but I sensed something about to happen, I felt circumstances changing, and that called for a bit of fellowship. I coaxed him. "Maybe a little one?"

"A little one, then."

"Bourbon okay or would you rather have something else?"

"That'd be fine, sir."

I called down and ordered two drinks. We sat on opposite sides of the desk and I said,

"I'm getting strong vibes from you, Mr. Young; like maybe we've met somewhere but I can't put my finger on it."

"I worked for Mr. Geiger."

I caught the past tense and I remembered. "You worked for Geiger for many years. I saw your pictures with Mrs. Geiger and Mr. Willis."

"Yes, sir."

"You were in a lot of them."

He nodded. "I was the ginney, sir. I was the groom."

"You were a young man in those early pictures."

"I was a boy."

"That would mean you had been with Mr. Geiger at least thirty years."

"Yes, sir. I never added it up, but that's got to be pretty close."

Again I got a sense of some deep hurt in his voice. "What happened?" I asked.

"I was let go along with the servants."

Now I could see the hurt in his face and I didn't ask why.

"So how'd you hear about me?"

"I do some occasional work for Miss Sharon. She said you were a policeman they hired to find out what happened to her mamma."

"Well, I'm not exactly a policeman and I

haven't been hired for anything yet. Otherwise she's got it almost right."

He smiled, affectionately I thought. "She's like that sometimes, especially when she's going on no sleep. She should use me more than she does if I might say so myself."

"What do you do for her when you do it?"

"Afternoon work. I muck stalls, soap tack . . . some of the same stuff she does herself in the morning. With twenty or thirty horses there's always something to do. I go over full-time three days a week. And once or twice a month we take the big truck and I help her get a load of hay."

There was a knock at the door. "Our drinks," I said.

I let the fellow in; took the glasses and the ice and the two tiny bottles and gave him a tip. The waiter left and I turned my attention to the liquor. "May I call you Louis?"

"Everybody just calls me Louie."

"Louie, then, if that's okay with you." I opened the two little bottles and began to run water out of the tap. "You really want a lot of water in this?"

"Better not make it too stout, sir, I gotta drive home."

"My name's Cliff and I'd be pleased if you dropped the sir." I cut the booze with some water and handed him a glass with ice. "So what's this all about?"

"Might I ask you something, sir?"

"Sure. But I may not answer if you keep calling me sir."

"Cliff," he said shyly.

"Thank you." I waited for his question and finally he said, "Would it be possible — can we keep this conversation private?"

"I don't know. Are you going to give me evidence of a crime?"

"No, nothing like that."

"Are you going to tell me something that would put someone in trouble if I sat on it?"

"No." But he looked uncertain and I waited without committing myself.

"Whatever comes of it," he said, "I'd rather it didn't come from me."

"I'll do my best."

That didn't relieve him either. He began to fidget with his glass and I said, "As long as there's no ethical or legal reason that compels me to tell someone, I won't." I didn't tell him that ethics would be my call or that I had long ago drawn my own lines on silly, restrictive laws.

"I'd just rather Miss Sharon didn't even know I came here." His eyes roamed around the room. "I'm not sure it's possible to keep it from her, but I had to try."

"What would she say?"

"Probably nuthin'. I just don't know if she'd be all that happy about it."

"And that matters to you."

"Sure it does."

"What would she do about it?"

He shook his head and I had the craziest notion. He seemed on the verge of tears.

"What would Sharon do, Louie?" I asked again, gently now.

"Well, I'll tell you this much. She wouldn't take it out of my hide. She's not like that."

"But you don't want to disappoint her," I ventured.

"Yeah. I'd do just about anything to avoid that."

"So what you're telling me is, she's a good woman. That's what I thought this morning when I met her. I had an impression of someone who is honest and caring and hardworking. A straight-shooter."

"I'd say that's a good sound judgment." For another moment he seemed lost in thought. Gradually then his eyes came back to mine.

I said, "I take it she confides in you."

"Well, I've known her a long time."

"Long time, meaning . . ."

"I remember the day she was born."

"That would be quite a long time in her

frame of reference."

"Even in mine. More than half my own lifetime ago."

A moment passed. "So let me ask you again, Louie, what is it you want me to do?"

"We want to hire you."

I groped through a tired brain for something intelligent and came up blank. "Oh," I said.

"We think she maybe could use somebody like you."

"Who's we?"

"Me, the house people. All of us."

"What exactly are you hiring me for?"

"Just to keep an eye on things. Just for a while, you know? Could you do that?"

"I suppose I could go out and see her again tomorrow."

"Would you do that?"

"If it would matter, sure." I watched his face, his hands, his fingers tapping lightly on his knees. "Would it matter, Louie?"

"I think she'd like that. She might not say so, but . . ."

He sipped his drink and said, "That gal's got a heart as big as Montana." His voice quaked and I was strangely moved by his words. Coupled with the look on his face they spoke volumes about this woman I barely knew. For half a minute his eyes got moist and he dabbed at them with his shirtsleeve. We sipped our drinks and an uneasy silence fell over us. At some point he said, "She hired us all after Mr. Geiger let us go. Maybe you heard about that."

I nodded and he said, "We go in three days and she pays us for the whole week. Quite a bit more than we got working a week for Mr. Geiger, and that was fair enough."

"Hey, who wouldn't like a deal like that?"

"That's just how she is. Man, there's nothing we wouldn't do for her. We'd be happy to work every day, but she needs her space . . . time when it's just her and the horses."

"I can understand that."

"We'd each toss in half a week's salary; that's how we'd pay you."

There I was, facing the same question I had asked Junior. "I'm still not clear what you'd be hiring me to do."

"Come out, talk to her, see what you think."

"About what?"

"Maybe it's just me. Probably just an old man's fears. But I can't shake the feeling she's in some kinda . . . I don't know . . . maybe some trouble she don't even know about."

"Are we talking about real trouble, Louie,

as in danger?"

"That's just it, I don't know. It seems downright silly when you put it that way."

"What could she be in danger from?"

"It's hard to get a handle on it. But I keep thinking about how her mamma died — sudden, you know. No warning."

I thought of that too. I thought of the wall of winners in Geiger's office and now in my mind I saw the changing faces. "Lots of people work for a man like Geiger over the years," I said nonchalantly. "Most of 'em not like you, there for half a lifetime."

"Yeah, they come and go. That's how it is on the racetrack. Come and go. Move away to the other Coast and maybe you never see 'em again."

"I saw the pictures on his wall. Tell me about them. Looks like a pretty steady crew."

"Yeah, Mr. Geiger always used just one jockey at a time. Raise him up from a bug boy. He had one ginney for each four horses. He'd teach a bug boy from scratch, pay him just a salary, and have his services in the mornings for workouts as well as the races in the afternoon. He'd get a weight allowance, five pounds off scale for using a bug boy, and if he win the hands would get something extra."

A bug boy would be an apprentice jockey, he said, in case I didn't know.

"Most of those boys got good pretty fast. Mr. Geiger was a great teacher back then, and his boys listened to what he said. If they didn't, they didn't last long. Lotsa big-name jocks started as bug boys with Mr. Geiger."

"Tell me about the ones who took the hard way out."

"Yeah, well, you know. There's always some of those."

Geiger's first boy for one, he said: "Not the very first one, I never knew that one, I'm talkin' about the kid who was here when I first hired on."

A word-picture of a ninety-eight-pound punk billowed up from the past. Johnny Brewer, his name was . . . a self-important fool who strutted along the shedrow, bossed the ginneys rudely, and rode recklessly when he thought he could get away with it. One day he tried to squeeze through on the rail where there wasn't any hole and caused a bad spill. He broke his back and had been in a wheelchair ever since.

"What about Sandy Standish?"

"Oh yeah, but that's different. Mr. Sandy was okay."

"You ever hear from him?"

"Miss Sharon keeps in touch. They was real close."

I scribbled some thoughts in my notebook. "Who else?"

"Some other fellas, they wasn't with us long."

I asked him what else he remembered and wrote down some names. "We had a good crew then," he said. "It was a real happy shedrow in those days. We had laughs, man, I thought I'd die at some of the stuff them daggone white boys pulled on us."

The only trouble with good times is they never last, I said, but bad news always seems to come around again. "Like now. I heard Cameron's come back."

"Yeah, I saw him prowlin' around the house last week. He got outta there fast when he seen me comin'. So I didn't see him to talk to."

"Did you tell Sharon?"

"Oh yeah, sure. I couldn't let something like that pass."

"What'd she say?"

"Sluffed it off. She's not afraid of anybody. But she needs to be more wary."

"Of her brother?"

"Maybe especially."

There was something about his voice, his face, what he was saying and what he hadn't said. An evil thought went through my head and the moment was pregnant with rank implications. "I heard Cameron was bad news."

"They all are. But yeah, he'd be the worst."

"Do you think he stole the books?"

"We got blamed."

"I know you did. But it might have been Cameron."

"That'd be my guess. Since you asked."

"Tell me more about Cameron and what he does."

He shook his head. "I don't understand . . ."

I think you do, Louie, I thought.

"What's the worst thing he's ever done?"

He was surprised by the question; I could see him struggling with it. Whatever he knew, it was not something he wanted to talk about. *What could that be?* I thought. Again a brutal, rank image crossed my mind and I didn't have to be Albert Einstein to see it.

"I'm not just asking this to shovel the dirt, Louie, it's a question I often ask. It helps if I know what a guy is capable of."

"Just figure anything. He'd do just about anything you can imagine."

"What's he actually done that you know about?"

His eyes looked away.

"We're not talking about money now, are we, Louie?"

He looked back at me and his face was a thousand years old. I could see the shape of it now, a dark secret he had never told anyone. I was guessing but in that moment I'd have bet a small bundle on it. I cocked my head and looked in his eyes. "Louie?"

"I don't know what you want. I don't know anything . . ."

Softly, I said, "Did Cameron do something to Sharon?"

He had been watching me edge closer to this moment. Now it was here and he was shocked. "Man, I can't talk about this," he said, and his voice quaked.

"How old was she when this happened, Louie?"

"I don't know . . . Jesus, I'm just a ginney; how am I supposed to know stuff like that?"

He looked in my eyes. What he really wanted was that nothing had ever happened. That Sharon would perhaps tell me something he himself couldn't say. That Cameron had never come back. That Cameron had never been born in the first place.

"Maybe I could come out in the morning

and talk to her some more."

"If you would just do that much. But don't tell her what we're talking about."

"Are we talking about something?"

"No, sir. We didn't talk about Cameron. He's . . ."

After a while I said, "What is he, Louie?"

"He's fishin' around for some way to approach her. He must be down to the end of his rope. I think he must need money really bad to come back here and show his face. That means he's gotta try something soon."

"I'll see you tomorrow morning then."

I would have to be there early, he said. "We're going over for a load of hay tomorrow, so she'll want to get the animals taken care of by daybreak. We'll be out of there at six-thirty."

He reached for his wallet. "I could give you something now, more in a few days."

"Keep your money, Louie, I've already been paid."

After he left I looked at my untouched drink. I dumped it in the sink and went to bed.

6

I awoke thinking of Sharon and her menacing half brother. The dream had faded even before my first awareness of the new day, leaving only a vague impression of the brother, a man I had never seen but who now made me think of the worst characters from Dickens. I saw him as a big hulking man, a bruiser who preyed on children, but even Dickens in his day couldn't write the stuff that lingered in my mind.

Again I was out well before dawn. The weather had finally cleared, the streets were still pocked with slushy puddles, but the forecast was for blue skies the rest of the week. I drove past the all-night café in the dark and went out along the road where twenty-odd hours earlier I had ridden as a passenger with Junior Willis. I got on the dirt road without a hitch, went past the KEEP OUT sign as if I belonged there, and soon I saw the lights of the old man's house.

I went on past and turned into Sharon's yard. Suddenly she was there in my headlights, walking around a big closed truck that had been parked at the side of the porch. The three dogs swarmed around her. She looked my way and waited for me to stop, then she came around and said hello. "I'm glad you came back. Come on inside and eat something."

Inside the talk was easy. I said I had come out to work again, she didn't seem surprised, and I figured I'd save the trumped-up explanation for if and when I needed it. We sat and had some coffee and a moment later the servants came in. It was immediately clear that whatever they had been at Geiger's, they weren't servants here. Sharon pushed her own place aside to make room for them at the table and they all sat down and hunkered close. "People, this is Cliff," Sharon said; "Cliff, that's Rosemary on the end, the young man beside her is Billy Young, next to him is Lillian Wheeler. That tall handsome gentleman next to the wall is Louie Young." I grinned affably, shook hands, and said hello to them all.

Sharon had made a large breakfast casserole; she brought it out herself in two trays, they all helped themselves liberally, and everyone ate with good appetites.

Lively, uninhibited talk flowed around the room. Rosemary turned out to be Louie's younger sister. She was most interested in the news of the day, presidential politics, and the coming day's work. Lillian had the loudest voice, rich, high-pitched, and full of infectious laughter. Billy was a strapping kid about twenty years old. He had two years of college under his belt, he wanted to get into law enforcement, and Sharon had told him about my police career. He asked how I had broken in and why I had left the department to go into the book trade. I couldn't sugarcoat that part of it, so I told him the shortest version, that there was a thug in Denver who was brutalizing a woman and wouldn't take no for an answer. "One day I pushed him into a fight, and maybe I shouldn't have done that. It was a pretty big scandal in Denver."

"What happened?"

"I was suspended pending the outcome of an investigation."

"How'd that turn out?"

"I quit before the final report was finished. The writing was on the wall."

"They were gonna sandbag you."

"There are some fellows in the department, including my old friend and partner, who'd tell you I sandbagged myself. There's one thing you've got to remember if you get in with the cops, Billy. Always do it by the book."

"What if you can't?"

"Then I guess you've got to follow your heart like I did. Just be ready for the consequences when they come down, because they will, and you've got to be at peace with yourself when it's all said and done."

Sharon said, "What about you, Cliff, are you at peace?"

I told her I had never been completely at peace with myself about anything. I accomplish something and then right away I get bored with it and I start looking for something new. "Looks like I was born with a restless spirit." Billy said, "I can't imagine being a police officer and being bored," and I told him it's like anything else in life, it's got its highs and lows. "The highs can be really high, but when the lows come — when you know a guy is guilty of really bad stuff, when there is no doubt and there's absolutely nothing you can do about it, and what's worse, you know he'll do it again — that can be pretty debilitating."

"What about now? Are you sorry you took on that creep?"

It took a while, but I finally said, "No."

"You don't miss it?"

"Sure I do, but that's a different question. That's why I still do some work on the side, to keep my hand in. But you're right, it's not the same."

"Have you ever had to kill a man?"

"Billy!" Rosemary said sharply. "What the hell kinda question is that?"

"I guess the real question," Sharon said, "is whether you'd go back to it if you could."

That was a strange moment: I had seldom allowed myself to consider such a possibility and now here it was in my face. It wasn't real and yet it was, and suddenly I was aware of the scrutiny of the group. "I don't know," I said, and in that moment, perhaps for the first time, I didn't know. "Maybe," I said. "The job would have to be right, wouldn't it?"

I hadn't ever let myself think that way. I had had a good career then and I had a good one now. In my mind, that was a thing for its time, but this lingering doubt had always nagged me.

Across the room a clock chimed.

"Quarter after six, boys," Sharon said. "Time to head 'em up, move 'em out."

Three of them were going on a sixty-mile trip, out to a farm where she had bought hay for years, and I would make it four if I wanted to ride along. She spoke to me privately in the hall while Louie went outside and warmed up the truck.

"I've been thinking about what Junior told you. Have you made up your mind yet about working for Junior?"

"I left it in limbo, but it doesn't look good. I can't work for a guy who won't talk to me."

"How'd you like to work for me instead? Same job with maybe a few new wrinkles, better working conditions, happier people, fringe benefits, time-and-a-half for overtime, a good pension plan, no pressure . . ."

We stood in the dark hallway for another thirty seconds. Softly she said, "Whatever he's paying you, I'll double it." Then I heard a door open and saw a light. She was standing about ten feet away. "Come here, I want to show you something."

I followed her into a sparsely furnished bedroom with a winner's circle picture on the far wall. Her mother looked out at us with deep intense eyes.

"Of all our pictures, this is the one that's really her. She's not putting on a face or trying to be what she thought he wanted. Come over here a minute."

We crossed the room and she opened a closet. Hanging there, looking like new, was the bookwoman's white dress.

"She died in that. They were out at the farm in California."

I stood waiting for whatever might come next. She said, "Go ahead, touch it," and I felt the silky-soft material.

"That doesn't prove anything, does it?" she said. "I just had a silly notion that if you touched it she'd come to life and you'd have to find out what happened to her."

It doesn't work that way, I told her. Having a burning mission doesn't automatically mean success.

"I know that. I'm prepared to fail, but I think you're the last best chance I'll ever have of finally learning the truth."

God help the truth, she was probably right.

"So what do you think really happened to her?"

"I don't know that, do I? My biggest fear is I won't ever know."

Out in the hall she asked me again. "Stay. Help me bury her once and for all."

"I'd have to think it over. Decide what the ethics are and whether I can do that. I took a fairly large retainer from Junior."

"Give it back to him. I'll give you a bigger one."

"That doesn't just make the ethical problem go away. In a way it makes things worse. All it does is turn me into a hired gun, for sale to the highest bidder."

We walked out onto the front porch. "There are ways around these problems," she said. "You're a smart cookie, Cliff, I know you can come up with something."

"I could work for you free. That would probably do it."

"Oh, be serious."

"I am serious, in a crazy kind of way."

"Okay then, I'll pay you *exactly* what he was paying you. Not a penny more."

"Good-bye pension," I said sadly. "So long time and a half."

She walked across the porch and stood looking into the black morning. "I happen to believe these are important questions, no matter who's raising them, who's paying the tab, or what their motives are. I've been thinking about it for years . . . more than half my lifetime. Now you're here and you're about to leave us. If I let that happen there won't ever be any answers."

She balanced on the edge and sighed loudly. "Look, I know there's no guarantee. It's a longshot any way you cut it, but now Junior's raised the question and I've got to try. All I'd ask is that you give it your best. If that doesn't work I'll have to find some way to forget her."

We were out on the road before seven. The truck was capable of transporting at least eight horses or many bales of hay. Sharon drove and I rode with her in the cab; Louie and Billy sat on a bench in the back. We passed a feed store, already open at that early hour. A sign on the building said FREE DELIVERY ON ALL ORDERS, and suddenly what we were doing made no sense. Why take four of us away from the farm for most of a day when the feed store was almost within spitting distance? But when I asked her, she said, "I've been dealing with this same farmer a long time, way before that feed store ever opened. Nothing wrong with the feed store, but I need the exercise and I want to do it this way." She said nothing more for a while, but I could sense her ongoing struggle to find the right words, some true thing that would make her a little less strange in my eyes. "I know a lot of people would find this odd," she said. "And I find it hard to explain even to myself. What we're about to do today is hard work. And it's got nothing to do with Louie and Billy. Before they came, I did it all myself. I had fewer horses then but at the end of the day I would go home just drained; when I hit the bed I didn't have another ounce of strength left in me. There were nights when I just lay there, so dead tired I couldn't move, still unable to sleep, and I'd think, *You're a strange, weird woman, Sharon.*" I told her those were just screwy words. "Hell, *I'm* strange, by any standard the world uses to define itself. Strange has at least two sides and a dozen shades, and from what I can see you're way over on the good side of it."

The farm was about ninety minutes from town, along a dirt road that led back from the highway. First there were fields, stretching out to the east; then we saw the barn, then the farmhouse in a grove of trees. We pulled up in a warm Idaho sunshine and she parked under a tree at the side of the house. The old farmer and his wife came out to greet us and we all shook hands. It was well after the cutting season: If we had come a few weeks earlier, the baled hay would still be in the field. Now it was stashed in that immense barn. "This makes it easier," Sharon said. "We might get out of here before noon."

The work began. It was much the same as Sharon and I had done at her place, only more of it. Louie and Billy tossed bales down from the loft, I heaved them up onto the truck, and Sharon stacked them tightly from the floor to the ceiling. The farmer's wife brought us coffee for a break at ten o'clock and we all stood around laughing and talking. The farmer, whose name was Adams, never once asked to double-check her tally. Sharon wrote everything down meticulously and rounded it off in his favor. At the end of the morning she gave him her total and her check. Hilda, the farmer's wife, insisted that we stay for lunch, and we sat around a large table on their back porch, talking about the old days of farming and horse racing.

Everything's different today, Adams said. In another thirty years there won't be any independent farms like this one. It's all going corporate.

And life changes, life endures, and life goes on.

There was one nice touch: They had a large shelf of books inside the old farmhouse, and I found a good one: *Oh, Promised Land,* by James Street, Dial Press, 1940. I had cherished this as a boy, loved it right up there with *The Black Stallion* when I was fifteen. It took me straight back to the early American frontier just to see the almost flawless jacket. The farmer's wife said she had loved that as well when she was young. "You've kept it in remarkable shape," I said:

in fact, the only problem was no problem at all, a slightest bit of fading to the jacket's spine. I hadn't researched it: all I knew was that I hadn't seen any hardback in years, and here was a gorgeous first edition. "I don't suppose you'd want to sell it," I said, and the woman took it from her shelf and tried to give it to me. I told her I'd give her five hundred and she almost fainted. I ended the day asking her to pack it carefully and ship it to me in Denver, and I wrote her a check for $525.

"That was fun," I said to Sharon in the truck.

"Yep," she said. "Couldn't do that at the feed store."

We were heading home by three o'clock. Sharon was tired and I drove while she slept soundly against the door. At quarter to five we pulled into her road and her eyes flicked open. "Somebody's been here," she said. She was still in the grip of sleep and I have never figured out how she knew that. Somebody in fact had been there. "Cameron's been here," she said.

7

That day I moved out of the hotel. Sharon had a tack room in the loft, which became my home of the moment. We didn't know if Cameron would return; none of us were mind readers, and even Sharon, who had somehow sensed his presence as we pulled into the road, could not remember what she'd been dreaming or if she had been dreaming at all. We did know, because Rosemary had told us, that Cameron had come calling three times; he had been increasingly insistent, and the last time he was abusive and threatening. He had come looking for a book. That was all they knew for now, but it was enough that I wanted to be here if he came again. I pulled my car into the barn and parked out of sight in the feed bin. I had my working police .38 in my bag and suddenly I was glad it was there.

Sharon and I still had no agreement written or implied: I had asked for no money and she seemed content to leave that topic alone and let it find its own place as time went by. We didn't talk about Candice that first night: I knew there was much to be said, but for now I stashed my bag in the tack room and set up the rollaway bed against the wall facing the door and left her alone. I draped my gun over the chair in its holster, within an arm's reach of the bed, and by dark I was solidly entrenched. It was like living in a cave of straw, primitive but pleasant in its way. I liked it, it was private, the bed was good, and I was as content there as I ever am anywhere.

The room was about twelve feet square with a shoulder-high window about eight inches by twelve that looked out toward the house. The window was simply for light and air: in case of fire, all you could do was go back through that wall of straw or roll yourself into a ball and kiss your ass good-bye. To get there I had to climb the narrow stairs and go through that feed room over the barn. There was a corridor of sorts, a tight squeeze between the bales of hay stacked on both sides, and a door with a lock that I would probably never use. A table and two chairs, a hotplate, and a small icebox — these were the only furnishings and appliances other than my rollaway. The hotplate was on a shelf under the window, far away from the hay and straw. "Don't leave it plugged in," Sharon said with an apologetic shrug as she stated the obvious. "There's coffee in that cabinet and some books there too if you're a restless sleeper." If I needed water I'd have to go down and fill my pots and canteen from the tap where we watered the horses. On dry evenings like this one I could leave the loft door open, squeeze through the straw to my room, or bed down in a sleeping bag in the dark loft, playing the radio, looking at the stars, or watching the road all the way back to the trees.

At quarter to nine that first night Sharon came over and told me to get my hunkus up to the house for something to eat. Lillian had cooked a stew. It was such a late dinner that I had almost forgotten about food, but the rich smell of it brought my hunger raging back again. Sharon had been on the telephone much of the evening, arranging for the six new horses to be brought in. "It was touch-and-go whether I'd get them," she said. "Some people would rather just sell them to the killers, don't ask me why, and the only way I can save them is to find out early enough and pay more money than a sane person ought to. But I can outbid anybody if they get my dander up."

She was expecting a mixed lot, half of them fairly sound, the others with various problems. "One of 'em's pretty sick and from what I heard we may lose him. We'll see how he is tomorrow." We stood in the yard at the end of our day and I felt at home with this woman I barely knew. Inside, we sat around the table and filled in the particulars on Cameron. He had arrived this morning, an hour after we left, driving up to the front door like he'd never been away. "I think he may have been watching the house," Rosemary said, "just waitin' for y'all to leave." She didn't know this for a fact but she could feel it in her bones. He was in an old Buick Eight with a crushed left fender, and the motor pinged like it was on its last legs. At first he was charming: a smiling jocular man with tiny hips and an enormous belly that drooped far over his belt. "You wouldn't know him now if you passed him on the street, even if he is your part brother," Rosemary said; "I'd bet a dollar he ain't seen his own dick in five years," and the table erupted with laughter.

He had aged badly. His skin was pale and pasty, craggy like some alien desert landscape. "He looks like he might have some little skin cancers growing around his nose."

148

One thing that hadn't changed was how he swaggered his way up the stairs to the front porch, "like he owns the world and the rest of us are just paying rent." Sharon nodded faintly. Of the three brothers, Cameron always did put on the best swagger. But Rosemary thought life had not been good to him: he had to make a big effort just to get out of that car and haul himself up the front stairs. To a casual eye he looked more like he might be Sharon's daddy or maybe her grandfather than her half brother. He had a fellow with him about half his age with muscles bulging under tightly rolled sleeves. Sharon asked if she had gotten a name for that one, but they had come and gone, each time there had been more tension, and there'd been no time for questions. "He just said he'd come for a book you owe him," Rosemary said.

"I don't know what he's talking about," Sharon said.

Both of them had approached the door that first time. Rosemary described it candidly, with no effort to be overly polite. "That cracker from Muscle Beach was what we always called white trash. He stood off flexing his knuckles like he'd just die for the chance to rearrange my bones then and there, like one word from Cameron and I'd be dead meat." They loomed there in the doorway, trying to intimidate, arguing for at least five minutes and getting more insistent all the time. "They just stood there trying to face us down. That's when I put politeness out the back door and told 'em they might as well get used to the wait, because nobody comes in Sharon's house when Sharon ain't here. Nobody."

So they had gone away, but less than half an hour later they were back again. Now Cameron was getting ugly. "God*dammi*t, Rosemary, you're takin' a helluva lot on yourself for hired nigger help." Sharon sat up straight in sudden hot anger. "Did he actually say that?" "Yes, he did," Rosemary said. "I didn't know whether I should tell you or not, you know I don't get outta joint over stuff like that, but yeah, he said it several times to both of us. He said, 'Maybe you think you be family or some such, but you ain't nuthin' but highfalutin house niggers.' " Sharon was red under the front room lamp. "Then what happened?"

Then they argued some more, maybe twenty minutes this time, with Cameron getting madder by the minute. "Listen, you!" he yelled at one point. "I ain't got *time* for this goddam song and dance, I got to be on the Coast tomorrow afternoon and

I ain't leavin' here till I get what's mine!" So Rosemary said, "Write us a letter about it. If it's yours Sharon might be inclined to send it to you." More laughter, like a soft cheering section, went around the table.

"He didn't like that business about the letter," Rosemary said, "but he left again, callin' me nigger names and cussin' up a blue streak."

This time he was gone till early afternoon. "Next thing I hear out of him he's there on the porch again, trying to kick the door down. I figure they snuck back somehow 'cause I never heard the car come up and never saw it either. We just sitting here like this and there he is, beatin' on the door with his shoulder and his feet till I can hear the wood starting to split. Then he says, 'Now you made me mad, nigger,' and he keeps on sayin' that like some crazy man. 'Now you made me mad, nigger, now you made me mad. You shouldn'ta done that.' "

Sharon shook her head and said, "Jesus," under her breath.

"That ain't all. You wanna hear the rest of it?"

Sharon nodded warily and Rosemary said, "That's when Lillian comes up with the 12-gauge pump gun. I jerk the door open and she fires a load of buckshot right over their heads. Blow a hole in the porch roof big as my fist."

"I'll pay for that," Lillian said.

"What happened then?" Sharon said.

"Then she jack another shell into the gun and they fall all over each other trying to get down them steps. Last we seen of 'em, they be going like hell down the road, about as fast as old Cameron can move. I felt like puttin' a load 'tween each of 'em's hind ends."

Again Lillian said, "I'm paying for the damage to the porch," but Sharon told her not to worry about it. I hadn't said anything all this time. Once I looked up at Sharon, our eyes met, and she looked away as if it shamed her to be part of our race. Lillian said, "I'd really appreciate it if you'd let me take care of that hole in the roof," and Louie made an aggravated motion with his hands. "Quit worryin' over the damn hole in the roof, Lil, me and Billy can fix it good as new."

We ate and talked some more, and afterward Sharon walked me back to the barn. "All of a sudden I'm nervous," she said. "No matter how careful I am, the books make me vulnerable."

"Would you be open to a visit from the guy at the Blakely Library? I'm not lobbying for him, but I know he'd like to see your stuff. And he's got a lot of well-heeled people in his corner, so he can get the money if you ever do want to sell it."

"I wouldn't want him to come all the way out here for nothing."

"He's a book guy, Sharon, this is what he does. He'd like to see it just for future reference, so if you ever do want to donate or sell it, you won't have to reinvent the wheel every time you talk. I imagine he'll want to make notes for his own information, if that's okay. For bibliographical purposes."

"And you trust this guy?"

"His word is like money in the bank."

"Okay, I'll see him," she said. "What's his name?"

"Carroll Shaw. The library is a private one; he's the director of special collections. I think it's an honorary job, which means he gets the satisfaction of putting it together and a lot of credit from book people all over the country. They've got some well-heeled backers and they're housing a world-class collection about an hour's drive north of San Francisco. Their whole mission is to protect books like yours, to preserve whatever's donated in the spirit it was given."

"Don't they all do that?"

"Not unless you nail them to the wall and

tack them down with Monster Glue. The first thing even a high-class library might want to do is sell off the dupes to generate revenue. I think it's vital from your viewpoint that the collection stay together. So whether you sell the books or not, listen to what Carroll has to say."

"I will, I promise."

"Don't do anything you might regret later."

"I won't."

"Swear to God," I said, and she made a sign in the air and we laughed.

We walked around the barn and stood in the shadows of the loft.

"What else are you thinking?" she said.

"I'm thinking I'll stick around a while. If that's okay with you."

"You think Cameron will come back?"

"Who knows what a guy like that might do? He's been here three times in one day and once he tried to kick the door in, so you've got to figure he's serious. Even if Lillian did scare him off for the moment, you need to know where he is."

"Then what?"

"Then we'll see."

The new horses arrived the next morning. She pulled off their shoes and turned them out and let them wander freely across the field. The sick horse was a sorry-looking thing, scrawny and scabby, trembly, with pus running down his face from an infected eye. He stood apart, wary as she approached him, but too sick to run away anymore. Her voice was almost mesmerizing, and after a while he closed his eyes and let her touch him. *Go ahead, kill me,* he seemed to say. She rubbed his ears and slipped a halter over his head and put the chain end of a lead shank through the halter and snapped it under his chin. All this time she kept talking, touching him, and I held him while she felt his legs. She hugged his head and ran her hands gently across his body till his trembles went away. This took a long time, but she went about it like she had nothing better to do with the rest of her life. I remembered what Junior had said about her hands but this was more than that. I thought she was treating him with her voice as well as her hands. *There you are, little guy, you're home now . . . you're home now . . . you're gonna be fine . . . my what a sweet little guy you are . . .* the same words over and over while she rubbed his neck and upper legs.

"He's got two bad tendons that never were treated right," she said. "Somebody fired him at some point but I don't think it did

155

him much good." I asked her what that meant and she said, "Basically you take a hot iron and burn holes in his legs. The idea is that all the healing properties in his body rush to that spot and help him get well."

Both front legs were bowed, she said, "and his lip's all screwed up where somebody had a mean twitch on him. Indicates a hell-raiser at some point, but there ain't much hell in him now. He's got bad feet: quarter cracks, a deep sand crack on that rear left hoof and a bone spavin on his right rear leg. Right now he's pretty miserable, he probably hurts everywhere all the time. He's mighty tired of living, but maybe I can coax some life into him after all. He might do okay here."

She put him in a stall and gave him a warm mash, and he ate like a starving castaway.

"Nothing wrong with his appetite," I said.

"That's the good news." She touched the side of his face, then lifted her hand a few inches and wiggled her fingers. "I think he's blind in this eye. I'll give him an antibiotic and see how he is tomorrow. Maybe all he needs is time and a new outlook on life."

She leaned toward him and made a soft kissing noise and he put his head on her shoulder. "Look at him," she said. "He's a real lover boy. He loves to cuddle."

"Does he have a name?"

"He does now. I think we'll call him Paul, after a fellow I once knew. Life treated him badly too."

We went up to the house and sat on her porch, and there I began to ask more questions. I wondered if she knew what the deal was between Junior and Damon: it seemed like an unholy alliance or at least an uneasy one. "It's really pretty simple," she said. "They've got a crackerjack three-year-old and some other nice horses they want to take out to Santa Anita this winter. But the will won't be settled for a while yet, so they'll want to get all of us together. Apparently Bax has told them he's fine with it. I'm the stumbling block."

"What do you think you'll do?"

"Don't know yet. I'm not sure I can do anything legally; the executor would probably side with them pretty quickly. There's two ways you can look at it. I don't particularly like racing, but these horses have been well-trained and they're fit, ready to run. This is what they've been aimed at; when HR was alive he and Junior were supposedly getting them ready, and I'm not sure I should step in now and mess that up. I doubt HR would actually have taken them racing, but this new crop they've got is exceptional. I watched Damon work one colt on our track and he does run like the wind, he could really be something good. If it was just Damon taking him I'd say no way, I'd fight him to the death. But believe it or not, I trust Junior. Maybe his bedside manner with people is lacking but I think he'll do what's right for his horses."

She remembered her mother in scattered episodes: here sometimes, gone with Geiger for weeks at a time. She had often been left with Rosemary during her school years. Louie had taught her about horses when they were home. "In a real way Louie and Rosemary raised me."

She was eleven when her mother died. "That's when they really raised me full time."

They were good teachers, she said. Rosemary taught her right from wrong and Louie showed her how to sit a horse properly.

But as time went on, her discontent deepened. "I never lost the feeling that my life would have been so much different if she had lived."

Gently I eased into the subject of her mother's death. "Where were you when she died?"

"I was here: it was the middle of the

school semester."

"Who was here then?"

"Rosemary, Lillian . . ."

"Your dad?"

"He was in California."

"There at the farm?"

"No, he had gone to a friend's ranch to look at some horses he wanted to buy."

"So she was alone."

She nodded. "HR found her when he came home."

"Where was Junior?"

"Out there at the racetrack. Junior was always there when HR went racing."

"What about your brothers?"

"Racing at Bay Meadows. Cameron was at some county fair."

All in Northern California, she said.

"Why did the cops out there assume Candice's death was an accident? Was there an autopsy?"

"Yes, it was the peanuts that killed her. That was never in question."

"The real question was, how'd she get them? The cops had to wonder about that."

She fell into a long silence, so long I had to prod her. "Sharon?"

"I think they suspected . . ."

"What?"

"They thought she might have eaten them

159

intentionally."

"Why would they think that?"

"Someone told them she was unhappy."

"Who told them that?"

"I never knew. Someone they talked to, and then they asked Louie about it. Someone had told them she was unhappy and that's how the question came up."

"So whoever it was, they got the idea she might have done it herself. And they never found any other theories or motives? Seems like they were pretty quick to make that call."

"Actually, they talked to everybody. I've got some of the reports. There came a time when they couldn't do any more."

"Okay, I understand that, I had a few like that myself."

I asked her to tell me about her brothers.

"Cameron's the oldest, but they're all getting up there now: When Candice married HR they were as old as she was."

"Did they resent Candice?"

"At first, I think. Then they learned she was far from a young gold digger, she could buy and sell them all fifty times over." Sharon laughed. "I'd love to've been there then, when that realization first came over each of them. Wish I had their faces on film. I'd play it back on my TV on Saturday st for amusement."

fternoon I looked through Sharon's
 while she made some telephone
checks. I wrote out detailed notes and
checked them against my earlier impressions from the old man's books. By late
afternoon Sharon had learned where Cameron had been staying: a flophouse indeed,
but he had already checked out. Before
evening we had begun to slip into a routine.
In the morning we did the stable work, and
after breakfast she made some phone calls.
Baxter was indeed at Golden Gate. "That's
where I expect Cameron to go if he goes
back to California," she said; "either to
Golden Gate or some county fair. I think
they're running at Pomona now."

She had made contact with half a dozen
horsemen she knew on the Coast. "If he
shows up anywhere out there, we'll know.
Then what?"

"I'll see what I can do."

I wasn't stonewalling her; I had been
thinking about it for days.

I talked with Rosemary and Lillian the
next morning, and with Louie early that
afternoon. At first they went on about how
great Candice was — nice but not particularly helpful. "They all think she walked on

161

water," I told Sharon. "They need to un̲
stand that I'm not here to sandbag you̲
mom, but I've got to get the names of any
people who had anything against her." This
might be difficult, I admitted: "I need you
to convince them to tell me the truth, no
matter where that leads." Sharon said she'd
speak with them, and the next day I went
through it all again. Now their manner was
cool but I thought I was getting at the truth.

Rosemary said Candice knew a few young
men, one who went back to her childhood.
"She had funny made-up names for 'em.
One was like Tricky Dicky, like that presi-
dent Tricky Dicky we had. That wasn't
exactly right, but it was something like that."

"Yeah, she made up names for lots of
people," Lillian said. "She had names from
her storybooks, and she'd slap one of them
names on somebody if she liked 'em and
the name fit. I forgot about Tricky Dicky,
but I remember it now."

I asked if they had ever seen any of these
people.

"I seen Tricky Dicky one time," Rosemary
said.

They had been at the farm in California
and this young man had been buzzing
around her. "I never seen him up close, but
sometime she'd walk down to the gate and

162

he be there and they walk under the trees and talk."

"She had a friend name Gail," Louie said. "I didn't know about none of them boys, but I remember Gail from down on the farm."

He couldn't remember Gail's last name, just a nice gal her own age.

I worked the phone. I called every book-seller I knew on both Coasts and some in the great Midwest. I used the ABAA direc-tory of top dealers in juvenile fiction, I called ILAB specialists in London and asked the same question. Had anyone ever, even years ago, come in with wonderful juveniles to sell? . . . the kind of stuff you don't ever forget. I worked from the boxes of reprints Sharon had stashed in the barn, and from the sketchy list I had made of missing titles that first morning with Junior. Yes, I told them all, there was a question of theft. You don't worry about dealers at that level unless you are truly paranoid.

In the afternoon I went down to the book room and lost myself till early evening. Just before dinner I went running, a two-mile sprint that took me well past the road to the Geiger ranch, out to the road and back. I looked for Junior but there was no sign of him.

On Thursday I told Sharon I had returned Junior's money by special delivery and I was no longer in his employ. "That's good to know," she said coolly. "If you need anything, holler."

I stayed with her ten days. Every morning I helped with the stable chores; every afternoon I made my phone checks. I spent hours in the late afternoon looking through her books. The book room consumed my thoughts: It was so easy to lose all track of time down there, and my roster of her books got more detailed every day. I was flying by the seat of my pants, giving everything the broadest possible value. "At least $50,000," I wrote beside one entry: "could be four times that, depending on how many copies there are in the universe." I made a supplemental note: "I suspect there will be none in this condition." I was conservative by nature, but now I wrote superlatives —"superb," "gorgeous," "marvelous"— until I got tired of using them. Then I began noting degrees of superb with small checks in the margins of my notes. I could have walked out of there with a quarter-million dollars under my coat and she wouldn't know it till she took some kind of inventory, if that day ever came. I felt the weight of her trust more every day.

I was drawn to the books with her grand-father's bookplate: every time I opened one it was like a thrilling new surprise. One morning I asked her the obvious: "You said you've been looking for these but you don't go into bookstores. You must have a dealer keeping his eyes open for you." She said she had several dealers searching constantly. One had a shop in Los Angeles and knew high-end dealers like Heritage, who might hear if something like that came on the market. I wrote all this into my notebook for future reference.

I had been in touch with the coroner's office in the little county where Candice had died. But it was hard to get the kind of information I wanted on the phone: another reason why I'd have to go there. This was a strange time. I was not working for Sharon and yet I was. She never mentioned money again; she just left me alone. The routine continued. Each morning we were out by sunrise, feeding and watering, going about the day's chores. We never left the house unguarded. Either I was there or Louie was: Occasionally we had Billy watch over things. I knew Sharon must be getting impatient, but she never griped, and until we found out where Cameron had gone, this was what we were stuck with.

There came a time when I ran out of people to call. It almost seemed like the missing books had fallen into some dark hole. Not a dealer, I thought: They were in some collector's hands, someone who hadn't sold them.

I sat for an hour in the open loft looking out over the farm. I did fifty push-ups in the barn three days that week, and by Monday of the second week I had increased my reps to seventy-five. For the first time my old wounds felt truly healed and I was whole again. At dusk I went up to the house for dinner and talk. Rosemary and Lillian kept each other in stitches and as Louie might have said we were a happy shedrow together. On Thursdays and Fridays they didn't work, and on those nights it was just the two of us, eating alone in that big house. I sensed a slight awkwardness on her part, though I stayed loose and tried to keep things easy.

"It doesn't seem right putting you in that tack room," she said one evening. "You should stay in the house. I've got lots of room, plenty of space upstairs where you'd have as much privacy as you need. One room's clear over on the other side: you wouldn't hear me at all." There was no hint that the offer was anything more than it seemed, but I liked it where I was. On Monday, my tenth day, Sharon and I met as usual just before dawn. "Cameron's turned up," she said. "He's at Golden Gate, trying to borrow money from everybody he knows." Her friend Sandy Standish had seen him in the stable area and had left a message on her telephone.

My time here was winding down and I still hadn't talked to Damon. I drove out along the road and turned in toward the house. It was mid-morning: The sun was bright and the day was warm, and I could see they were still up at the track, Junior and Damon, watching a horse gallop. I could see their ginney, standing by at the barn waiting with a bucket of water. I stopped the car well short of the track, got out, and said good morning to the ginney. He said, "How you doin', sir?" almost as if he knew me well. I asked if I could go up and talk to the gentlemen at the rail and the question seemed to baffle him for a few seconds. Then he said, "I wouldn't mess with 'em while they workin', sir. They be right back, and this be our last horse this mornin'." So I waited.

It wasn't long. A few minutes later the boy turned the horse through the gap and they came up the road together, Junior and Damon on opposite sides of the horse, saying nothing for the moment. I knew this was not going to be pleasant; it was one of those things that had to be done and one of those times when I missed the authority of my badge. Damon saw me first: He raised his head and there seemed to be some kind of amusement on his face. He was probably younger than Junior but not by much. He had a gray beard and today he wore a cap and jeans and a flannel shirt. He said something; Junior looked up and stopped dead in his tracks.

They talked for what seemed like a long time. At some point Junior turned away and Damon came on alone.

"Mr. Janeway."

I nodded.

"What can I do for you?"

"I was hoping we could have us a talk. I guess Junior and I got off on the wrong foot."

"If Junior had eight legs like a spider you'd get off on eight wrong feet eight times running."

I laughed politely.

"I think you understand old Willis," he said. "Junior wants to rule the roost, and he never knows what side his bread's buttered on."

"Maybe he should take lessons in deep breathing."

"Oh, Junior's not all bad, he's trying to do better even as we speak."

"Didn't look like it from here."

"I'm telling you he's having a change of heart. He wants you to come back on board and see what you can find out. No strings attached this time."

"Can't do it, though. I've already taken a job with Sharon."

"Doing what?"

I didn't want to tell him what my job with Sharon was, but I gave him this to keep him talking. "She's mainly interested in finding out what happened to her mother."

"I can't help you with that. I don't think anybody can. That was a long time ago."

"Junior mentioned the possibility that she'd been murdered."

"Junior's got diarrhea of the brain cells. That's an old theory; I thought it had been put to rest years ago. He was just trying to rankle you because you were a big-time city po-lice-man."

"So what do you think happened to her?"

"I barely knew the woman. But if you want my guess, she ate them peanuts on purpose."

He waited for my reaction but when I had

none, he said, "My old man wasn't easy to live with in the best of times. When he got older he was impossible. What else can I tell you?"

"I was wondering . . ."

"What I meant was, there's nothing else I can tell you. If you're looking for Candice, I don't think she's here. I don't know anything about her and I barely talked to her when she was alive."

"And you had no opinions about her?"

"She was a whore. Other than that, what's to know?"

I blinked. "A whore? First time I've heard that one."

"Everybody thought she was such a goody two-shoes, but we-all knew better. She wasn't the plaster saint people thought she was, that's all I'm saying. She had her flings the whole time she was with the old man."

"Who'd she have these flings with?"

"That I guess was her ugly little secret."

"Then how do you know about them?"

"Ask around, you might get an earful."

"Ask around where?"

"Wherever your nose leads you. Look, this is all very old news, it probably does no good to rake it all up now. You asked me my opinion and I told you, but what's it prove all these years later?" He looked at his watch. "I've got to go in now. I've got things to line up."

"What can you tell me about your brothers?"

"Nothing you haven't already heard. Baxter's a refugee from a loony bin; Cameron's a born loser. I guess that leaves me as the only normal one."

He shrugged. "I'm a simple horse trainer, that's what I know. Other than that I got nothing to say."

That afternoon I left a message for Erin, that I was heading for California and I'd call her from Golden Gate. At dusk Sharon and I went out to eat. She took me to a place called the Sandpiper on the Snake River and we sat and talked about everything. The waiting game was finished. She watched me watching everyone else, and once when our eyes crossed paths I winked at her and she smiled. "Mr. Suspicious," she said, and we laughed lightly. But I had spent a good piece of my life being suspicious and it was late to start changing now.

After supper she came out to the barn. I was all packed up, ready to go.

"Looks like you're leaving us."

"I don't know if there are any answers out there, but that feels like the way to bet."

I told her I would check the records on her mother's death and send her a report.

"Well," she said, suddenly uneasy again. "Keep in touch." She handed me a thick roll of money, five thousand in hundreds I later found out. I put it in my pocket without counting it.

"Sorry about Junior," she said. "I'll see what I can do with him after you're gone. I think at some point you'll see both him and Damon out there, and maybe you'll get another shot at them."

She stared at me for another moment. "Ask for Sandy Standish at the stable gate," she said. "He'll be expecting you and he'll get you in and put you on his list so you can get a license. Once you're inside, you can go just about anywhere."

I left before dawn the next morning. We said our good-byes in the yard at the side of her house. She hugged me impulsively and in that same spirit of adventure I patted her on the back. I drove off into the blackened west, and after a while the last phantoms of the night came calling.

When I was younger I had answers to everything. Right always won out over wrong, good stood up to evil, and I was the double-edged weapon that dispensed justice. I had unlimited faith in my own power,

I knew what I could do and I feared no one. Such is the foolishness of the young, so goes the ego of the strong.

The land ahead began to brighten and soon the sun at my back lit up the highway like an incandescent ribbon. By daybreak I was well out on Interstate 86, heading west.

8

I picked up Highway 93 south, crossed into Nevada, and got on I-80 westbound. From there into Reno, I encountered no effective speed limit: I had seldom seen cops on this desert run, I had always made good time, and I rolled into the biggest little city in the world well before six o'clock. I had gained an hour crossing from Mountain to Pacific Time, and now I stopped to eat and gas up before making that last link over the Sierra Nevada, and down into Oakland.

I browsed a few junkshops and prowled through their bookshelves. Bought two mysteries from the mid-forties, nothing wonderful but I liked the jackets, and the short breaks helped keep me awake for the final push to the west.

Snow was falling as I headed up the hill toward Donner Pass. The sky was dark in the east and I was beginning to think of Sacramento as a stopping point. I knew I could make it to Golden Gate tonight, but Sharon's friend Sandy might not be there again until tomorrow anyway. That might be the time to catch him — after the work, before he took off at noon. So I put up in a motel, read a few chapters of a truly atrocious novel, and I turned in around eleven.

In the morning I made the trip down to the Bay Area after daybreak. The snow of the high country had become a miserable rain on the Coast: steady, relentless; maddening, I imagined, if you had to race in it unless you had a great mud horse. Then it lit up your life and became something special. Golden Gate Fields sits on the east side of the bay, right on the water in Albany, just north of Oakland. Its blessing is a wonderful environment for a racetrack; its curse is the same environment, which will seal its doom. I don't know this for a fact, but I imagine a day, sooner rather than later, when money will change hands and a group of condos will occupy the ground where, once upon a time, crowds had thrilled to the sounds of the race, the announcer's call, and the illusion of easy money. It is a colorful way of life that will disappear without a trace.

I got off the freeway in Richmond and drifted south. I was early and I still had time to kill, so I killed some of it riding down San Pablo Avenue. Occasionally the rain slacked off and I got out and walked a few blocks. I found an open newsstand and I bought a copy of the *Daily Racing Form,* where I learned that Sharon's friend Standish had a horse in the second today: a $10,000 claiming race for three-year-olds and up. I got in my car, turned west on Gilman Street and drove the few blocks out to the bay. The stable area was directly on my right and there was a parking lot on my left. I found a small café under Interstate 80 where it passes over Gilman and a parking space almost adjacent to the front door. I stopped and went in for coffee.

The place was crowded with grizzled old men in jeans and boots and flannel shirts; more than a few of them I figured were horsemen, and the rest were horse players waiting for the gates to open sometime before noon. Some might know Sandy Standish; one of them might even be the man but I doubted it. The fellow Sharon had described had better things to do than gossiping with old farts during working hours. I sat quietly drinking my coffee, looking at my newspaper, and soon I heard racing talk behind me. Again I turned to my *Racing Form* and found the race they were discussing. A four-year-old named Green Money Machine was said to be a sure thing in the fourth. It was six furlongs and he was a killer at this distance against this kind of company. He would go off at about 3-1, the *Racing Form* predicted, and one old man said, "If he gets clear and comes into the turn on top, they can kiss his hiney goodbye. He's the best thing going today." There was ominous talk of his long layoff — he hadn't run in four months — and that's why the odds were good. But he was in easy, dropping in price from his last start in early summer, which he had won in a walk from better horses than these. He loved an off track. "He'll eat this field alive," the talkative one said: "These horses can't run fast enough to scatter their own shit."

I coughed to cover a laugh and looked at the form on Sandy's horse, a big red gelding named Pompeii Ruler. He was a 9-1 shot in the early line; his bloodline went back a few generations to Bold Ruler, one of the great studs of our time.

I finished my coffee and went outside: parked in the lot across the street and backtracked through the rain to the stable gate. A suspicious-looking man leaned out of his window and I asked for Sandy Standish. The rain was coming down heavier now and I huddled against his outer wall as he turned away and spoke into a microphone. *"Sandy Standish to the stable gate . . . Sandy Standish, you have a visitor at the stable gate."* I waited for several minutes, until the wind shifted and there was nowhere to hide; then I got up against the glass and gave him my hangdog look. At last he opened the window and said, "You want to wait in here?"

I thanked him and went into the little guard shack. He motioned me to a stool and I perched there out of his way while cars came through in a steady parade. Mostly he just checked for licenses and they went on in without a hitch. Occasionally there was a question — "Who're you with, sir? Who did you want to see, ma'am?" And this or that car was made to pull off to the side until the owner or trainer could be summoned. I sat on the stool patiently through all of this. Ten minutes passed. The guard said, "I'll give him another call," but I said no, "He's probably busy, give him another fifteen minutes." He nodded and I sat watching the cars go in and out. And suddenly I looked up and there in the guard's face was Cameron Geiger.

I had never seen him before that moment, but I had no doubt who he was. First I heard the sound of his car — he was sitting behind the wheel of an old Buick that had a wicked ping. At least two of his eight cylinders were sticking. At the same time I saw the younger man with him in the front seat. As I scanned the car I saw the crushed fender. He said, "Call Bax again. Come on, Alvin, get the lead out of your ass." The guard looked at me and rolled his eyes. Wearily he picked up the microphone and said, *"Baxter Geiger to the stable gate, please; Baxter Geiger, you have a visitor at the stable gate."* Then the guard asked Cameron to pull his car over to the side and please wait. The word *wait* was not in Cameron's vocabulary, but he pulled off the road in a snit and sat in the car with his companion until its windows fogged over. This took maybe ten minutes; then Cameron got out and angrily approached the stable gate on foot. So far he was living up to his advance billing. His huge belly was the most conspicuous thing about him; his hips looked almost brittle in support, and he shuffled along in obvious pain. The other fellow stayed in the car. The stable gate man was busy checking cars coming and going and he never looked back, but I tracked Cameron all the way in as he limped toward us through the rain. Suddenly he jerked the door open and came inside, bellowing. "So what're you gonna do, Alvin, make me sit out in this rain all goddam day? Where the hell is Bax?"

"How am I supposed to know where he is? I don't keep his appointment book."

"Then how about I go in and get him? I can find him in five minutes."

"You know the rules," the guard said.

"Rules are for gooks. How many years have I been coming to this racetrack?"

"That's all well and good. But if you want to get in today, you've gotta have a valid license or get somebody who's got one to come get you. Come on, man, you know this as well as I do, so maybe you should just go in through the other side and get your license now."

"Maybe you should eat *this*."

I didn't look: It wasn't any of my business what Cameron wanted Alvin to eat. A moment passed. Cameron said, "What the hell harm can I do in five lousy minutes?" The guard said, "You can get me fired in five minutes. Is that what you want, sir?" Cameron glared at him and his look said he didn't care what Alvin did. He turned his head and saw me watching him. "So who're you and what're you waiting for?"

"Don't bother him," Alvin said. "He's

here to see someone."

"Well, *pardon* the hell out of me. Am I bothering you, mister?"

I shook my head. The last thing I wanted was to get in the middle of a running shitfight with these two.

"Who are you here to see?" Cameron said.

"Sir . . ." Alvin said.

"Don't give me that sir bullshit. I was racing horses here when you were still pissing your diapers." To me he said with exaggerated manners, "I only ask because I know everybody who's raced here in the last twenty-five years. If there's a problem I might be able to help."

"I'll be fine," I said.

He bristled. "If that's how you want it, pal, you just sit there and suit yourself."

He settled in the corner and the glass began to frost over. Alvin now spoke to him by his first name. "You're gonna have to leave, Cam. I'm sorry but you're interfering with my duties."

Cameron didn't move.

"I don't think you want me to call security," Alvin said.

"Tell you what, Alvin, I've got bigger things to do than sit here worrying about you. I don't care who you call."

"You know if you get kicked out of here

again you might have a helluva time ever gettin' back in." Alvin looked at me. "Maybe you should leave as well."

"Sure," I said. "I'll wait in my car."

I got up and started for the door. Cameron slid his chair over and blocked my way.

"That's it, Cameron," Alvin said. "Get out of the way or I'm calling security."

"Listen, you," Cameron said to me. "I tried to do you a favor here and I don't appreciate it when a deed like that gets thrown back in my face."

"Don't start anything with this man, Cameron," Alvin said.

"What's he gonna do about it?"

"Look at him and compare him to you. He just might kick you a new asshole."

"Hey, buddy," Cameron said: "you really gonna kick me a new asshole?"

"I wouldn't know where to start."

I regretted this as soon as I said it. Alvin laughed, making it worse, and Cameron sized me up, seriously now. Then he got up from his chair and stomped out.

"Sorry about that," Alvin said.

"Hey, stuff happens. For the record, you done good."

"There won't be any record. I'm not worried about him filing any complaints." Alvin passed two fellows into the stable area.

"Nice line back there," he said. "That man is all asshole, all the time. He thinks racing owes him a living."

"Comeuppance comes hard sometimes."

He looked at me a little more closely now. "What'd you say your name is?"

I hadn't said but I did now and we shook hands.

"I don't know what's taking Sandy so long," Alvin said. "I know he's here. He came through about four-thirty and he hasn't come out again."

"Then he'll come when he can. He's got a horse running early today, maybe that tied him up. Don't hassle him, I'll go wait in my car. I'm the silver Chevy at the edge of the lot."

I got out of his hair and sat in the car playing the radio with my eyes closed. The next thing I knew, the sound of tapping on my window brought me out of a dream. I opened my eyes and there was a face in my window. Not Sandy's: This fellow was young. I motioned him around and he took off his raincoat before flopping on the seat beside me.

"I'm Obie Mays. I work for Sandy. Sorry about the delay."

We shook hands and he said, "Might as well drive down. We're way over on the backstretch rail near the turn. No sense getting wet."

He directed me across the street, where Alvin stopped us and came out of his shack for a look. He had me sign in, motioned us through, Obie told me to hang a left, then right, and I pulled up at the barn and parked at the end. I saw Sandy at once as I came under his shedrow. He would be the tall gray-haired fellow standing at a stall door near the middle of the barn. "They had to do an emergency tracheotomy on this old mare," Obie said softly: "That's why Sandy couldn't come for you right away. This horse isn't worth much but Sandy's always been partial to her."

"What happens to her now?"

"We'll ask around, see who might want her for a lead pony. She's really a sweet-tempered old gal. If we can't find anybody for her, I imagine Sandy's friend Sharon will take her."

We walked up the barn together and Obie told me the troubled history of this old horse. She had always been a cribber, prone to sucking air. "Usually that's not a big problem, but she's been getting worse this year. This morning she went into a sudden choking attack. Sandy had gone on up to the kitchen for coffee and none of us ginneys knew what to do. So here we were, trying like crazy to help this poor horse, and I thought we'd lose her sure. Then we got lucky: Dr. Tate came by in the barn across the way. I saw him and called him over. She'd have died in another few minutes."

We had reached the stall. A powerful light had been hung there from the top of the door.

A man wearing bloody surgical gloves crossed in front of it: He was a fellow in his sixties with short-cropped gray hair. I glanced over Sandy's shoulder and saw a sad-looking horse that stood trembling in the back of the stall. Her front legs were coated with drying blood and there were pools of blood in the straw around her head. Implanted high on her neck was a small, round device with a breathing hole in it. I heard Sandy say, "Well, Doc, that's another one I owe you."

"That's what I like about being a vet." Dr. Tate clapped Sandy on the shoulder. "You get to battle God with God's own creatures and occasionally you even win one."

"Make sure you send me a bill this time."

We moved out of the doorway. The doctor was instructing two ginneys on the removal of the tube, which had to be done every week to keep the passage clear. Sandy had not yet said a word in my direction but now he turned and our eyes met. He nodded slightly and thanked everybody on behalf of his stable and his horse. The tiny crowd broke up and only then, when people were well out of earshot, Sandy said, "Mr. Janeway. Sorry I kept you waiting." We shook hands and went into a tack room at the end of the barn. He closed the door and nodded toward a chair.

"How's Sharon?"

"She was fine when I left her yesterday morning."

The moment stretched. There was a feeling of discomfort between us as if each of us was waiting for the other to get the ball rolling. At last I said, "She tell you why I'm here?"

He nodded. "Good luck. That's a cold trail you're chasing. Any reason to think you can pick it up and find out anything?"

"You never know. Sometimes a new pair of eyes can make a big difference." I shuffled through some notes. "If there's a victim I usually start with who she knew. Who saw her last, who knew her best . . ."

"Is that what you think, Candice was a victim?"

"That would be one of the things I'll have to find out. The possibility's been raised that

Ms. Geiger was murdered. Sharon doesn't think a lot of effort went into that investigation."

"I was truly surprised at that; I had no idea she had these doubts."

"She never told you?"

"Not a word till now. Look, if anybody other than Sharon was raising these questions, I'd put it in the same corner of my mind where I'd keep conspiracy theories in the Kennedy murder; I just wouldn't give it the time of day. But Sharon's always been such a steady girl. Even as a kid, her judgment was sound."

"And she has a certain knack," I said. "She does seem to sense things."

He didn't ask what she sensed or how, and in that gap a minute went by. Through the closed door we heard a horse nicker and a feed tub clatter to the ground. One of the boys yelled, "Dammit, help me out here!" and the voice carried through the wall. Whatever it was it didn't move Sandy from his perch. He was sitting on a saddle trunk facing the door, deep in thought. Then he said, "How can I help you?"

"If I could start by asking you a few things. Get my bearings, if that's okay."

"Sure, go ahead."

"How well did you really know Candice?"

My question knocked him back on his ass and he blinked. I saw his hand tremble and he clutched it with his left hand and still he couldn't stop fidgeting. His eyes watered and he tried to look away.

"Mr. Standish?"

"My God, does Sharon think I killed her?"

"Did I miss something here? Nobody's said that."

He nodded but his face was pale. "Wow," he said. "As opening questions go, that one's a lulu. Did Sharon tell you to ask me that?"

"Sharon didn't tell me to do anything. To me it seemed like a natural place to start."

He still looked winded, but he forced himself to be calm. "It's just . . . I guess it was that word *really* that set me off. I've never been asked that question that way before."

"I wasn't aware I had any kind of way with questions."

But I waited for him to answer it. He gave me a thin little smile and said, "I knew her very well. She was a great woman and I had a lot of affection for her. I don't know how to describe those days except to say she was a close friend."

"That was quite a difference in your ages."

He paled again. Now I had questioned a

relationship that hadn't been in doubt until this moment, and he had trouble looking at me. "She was seven years older than I was," he acknowledged. "I wouldn't call that quite a bit. Damn, Janeway, I had no idea you were thinking these things."

"I wasn't thinking anything."

But I am now.

I said, "Did the age difference seem to bother her?"

"Why ask that? What difference does it make?"

"Just that she had always preferred older men."

"Maybe she was trying to break that pattern. Christ, what do you want from me, I wasn't a mind reader." He was looking at the floor as he spoke, and in that moment something had happened. I had had this reaction with others in my police career. Dozens of times I had looked at people and asked the hard question — *Did you kill her?* — and some of them had melted like wax too close to an open flame. Now it seemed to be happening and I hadn't asked the question yet.

Then he said, "I loved her," and the way he said it and the way he looked made me want to believe him, at least for the moment. "I've never told this to anyone," he said. "I sure didn't intend to say it here and now, but it's true. Haven't you ever known a woman like that?"

"Like what?"

"Where you know it's star-crossed right from the first minute and you still can't stay away from her. I'm talking about a woman who can make you dream about her years after she's gone . . . and when you first met her all she did was say hello and your storm warnings went up."

"Sure, I can understand that."

"I thought I was ready for this," he said. "Sharon called and told me who you are and what you're doing, and I thought, *I can deal with this now; I can answer the man's questions.* But then you come in here and ask me how well I knew her, and I feel a lump in my throat and I can barely talk; I'm right back in those days, my hands tremble when I think of her, and I don't know what I can tell you."

He tried for a smile but it came up short. "God, I just loved her," he said again. "When she died, all the joy went out of my life. She took that away when she went."

"She seems to have had that effect on more than one man."

"Can I ask you for a favor? Is it possible to keep this between us guys?"

"That's going to be a tough one, Sandy."

"I know it is. I hear what you're saying."

"You're asking me not to tell Sharon. But she gave me a chunk of money to come out here and uncover some facts."

"I have no right to ask any favors. I understand what kind of position that puts you in."

"I could leave it to you to tell her," I said. "That's the best I can do."

"I don't know if that makes it easier or harder. It does change things. This is something I have never talked about with Sharon. I just assumed that's how she wanted it. And now . . ."

He put up his hands in a surrender motion. "I loved her mother from the first day HR brought her to the racetrack, just after her father died. I remember it like it was yesterday. Mr. Ritchey died and HR began squiring her around within a few weeks."

He looked at the ceiling and in that moment I could see how vulnerable he was. A fool could see it. I could ask him almost anything now and maybe another little piece of unwanted truth might come out. I could sense it back there in his head, down in his heart. He had lived with a ghost for a long time and now here it was in a stranger's question that hadn't even been asked yet.

"Sharon has never mentioned this," he said. "She has no idea . . ."

"Don't be too sure of that."

His eyes opened wide. "Did she say something?"

"Just that you'd be worth talking to. That you'll help me get around."

"I will . . . hell, I'll be happy to do that . . . no matter what you decide. But you know . . ."

I cocked my eyebrow, waiting for him to finish his thought. He said, "That kind of comment from her might mean anything or nothing at all."

"Sharon's a clever young woman," I said. "All I'm saying is, don't be too surprised if she's figured out some things on her own."

"She's never said a word to that effect. Not to me."

"Maybe she's too much of a lady to bring it up. It's a touchy subject, maybe she's waiting for you to say something."

"Yeah, tell me how touchy it is." He nodded. "Anyway, you've made your point."

"So did you have an affair with her mother?"

I tried to say this kindly — a soft question from a man who might have been in that same boat himself once or twice. A woman he absolutely shouldn't touch. Consent

192

implied in her words. The raging hormones of youth. The next logical thought wafted up from somewhere: "Are you Sharon's father?" I asked, and his face went ashen.

"Damn, you do get right to the point, don't you?"

"I know it's a sticky question but it had to be asked."

"It was only for a short time," he said. "We were only together . . . a little while."

"Once is all it takes." I looked at him steadily, without wavering, with what I hoped was a fair piece of understanding. But he wouldn't meet my eyes, so all that effort was lost.

"How's the timing?" I said.

He nodded to the wall. Yes, it could've been him.

He looked up at me: another mighty effort to make eye contact. "I've thought of that almost every day," he said, looking away.

"And you still think Sharon doesn't realize what might have happened?"

"Then why didn't she ever say anything?"

"Why didn't you?"

"I couldn't, not while the old man was alive. But then he lived so long it had become our way, what we were." At last he forced himself to look at me. "I was very young. Candice was . . ."

I waited.

"My first," he said. "In a way it was like that for both of us. Her first real fling."

I thought this was doubtful, but I said, "I'm not here to pass judgment, Sandy."

"But now you've got to tell Sharon. I suppose she's absolutely got to know?"

"There are ways to find out today. Tests that didn't exist thirty years ago."

"Jesus." He quaked at the thought. "How much time will you give me to decide?"

"It's not your decision to make. It might come up any minute and I can't lie to her."

"So the clock is already ticking."

"I think so. She needs . . ."

He groped for a word and I found it for him. "Closure." This is an old word with a modern meaning that I loathe and never use except in sarcasm. He stared at the wall and didn't notice.

"Of course she does," he said finally. "She needs closure. God knows she deserves that, and I do want to help her. If you doubt that, remember this. If it ever comes out that I got you in here under false pretenses, I could be in real trouble with the stewards."

"I won't tell and I'm sure Sharon won't. I'll work my shift like anybody else."

He looked at his watch. "I'm sorry, I'm

running into a time problem, I've got two guests coming out to visit. Helluva day for it, but I've got a horse in the second race."

"I'll be fine here."

"We'll get you a license this afternoon," he said. "Count on Obie for everything, he's solid. You can bed down with my boys, if that's what you want. I'll put you on as a hot walker. That would leave you time to poke around."

He opened the door and walked away; then he turned to give me one last look. I thought he was about to say something, but when he did it was only a racetracker's tip. "My horse is ready to run today, in case you've got a little change burning a hole in your pocket." Then he was gone. I went out into the shedrow and watched him leave. For a moment the barn felt absolutely still, but slowly the sounds of a living world returned to us. I heard a horse nicker and the rain rattling on the roof. I could hear the noises of men and boys talking and working in the next barn. One of them came limping past the gap and in that second before I saw him, I knew it was Cameron. He stopped and turned my way and we stared at each other briefly across the thirty-odd feet of the rainswept tow ring. I looked away first. When I glanced up again he was gone.

9

I was settled in the corner tack room before noon. By twelve-thirty I had been photo-graphed and fingerprinted, I had a ginney's license issued in my name and I was official; I could now get into the stable area any time day or night without a guide; I could talk to anybody about anything. I was standing just outside the paddock, watching the horses being readied for the second race. The steady rain had made the track a sloppy lake. Sandy came into the paddock and stood in the dry stall, waiting for his horse. He saw me lounging near the rail, but he didn't nod and neither did I. He wore a coat and tie despite the weather and his pants had been pressed to a razor-sharp crease. The horses arrived: Obie led Pompeii Ruler around until Sandy told him that was enough; then they turned into the stall. The riders came out: There was barely any conversation between Sandy and his jockey

— this boy, I later learned, had ridden this horse in ten races, had won five and knew him well. He would go off in blinkers, which Sandy was putting on him now. The race was a mile and seventy yards, a bit of a stretch for this animal, who liked to run on the lead and was good at any distance under a mile. That's why the odds were so generous — the tote board had just taken another bump, knocking him back to third choice at 12-1. The *Form* on him looked solid in sprints, but he had raced only once at more than a mile since early last year and had finished sixth, fading fast in a ten-horse field. He was getting no confidence at this distance — the *Form* doesn't cut racehorses any slack for headaches or mood swings, menopause, or the occasional bad-mane day. I remembered an old saying on the racetrack from years of following the races in Denver: *Play the trainer, not the horse.* I dropped $100 on his nose and swore I wouldn't bet again until I had some kind of break on this case.

Thirty minutes later, I cashed my win ticket and came away with $1,350.

I walked back to the stable area with Obie and the horse. The rain was relentless and we were all grubby now: I could see the dirt caked between the horse's legs and I felt it on my face and neck. We arrived just as Sandy got there with his guests. She was a handsome woman in her sixties; the guy I pegged as her husband. They might have been a couple of millionaires celebrating a Derby win from the look of them: there was lots of happy talk between Sandy and the lady: lots of camaraderie, lots of laughs. He called her Barbara. I heard her refer to her guy as Charlie. She wore dressy clothes and a colorful hat and carried an umbrella. Sandy passed through his circle of boys and handed out twenty-dollar bills and the lady looked on with kind amusement. "Did you play this horse, Janeway?" Sandy said, and I told him I had indeed and I thanked him for the tip. He gave me the twenty anyway and I damn well took it: I didn't want to stand out from the others in any way, and soon enough they would all know why I was there.

Sandy got out some folding canvas chairs and he and the lady sat in the feed bin, out of the rain but near enough to see what was going on. Her husband had drifted away down the shedrow and around the corner, to see what he could see. "Sandy always stays to watch his horse cool out," Obie said. I held the lead shank while Obie sloshed hot water on his horse with a sponge. The steam almost obliterated us, and Obie's voice was like some disembodied entity wafting up from the other side, as if the horse, not his ginney, was suddenly doing the talking. "Man, I love this horse. You can see the intelligence in his face, the pleasure he gets from a hot bath." He washed the animal's private parts and scraped the water off his back, threw on a heavy wool cooler, and I started him around the shedrow.

Here he was then, my first walk, and it was a cold one under the barn's overhang. I didn't have to learn anything, just walk. I snuggled down inside my jacket and still it was cold. Around and around we went: I lost track of the time and forgot about the cold as I walked. This was indeed a nice horse, so gentle and well-mannered, such good company on a bad day, impossible not to like. I stopped him occasionally to look in his eyes and fondle his head and say a few words. At thirty minutes Sandy took off the wool cooler to run a hand over his flank and cover him with a sheet. He was slow to cool and all this took most of an hour. During that time someone from the stewards' office arrived and stood at the stall while I held a small jar on the end of a stick and waited for the urine sample. "Whistle to him," Obie said, and I did: just a monotonous series of high-pitched one-note birdcalls. After three minutes of this he was ready to pee, and from this flood we collected the tiny urine sample. The man sealed and labeled the bottle and left.

Sandy was off to an early dinner with his guests. I thought he might say something more, since we had barely made eye contact during the whole time he was in the barn. He's spooked now, I thought: all this talk about the bookwoman had given him too much to think about. This might mean something or maybe nothing at all: anyone's guess was as good as mine. I could hear the horses being called for the seventh race when Sandy said good night to us all and he and Barbara went around the barn to find her elusive husband.

I put Pompeii Ruler in his stall. Obie felt his legs and picked the gunk out of his feet, then filled his bucket with water. The horses ran past in the seventh. I could hear their hoofbeats briefly and I heard the call wafting over the stable area in a muffled monotone. But the crowd had left early and now there was no spectator noise. The horses for the last race were called to the paddock as an early dusk fell over the bay. I heard thunder as Cameron limped quickly past the open gap and disappeared into the tack room opposite mine.

I stood in the open door and looked down our shedrow. There were seven of us in Sandy's barn: twenty-three horses, six ginneys, and me. I was the only full-time hot walker. Sandy no longer carried a jockey on his payroll: he preferred to pick his boy or girl from the pool of available riders as a race drew near. "We used to have a full-time bug boy but the old man's partial to girl jocks in sprints," Obie said as he showed me around. "He says they're smarter and less prone to use cowboy tactics. But in longer races, he still wants a man." Obie was the unofficial stable foreman. He was young but he'd be the one they'd all look up to, his word would be final if something came up and Sandy couldn't be reached. In the room next to mine was a Mexican kid named Milo and a pint-sized Texan who played the harmonica and guitar simultaneously and sang country songs about jilted men and the women who broke their hearts. Halfway down the barn was a fellow named Bob from Boston, a serious student of the game who was saving his money to buy a horse. Bob was a drummer; he carried his drumsticks in a bag with his clothes, admired the Gene Krupa legacy, and could beat out a mean rhythm on the flat part of a chair. He had a notebook where he had written down everything he could remember that Sandy did and said. "Sandy's the best trainer in the state," Bob said.

I met them all that first day. The day waned quickly under its deep black cloud cover.

I raked up the shedrow and did some other chores. All along the row the ginneys were at work with their pitchforks. Filling their baskets with muck. Getting ready for the night. At loose ends in the murky day.

The wind picked up and an early night fell over the bay. All of them had apparently accepted me as just another racetrack drifter; only Sandy knew the truth. Obie might suspect something — once I saw him looking oddly in my direction — but it was one of those hypnotic stares that sees nothing. The days of Candice Geiger were long past and I wondered if any of them had ever heard her name. At last he looked away and beyond me. He might have been staring over my shoulder at a crack in the wall, reliving the race in a dream.

Thunder rumbled across the sky. The rain fell steadily, relentlessly.

The crew felt the weight of the stake Sandy had dropped on us. The extra money seemed to burn holes in every pocket. It called for a night out, but no one wanted to brave the storm even for a run to the kitchen. All during the dinner hour the rain came down in sheets.

By seven o'clock we had decided to stay home and eat our simple racetrack fare: fried egg sandwiches on plain white bread with mayonnaise, and beans in a can. Hobo food, which at the moment sounded elegant as hell. The sizzle and smell of twenty eggs frying on hotplates filled the shedrow and we sat in the canvas chairs and ate, feeling like rich horse owners.

We talked and cracked jokes. I felt insulated, far from the real world, with only a hazy light to tell us that life might exist on the next planet, in the shedrow just across the way.

Tex played his harmonica and Bob kept rhythm with his sticks. They all sang songs of cheatin' women and old-timey horse races, and nobody asked about me. As far as they were concerned I had no life before this one. I felt a growing sense of unity with these guys. Amazing how quickly I had blended in with them. None of them cared where I had been or what I had done, none of them asked, and this was good. I didn't have to lie and then remember the next day what my story was. The good cheer was spontaneous. There was no need to reveal more of myself than I already had, and soon the songs of fickle love and heartbreak gave way to musical tales of ginneys with legendary peckers, of cocks that stood up and yelled *heee-haw*, said *mamma*, and saluted the flag. We laughed at everything and nothing. For the moment we were happy in this bawdy male universe, sealed in by the rain and the good feeling of money unspent from today's winner.

We had no past. The future was unknown, not to be probed or pondered.

Obie walked along the shedrow and checked on his horses. Cleared his throat and said he was going to bed. Four o'clock comes early. But a few of us sat up talking, reluctant to give up the day.

"Tell you what, boys, I've had enough of this weather," Tex said. "Maybe I'll get to be the lucky one goin' south."

Everyone but me seemed to know what he was talking about, so eventually I asked.

"Sandy's going to Santa Anita after this meet's over. He's only takin' one ginney with him."

"He's gonna train Barbara Patterson's horses," Bob said.

I looked perplexed, which wasn't difficult

at the moment.

"That's the lady you just met," he said.

"Where the hell you been all your life, Janeway?" Tex said. "Maybe Sandy's time has come. I don't think Ms. P. is running short of cash, and cash money speaks out loud to just about everybody anywhere. Anyways, you can bet me."

"Ms. P.'s got a stable full of really nice horses," Bob said helpfully. "Got a nice ranch about a forty-minute drive from here."

"Got a dynamite undefeated two-year-old geared up for next spring's Santa Anita Derby," Tex said. "If he runs good there, it's almost a sure thing she'll ship east for the Triple Crown races."

"So why'd she get rid of her old trainer?"

"Real question is why she ever hired that moron in the first place. He's screwed up more good horses than most of us'll ever see."

"This is all on the q.t. for now," Bob said. "Word to the wise."

"We let Sandy make his own announcement in his own time," Tex said. "Gives him a feeling he's running things around here."

They laughed.

"You all seem to know a lot about what's really going on," I said.

Bob held his finger to his lips. "Back-stretch scuttlebutt."

I looked for a way to mention Cameron but nothing opened up. I looked for some door that might open innocently into the topic of Candice and her books, but it didn't happen. Someone suggested a card game but he had no takers. "Damn, boys," said his voice, somewhere in the ethereal night. "I can't give this money away."

A light flickered. The tack room across the way went dark and closed down for the night.

The rain picked up again.

I let go my part of it and went to bed.

Deep in the night I heard the muffled sounds of people talking. I opened my eyes. The little clock radio said the time was one-thirty. I got up and cracked my door: looked out at the new day, which at the moment looked much too much like the old day. The sky was still black and would be for another five hours. The rain had slowed to a steady downpour and I got the sense, though I couldn't see it, that the tow ring was un-walkable, filled with lakes of mud.

The talking persisted as a faint mumble. I pulled on my pants and cracked open the door. Suddenly the voices were louder. A shadow-man stood just inside the shedrow in the barn across the tow ring. He was huddled in conversation with another guy I couldn't see at all, and their voices carried amazingly well over the rain. The shadow said, "If Bax asks, you don't know where I am. Do not mention the farm. The last thing I need is him busting in on me." They both came out and went past me in the drippy morning. I watched from there until they disappeared around the corner, then I eased across the tow ring on the other side, water over my shoes, up to my ankles in it, and struck out in the general direction I thought they had gone, out toward the stable gate and the parking lot across the street.

At the edge of a barn I saw their tiny light bobbing on the road forty yards ahead. A truck came in through the gate and its headlights illuminated the two silhouettes. One of them limped distinctively in the glare from the truck. I moved over into the darkest place on the road — couldn't see the gate from there, but I pushed ahead anyway, slowly, and eased around the corner. There they were, chatting and laughing with the night man inside the stable gate.

In a while Cameron went outside and crossed the road to the parking lot. When he came back he had a small bag, which he passed through the window to his pal. The night man asked to look at it and seemed to be satisfied. I guessed it was the other guy's clothes, meaning what? . . . that Cameron was going away for at least a day? Cameron had a few more words to say and they all laughed; then he went across to the lot again, got in his car, and drove away. The muscle man stayed another fifteen minutes, talking to the guard. When he did come out he hurried back through the stable area in the rain. I followed him at a distance and lost him briefly, but when I came into my shedrow I saw him about twenty yards away, in his own barn across the tow ring. The night was almost completely black and I saw him only because he was standing directly across the way, having himself a smoke. I waited in the dark until he apparently called it a night. The light went on briefly in Cameron's tack room and went off almost in the same breath.

Inside my own room, I stripped off my wet clothes in the dark, hung them across my chair, and lay down shivering under my blankets. I was asleep almost at once.

I dreamed of wicked things.

Monsters who looked like men.

Killers I couldn't catch, couldn't see, who

wore masks of smiling friendship.

I opened my eyes and saw light trickling in from somewhere. I got up, pulled on my pants, and looked over at the clock radio. *Four forty-two.*

I cracked the door, just enough to see Cameron's pal across the way. He was mucking a stall about thirty yards straight across the tow ring . . . the same stall Cameron had done last night. In our shedrow I saw Bob and Obie already hard at work.

I opened the door wide and walked down the row. "Anybody got horses to walk?"

They all did. Obie looked at the chart Sandy had made and said I could start with Pompeii Ruler. I hitched a shank to his halter and away we went. As I came around the first time I heard an angry voice across in the next barn.

"Whaddaya mean he had to go somewhere? What the hell's that supposed to mean?"

"I told you, an emergency came up."

"Emergency, my ass. Goddammit, does he want this job or not?"

"Sure he does. Didn't he leave me to cover for him?"

"If I wanted you to rub eight, I'da hired you for eight. One man can't do a decent job with five head, let alone eight."

I made another trip around the barn and the guy across the way was still steamed. His voice carried clearly over the tow ring "He's got a problem? *He's* got a problem? Don't tell me about Cameron and his problem, Rudy, I don't wanna hear it. This is what I get for hiring that guy, I shoulda known better, everybody said I'd live to regret it. Who the hell just disappears his first day on a job? I could hire a skid row bum and get more out of him than this."

By then Sandy had arrived. He paid no attention to the ruckus in the next shedrow: he went about his own business and pushed on into the morning. "Let's walk 'em today," he was saying. "All but Erica's Eyes. She needs the work even if it is miserable out there. I'll start 'em, see if we can get this done at a decent time."

I moved on down the row. On my next trip around, Sandy fell in behind me. He had been standing with his horse in an empty stall, waiting for me to pass. He still didn't say anything and neither did I: we just did our half-hour walk and started two more horses, but I was aware of his presence the whole time. Now the shedrow across the way was quiet. Once I saw Cameron's pal Rudy drag out a muck sack and dump it into the bin between the barns, but he didn't look up and we never made eye contact. At some point I was aware that Sandy had dropped off. I went around one more time and he was standing in the shed-row, waiting. He didn't say anything: just cut his eyes back toward my tack room. I nodded and turned the horse into his stall. Obie took him and ran a rag over his gleaming coat.

"Where you goin', Cliff? I got a whole bunch of work for you."

"Sandy wants me. I'll be back."

I found him inside the tack room, sitting on the same saddle trunk, looking over his training log. "So what's been happening on your side of things?"

"Nothing much yet," I said. "I'm still getting my feet wet."

He tried to smile at the unintentional pun. "Sorry if I got my tit in a wringer yesterday."

"Hey, you're entitled. What's your thinking about Sharon this morning?"

"I think I've got to talk to her myself."

"For what it's worth, I think that's a good decision. Just don't drag your feet."

"I left a message for her last night. Jesus Christ, Janeway, Rome wasn't built in a day."

"I'm just telling you, if she asks me I've got to tell her."

"I *know* what you're telling me."

I decided to leave him alone and let the story work itself out. "Look, I can't help being upset," he said. "I don't want to lose her friendship over something that might not even be real."

I wanted to tell him that wouldn't happen but what did I know? I had met Sharon only two weeks ago and he had known her all her life. "I can't imagine anything good coming out of this," he said nervously. "But we're in it now, and I guess I'll hear back from her this morning."

I said nothing for another moment. Sandy hadn't moved from his perch on the trunk and I watched him fidget with a piece of rope. "Everything comes home to roost, doesn't it?" he said.

"Sometimes that's good. It can be liberating. By the way, how long did you work for the Geigers?"

"I worked for the old man. I was with him about two years when I was just starting out. I was to him what Obie is to me. Rubbing horses for old Geiger was the best education a kid could get. Too bad the sons didn't learn what the old man knew."

"That's usually the way, isn't it? Offsprings' got to find their own light."

"Or spend their lives trading on the old

man's name. Resenting his real accomplishments and wondering what it's all about."

Abruptly I changed the subject. "Did you ever hear Candice mention a character called Tricky Dicky?"

He shook his head. "Sounds like something from her storybooks."

"And she did a lot of that."

"All the time. If your name or personality struck her a certain way, she'd call you that. She called me Pooh."

"Wasn't Pooh a short, fat bear?"

"She thought I was a worrywart. Whenever I started naysaying, she'd say, 'Oh, Pooh,' and give me a shove."

"Any others you knew about?"

"She had a friend she called the Mad Hatter."

"You ever know who that was?"

"No. I only heard her mention him once."

"But you remember it all these years later."

"She was special to me. That's not hard to understand, is it?"

He asked again if I had made any progress and I told him I might know more tonight. "I guess there's no use asking what's happening tonight," he said.

"Sure, you can ask. Cameron's gone missing." I watched his face, which now showed surprise. I looked at his eyes, which had opened wider.

"Gone missing how?" he said. "I didn't even know he was still here."

"He took a job yesterday, rubbing horses for the stable across the way."

"That doesn't sound like him. Wherever he is, Cameron likes to be boss."

"You've got to have some gas in your tank to be boss, Sandy. Looked to me like he was running on empty. The man over there sounds pretty pissed this morning."

"I don't blame him. If he came to work for me and did that, he could keep on walking."

"Any idea where he might have gone?"

"How would I know that?"

"I heard Geiger had a farm not far from here. Would Cameron have gone there?"

"I can't imagine why."

"Do you know where it is?"

"I worked there for a few weeks myself, but that was thirty years ago."

"Can you make me a map?"

"I can try. I'll do the best I can."

He pulled up a chair and began to draw a rough sketch. "It's just a little holding farm with a training track, a house, two or three barns, some pasture, and a storage shed. When you get off the highway at the gas station, it's about ten miles along this road. Then you'll see a dirt road leading off to the east. Once you're that far you can't miss it."

But he gave up the map reluctantly, as if he might change his mind and snatch it back. I had to reach to take it from his fingers. "There's no telling what it's like down there now," he said. "It might be a shopping center after all this time."

"I don't think it's a shopping center, Sandy. Sharon says they still own it."

Slowly he nodded his head. "No, they wouldn't sell it. I remember now, Candice bought it for Geiger's birthday. Did you know she died down there?"

10

I left three hours after daybreak and drove south in the rain. I knew that at some point I would want to check the records in the coroner's office on Candice's death, but now I wanted to see the farm where she had died. The storm had an eerie intensity, almost like one I remembered in Seattle, and I was glad I had brought one of the raincoats from the tack room. The sky to the south looked worse than the sky north but the black clouds retreated as I drove toward them. Then the rain eased up and by the time I made the loop around the bay it had almost stopped. I struck out to the east.

Suddenly things were looking up. The sky was now white with only an occasional streak of gray. A fine mist coated my windshield as I pushed on, but the heavy rain had gone, at least for the moment. I looked again at Sandy's directions. I figured the dirt road leading back to Geiger's place should be about ten miles straight ahead. My spirits were lifted by the undeveloped landscape: I had seen few houses and one country store; the rest was sporadic woods and open fields. The road was still gravel mixed with dirt, just as Sandy had remembered it from long ago. I came to the road I sought; it was lined by trees and set off by a large mailbox. Nobody was around: no cars approached from either direction and I could already see that the mailbox had the name GEIGER painted clearly on the side of it. There was a spic-and-span neatness to most of it, but Geiger's mailbox had been here so long that it was almost red with rust. I stopped and looked both ways; opened the mailbox door and saw a small stack of recent mail. I leafed quickly through it: ten pieces, all addressed to Cameron Geiger, all dated within the last two weeks, most postmarked here in California or up in Washington state. Bills, bills, a collection agency, more bills. I put it all back the way it was and sat in my car at the side of the road.

This did not bode well. If Cameron had come this far he had gone on past without picking up his mail. Unlikely, I thought. But given the nature of the mail and the character of the man, it might mean nothing. I turned the car into Geiger's road and drove back through the trees. The road went about half a mile and dead-ended at a locked gate, where the initials HRG were cut ornamentally into the white-painted wood. I could see some shacks off to my right, outside Geiger's property along a single-lane rutted road that skirted the fence. The road had been wet but now it was pretty well drained; there was no standing water and no tire tracks in the mud. As I continued along outside the fence, I could see some of it now — a rolling field, a road separated in classic horse-country style with white wooden fencing, and the gable of a house maybe a quarter-mile away. This was more than Sandy had remembered: much more than just a holding farm. I could see no obvious end of it — no fence to the south or the east — and this suggested a sizable spread, maybe a hundred acres or more, a nice little present from a loving spouse. There was no telling from this limited vantage point whether anyone was now living here, but the grounds looked immaculate and well cared for. To a man with no end of money this would not be difficult: just hire it done, get a man, two men, or half a dozen to come in once a week or twice a month and see that it was kept shipshape. Why? *Because it's her house,* I thought. This was how he would see it: *her house, her gift,* and he would maintain it exactly as it was then. I was optimistic again, even though this was just a thought, even if there was little reason for any celebration. I had still discovered nothing.

The house was now almost in full view. It was plain but well-painted, standing up on brick supports about six feet off the ground. There was a generous front porch that looked out over the fenced pasture, and from where I was the pasture seemed to continue on over the next hill. The illusion was forever: a nice country estate, still no telling how far it went. My road got ugly, and now there were deep ruts. I felt the bottom scrape and I saw some serious-looking water-filled potholes ahead. At the next wide place, I pulled off and parked the car in the bushes under a tree. From there I could look down at the house, into the backyard, and partway around the side. I saw the back of a car parked on the far side of the house, just the blue fenders of an older GM model, and this was enough to make me sure it was Cameron's Buick.

I had a sudden dark thought, that this had all happened before in another time and place. I could look back over two decades and see half a dozen times when I'd had to go in alone after someone who might be armed and dangerous. I had no reason to think this now, but I always gave myself high marks for intuition. *Always call for backup* — that was the rule, but here I was and there was no backup. I got out in the woods and put on my raincoat. I zipped it up and tied my hood tight under my chin. Just for the hell of it, I got my smaller gun out of the trunk, then I started ahead, ducked between the slats of the fence, and ran in a half-crouch across the open space to the back of the house.

All the blinds had been drawn over the windows, I saw as I ducked under the house. Same old stuff. Just once it would be nice to go into one of these things and not be the only man visible. The place looked deserted; to a casual watcher it looked like a painting, perhaps of another time. The house, I guessed, might be any age from forty to eighty years.

I stood quietly in the deep shadow under the house, the silence deafening. I heard nothing from above: no telltale walking, no noise whatever. I went deeper under the house and came to a large brick column, a strange fireplace, which I guessed opened into the real fireplace in the upper room. I certainly had no reason to think Cameron was *not* upstairs: he might be asleep, but again I had a hunch that he wasn't here at all. This wasn't the way to bet, it was just my hunch.

A moment later, pushed on by my craziness, I decided to walk up and knock on his door.

But I didn't do that, at least not yet. That hunch kept battering my insides and I stood my ground until I became almost a basket case from the quiet. I eased around to the side and there was a walk-out opening. I could now see Cameron's car from the trunk to the crushed fender. I looked across the field and I could see what seemed to be the end of it, five hundred yards down the slope. To my right was a set of wooden stairs that led to a small porch and the side door. Slowly I started up.

Nothing.

I was at the top, staring into a kitchen that opened on one side into an airy room and straight ahead into a dark hallway. Slowly, carefully, I backed down the stairs and went around to the front porch. I knew enough law to figure I was in a mildly compromised position. Even if I walked up to the door and rang the bell, I might have some explaining to do, how I had gone through a locked gate and showed up suddenly on his porch. The hell with it; it wasn't a capital offense, so I went up and knocked on the damn door.

Again, nothing. I waited and knocked a bit harder.

I peered in through a set of flimsy curtains. I could see the fireplace in the center of a large living room; I saw a TV set across the room, one of those consoles, I thought about twenty-five years old. What I could see of the furniture looked old as well, the kind of new-old that says, *I may be old but I've been used kindly.* Not many people had flopped on that sofa in the years since it had been put here. I had Cameron pegged for a slob, so he had either slipped out of character to keep this place looking good or had not used it much at all. I walked to the end of the porch and looked down at his car. Then I went down the stairs and stood beside the car, looking in the windows. I could see the keys dangling in the ignition. This was too much temptation: I pulled on a pair of gloves and opened the door, took the keys, and opened the trunk.

I don't know what I expected to find there. There was nothing; just a jack and a flat tire, but in that half-moment I almost expected to see a dead body and I thought, *Janeway, you've been to too many homicide scenes.*

But I couldn't shake the doomsday feeling that had come with the turf. I got back in the car and looked in the glove compartment. Nothing there but motor vehicle papers, and oh, a wicked-looking gun, loaded and ready for something.

Wrong tense: the gun had already been used; I could smell it the instant I opened the little compartment door. Gloves or not, I didn't want to put any prints at risk, so I picked up the gun carefully, held it with a pen stuck down the barrel, and sniffed it at closer range. The smell of gunpowder filled the car, and now I looked closer and saw that one shell was gone: the one under the firing pin. I smelled the barrel again. Strong gunshot stink: fired as recently as today. Not here though. No blood in the car: no spatter anywhere, inside or out on the grass.

I looked at the papers, moving them as little as possible. In addition to the registration and a few other things there was a traffic ticket for speeding, written yesterday, somewhere between the racetrack and here. Mr. Cameron Geiger had been the lucky recipient. Out of long habit I copied all the information, including the officer's name. I put everything back just as it was and figured it was time I got the hell out of there.

I never made it past the hedge. I had just turned the corner when some dark shadow rose up behind me, came from under the stairs and whacked me behind my right ear with something hard, a poker it turned out.

I opened my eyes and knew I was in trouble.

I knew some time had passed and I was somewhere in the house. The room was dark; the door was closed and only a little light got in around the curtains. In fact I had no idea where I was or what curtains I was thinking about or how long I had been there. For at least a full terrifying minute I couldn't remember my name.

I had never been kayoed like that in my whole rough-and-tumble career. I had been in more fights than I could remember; I had been whacked by brutes when I was ready for them and sucker-punched when I wasn't. This was different. I didn't know how different it was or why it was different, I just knew I had to get out of there or die trying.

I rolled over on my side and two things happened: I knew why and I began to remember my name.

I was a cop; at least I knew that. My

partner Hennessey and I had been ambushed and I had been shot. These things will sometimes happen to a cop, but I had never been hit with such obvious intent to kill. Whoever had done this had meant to do serious damage.

My name was Cliff.

Heathcliff.

My voice came from somewhere in the deep past: *Me Tarzan, you Janeway.*

The literary references should have told me something, but at the moment only nonsense wafted through my brain. Then I knew I had not been shot and I was not in that bedroom. But the more consciousness returned, the less I could see. No curtains, only black in this room. For a terrifying moment I thought I was blind.

I was in the trunk of a car, eating rubber. I felt the flat spare tire under my cheek and the jack beside my arm and finally I figured it out. I was in the trunk of Cameron's car.

I still couldn't remember Cameron's last name or who he was.

Geiger.

Mr. Cameron Geiger was a horse trainer. He had a brother I had never met and his father was two hundred years old. A page from *Ripley's Believe It or Not* fluttered in the wind.

I had a concussion at least. This had a floating dreamlike quality. Sometimes I floated; sometimes I spun, like something from a movie.

Like *Vertigo.*

I heard footsteps. I heard him cough and hawk up a spit. The perp, whoever he was, got into the car and tried to start it. He kept grinding away and I was just about to give up on his behalf when it caught, coughed, backfired, and started.

This was not good news. I reached for my gun but of course he had taken it.

I remembered I kept it on the other side. Carefully, making no noise, I shifted my ass and reached for it, but he had taken it from there as well.

I felt around on the floor of the trunk. The only thing I could use for a weapon was the jack. That made a lousy fit in my hand, it would be awkward in small confined places, but I gripped it and waited for Cameron to come open the trunk. Instead I felt the car jerk forward. I could almost see where we were going by how it felt. The car made a left turn and I could see the road in my mind's eye, I could see he was going around the house. There was another road up ahead, the road out through the gate. He would turn left here, but he turned right

227

and I knew I was still working through the effects of the concussion; I knew he had stopped and turned left after all, it was left he had turned and I was simply in no shape to know the difference. He had stopped and turned *left,* goddammit, left was what he had turned, and now we were rolling down that short road to the main gate.

He stopped again. I heard his keys jingle and a moment later I realized that the car had been turned off. The door opened and slammed shut on the driver's side, at least I *thought* it was the driver's side, it could have been God driving his angels across heaven and I wouldn't have known the difference. I pictured him standing at the gate in his long flowing robe, fumbling through his key chain, his lovely white beard billowing in the breeze like an endless ribbon around the world, his eyebrows bushier than Andy Rooney's, furrowed in anger. Angry God. Impatient God. He could just say, *Let there be the damn key in my hand,* or, *Let the nitwit gate be open in the first damn place,* but he had bigger stuff on his mind and he didn't do that. None of this was funny, it's just part of the craziness you see when your brains have been scrambled. I saw him in my mind's eye as he opened the gate; he came back to the car and got in and started it. It started easier this time. He pulled forward a few feet, stopped, and got out to lock the gate. Then he was back and we were off down that dirt road out of there.

I turned over and lay my head on that soft, airless tire. I was careful; didn't want to make any noise, didn't want him to know I was alive let alone awake. I thought I was starting to get my wits back now. I knew enough to know I was in a bad spot. Two or three things could happen, none of them good. I knew he wasn't going to help me out of the trunk, brush me off, and send me on my way. When he opened it, I had to attack, fast.

Now I could hear the radio playing: some vintage country music station with a hayseed announcer who droned on and told bad jokes between such ancients as "The Race Is On" and "Please Help Me, I'm Fallin'." I had a moment of absolute clarity, maybe a full minute when I knew everything, and I saw Sharon's face so clearly I could almost touch her; I thought of my bookstore on East Colfax and I remembered my old pal Hennessey from Denver homicide; I visited the other booksellers, Seals and Neff, who used to be up the street; and for a long minute I was back in my childhood with my friend Vinnie. Rita McKinley was clutching his arm and Trish Aandahl stood apart like a good reporter and took notes. Vinnie and Rita were getting married and Trish was the society page reporter sent to cover the affair for the *Seattle Times.* Finally I thought of Erin d'Angelo and I wondered if I'd ever see her again. Oh, Erin! This trip did not have a good feeling to it, but here I was and I couldn't do a damned thing about it. When the moment came I had to attack the bastard hard.

Again I had forgotten my name. Slowly it all began coming back.

I stretched out my arm, which had gone numb, and my hand touched the poker. I knew right away what it was; I remembered seeing it by the fireplace in the living room as I looked in from the front porch. A poker is a helluva terrible weapon. And a mind a terrible thing to waste.

Forget the jack: Give him a taste of his poker. Poke his guts out, then hope I could get up fast enough to take a real swing at his head.

I closed my eyes and the vertigo returned.

Incredibly, I must have slept. I opened my eyes to the headache of the world. I still couldn't see but for the moment I could think and I could hear the steady drone of the car. I was being taken for a ride in all the worst uses of that term; I was going for a ride, as somebody named Nitti or Capone might have put it.

I thought I still had a good sense of time. I had always been able to wake from a sound sleep and know about what time it was. My gut told me this was mid-afternoon, we had been on the road two hours, and that meant we had traveled a hundred miles or more from the farm. If he had gone northeast he might be close to the racetrack now. Maybe that's where we were going: he was planning to dump me near Golden Gate Fields in his good deed of the day. But I knew that he might not have gone northeast at all, he might be going south by southwest, in which case we'd be some-where down the Coast, past Steinbeck country, maybe headed for San Luis Obispo. I had no way of telling, but that country station was still blaring on the radio, I heard the call letters and static, which probably meant he was heading away from the sta-tion's broadcast area, wherever that was.

I thought about my life. It all passed like they say it does for a dying man, like a fast motion picture. It went much too fast, because suddenly my time ran out.

The car had stopped. I heard him get out; I felt the car rock but he closed the door softly, with the slightest click. He walked around to the trunk, rapped on it three times, kicked the tire. *What's that prove? Not a damned thing. He's trying to see if I'm awake, if I'm alive, if he can rattle me. He's not sure now whether he killed me; he figures if I'm alive I'll be a basket case by now and I'll start clamoring to get out. He's partly right; I am that basket case.*

I couldn't afford any weakness now; I couldn't let him see me blink, couldn't let him hear me breathe. But that goddam radio kept whining, filling the air with its corn-pone disc jockey and its whiny shit-kickers. Country music may have a certain charm, but not when you're about to die. No one should have to listen to shit-kicking nonsense when someone has come to kill him.

I could feel his presence, looming over the trunk.

He's trying to decide what to do and how to do it.

Then I heard the sound of liquid being splashed. Johnny Horton was singing "The Battle of New Orleans" and the smell of gasoline was seeping down around the top of the trunk.

He's gonna burn it . . .

. . . burn it . . .

He's gonna burn the fucking car.

I heard it blow, a *poof* sound as unmistakable as a gun being cocked. Almost at once a crackling noise came down like the forest fire that almost killed Bambi, and in a few seconds the heat was terrible. I turned in the cramped space and all I could think in that desperate moment was *gotta get out.* I couldn't go through the trunk door, couldn't rip up the floor: only one thing I might do, kick out the backseat and go that way.

I wiggled around and doubled over; got my legs against the partition behind the seat. I pushed with my legs and it gave a little: then I kicked it, kicked it again; I kicked the hell out of it and the seat flew out of there. Smoke and heat poured in and I rolled over and around and crawled into the car. I still couldn't see: it was night, my timing had been seriously off, it was pitch-black dark except for the fire, which was suddenly everywhere. Crawling through it was like crawling through the end of the world into hell. I gripped the back door handle and wrenched it open and the cold air gushed in. I had the poker in my hand — didn't remember picking it up again or maybe I had never let it go — and I rolled out of the car and fell on the cold sweet earth. I rolled and I kept rolling until dizziness made me stop.

I lay flat in the snow and watched the fire burn.

No idea where I was. No clue where *he* was. Not a hint whether he had stayed around to see the end of his handiwork or hauled ass out of here as soon as he lit the fire.

I raised my head. The world spun out of control. I flattened out in the snow as the car exploded and rained fire around me.

I rolled out of the freezing snow onto a stretch of grass that felt almost dry. Then and for the longest time I didn't move. When I looked up again the burning car seemed cold and far away, like something in an astronomer's telescope.

11

In the beginning I was alone in the black universe. The fire was the exploding galaxy and it would burn till it stopped, as other stars had done and would do for trillions of years. I knew I was hurt but I felt no pain. I was cold but I felt no chill. I felt no alarm, no heat, or relief. I had no thought but that I had somehow made it through the endless night. I could feel the firmament but I had no sight except for that fire-thing swirling off in the distance. I had a thought, what the first man might have thought coming to life after that long dark night. *Where am I?* But still the night showed no sign of ending and the universe swirled in its blackness as it had forever.

I was most aware of the nothing. It was deeper than the black; I could feel some small part of the black, but the nothing went on and on beyond my ability to imagine. If I had been able to stand I might have wandered in the wilderness, gone off a cliff, fallen into the nothing, and blundered into the next vast abyss. This darkness would drive a sane man mad; trying to penetrate it was like pondering the Creation without any compass or moral guide, without even a hint that there was any true way or direction. There was no up, down was only what I lay on, and for now this was all there was.

In some part of my brain I knew there was another man somewhere. There was a man in the nothing trying to kill me. Gradually over decades and centuries I had retrieved enough sense to remember that. The man walked with a limp and his name was Cameron.

Years later I opened my eyes and saw a pale outline against a black universe slowly turning blue. *A mountain.* I still felt pinned against the earth, weighed down by God's heavy boot on my back, but I had seen the mountain and I knew I would survive. I had rolled over and now I lay on my back. *Oh, wow.* I clearly remember thinking this thought; I knew I'd had a dream and in it I had been a deity, a ruler over the earth. But tonight I was a wounded one and here I lay. *Here I am, limping man: Come and get me, you son of a bitch. But if you do, you come at your peril.*

The sun rose slowly over the mountains, the valley became eerily visible through a thick fog, and now I knew some other things. *The sun was like a great red wafer pasted in the sky.* This was a line from a book, and it told me I was a reader. I thought it was *The Red Badge of Courage* by Stephen King, but I still wasn't sure of anything. I thought the mountains were to the east; there were hills behind me, and that was the west. I turned over on my side, an excruciating effort; but then, having come that far, I knew I could do anything. I made the big effort and pulled myself through my pain, and through the fog I could see the road and across the way the place where the burned hulk of the car still gave off a wisp of black smoke.

Now it all came back. Sudden clarity returned and I knew I still held the poker in my right hand with a tight grip. I knew I had been sleeping on it. I knew these things before I felt the numbness in my arm and the ache in my ribs. I shifted the poker into my left hand, but this was not easy. The right hand held on and I had to force my will over it.

I would have a helluva time standing; it would be a challenge figuring out where I was and where I had been going, but at least

I was alive. He had left me for dead and that was the worst mistake he would ever make.

Slowly I got to my feet. I suffered through a new wall of dizziness: then I began to walk down to the road, one step at a time.

I stood on the road, still unsteady. I was vaguely aware of a car passing as I closed my eyes and held on to a road sign. The next car that came, minutes or hours or days later, stopped.

I never did get her name. I thought she said Cathy, but that may have been another part of my Heathcliff dream. She remains in my fractured memory as a voice, a strong arm over my back, a wisp of bright red hair, and a Vermont license plate.

I think I told her I had been in an accident. She drove me to a town and took me to a hospital, handed me over to a man in a doorway, and disappeared.

Modesto.

I was in a hospital in Modesto, more than halfway across the state. In addition to the concussion I had second-degree burns on both arms. I spent a good part of the rest of my life filling out insurance forms, signing my shaky name, promising to pay if Blue Cross decided not to for any arbitrary reason they chose to invoke. They were sending an agent out to get a face-to-face statement of what had occurred, and I took this as an omen that my rates would go up whether they paid the bill or not.

I listed Erin d'Angelo as a responsible party who could be called in an emergency. A cop came to my room and took a statement. I didn't ask; he just showed up. This was the hospital's doing and it turned testy when he teetered on the verge of threatening me with trespass. The next day I was told they had found the remains of Cameron's car. They were trying to find its owner. Lacking any further motive or more physical evidence, this was probably all they could do. Cops are overworked almost everywhere.

That afternoon I called Sharon at the ranch in Idaho and left a message on her answering machine. I told her I needed written permission to enter the grounds of the farm and the house, and I needed keys to the house and the gate as well. I needed these as fast as she could get them here.

I told her Cameron was missing and Louie and Billy should be extra vigilant.

I left a message for Sandy at the racetrack, saying I'd had an accident and would be back in as soon as possible.

I slept. Watched part of a boring news

conference on the TV, then an old movie, a program of Roadrunner cartoons, and some *Beverly Hillbillies* reruns. At eight o'clock I closed my eyes and slept through the night. When I opened them again, Erin was sitting in the chair beside my bed.

"Hey. What brings you here?"

"I'm the gas girl, here to read your meter."

This was an old joke between us. I smiled and told her my meter was broken and she leaned over and kissed my weary head. "At least your brains are becoming unscrambled. I expected much worse."

The hospital had called her to verify information, "and here I am."

Bless the hospital. "How long can you stay?"

"As long as I need to."

She was calling in her Brownie points for all the overtime she'd been working at the law office. I told her everything that had happened and we talked far into the morning. "The best thing you can do is come on home to Denver, send this Sharon her money back, and forget about it. But of course you won't do that."

"No." Now I needed to find Cameron. Now it was personal.

Two days later someone in a white coat said I was being released. I was still having occasional episodes, as he put it, but if I took things easy I could go. This would never have happened in the days when doctors, not insurance companies, made these decisions, but I was glad to get out of there.

12

We drove across the state and picked up my car. It seemed untouched from when I'd hidden it in the trees outside the farm, and I felt reasonably coherent, well enough to drive cautiously on to Richmond. Erin followed me and we took a room there, not far from the racetrack. I slept through the night and awoke well before dawn with a headache. A few painkillers brought me to life again, and we sat in an all-night cafeteria over breakfast and talked about how to proceed. She was in it now; I knew her well and there was no turning her back unless I went home with her. I was itching to get out to the racetrack — for herself she suggested taking my list and trying a few of the San Francisco bookstores that I had not reached with my phone checks. That part of the hunt had begun to look bleak, like shooting at the moon with a BB gun, but I had learned never to underestimate her energy, ingenuity, or stamina, and I sure welcomed her viewpoint. Maybe she would ride up to Blakely and visit Carroll Shaw at the library there. "He sounds like a fellow who can educate me if nothing else. I'll see how the day goes." We would meet that evening at five o'clock in the same café on San Pablo Avenue.

It was still on the early side of six when I arrived at the stable gate. I showed Alvin my license, he nodded me through, and I walked along a ridge above the mud and turned into the stable area. Already the clatter of feed tubs was a familiar sound as I crossed between the barns, and I blended right in. I passed a few words with Obie; then I started Pompeii Ruler around the barn. Dawn was breaking when I finished his walk: a brilliant sunrise that lit up the world.

Sandy arrived late. I told him I was fine and he left me alone for the moment. The tow ring was still a river of slop, but the rain had gone and I took that as a good sign. Again the ginneys and I walked the whole stable under the shedrow. As always I seemed to gain strength in work: I walked five miles; then I sat in the chair outside my tack room and let the boys finish up. Everyone was sympathetic: they had heard I had

had an accident and were happy to take up my slack. Sandy pulled up a chair and asked me for an account of my trip east, as he put it, and I told it to him straight. Cameron hadn't shown his ugly face again but his pal Rudy was still working in the opposite barn. No one had approached him; no one as far as Sandy knew had asked him about Cameron. I doubted this. If the cops had not at least sent someone to talk to him, this investigation would set new records for shabby ineptitude. I asked Sandy how his conversation with Sharon had gone, but he said they had been playing telephone tag all week and he had not yet had that pleasure. I was annoyed at this news and we had a short, terse exchange over it. I said, "You know if she asks me what I'm finding out about her mom, I'm gonna have to tell her," and it went downhill from there. He said, "Look, I've got one or two other things on my plate right now. I've got a horse running this afternoon, I'm not sitting by the phone all day, and I'm sure she's not either." I said, "That may be, but I'd put a priority on this if I were you." He said, "Dammit, Janeway, I'm not accustomed to taking orders in my own shedrow," and I said, "Then let it ride and we'll see what happens." He got up from his chair. "That sounds almost like a threat." I closed my eyes. "I don't like threats any more than you do, Sandy, but if you don't tell her soon, I will, and I'll bet I can get her on the phone pretty quick. That's not a threat, she just needs to know."

There was a moment when I didn't know whether he was going to continue with this, break out laughing, or chase me out of there with a buggy whip. I gave him what I hoped was my apologetic look, but I knew he had been dragging his feet and he knew I knew; he had done nothing the whole time I had been in the hospital.

"I'll tell her," he said defensively. "I said I'd tell her and I will."

"Please," I said as he walked away.

He had left me irritated and headachy. I sat watching the barn across the way. I could see that the trainer had hired another young stud like Rudy to rub Cameron's horses. Rudy was assuming authority over the new hand and acting bossy. But I still figured Rudy was all strut, no waltz, and I made up my mind to pay him that visit. I was not quite my old self yet, but right now what I felt like doing was goading him into taking a swing at me.

At ten-thirty another man arrived across the way. Obie saw me watching and said, "Cameron's brother, Baxter." He was a smart guy, Obie, I decided again: he knew when something was up. "Bax has a stable over in Barn 14," he said without being asked. I could see the Geiger resemblance in Bax even from there. I wondered if the brothers socialized much: I had heard they were not on friendly terms. "Cameron will always take any opportunity to be a pain in the ass," Obie said, "but you already knew that. I think Bax has got his craw full of it in recent years, but he's no plaster saint either. And they are still brothers after all."

I could only hear part of what Baxter was saying. His voice carried across the tow ring in snatches and he seemed to be asking everyone in the shedrow if they had heard from Cameron. No one had, and after a while he left. I didn't move from my place in the sun for much of what morning was left; it felt too good just to laze around and take pleasure in being alive. At eleven-thirty I walked up to the kitchen and found a copy of today's *Daily Racing Form* where someone had left it on a table. I glanced through the races and learned that Sandy had Erica's Eyes in the fifth. It was a five-furlong dash for maiden fillies, which I knew meant a cavalry charge for fillies that had never won a race. In fact, Sandy's horse had never raced anywhere, but somebody must have known something because she was an even-money favorite in the morning line. This had come about as always by some mysterious ripple process. Since she had no form, the railbirds were going by her workouts and maybe the reputation of her trainer. I toyed with the crazy idea of putting my whole load on her nose, everything I had won on Pompeii Ruler last week. A sucker's bet, but it was all found money, never mind the vow I had made to bet no more. For a moment I was tempted to ask Sandy how she looked but things between us were suddenly chilly and now the cop in me didn't want to owe him anything.

I had some lunch and over the noon hour I felt a little better. I wasn't all there yet but I could almost feel the strength oozing back into my muscles and bones. I checked in at the barn. Erica's Eyes was Bob's horse. He was sitting in the straw, wrapping her legs. I leaned over the webbing and watched him work. I asked him how she was feeling and he smiled and gave me a wink. He had been her ginney for more than six months, and right then, on nothing more than that, I decided to play her all the way.

We were now into the early afternoon. This was the quiet hour, when ginneys with nothing going could catch up on a little sleep. Again I thought of having that little talk with Rudy across the way. I had a hunch that was growing stronger by the minute. If Cameron had turned up nowhere by now, my cop's instinct was to follow him through Rudy, the last man known to have seen him, so at one o'clock I hauled myself out of the chair and started across the tow ring. A few horses watched with keen interest as I walked into Rudy's shedrow and gave him a bold look through his screened door.

He was sitting on his bed looking through a *Playboy* magazine. Slowly his eyes came up over the pages. "You looking for something?" He got to his feet and came toward the door, said, "What's goin' on, dude?" and now there was a hesitance in his face. He had come just two steps and stopped. "I'm looking for your pal Cameron," I said.

"He's no pal of mine." In a bellicose voice, he added, "I'm not his goddam secretary, either. What makes you think I know where he went?"

Until that moment I had no idea what I was going to do but suddenly I did what I'd always wanted to do as a cop: I opened the screened door and took a full step inside. This would have been just enough to put a cop's case in jeopardy if I had been a cop building one, but at the moment the game was between Rudy and me. It was enough to surprise him and he backed around the edge of his bunk. "Wait a minute, goddammit, I didn't say you could come in here," he said, but his voice quaked and gave him away.

"A guy across the way said you're looking for somebody to play rummy with."

"What are you, some kinda nut?"

"Go find Cameron, then we'll have us a third. Maybe you know somebody else, then we'd have enough for a game of bridge."

"I don't know what the hell you're talking about. I don't even play cards."

"Cameron's brother Bax could be our fourth."

The anger that skittered across his face was again tempered by doubt.

"Man, this is *my* room. What right have you got barging in here?"

He was still trying hard to be tough but I could see he was a frightened liar. His face said he was stonewalling and his voice said he was afraid.

I could almost smell the fear on him. I took another step and suddenly the rules changed from rummy to Grab-ass, the new Parker Brothers board game. I said, "Okay, maybe we won't play cards. Instead I might just kick you around a bit and worry about my rights later."

"What the *hell* are you talking about? Jesus, I don't even know you."

"Then I guess you're gonna find out about me now."

His mouth opened like a gaffed fish. I cocked my head and tried to look bored. "You don't get it, do you, Rudy? I throw you my best lines and they're lost on you. So listen to me. Sit down and shut your mouth and listen." I pushed him and he slammed hard against the wall.

"Jesus Christ! Who do you think you are?"

"I'm the guy who got worked over looking for your pal Cameron. Somebody whacked the hell out of me with a poker and tried to roast me for dinner. But I guess you wouldn't know anything about that."

"I don't know anything about anything."

"Generally speaking, let's say I think you're a liar and a pretty bad one. I think you see yourself as a tough guy, but I've met guys like you dozens of times before. When the chips go down you're just another scared rat."

"Man, I don't have to take that shit."

I smiled, venomously I hoped, and he made one last attempt to gain the high ground. "You know if I report this you'll get deep-sixed out of here fast."

"Then I'll have to convince you not to do that."

Sudden alarm spread across his face. "What the hell's that supposed to mean?"

He tried to crawl away but I grabbed his shirt and tightened it into a knot over his Adam's apple. Slowly I drew him forward, struggling on the bed, until I could smell his smoker's breath. "Rudy, you are really starting to piss me off. You know why that is? Because you're turning me into a bully. I hate bullies worse than anything. I even hate myself when I've got to resort to tactics like this, you know what I'm saying?"

He sat mute and softly I added, "But that won't stop me from kicking your ass."

He looked away as a mouse scurried around the corner.

"Are you gonna talk to me, Rudy?"

"I don't . . ."

"Wrong answer." I raised my hands suddenly, like a Halloween spook yelling *boo*, and he cringed back into his bedding with a sharp cry. "*Wait* a minute!"

I waited, somewhat less than a minute. "Rudy?"

"Hey, Cameron's no skin off my nose. What do you want to know?"

"Good man." I smoothed his shirt,

brushed him off. "Mainly I want to know where he is and why he went away and what he wants and when he's coming back. If you tell me these things, we can be buddies again. But if you say you don't know, that would be a mistake. Now, answer a few questions and I'll get out of your face. Where's Cameron gone?"

"Down to the old man's farm. What's that got to do with you?"

"That's one of the things we're trying to find out. Why'd he go down there?"

"Said he had to see somebody."

"And who would that be?"

"He didn't say, I didn't ask. If you don't believe me, ask him yourself."

"Maybe I'll do that if he ever shows up again. What's he after?"

"I don't know."

"Rudy . . ."

"I don't *know,* man! So we travel together, that don't mean I know everything he does."

"When's he coming back?"

"I figured he'd be back three days ago. That's what he said, but now he's missing and even the cops don't know where to look."

"Cops are looking for him?"

"Well, yeah, as much as they look after anybody that drops off the earth."

252

"But you don't know who he went down to the farm to see?"

"He went to see some dude who's gonna give him a bunch of dough."

"How big a bunch?"

"Big enough to stake him till he gets on his feet again."

"But he didn't tell you why this fellow is giving him all that money?"

"He tells me nothing about his business. This is God's truth now, I swear it is."

"You ever known him to traffic in books?"

"Books? What the hell kinda question is that?"

"You know what a book is, Rudy. I don't expect you've ever read one on your own, but I think you've heard rumors of their existence."

"Man, you're outta your mind. Are we talking about the same guy?"

"Don't lie to me, Rudy. I know you boys tried some grab-ass stuff with Sharon's crew in Idaho, and I know you were looking for a book. This may be your last chance to level with me."

"So he was looking for some old damn book. So he's weird. Am I supposed to know what that's about?"

"He didn't tell you?"

"Hell, no. Just said it was worth some dough."

At the doorway, I turned and said, "Naturally, if you're lying . . ."

He turned his hands up, a picture of helpless innocence, and I left him there.

I walked over to the saddling paddock with Bob and stood outside the ring and watched while Sandy saddled his horse. To make the wait interesting I dropped my entire winnings on Erica's Eyes. She went off at only four-to-five but won in a breeze by six lengths. Her jock never had to touch her with the whip. He just waved it at her, she blew away the field at the top of the stretch, and was still pulling away under a tight hand-ride to the wire. If they had gone around the track, I thought, she'd have lapped them.

This was more than two grand back to me on my $1,200 bet. Again Ms. Patterson came out to the shedrow with Sandy, this time without her husband. Hmmmm, I thought evilly. She had to be impressed: If she was looking for a new trainer, Sandy's record the past few days was persuasive. They said nothing about this within my hearing, but Sandy was charming and apparently funny; they laughed it up and looked to be old backslapping pals by the time Erica's Eyes was cooled out. Hmmmm, I thought. Again he passed out money from a roll of twenties. I shook my head but he pushed it on me. Suddenly he was chummy again: the man had more faces than Lon Chaney. I had been upgraded to Cliff, so the hell with it, I took his twenty dollars. He left early with Ms. Patterson in tow; I walked our winner and Bob checked her cooling-out periodically as we came around. By quarter after four I was able to break away and walk back through the stable area. I stopped at the mail room, where I had an Express Mail package from Sharon. Two keys and a short note — just what I needed to get in trouble all over again.

13

That night I met Erin in the café on San Pablo Avenue. She'd had an uneventful day tramping through bookstores on both sides of the bay. This had left her no time to go up to Blakely, but "that's what tomorrow's for." She asked about my day and I told her all except the arrival of Sharon's note and the keys. I was uneasy keeping this from her — I had never been able to lie to her effectively — but there was no way I was taking her down there and I knew she wouldn't sit still for having me go alone. We watched a boring television show in our room, retired early, and in the morning we struck out again on our separate ways. I got to the track at five o'clock: by then they all knew I was not just a hot walker, I had too much leeway, I must be doing something for Sandy, but no one asked what. I tried to do my share of the work, walking six horses before I bailed out and headed south at

eight-thirty. It was a far better trip without the rain. I made good time, turning into that graveled road just before eleven. The road was like a still painting in oil, at first unchanged and unchanging, and suddenly this had all the earmarks of a wasted journey. But as I got closer I could see that the gate was open. I stopped the car and sat with my motor idling: tried to remember how it had been left. I had been in the trunk and he had stopped to open the gate; then he had gone on through and stopped again to close and lock it. I was almost certain this was what had happened. He was a careful killer, and the gate had been left locked.

He had a key. It had been on his key ring.

I pulled off into the trees and got out of the car. I got my .38 and walked back up the road to the gate. I could see the road continuing beyond the open gate, the place where it turned back toward the house. Even the trees were eerily still: not a breath of air to stir them. From the gate I could almost see the house, and when I walked along outside the fence I could see that somebody was home. Whoever was there had lit the fireplace. Smoke curled conspicuously from the chimney. Standing under a densely leafed tree, half hidden by the shade and half by the tree trunk, I could make out

the shape of a man out at the edge of the front porch. He had lit the fire and then come out to stand in the cold.

I shifted the gun around till it was hidden on my rump under my coat. I moved away from the tree and soon I could see around the porch — that part of the backyard where Cameron had parked his Buick, where now there was a pickup truck. I stood there for at least ten minutes. There was no more movement from the porch: The man, whoever he was, was gone. I came as close as I dared; then I stepped back into the under-brush and stood there watching, but it was like trying to peer through a fluttering green curtain. Occasionally I could see someone walking inside, past a window, but no more than that, just a flashing change of color. I looked at the sky, which was white through the trees.

I moved slowly now, and the house took on a darkly familiar shape beyond the flut-ter of the trees. I heard a door slam and I got behind a tree as someone came to the door and opened it. Minutes passed in near silence. Only the rustle of the leaves as I squirmed back against the tree trunk. Then the door opened wide and Baxter Geiger came out onto the porch.

He didn't seem to be doing much of

anything: just in and out of the house with an antsy restlessness. I stood still until he went inside again; then, impulsively, without making any conscious decision to approach him, I hustled along the road toward the house. *Up the porch steps on the balls of my feet, across the porch as quietly as I could go, but that didn't matter now, he must hear me coming.* I knocked on the door and I heard his heavy footsteps. He stopped suddenly and spoke through the door. "Who's there?"

A tense voice: nervous, loud.

"My name's Janeway. I'm looking for Cameron Geiger."

The door opened a crack. I saw one eye and a beard, part of his heavy plaid shirt; a big fist gripped the door, and across the room, a rifle leaned against a wall. "Join the club," he said. "What do you want with him?"

He didn't seem to know me by sight: If he had seen me across the tow ring, my face hadn't made any lasting impression. "I'd like to talk to him," I said; "see where it goes from there. But nobody seems to have any idea where he might be."

"So you came down here on a blind, is that it?"

Now he did begin to put my face together

with something. I could hear his slight intake of breath, but enlightenment came slowly. His eye roamed up and down the crack in the door and at last he opened it wider until I could see the pistol in his right hand.

"Janeway. I've heard that name some-where."

I let him play with it and then he remembered. "You're the guy who almost got turned to toast in Cameron's car." He looked in my eyes. "I saw you in Sandy Standish's barn yesterday." I nodded slightly, just the barest movement, and he said, "What the hell were you doing here? What are you doing here now?"

I looked down at his hand. "Put the gun away and I'll come in and tell you."

I saw a flicker of a smile on his face. "Afraid I'm gonna shoot you?"

"You never know, the way things have been going."

He gave a little laugh. "Guess I'd worry too if I was in your shoes."

He opened the door but he didn't give up the gun. I stepped in anyway. He backed away from the door and I moved with him, nothing quick or threatening but I was close enough that I had a chance against him if he went suddenly crazy. He looked damned unstable. His eyes darted from me to the corner of the room and back again. I said, "I've got a letter from your sister, giving me permission to look through the house."

"My sister?"

"Sharon."

"I know her name. I just never heard it said . . . quite that way."

"Would you like to see the letter?"

He nodded and, without taking my eyes off him, I fished out my wallet and got him the paper: handed it to him and stood still, hardly breathing until he had read it.

"Sharon's always been a good kid," he said.

And that was how we came together on that extraordinary day.

Now came a quick surprise: He apologized for having no manners or food in the house. At that point he did put away the gun and I breathed a little easier. I moved back, slightly out of immediate striking range, and we sat at the kitchen table over coffee that must have been five hours old. I told him what had happened to me earlier, how I had gotten out of the trunk, and some version of why I had come here in the first place. He poured more coffee and said, "You must think we're all a bunch of lunatics. Have you met Damon yet?"

"He was out at the ranch in Idaho."

"What are you, some kind of cop?"

I told him what kind of cop I had been. But for now I told him as little as possible.

"I guess you're wondering what I'm doing here," he said uneasily.

"If you feel like telling me. But you're family, I assume you've got a right."

He drained his cup and stared off into space. "Don't assume anything with us," he said after a long pause. "I've got a set of keys but that doesn't mean squat. We all know this place is going to Sharon if they can ever get the will figured out, so I guess you've got as much right here as I have."

I didn't push him on that point. I'd had all I could drink of his coffee, but we were still fencing, feeling each other out. "Hell, I'm doing the same thing you're doing," he said. "Groping around. Looking for Cameron."

"You got reason to think he's here?"

"There were places we went together, years ago," he said quickly, "before bad temper and other things drove us all apart."

"What places?"

"There's a canal that cuts along the edge of the farm, and a stand of trees across the back road where the woods are thick. We used to shoot birds there a hundred years ago."

"You really think he's there now?"

He blinked and took his time. "I don't know what I think. But I thought he might be."

"And that's why you came out here?"

Almost a full minute passed before he said, "Maybe I'm the crazy one. I came here thinking he might show up, and I've been shivering in the house for three hours. What do you make of that?"

"Jitters . . . everybody gets 'em at some point in life."

"This is more than any jitters. I told you I've got a hunch."

"About what?"

He didn't answer — just looked at me hard across the table, said, "You wanna take a walk?" and suddenly I shared his hunch, that something had happened even if we didn't know what. I said, "Sure, I'll take a walk with you." Then, to my own unease, he picked up his gun and motioned me ahead of him through the door to the porch.

Out in the yard he tucked the gun into his belt and draped his coat over his shoulders. "Your lead," I said, and he struck off at once, through the fence and across the field. He walked with long decisive strides, eating up the ground, and I kept pace a step behind him. His breath floated out of him in small white puffs, swirling and disappearing into the air. We started up the hill. The place had an air of eternity, as if it had been sculpted out of the plain in some former lifetime. I said as much but he only grunted a response. We had gone halfway up the hill when he said, "Yeah, they were always workin' on it when Candice was alive: hiring landscape people, having trees planted along the road; shrubs and stuff." I wanted to ask what he thought of Candice. The moment didn't seem right but I backed into it anyway. "Candice sounds like a fascinating woman."

Again he took his time answering. We had almost reached the top when he said, "Oh yeah, she was a doll," as if his brain had slipped into some kind of slow-motion mode, almost as if he had been taking a hallucinatory drug. We crested the hill and on the other side was a long downward-sloping pasture that ended in a wall of trees. "That's the canal," he said. "You can't see it yet, but it goes there through the trees." He was walking fast now and I had to hustle to keep up with him. I could hear his breath coming hard; I could see it clearly in the frosty morning, puffing around his head like smoke from a train. Suddenly he said, "Yeah, Candice was a living doll," and he veered left toward the woods. I could see a small building there in the trees, and off to the left of that, a number of corrals and another smaller house. "They used these for feed houses when she was alive," he said. "The house straight ahead was to store hay in." We were now on a rutted road, which cut through the field to the feeding area. He stepped nimbly for a big man, dancing around the water-filled potholes, slipping once but getting his footing without missing more than a step. "Candice would be proud if she could see it now," he said.

He stopped suddenly, I came up on his flank, and we collided gently. He cocked his head and again had that strange time lapse in his thinking. "She brought new life to the old man and that had to be a good thing. This place cost her a pretty penny even then, but she didn't care. Nice having money like that, huh?"

"Seems like she used it well."

He nodded and I said, "How well do you remember her?"

This time he answered immediately: "I remember everything about her." He looked at the sky over the hay house. "I remember everything." He watched a flock of birds circling over the woods. "Like it was yester-day," he said.

I doubted that but I let him talk. He started walking again, slower now. "I heard she took this walk every morning when she was here. She loved the fields and the trees. She put up with Idaho, but she liked it best of all down here."

He opened the door and we went inside. It was a four-room house, the rooms still had hay residue on the floors, and there were a few old bales of straw, smelling dry and stale. "Like it was all yesterday," he said as we crossed into the back rooms. We went out the back door and looked inside the smaller house. "So much for hunches," he said.

He turned and started back up the hill. But we had only gone a dozen steps when he whirled around and said, "Wait, I want to see the canal," and he doubled back past the corrals into the trees. There was an old path, mostly overgrown now, but he found it as if he had never left here, "like it was all yesterday," he said again. I followed him by about ten yards, and soon I saw the water running slowly in its bank just ahead. We came into a clearing and he went to the edge and stood transfixed, looking at the water. "Don't know what's wrong with me," he said. "I feel cold." I told him it *was* cold, but I knew that wasn't what he meant. "That crazy bastard," he said, striking off along the bank. We went two hundred yards and he stopped and wavered in the gentle breeze.

"Oh, God," he said, covering his face with a handkerchief. "Oh Christ, I'm gonna puke."

Then I smelled it too, a rotten stench that hung over the cut like a shroud. I came out to the edge and there was Cameron, draped over a piling, half in and half out of the water. The birds had been at his eyes and his head had been blown open, the wound full of maggots. His body swayed in the water, his hand making a macabre little ebb-and-flow greeting, like a man saying hello to people he barely knew.

14

Erin sat coldly through my account that night. The police had arrived at two o'clock with the coroner's men on their heels; Baxter and I had been questioned in separate rooms; I explained why I was there and showed them my note from Sharon; I told them about my own adventure in the trunk of Cameron's car and the gun, recently fired, that I had found there. I was released after two hours with the usual polite request to keep in touch. They were still questioning Baxter as I left. I knew they weren't satisfied with his part of the story: If he had told them what I had seen or heard from him, I wouldn't be satisfied either. They would ask, for example, how he had suggested a walk and then led me almost straight to his brother's body. I hadn't told Baxter about this likelihood: the last thing I wanted was to coach the suspect, if that's what he turned out to be, but this was one of those times when I longed to be on the other side of the badge. I did take his gun away from him when he put it on the table: I picked it up carefully, put it on another table across the room, and left it to the cops to deal with when they arrived. Other than a few brief comments, we had nothing else to say until the police came.

"I didn't kill him," he did offer at one point. "How long's he been dead do you think?"

I didn't say but I thought it could be a week on the long end.

"I've been up at Golden Gate till early this morning."

People could verify that, he said, he was well known up there. "Besides, why would I kill him?"

Now, hours later, Erin listened to my story without a word. We ate our dinners in that awful silence, and at last I said, "Okay, if you're gonna chew me out, let's have it."

"Would that do any good?"

"In what context?"

"Don't be dense, Janeway, it doesn't become you. I'm just very calmly asking if you'd do it again under the same circumstances, which of course you would, like a bat out of hell. I thought we had all this out months ago. *Years* ago."

"If it makes any difference, I did bring my sword to fall on."

"Which means nothing when push comes to shove. I predict one of these days we will have us an ugly parting over something like this."

A scary thought. I pondered it and said, "But what would we do without each other?"

"That is the question, isn't it?"

That was indeed the question. I had once come so close to losing her that now I got edgy if she was running late in traffic, tense if she failed to call. I was nervous in all those harmless down times where before, in my old life, I had felt invincible.

"You worry way too much," she said. "You're becoming . . ."

She fished for a term and I gave it to her. "A pain in the ass."

"Thank you. I was thinking of a mother hen but your description is better."

"So," I said expansively; "what do you think of our little dilemma?"

"I don't think with all your scratching around you've done much to further your cause."

"Getting brained with a poker and left for dead; finding Cameron's body — you don't count that as progress?"

"You've demonstrated again that you have an uncanny ability to stick your head in front of hard, fast-moving objects. I admit that's a nice talent, but what did you learn?"

"Somebody killed Cameron."

"A fact that surely would have materialized anyway, but yes, you did let the brother lead you straight there, I should give you points for that. That does make the brother the top suspect. So far, however, your footwork has been lagging."

I glared at her.

"Far be it from me to tell you what to do; your experience as a cop far outweighs mine. But forget about Cameron for a moment. Doesn't sound like anybody will miss him anyway, so, unless his death is connected to Candice somehow, what's the point?"

"I believe it is connected. It's not often that you get two unrelated murders in the same family. Rare, actually, as people like to say in the book business."

"That's an overused term in books as well. *Where* is the connection and *how* are they connected and why? Did someone kill her, did she do it herself, or was it an accident? We still don't know these things yet. I'm sure it must have occurred to you to question some people if you have any hope of finding out what happened to that woman all those years ago, but so far the only ones you've pushed at all seem to be Sandy and that dumb guy across in the next barn."

"There's a reason for that. Can you guess it?"

"You're reluctant to give up your under-cover status."

"That's true. Once you go public, so to speak, you can't ever change your mind and tell people to forget it, you really are just a racetracker like them."

"Okay, but what's the harm?"

"I'm afraid if the stewards find out they'll kick me out of there. Where would I be then?"

"Hmmm," she said. "I admit that's one argument I hadn't figured on."

"No, but you were starting to have some great fun at my expense."

"Would they kick you out?"

"For coming in under false pretenses? What do you think?"

"Hmmm."

"Sandy might get in trouble as well. Now maybe you see it's more complicated being a cop than a lawyer. Especially if you're a cop without a badge."

She ignored this dig. "What about that guy you hassled . . . what's his name?"

"Rudy."

"Yeah. Won't he tell?"

"Rudy can't tell time without help. He has no clue who I am."

"But he knows you're somebody now."

"You give him way too much credit. I don't worry much about a guy who struts around and then, when some inevitable showdown happens, hasn't got the balls, pardon me, to back it up. I doubt if he's had a real thought in thirty years. His act is his whole life."

We sat for a while in a ponder-mode, saying nothing.

"Hmmm," she said. "Want some dessert?"

"No thanks, but you go ahead." I looked at her with admiration. "You burn calories like other people breathe and you never gain a pound."

She smiled sweetly and ordered a piece of lethal-looking chocolate swirl cheesecake.

"So," she said. "This does make it difficult. This will require some deep thought."

We thought deeply, but in the end she said, "You can't just keep coasting. At some point you'll have to take a chance and shake things up."

Of course I knew that. Meanwhile I asked how Blakely was and her face lit up.

"Incredible library, fascinating stuff; what

can I say? Your friend Carroll Shaw was cool, too. But you know all that."

"Actually I've never been up there. I've always done business with them by telephone."

"Do yourself a favor and stop on your way back to Denver. You could spend days and never see a fraction of what they've got."

I asked about Carroll and she said, "Nice man. Spread a little thin when I dropped in on him out of the blue so he had an assistant show me around. He did say hi to you."

She had picked up an artist's drawing of the new library, which would break ground next year and be finished in 1998. A pamphlet integrated its mission statement with drawings of the various rooms and listed its current officers and benefactors. Lots of old money, plenty of public spirit. I recognized many high-class horse owners among the board of directors: Gallaghers, McWilliamses, Adamses, Wentworths, and in fact Sandy's friend Barbara Patterson was on the board.

"There's a woman who gets around," I said.

"Good to have a busy life." She pushed her dish across the table. "Last bite of the cheesecake."

I shook my head and she ate it.

Later, as we prepared to call it a night I said, "You wouldn't leave me."

"Not till the pain really outweighs the joy."

15

Baxter Geiger had his horses stabled in Barn 14, a few rows over from my tack room. He had already arrived when I walked into his shedrow at quarter to four the next morning, a solitary figure standing in an open tack room drinking coffee from an old porcelain mug. I could hear his ginneys stirring about in the other rooms: I heard an alarm clock ring and a radio softly playing elevator music nearby. Bax stood like a statue and watched me come to him. I came up close and said good morning and he grunted out a response. "Thought they threw you in the clink," he said.

"Is that what they told you?"

"They didn't tell me anything. But you weren't there when I came out."

"And you had me figured for Cameron's killer."

"Just like you figured me."

"I try not to jump to conclusions like that,

Bax. If you do, it leaves you with egg on your face when the truth comes out."

"I told you I didn't kill him. But you didn't believe me."

"Didn't believe or not believe. I had just met you, what did I know? But you don't seem too broken up about it."

"Cameron's a hard guy to mourn, even for a brother. So what do you know now?"

"Not much more. I was wondering if we could have a little talk."

"Got to be after work this morning. This rain's played hell with my schedule."

"You say when."

"Come back around noon, I'll talk to you then."

I crossed over to Sandy's barn and began the morning's work. Again he was moody and tense. He was short with his ginneys and the bug boy but said nothing to me. I heard him raise his voice as I walked Erica's Eyes down the shedrow: "Jesus, Obie, hold him still; can't you even keep his head straight?" I turned my horse into her stall and hugged her head, then started another walk. The tow ring had dried considerably and we were able to walk in the sunshine as the morning spread its glory over the back-stretch and on across the bay. It was a crisp cold autumn day. Sandy took ten horses to the track, six to gallop and four to work. This made the morning busy for his hands. I walked without letup, around and around, yet my mind was full and I never got tired or bored. The horses were alert and feisty, they kept me on my toes, and so the hours passed.

At the end of the morning Sandy came up to me and said, "Let's talk." We went into the tack room and he closed the door. "How's it going?" he said.

"Slow."

"You got anything solid yet?"

I shook my head.

"I heard you found Cameron yesterday."

"Yeah, Bax was with me."

"Well, I wouldn't mind having a progress report now and then."

"What kind of report do you want, Sandy? I haven't even had time to call Sharon yet." I looked at him, expecting the worst. "She is my client, after all."

His face boiled over with anger. "I *know* who she is. I shouldn't have to remind you that you are here in the first place as a personal favor to her."

I nodded, warily, but I hoped pleasantly. He said, neither warily nor pleasantly, "So from now on I want to be kept better informed about what's going on."

"Sounds like you're already pretty well informed."

"Goddammit, Janeway, don't play games with me. Everybody on this racetrack knew what had happened before I got here this morning."

"I'm sorry about that. But surely you don't expect me to chase you down every time something happens, just so you can hear it first."

"I expect you to use a little courtesy and respect. Is that too much to ask?"

"I don't know, it might be. Depends on what it means."

A long thirty seconds passed. He held his ground and I could see he was trembling mad. He got up from the saddle trunk, walked to the door, and turned to me. He said, "I'd like you to wind this up as soon as possible."

I smiled, the soul of reason. "So would I."

"So I'm *asking* you how long this is gonna take."

"And I'd tell you if I knew. I can't even guess at the moment."

He opened the door and the shedrow stretched away into the distance. I saw Obie and Bob watering their horses. Wisely, they didn't look up, but Pompeii Ruler was curious as usual. Sandy hovered in the doorway as if he couldn't make up his mind what to do. Finally he said, "I want this done with by early next week."

"A week seems to be everybody's time frame," I said. "First Junior wants me gone in a week; now you." He walked away without another word.

I tried Sharon from the pay phone in the kitchen and got her on the first ring. We talked about Cameron. Like Baxter, she was finding it difficult to care.

"But something ought to be done for him," she said. "He's their brother, for God's sake. They'd be just as happy if he was thrown in some potter's field in an unmarked grave."

She would have him cremated, and the ashes buried up in Idaho.

"How are you doing?" she said.

"Not as well as I'd like. If Cameron stole those books, only his killer knows for sure."

"You still think Mamma's death is tied to the books."

"Yeah, I do. Just don't ask me to prove that in a court of law." I took a deep breath. "Your friend Sandy is getting impatient."

"Would it do any good if I talked to him again?"

"I don't know. What would you say?"

"Ask him to give you some more slack."

"Let's play it by ear for now. If he actually runs me out of here, I'll let you know."

"Then what?"

"Then I've got to drop back and punt," I said, but in fact I didn't know what. I had never worked like this before. All the people I needed to see were in a closed, protected environment where I had no official standing. I was here by permission that could be revoked at any time. I had already offended some of them and would probably offend the others the first time I asked a question. No one had to talk to me about anything. "I don't know whether to walk on eggs or come out swinging."

"Follow your heart. Whatever you do, it'll be fine."

"That ain't necessarily so, Sharon. But I'm going to see Baxter in a little while. What else is happening up there?"

"I'm playing telephone tag with your friend Carroll. He wants to come out here in a few weeks and see my books. You do think I should do that?"

"I think he's worth knowing even if you never sell or donate them. Sometime I'll show you that bibliography he wrote. Incredible piece of work."

"It would be nice if you could be here. December tenth was mentioned."

I wrote it down but I had no idea where I'd be then. Almost as an afterthought, she said, "By the way, Junior knows where you are. He got a call from some California policeman, asking questions. They talked to me as well."

"What'd they ask?"

"Questions about you, a few about Bax. Mainly they wanted to verify where you'd come from and what you were doing."

"How are you getting along with the junior one?"

"He never gives me any grief. Yesterday he actually appealed to my sense of reason. He and Damon want to come out to Santa Anita and bring HR's horses. So if you go that way you'll see them there before too much longer."

I wondered again if they could just do that on their own.

"Unless I raise a fuss, who's gonna stop them?" Sharon said. "Even if I do, my lawyer tells me they'd probably win. Junior's the manager. He'll argue that this is in the estate's best interest. These horses have a definite racing life span, two years, maybe three, and if any of 'em do well their value could go up enormously. So theoretically at least, the clock is ticking."

"Try to talk to Junior before he comes.

Tell him if he screws up what I'm doing it'll work against him in the long run."

"What do I tell him if he asks what you're doing?"

"Tell him nothing."

"He won't like that."

"Then I guess you'll have to get tough with him."

Bax took a long drag on his smoke. "All I can do is tell you what I told the cops. Hell, I don't know what happened to Cameron. But yeah, I'm sure I looked guilty as hell."

"You look better today," I said.

"I am better. But before you walked in on me yesterday, I had been down to the cut."

"So you found the body before I ever got there."

"Christ, I'll never forget it. I've never seen anything like that. I was shocked. I mean listen, there hasn't been any real love lost between Cameron and me for twenty years. But seeing him there in the water with his head blown open . . . and those worms eating his brains out . . ."

He shivered. "I couldn't move for five minutes; couldn't move, couldn't look at it. Then I turned and ran like hell. Man, I'm telling you, I never ran like that. Thought I was gonna drop dead myself."

We had walked up to the backstretch rail to talk in private. He leaned on the rail and lit another thin black cigar. "Then I got to the house and I just . . . froze again. I could barely breathe when I thought about it. You ever see a dead man?"

"I was a homicide cop," I said with a dry little laugh.

"You would have then, wouldn't you?"

"Once or twice."

"I never have. Somehow the thought of death has always made me squeamish. I have a helluva time putting a sick horse down, gotta get the doc to do it. I hated being Candice's pallbearer, and I didn't even go over for the old man's funeral. Didn't want to see him, all waxy like that." He blew a cloud of smoke. "Cameron was the first I ever saw."

"It gets easier after the first dozen. You close your mind and just do the job."

"I can't imagine. I don't know how anybody does a job like that." He put his head down and said, "Whoever did that to Cameron never meant for him to get up, did they?"

"Doesn't look like it."

He shook his head. "You ever know anybody like me?"

"Sure," I said. "It's the fear of death. I

believe it's called thanaphobia."

"You mean I'm not the only one?"

"Not hardly."

"I used to go shooting with Cameron, but that was all for show. I never shot anything. Cameron used to say I was the lousiest shot in the U.S. of A."

"Where'd you get the handgun you had out at the farm?"

"It was the old man's. I remembered where he kept it; it was still there. Just for show, like all that other shit I did. It wasn't loaded."

We stared out across the racetrack at the grandstand. "Now you know my secret," he said. "Nobody else knows. I've been ashamed of it all my life."

"Now you'll have to kill me," I said, and we both laughed.

We stood there in the warming day and I watched the early birds beginning to fill up the lower grandstand. "You feel up to a few questions now?"

"I guess." He shrugged. "But I might as well tell you right off, I don't know anything. Whatever Cameron was doing down there is anybody's guess."

"What's your guess? You must've had some reason to go down there."

"I knew he stayed there sometimes. Where

the hell else would he be? He wasn't about to spend money on motels, even if he had it to spend."

"So you went down there because you couldn't think of anywhere else."

"That's about the size of it."

"Were you worried about him?"

"When he just disappears like that, hell, a brother's got to do something about it, even if the brother's Cameron."

"But you never expected foul play?"

"I thought I'd find him there, counting his money from some big score."

"You just lost me." I cocked my head. "Run that by me again."

"Cameron always lands on his feet. You think he's down and out and up he comes with some money."

"That's a nice talent. How does he do it?"

"Don't ask me. I just know he does."

I fired a shot into far left field. "Maybe he still had access to the books."

"I'm afraid you just lost me, pardner."

"That's all right, I'm just trolling. You talked to his friend Rudy?"

"He's an idiot. Cameron's always got some moron like that hanging around, picking up his mess. Rudy's got no idea what Cameron went to do or why."

"You told the cops this?"

"Yeah, sure."

"And you yourself have no idea. Not even a wild-hair notion?"

"Nope."

"Well," I said after a while, "unless he had a printing press, he was getting whatever he had from somebody. Did he ever mention owing anyone big sums of cash?"

"He wouldn't tell me something like that. He owed me some."

"Could I ask how much?"

"Ten grand."

"That's a fair sum."

"It adds up over the years."

"And he never paid you any of it back?"

"After a while you just knew. If you loaned it to Cameron, you could kiss it good-bye."

"And I imagine after some years of that, sources dry up."

"You got it. When your own brothers won't loan you a dime, where the hell *can* you go?"

"He was tapped with Damon too?"

"Oh, a long time ago. Damon's got a lot more brains than I have." He lit another cigar. "You ever known anybody who's broke one day, flush the next?"

"As a matter of fact, yeah." I told him about a bookseller whose shop was just up the block from mine. "Somehow he always had the money to score some books, but then he couldn't get Public Service paid so he could turn on his lights."

"That would be Cameron, if he'd been into books."

I asked him again what he remembered about Candice and he said, almost in the same breath, "Finest woman I ever knew. I think my dad was one lucky old bastard. Always did think so."

"What was she like?"

"Well, hell." He scratched his chin. "She was honest, pretty, I always thought a straight-shooter. What else can I say?"

"You never had a disagreement with her? Never any cross words?"

"I wouldn't do that, and you know what? Neither would she. She was incredibly easy-tempered. Just a nice woman all around. It would be like picking a fight with one of God's angels. I know that sounds corny."

"Damon said she slept around. You know anything about that?"

"She never slept around with me, if that's what you're asking. Look, I made it a point not to talk about her."

"And you've got no idea why anyone would've harmed her."

"Oh hell, no. I don't know where you got that idea, but you can forget it. It was an accident, pure and simple."

"What about her relationship with your dad?"

"They lived for each other, as far as I could see."

"Did you see them much?"

"Not at all the last ten years. They were in Idaho a lot; and even when they were out here I didn't see 'em. I did a lot of meets in the Midwest then, and up in Washington."

"What about Sharon?"

"What about her?"

"Do you like her?"

"That's a funny question. Why would I not like her?"

"No reason. Just a question."

"I think she's a little weird, since you ask. I mean, why would anybody with all her money lock herself away on a two-bit horse farm like that? But yeah, I like her fine."

The announcer called the horses for the first race.

"You got anything running today?"

He shook his head. "Two tomorrow, though. But I'm just about done here — gonna break camp this week and take my horses south."

"I didn't know you ever raced down there."

"Somebody's got to ride herd on Junior

and Damon when they bring our good ones out."

We stood quietly for a few moments, watching the crowd now building quickly across the way. "I imagine I'll want to talk to you again," I said.

"You know where I'm at."

"I'm on a pretty short leash. Sandy wants me to wind it up."

"Tell him where to stick it. Hell, if he fires you, you can come down to Santa Anita and walk horses for me."

In my tack room I lay on the bunk and thought about my shifting fortunes. Baxter had become a pleasant surprise. Sandy was turning unpleasant. Junior would soon be here. I thought about the strangeness of the human animal, about his quirks and phobias and manias. I thought about the many faces of bibliomania and I dozed lightly until the call for the third race.

I spent all afternoon asking questions. Suddenly I felt free of Sandy's heavy boot on my back, and by the time I struck out across the stable area I had recaptured the attitude and swagger of a young cop. This might be an illusion, but for now Bax had given me a breath of fresh air. I drifted through the barns talking to grizzled old horsemen, ginneys, anyone of a certain age who might remember old Geiger and his glamorous young wife. I put a note on the office bulletin board, "Seeking information on Candice and H. R. Geiger, contact Janeway, Barn 26." A risky tactic, I thought, but I went with Erin's words echoing in my head: *Take a chance and shake things up.* That's what I did, and in no time I was back in my natural frame of mind.

I found surprising numbers of people who remembered Candice. I talked to two old trainers who claimed their memories were as vivid as yesterday. They could still see old Geiger sitting with his pretty wife in the shedrow of Barn 28. "He had that barn every year for a while, and he'd sit in the shade for an hour or two almost every afternoon and talk with just about anybody who came by," said Woody Benton. "I remember when I was a young upstart just getting my act together; I remember taking a gimpy horse past his shedrow and saying, 'Hey, Mr. Geiger, can you tell me what's wrong with this horse?' And he looked up and said, 'Trot him down the shedrow,' and I did. Then he got up and felt the horse's legs and said, 'He's just burnt out, needs to be rested a while. Find a place where you can pull off his shoes and just let him find himself.' But of course we couldn't do that. I was working for old man Sapper then, and we ran them claiming horses back every week, stood 'em in ice and just ran the bejesus out of 'em. That horse still had no end of heart, man — he'd just run and run till he broke down, and that's what he did. He run his heart out for us and Sapper sold him to the killers."

"What about Mrs. Geiger?"

"A real sweetie. She came out of the tack room while the old man and I were having that very conversation, and said, 'Afternoon, Woody.' Hell, I didn't even think she knew my name, and I stammered something stupid and got out of their way. But I always remember her, every time I pass that shed-row I think of those days and what she was like. A lovely, classy, kindhearted woman."

"She knew everybody's name, from the ginneys across the way to the jockeys who rode for them," said a trainer in the next barn. *Class* was the word that came up most often. "She had buckets of class and that's something you can't ever fake. Class never lords it over the common man, and she treated everybody alike. Insisted on us all calling her Candice, never Mrs. G. I never got used to that, but that's what she wanted and that's what we all did."

"Candice," said an old man I found up near the clocker's stand. "She'd scold you if you forgot to use her first name, but always in a good-natured laughing way."

None of them had any idea about her interest in books. They knew nothing about her life as heiress to the Ritchey fortune. They knew her as Geiger's pretty, young wife who died young.

Candice. The woman in white.

I took detailed notes: names, recollections, barn numbers.

She would've been in her thirties then, just a damn striking figure in that white dress. Young enough to shine, old enough to have that edge of authority. You don't ever forget someone like Candice. Not ever.

Jerry Bryce, Barn 9, stared off into space and remembered the days of Candice.

I never did get my own stable. Still rubbing horses for other guys after forty years. Seems like I worked for most every trainer who ever raced in Northern California since the fifties.

I worked for Geiger in the mid-sixties, I was his head ginney, which means I was in charge of that barn when he wasn't there. We were all in love with Candice; the whole goddam shedrow came to a dead stop when they arrived. You'd see her out of the corner of your eye; that's all you dared to do, you never wanted to be caught gawking. Geiger had eyes like a hawk, he didn't miss anything when she was around. He watched her like he'd watch a prize filly.

We all loved her. Me more than most, with good reason.

In 1966 she paid for my son's funeral. Nobody was to know, and nobody did know till now. Guess she's beyond caring. My son Jason got kicked in the head by a horse and she gave me a check to cover the expenses. It was signed Candice Ritchey, I remember that. Candice Ritchey, not Geiger, but it went right through without a hitch. I never knew anything about the name Ritchey. But long before that, I always thought she was something special.

I even tried to read that book about the woman in white, but I couldn't get past first base. Too much flowery bullshit for my taste. Then somebody gave me the Classics comic book and I read that. Tried to imagine her in that part and I just couldn't put her there. She was way bigger than that ghost story. But I've still got the comic book. Go figure.

I asked them all if they remembered ever hearing her use the nicknames Tricky Dicky or the Mad Hatter for friends, but none of them did. At the end of the day I stopped at the office to check the bulletin board.

Someone had ripped my note down. I wrote another and this time I added the word REWARD in large red letters. Baxter's offer was a nice hole card in case Sandy became impossible, but I had a feeling of growing urgency. If there was any shaking to be done, this was the time.

I felt better. I was moving again. I hurried into the gathering dusk to meet Erin.

16

She was late. I sat at the restaurant's bar and cooled my heels for almost thirty minutes before she came in. I raised my hand and she saw me, changed her course on a dime, and drifted over to plop on the open stool next to mine. "You look frazzled," I said.

She ordered a gin and tonic and smiled sweetly. "I should be, I've been working like a dog all day on your case."

"Did you wrap it up yet?"

"Not quite, wise guy. But speaking of dubious accomplishment, how did *you* do today?"

I told her and she nodded her approval. "Now you seem to be getting somewhere; I must atone for my snide remark. And you didn't even need to refer to your notes to tell me about it."

"Notes are for sissies. You may not know this but I have full recall of every interview

I've ever done."

"Wow, how impressive, I *didn't* know. They must run into hundreds."

"In fact, thousands. But tell us, doll, how did you really waste your time today?"

"Doll?" She gave me that bitter little smile she has when there's a cat about to come out of a bag. "I want you to remember you said that when I tell you what I really did today."

Suddenly I sat up and paid attention. I always pay attention when she takes on that tone.

"I want you to remember the dismissal and derision I've had to put up with. The snide attitude, the innuendo of your silence."

"My silence has innuendo?"

"*Oh,* does it ever."

"That was a completely respectful silence. I'd even call it reverent."

"Well, try your reverence on this. I went down to the farm today."

I stared at her.

"Not a disparaging word from you, Cliff, I'm warning you," she said. "Not . . . one . . . word."

"May I at least ask why? Did you do this to teach me a lesson?"

"That must have been it. I guess I wanted

you to know how it feels to be pushed aside and left behind and told nothing. To fly all the way out here and not even be told where you're going."

We stared at each other in the mirror. She sipped her drink and continued to look frazzled. Then she broke into that lovely smile and I waited tensely for the punch line.

"Actually I had a hunch," she said. "You know, one of those things you're always getting between the snide attitude and the silent innuendo."

I nodded silently, warily.

"It occurred to me, while you were giving me all the safe tours of duty, that you might not be finished with that farm yet. So I drove down there to take a look at it."

I closed my weary eyes and lapsed into silent innuendo. Unfazed, she said, "I also stopped in to see the coroner."

That had been on my list of things to do before I'd had my brains scrambled.

"I've got a copy of his report for you," she said, drawing me along.

I thanked her politely, still waiting for her punch line.

"It doesn't say much anyway, so I wasted some time."

"Kinda what you're doing now."

"Eventually I went on out to the farm. At first I thought I'd drive up to the gate and look at it. You know, just to rattle your cage. It was obvious there was no one home, but this hunch of mine kept nagging away."

"Please tell me you didn't climb over the gate."

"I just watched it and all the time I could feel that hunch growing, like *there's something else here,* like *he didn't get it all yet.*"

"You're really enjoying the hell out of this, aren't you?"

"Yes, I am. And I should warn you before we proceed, you are going to have a huge pile of egg on your face. Now, knowing all that, do you wish to continue anyway?"

I sighed loudly but my heart was going like a trip-hammer. She said, "Was that a yes?" and I nodded wildly with my eyes rolling back in my head.

"That's when it occurred to me to check out the neighbors."

"What neighbors?"

"Why, whoever's there, *doll.* And it turns out there *is* another farm about half a mile on down the road. It's smaller, more like a country estate than a farm. You can't see it from the Geiger place; you've got to go back out to the main road, drive till you see the mailbox, and turn in there. The road doubles back until that place backs right up to Geiger's. If you had gone to the end of that field, you'd be right on the edge of it. Then you'd walk up a short path through the trees and presto, you're there, right in their backyard."

I made a *go on* gesture with my hands.

"It was owned by a man named Medill Ronda. He died and his daughter has it now. She's what people in less sensitive times used to call a spinster. Sixty but doesn't look it. I know she's sixty because she told me she and Candice were born in the same year."

"She told you about Candice?"

"They became close friends."

For once I was speechless.

"She was the first real friend Candice ever had her own age."

"How'd she know that?"

"Candice told her, silly. Do you want to hear this or not?"

I nodded lamely in her direction.

"They became friends very quickly and were soon chums, walk-across-the-field-and-share-your-most-intimate-thoughts-type friends. You ever had a friend like that?"

"Only you, you lovely warm and cuddly woman."

"Now you're getting back in my good graces."

"Damn, I'm trying."

"Candice was unhappy in her marriage."

"And this woman told you that."

"Among other things. It wasn't quite the idyllic love nest we've heard it was."

She sipped her drink and looked at me in the mirror. "Her name is Gail."

My eyes opened wide in disbelief. The woman Louie had remembered was named Gail. Candice and Gail had become tight friends.

"She came all the way up here with me just to talk to you," Erin said. She covered my hand with both of hers. "Let's go, I'm starving."

She had put Gail Ronda in a good hotel overlooking the bay: the least we could do, she said. "Once I told her you're looking into Candice's death, she wanted to come; in fact she got fairly insistent. I think she's been bothered by this for years."

She was a tiny, fit-looking woman with straw-colored hair and pale blue eyes. I shook her hand warmly and we booked a table at the best restaurant we could find, a place in Berkeley that came highly recommended by both the hotel desk clerk and the concierge. In the car, she said, "Erin tells me you were a police detective and can find out about anything."

"I like to tell people that. But it took Erin to find you."

"Oh, he'd have found you eventually," Erin said wearily. "He was just getting started when they discovered Cameron. Then the place was full of cops and off limits for a while."

I looked at Gail in the rearview mirror. "Did the police talk to you yet?"

"Yes, they came out that same day, but there was nothing I could tell them. I didn't hear or see anything. I have no idea what happened to him."

"Did you tell them about Candice?"

"Yes, but they didn't see the connection. Candice had very little to do with any of them, especially Cameron. And the police have always accepted her death as an accident."

"But you don't believe that."

"*I* don't know," she said. "I'm sorry, I don't mean to be short, but how can I know that? Obviously it still bothers me even after all these years. Candice was much too careful to eat anything without knowing exactly what it was, and she always had her antidote within reach."

"Do you know if she had it that day?"

"They said it was there on the table beside her, but she never used it."

"Maybe she was overwhelmed, maybe the allergic reaction was so sudden she never had a chance."

"That's what they all thought. And I suppose that's possible."

"But you didn't believe it," I said again, and this time she only shook her head.

I turned into Berkeley and a few minutes later we reached the restaurant. She didn't drink and we didn't need to, so I had them seat us at a corner table well away from the noise of the bar. We chatted about the weather, the sorry mess in Washington, the 49ers. She was a news hawk and an avid football fan and I liked her, more as time went on. She had a reluctant smile that I soon discovered was a symptom of shyness. We put in a dinner order and at last we got back on point. "Did Candice ever mention her books?" I asked.

She shook her head. "Not in any detail. She was always too polite to bring it up."

"Embarrassed by her wealth, maybe?"

"And by the fact that I had nothing even remotely like that in my own life."

"Do you remember how the subject came up?"

"No, but I do remember her looking at my bookshelves one day. I've a few common books; they're well read and tattered. *Little House on the Prairie. Bobbsey Twins. Five Little Peppers.* Things from my own childhood. She asked what I liked, what I'd read. Later she said she had always loved books and had a few things as well."

"Wow, she *was* modest," Erin said.

I made some notes and moved her back to Candice and Geiger. "Most of the people I've talked to would be surprised at what you told Erin about Candice and old Geiger," I said. "I hear everywhere how happy she was."

"She could make you believe that. But how many of us really know what goes on between two people?"

"So what did go on?"

"As time went on, he became quite controlling. And Candice, who had been such a happy person, began to have times of moody despair."

"Do you know what happened to cause such a change?"

"I had my suspicions, but it's not something I like to talk about."

I raised my eyebrows and blundered onward. "Are we talking about sexual problems?"

Her cheeks reddened.

"I only ask because that happens to a lot of guys, some even younger than he was. It's nothing to be ashamed of, but some men still can't face it."

"Well, for whatever reason, he became much more possessive. He wanted her with him all the time. They had a private box high in the grandstand, and afterward she would go to the barn and sit with him while the horses cooled out. She always wore that white dress he had bought her and they went through the strange ritual of having her in the pictures."

"What did she think of that?"

"She did it because he wanted her to. She tolerated it; then she endured it. He tried to make her go racing with him as often as he could. That became less and less. Whenever one of his stablehands spoke to her, she felt his eyes watching them."

"Why didn't she leave him?"

"She didn't think that way. What good does it do to have all the options in the world when you don't believe you have any? She was always terrified of being alone after her dad died."

"She should've known better. Even without the money, she'd be a prize catch."

"But what difference would that make if

she didn't believe it?"

"Yeah, it's easy for me to say."

"For me as well. I used to tell her what an exceptional woman she was, but I think it only embarrassed her to hear things like that."

"She didn't believe it."

"No. I remember once she said, 'There are days when I wish I had been born without a dime.' But then almost in the same breath she'd say, 'But my God, what would I do without Daddy's millions?' She hated the thought of becoming a whiner. Little Miss Rich Girl feeling sorry for herself, that kind of thing."

"Doesn't sound like her dad did her any favors in life."

"You're probably right. If he were alive and heard this I'm sure he'd die all over again. My own father was a lot like that, so I know. That may be part of why Candice and I became such friends so quickly. Our fathers wanted the best for us, they absolutely did, but they looked at the world differently after we were born. They saw threats everywhere. A man like that can cripple a girl's growth."

Our dinners arrived and we began to eat. "This salmon is wonderful," Erin said, but I had barely tasted it. "C'mon, Cliff, relax and eat something."

Suddenly I said, "Do you think Geiger might have killed her?"

I thought she'd be shocked but she wasn't. "No," she said without hesitating. "No way."

"Wouldn't be the first time something like that's happened."

"He'd need a reason, wouldn't he?"

"Maybe he had a reason. Unless he was a total whacko."

"He wasn't like that. He was possessive, not crazy — my opinion, for what it's worth."

"But you didn't know him particularly well."

"Maybe not. But if you're asking me what I think . . ." She shrugged.

We ate some more and a period of quiet fell over the table.

"Was she ever despondent enough to harm herself?"

"No, no. Of all the things I *don't* know, I'm sure of that."

I returned to the premise. "And Geiger had no reason, right?"

We looked at each other and Erin watched us both.

"I'm telling you he didn't kill her," Gail said. "He loved her. I'm convinced of that."

"Well, if he didn't, and she didn't, and it

wasn't an accident, then somebody else did. Any idea who that could be?"

"No."

"No idea at all?"

She looked down at her plate. "I'm sorry. I shouldn't talk about her. I shouldn't."

"I appreciate that, Gail. But if anybody's ever gonna get to the bottom of this, and I'm the only one trying right now, somebody will have to tell me what she knows."

She shook her head.

"Did you ever see her with other men?"

She looked away at the kitchen.

"Gail," Erin said, "you didn't come all the way up here not to tell him."

"I know you're right. It just seems like such a violation of her life."

"The real violation of her life," I said, "was if somebody killed her and nobody does anything about it."

Suddenly there were tears on her cheeks. I reached across and put a hand on her shoulder and told her I was sorry. She dabbed at her eyes. "I'm having a harder time with this than I thought I would."

"Take your time. Finish your dinner."

The food truly was exceptional, and even Gail ate with good appetite. As we were considering dessert, she said, "There was a man. I wasn't supposed to know, and really,

I shouldn't have known. I wasn't spying, I swear."

"It would never have occurred to me to think you were."

"I felt so bad afterward . . ."

"After what?"

"I saw them . . . kissing . . . in the woods."

I nodded. "Any idea who he might have been?"

She shook her head.

"This may be important. Did you see him clearly?"

She nodded her head. "Pretty well."

"Did he see you?"

"No."

"You're sure."

"Yes."

"Could he have seen you without you knowing? Did you look away at any time?"

"I felt so guilty watching them. I did look away, and I thought, *I've got to get out of here.* But then I couldn't even pick up my feet to walk away."

I squeezed her arm. "It's okay."

"No, it's not. It'll never be okay."

"It's time you stopped beating yourself up over it."

She drank a small sip of water.

"Can you describe this man?"

"He was younger than her but quite a bit

taller. He wore a sport coat open at the collar and a black hat, one of those old-style hats you sometimes see in old movies from the forties. And at one point he seemed annoyed and started to walk away. And she yelled after him, 'Oh pooh!' "

"Sandy," I said.

"You know who he is?"

"I know somebody who fits. And he did have an affair with Candice, and she called him Pooh. But he told me about that. Would you know him if you saw him again?"

"After all this time, I'm not sure."

"When was this? When did you see them?"

"Not long after I met her." She shook her head. "I'm sorry, I'm terrible with dates."

"Anything might help."

"At least thirty years ago."

"Were there others?"

"A few, I think."

"Did you see any of them?"

"I hope you don't think I was in the habit of spying on her."

"Not at all. But sometimes accidents happen."

"I never saw her with anyone else."

"But you knew there had been others?"

"She told me."

I leaned forward and looked in her elusive eyes. "In what context did she tell you?"

She shook her head. "I don't understand the question."

"Did she suddenly tell you for no reason, like a confession, or did she seem to know that you knew? Just tell me how it came up."

"We were out in the field one day and she said, 'My God, Gail, I'm having an affair.' "

"Just like that."

"Yes, it was shocking the way it came up, so suddenly. Then I realized she was very troubled and was asking for my advice."

"What did you tell her?"

"I said I would never presume to judge her about anything, I believed in her always, and I did. I knew she would never do something like that frivolously, and if I could ever help her, even if all I could give her was a shoulder to cry on, she should feel free. Then she hugged me tight and said thanks. Said she loved me and I felt my own tears start."

"She never mentioned any names?"

"No."

I said, "What about nicknames?" and she smiled affectionately.

"She was always doing that. She called me Tinker Bell. Her daughter was Goldilocks. She remembered her father as Geppetto, very affectionately."

"Any others?"

"Fagan. She called her husband that when she was annoyed with him."

"But not to his face?"

She shook her head, definitely no.

"Did she ever talk to you about her men friends again?"

"Never." Her hand trembled and she said, "I'm really only guessing about others, but I think I could sense when she was troubled like that. I know her conscience bothered her terribly, I think she had some very bad nights. But she never mentioned it to me again."

She took a deep breath. "That day I saw her. I think it was her first fling."

"Maybe so," I said. "Now the trick is to find out about her last."

17

That night I bunked in the tack room. Erin wanted to stay with Gail and drive her home in the morning and I wanted to touch base with Sandy. "Keep away from that farm," I said, adding "please" as an afterthought. She crossed her heart, we picked up my car, and I watched them drive away together in Erin's rental. Ten minutes later I was at Golden Gate, passed into the stable area by the night man.

I stopped at the office. My note was gone again and I put another up and red-marked the word REWARD. Then I walked off into the darkness between the barns and a moment later I arrived in Sandy's shedrow.

Tonight it was deserted: the ginneys were probably still off somewhere at dinner, and I opened my room and put a chair in the doorway where I could look down the shedrow and see the whole length of it. There I sat, thinking about Candice and her short

troubled life. I thought about Candice and
Sandy and I wondered, not for the first
time, how Sandy fit the mold of a killer. He
was skittish, nervous, and, like Junior, had
moments of real temper. Clearly he didn't
want me nosing around anymore. Who else
did I have? . . . Junior? . . . the brothers?
Baxter was suddenly chummy; maybe, given
the eccentric things I had heard about him,
too willing now to accommodate my questions. I sat there for a long time and no
strokes of brilliance occurred. The shedrow
was deadly quiet: not even the eternally
curious Pompeii Ruler stuck his head over
the webbing to see what I was doing.

I sat still, contributing nothing to break
the stillness of the night. I had been there
fifteen minutes more or less when I saw a
movement down at the far end of the shedrow. A man appeared. All I could tell about
him from that distance was that he was not
one of ours. He walked with a shuffle, as if
life had beaten him down over the years: an
older man, I thought, when he was still just
a shadow half the barn away. He came
under one of the lightbulbs and I saw that
he was wearing a red flannel shirt and a
ratty pair of Dickies-style pants. He had a
hat such as it was, an old fedora that nobody
wears today, which made me think of the

man with Candice long ago. His hat was battered like the rest of him. He came reluctantly, slowly, and as he passed under another light I saw that the right leg of his pants had broken up the seam to his crotch and was held together with half a dozen safety pins. A ginney's seam job, I thought. I had seen others wearing pants like that.

He stopped thirty yards from my open door.

"You the guy that's been leaving the notes in the office?"

His voice was raspy and he coughed when he spoke. I could see now that he had one of my notes in his hand. I said, "I left the notes," but still he came no closer. I couldn't quite make out his face yet: that wide brim of his hat kept him in shadow. He held the paper up and said, "This says there's a reward." I said, "Depends on what you can tell me," and he took a step back out of the light. "I'm trying to find out who Mrs. Geiger knew back in those days," I said. "Did you know them?" He seemed to totter unsteadily as if he'd been drinking and he backed off another step. But when he spoke again his voice was steady and clear. "I knew them. Knew her, I should say."

This seemed unlikely, but almost at once I realized that more than twenty years of bad luck could make a big difference in how a man looked, dressed, smelled, and approached the world. He said, "I need money. I need to know now if you're serious or blowin' smoke."

"I'm damned serious," I said.

"Then tell me how much money you're talkin' about."

"For the right information, substantial money."

"You're still dancing around. There's no way to know what that means or if you'll pay me anything after I tell you what I know."

"I'll give you a hundred dollars now, whatever you've got to say; more later if it works out."

Again he wavered. I could tell he was tempted but he said, "I have a need for quite a bit more than that."

"Come on over here and let's talk."

But he stood his ground and held the note loosely at his side. "I need a thousand," he said finally.

"I can arrange that. But the information's got to be worth it."

Now I guessed he'd be refiguring it: I had jumped at his thousand dollars too soon, and sure enough, he said, "What if what I know is worth more than that?"

"Then I'll pay you what it's worth."

"How do I know that?"

"There's no way to tell till I hear it."

I thought for a moment I'd lose him. He did a slight half-turn in the shedrow and took another step back. "I trust nobody," he said. "You wouldn't either if you were me."

"On the other hand, who else is buying?"

Almost thirty seconds passed while he thought it over. "You want me to tell first," he said. "Pretty good deal for you."

"I don't lie."

"Neither did Brutus," he said, surprising me.

"Two hundred now," I said. "Cash on the barrelhead."

"Two hundred just for talking to you. You must want something really bad."

I knew then he was going to take it. I said, "Give me some general hints. No specifics, just an overview of what you've got. Then we can talk terms."

"What if I dictate the terms?"

"Go ahead and we'll see where we are."

Again he seemed reluctant, like a man sitting on an oil well who's being offered a price for cheap desert land. "How high will you go?"

We were getting nowhere. "You mean on a blind like this? I can't be a fool any more than you can."

"Three hundred now," he said. "More later. Maybe a lot more."

"Or nothing later, depending on what you say. Or don't say."

"But three hundred now. I get to keep that, no matter what."

"Two hundred cash, in advance," I said. "Another hundred if I like what you've got to sell. Then we negotiate the specifics."

"Gimme the money."

Sometimes you've got to go with your gut. I reached in my wallet and fished out two bills. He came forward slowly, like an enemy expecting a trap in an alien land. He held his head down, keeping his face in shadows, but it didn't matter: He was here, obviously a racetracker; this was a small world and I'd be able to find him again. I handed him the two bills and had a brief clear look at his hands. Rough hands they were, caked with dirt under the nails. He had my money now and he backed away again.

"So," I said, "what is it you're selling?"

"Not now, I got to do something else tonight. Meet me tomorrow night at the Santa Anita. That's a bar down the road on San Pablo."

I had seen its lights several times on my way in and out. "Do I at least get to know your name for my money?"

"Cash on the barrelhead, you don't need my name." But then he said, "Call me Rick."

"Where can I find you . . . in case, you know, you don't show up."

"I'll show up."

"Okay, Rick. What time tomorrow?"

"After work. Say six-thirty."

"All right, I'll be there. But you be prepared to say something."

"And you bring that other bill."

He turned and walked away. I felt like a fool, but whatever happened I had asked for it.

"Hey," I said when he was thirty yards away. He stopped but didn't turn again, leaving me looking at his back. "How well did you really know her?"

He didn't move: just stood there looking out at the night. "I knew her for years." He coughed. "I know everything about her worth knowing."

"That could cover a lot of living."

"Worried about your dough?"

Suddenly he heard voices down the shed-row — our crew coming back from chow. He turned and walked across the black tow ring to the barn across the way. He disappeared and in almost the same instant Obie and Bob came around the corner.

■ ■ ■ ■

The shedrow came to life. We sat in the cool evening air talking and laughing, but my mind wouldn't stay focused on the usual hijinks. I was thinking of Erin and Gail and I owed Sharon a report. *Tomorrow,* I thought. *Maybe then I'd have something real to tell her.*

It was a long night of little sleep. I lay awake reading into the early morning. At last I turned off my light, but even then sleep was elusive, difficult, poor.

I opened my eyes to the usual morning shedrow racket. Horses nickering, feed tubs rattling, ginneys talking. I started walking a blood bay filly I had never seen. "Be careful with that one," Obie said. "That's Ms. Patterson's little lady."

"I'm careful with all of 'em," I said. But of course he would know that, and I knew there was a message hidden in the warning. "What's her name?"

"North Hills, and she is one classy gal. Undefeated, won six in a row from real stakes competition."

"Sandy training for Ms. P. now?"

"Looks like it. She's gonna ship this one south pretty soon with some others."

"Then what happens?"

"All's I can do is guess."

I could guess as well. Then Sandy would leave his own horses with another trainer and go have his fling at the big time. I said, "You got a trainer's license, Obie?"

He smiled and I wished him luck.

I took North Hills out into the tow ring. The dried mud had been crushed down by now and the walking was easy, a welcome relief from the gloom under the shedrow. Sandy arrived with Ms. Patterson about twenty minutes later. Again her husband was missing in action. Sandy spent most of the morning with his head in the work. It was impossible to read him at that point: If he looked at me at all I didn't see it. The bug boy came and Sandy took Erica's Eyes to the track. Ms. Patterson walked up with him and they watched together from the rail. The sun was just breaking through the pink clouds in the east and the shedrow across the way was coming to life. I heard a voice I knew: Rudy, touting his best bet of the day.

Pompeii Ruler worked a fast half-mile. Eight others were breezed a mile. The last five were walked. When I finished, Sandy and Ms. P. were gone.

I called Erin at the end of the morning.

They were sitting on Gail's veranda drinking coffee. I talked to Gail briefly, asked if she had ever heard Candice mention the name Rick, but no, she hadn't.

I killed the afternoon watching the races without making as much as a two-dollar bet. I tried Sharon and left a short message saying I'd call her again tomorrow.

That night I found my way to the Santa Anita bar. Rick wasn't there, the son of a bitch. I waited till the cows came home, at least ninety minutes, but he never did show.

18

By eight-thirty I had Rick's barn number, 15, and his full name. The name he went by, working for Cappy Wilson, was Richard Lawrence. He was easy to trace: The fedora was a dead giveaway, he was the only guy on the racetrack who wore one like that, and the night man on the stable gate told me where to look. I walked into Cappy's shedrow and found three ginneys sitting in a tack room watching TV. They looked up when I appeared suddenly in the door and one of them said, "You lookin' for work, we all filled up."

"I'm lookin' for Richard Lawrence."

"Lots a luck. He left here with money in his pocket. Be lucky if he makes it back tomorrow morning."

"Tell ya one thing," said an older man across the room. "He doesn't make it back, he can keep walking."

"I take it Richard's got himself a drinking problem."

"That's like saying the *Titanic* sprung a slight leak."

The buddy to his left said, "He's burned his bridges. Cappy gave him a job when nobody else would, but there's a limit to how much bullshit even a good guy will put up with."

I talked to them through the screen. "Anybody know what time he left?"

"It was after feeding. Maybe six o'clock."

"Any idea where he went?"

"Try the bars out on the drag. I don't think he'd go far without stopping somewhere, and once he stops he's there for the night."

"Thanks."

I was halfway down the shedrow when I heard the door open and the voice of the helpful one behind me. "Try the Hideaway," he said: "It's just like it says, hidden away off San Pablo about six blocks south. You better go now if he's a friend of yours. Water's full of sharks."

I got my car; rode out to San Pablo; turned south.

It was a rough-looking gin mill on the side street with a flickering red neon sign. I pushed open the heavy wooden door and went into a smoky room full of shrill babble. When the bartender came over I fingered a fifty and said, "I'm looking for Richard Lawrence."

"He left here about fifteen minutes ago."

"Was he alone?"

His eyes shifted and I folded the fifty and put it in my shirt pocket. "I'd really like to give you this, pal, but it's important for me to find him ASAP."

"I know what you mean. Rick talks too much when he gets a few drinks."

"Tell me about it."

"He had three guys who came in with him and they were with him when he left."

"Did Rick say where they were going?"

"He made some noise about the Nineteenth Hole and buying drinks for his pals."

"So where can I find this Nineteenth Hole?"

"Three blocks thataway and hidden like this one, half a block down."

I gave him the fifty and walked along the street. At the third corner I stopped, looked into a dark narrow street, and saw a crummy little dive across the street in the middle of the block. The whole block was deserted as I started across: not a soul stirring, not a voice or a footstep anywhere. I blended into the shadows and felt my way along. I had gone maybe thirty yards when I heard the sounds of a man hurting. I heard him retch and he tumbled out of a doorway. Rick had never made it as far as the bar.

He was trying to walk — two steps, three, and down he went, crashing into a row of garbage cans and rolling over on his back. When he looked up I was standing over him.

"Got no mo' money." He coughed and spat up something red. "Goway, I got none left."

I crouched beside him, rocking back on my heels. His face was still in darkness but I could see he had lost his hat.

"You know who they were?"

"Hell difference that make now?"

"Tell me and maybe I'll go get the money back."

"Sure you will. That goddam Everett will eat you for breakfast."

I got up and kicked around in the darkness till I found his hat. "Here," I said, tossing it in his direction. "See you around, loser."

"Where's my other bill? You promised me another bill."

"You really do have brass balls, Rick. Let's just call us even and I'll try to forget you said that. Maybe by morning I can forget you altogether."

"I knew you'd welsh me out. You're a liar just like them."

"Like who, Rick?"

"Them three as . . ." He belched. ". . . sholes."

"Tell me who they are."

"So you can do *what?*"

"Look, I'm not gonna stand out here all night arguing with you. Let 'em keep the money, and you can go back to wallowing in your own puke."

"Wait a minute!" he yelled.

I walked away.

"God*dammit,* wait a minute!"

I wanted to keep going but I could almost feel his desperation across that black gulf. He said my name, just "Janeway," and his voice ached like the rest of him. But I had known drunks in my life and this was no time for sympathy. "You got anything to say to me, say it now."

"I'm trying to tell you if you'd just wait a minute. They live in Barn 18."

Racetrackers.

I stood there for a moment: heard him struggling to get a leg up in the dark.

"Parker and Sidney always go together. Everett's a big mother; a professional bad-ass."

"You know where they are now?"

He tried to laugh, but his voice cracked and turned into a sob and he broke down. I let him cry for a minute or more. Then I touched his shoulder. "Where'd they go, Rick?"

". . . sonsabitches took my money . . . went back to the racetrack."

"How much they take from you?"

"Whatever I had left from them two bills."

"Okay, let's go get it back. And, Rick . . . please try not to throw up in my car."

By the time we got to the racetrack he was on his last legs. I left him on his bunk and walked over to 18 alone. I could see the narrow line of light under the door as I came into their shedrow. I could hear them yukking it up through the closed door. Stupid, stupid guys. A complaint would have them all in Dutch tomorrow, maybe deep-sixed out of here. They probably knew Rick wouldn't complain, but right now I didn't know or care.

The night was still as I approached the tack room door. Far away I heard laughter and someone yelling in Spanish. I heard the nicker of horses as I walked past their stalls. I was almost happily calm as I pushed open the door and went in without knocking. They were sitting around a folding table with the money there between them, and I could see the shock on their faces. I said, "Hi, boys," and my eyes took in the money and let it register in my brain. I could see the big bill and some chicken feed, about $135 total.

"I'm looking for Everett," I said, but I had already singled him out. I knew he'd be the big lumbering guy with muscles up his ass. "That's my money you got on the table, Everett. I do appreciate you boys hanging on to it for me, but now I came over to pick it up before something else happens to it."

Everett got up from his chair. "Now that is total bullshit, whoever the hell you are."

"My name's Janeway, Everett. I work over in 26."

"He walks hots for Sandy Standish," one of the others said.

"I don't give a fiddler's fuck who he walks for, he can't just come busting in here and jack us around." He looked at me and said, "You must be fuckin' crazy."

"Correction, Everett, I *am* in here, and right now I'm getting annoyed at what you three did to my pal. That was my money he had on him tonight." I looked incredulously from one to another to another. "You guys really want to push this?"

"What do you think, we're gonna let you

take our money on the word of some drunk?"

"You still don't get it, Everett. All that's stopping me are two ladyfingers and a bucket of dog turds, which would be you."

He snorted, maybe a laugh, a bluff, or a plugged nose. But I could see that Parker and Sidney were already nervous. One said, "Let him have the fuckin' money." Everett said, "In a pig's eye," and for a moment nobody moved. I turned my face slightly toward Everett and watched his eyes. "Tell you what, Everett," I said, "I'm gonna ask your two clowns which one wants to pick up my money and hand it here. Then we can let this all blow over and be friends again." But Everett said, "Bullshit," and I added, "Otherwise, we can let the fellas in the racing office figure it out."

"Goddammit, give him the money, Everett."

"Shut up, Sid, he can't prove a goddam thing."

"Or," I said, "you boys can fill out a change of address for him at the post office and have his mail sent to the city hospital."

"Big talk for a goddam fool," Everett said.

Suddenly he made a move toward the table and in that tiny flash of time when his eyes were on the money, I took a step his way and kicked him hard in the balls. He gave a cry of pure agony and slipped to the floor. Parker and Sidney had backtracked all the way to the wall and we watched together as Everett tried to roll over and get up. "I will *kill* your sorry ass," he whispered, but the moment trickled away and Everett was still down and my sorry ass was still standing. "You," I said to Sidney. "Pick up the money and hand it to me." He stood frozen to the spot for about five seconds. "*Now,*" I said, and he leaped to the table and started scooping up the bills.

"Some of that was ours," Parker said.

"How much?"

Parker said, "The C-note" and Sidney said, "Fifty bucks."

I shook my head sadly. "You boys can't get anything right. You were lousy thieves and you're lousy fighters, and on top of that you're lousy liars." I wadded up thirty and threw it on the floor. Damned generous under the circumstances.

At the door I said, "I'll be back if you boys ever hassle my pal again."

19

I was in no hurry to get back to Rick; I knew he'd figure things out and come to me if he ever sobered up, so I went to bed and slept all night. In the morning I walked my horses and at some point Sandy blended in beside me. He was in no better mood than the last time I'd seen him. He said, "I want this cleared up, Janeway, I don't know what Sharon expects from me, but I need you out of here by early next week." I said nothing; just kept turning left. Later I saw him take Ms. Patterson's filly to the track and I heard him tell the jockey to gallop her six furlongs. Ms. P. arrived as Sandy had, out of nowhere. I heard her rich belly laugh and then I saw her, walking around the tow ring and following him up to the backstretch rail. They returned together and I held the filly while Bob gave her a hot soapy bath, rinsed her, and scraped her off. Sandy and Obie took Pompeii Ruler to the track and they huddled there in serious conversation. I started the filly around and Ms. P. sat on a folding chair to observe her baby's cooling out. Twenty minutes later Bob took off the cooler, covered her with a light sheet, and said to me, "Give her another fifteen minutes."

Sandy and Obie were still up at the rail, talking. At some point Bob took the sheet off and I walked the filly in the warm sunlight. She was truly a beautiful animal, gleaming brightly in the new day. Most of the time even I could tell a really classy horse. So I thought, but what did I know? I thought of Seabiscuit, an ordinary-looking champion of the thirties, whose trainer finally figured him out and soundly defeated War Admiral in their celebrated match race. You never knew, with horses or women. Ms. P. got up off her chair and followed me on another few rounds like a doting mother. I put her baby in the stall, Bob picked out her feet, rubbed her down, and Ms. Patterson watched over the webbing. I had nothing to lose so I ventured a comment.

"This is one special lady you've got here."

"She sure is. She's a dreamboat."

"She's got the look of eagles." I had read that line somewhere long ago, it seemed like something to say, and my risk saying it now was small.

"Yes, she does. What's your name?"

"Cliff."

"Well, Cliff, it's good to meet somebody who knows a good one when he sees her."

"I've got a hunch about her," I said to keep things going, hopefully my way. "I think she'll be a great one."

"You're a man after my own heart. Are you going with us to Santa Anita?"

"Don't know. Haven't asked Sandy yet."

"If you want to go, go, Sandy won't mind. I like it when people who handle my horses appreciate them. Then it's not just a job and the horses know that and they do better."

"Yes, ma'am, I believe that as well."

"You rub them too or just walk?"

"Just walk, but that's fine. Gives me time to get to know them, they're not just another leg to be wrapped. I talk to them in the tow ring."

She looked amused. "What do you say to them?"

"How pretty they are, how they stand out. Stuff like that."

"Do they answer you?"

"Oh sure, all the time."

"How do they do that?"

"Sometimes with a friendly nuzzle." I

remembered the horse on Sharon's farm and I stretched a point. "Once I had one who used to lay his head on my shoulder."

She watched as Bob put a shine on her filly. "I think with your attitude you could bring us luck. I'll talk to Sandy."

"When are you leaving?"

"Sometime soon. I imagine you could come with us if you wanted to."

"That's very generous, Ms. Patterson . . ."

"Call me Barbara."

Before I could call her anything, Sandy and Obie arrived from the track. Barbara said, "Cliff's going south with us, Sandy; isn't that great? He loves my baby and I've got a hunch about him; I think he'll bring us luck." Sandy turned to the wall and said nothing. He felt the filly's legs and frosted me with a look as he crawled under the webbing and walked away with Barbara. They were barely out of earshot when Bob began razzing me.

"Oh, I just LOOOVE talking to them. I whisper sweet nothings in their pointy little ears, I kiss them here and there, just every-little-old-where."

I laughed with him.

He brushed off his horse's legs. "You *dog*."

Noonday came and went.

Sandy and Barbara seemed to have left

the premises. I called Sharon from the pay phone in the kitchen and told her what was happening. On her end, the executor had finally approved the move to Santa Anita. "I think they're leaving in a couple of days," she said. "They want to get the horses accustomed to the track as soon as possible."

In the afternoon I pressed my hunt for people who remembered Candice. I walked through the barns and asked my questions; I shot the breeze and congregated with old-timers wherever I found them. So far my hunt had been sporadic, but I'd had such good luck on the first day I thought there had to be others here who had memories of the woman in white. If so I didn't find them. At four o'clock I arrived back in my tack room, tired from the long day. I kicked off my shoes and lay on my bunk, thinking I'd rest a few minutes. When I opened my eyes the clock said five-thirty and someone was tapping on my screened door.

Rick.

"It's not locked, come on in."

He sat on the chair facing my bed, a ruddy-faced man, jowly and aging badly with dull washed-out eyes. This was my first good look at him in the daylight, and he looked like he'd lived a hundred hard years. A shiner was growing under one eye and both lips were split. His nose was fat and red. In a year he'd be lucky to be alive. His first words were raspy and predictable.

"You got my money?"

"It's right there on the table."

He looked at it. "What's the catch?"

"Hey, *I* keep my word. Now take it and get out of here before I change my mind."

He picked it up with trembling fingers. But he didn't move from the chair.

"I hear you put Everett on the ground."

"So what? Everett struts around but he's got a paper ass." I closed my eyes. "I've seen a hundred guys like him. All of 'em put together don't amount to a sudden fart in a hurricane."

A long minute passed. I knew he was still there because I could hear him breathing. And I knew sure as hell what would come next.

He worked himself up to it. "What about my other hundred?"

"Don't press your luck, Rick. Take your money and scram."

"I could still tell you some things, Janeway." His voice trembled now and I knew he had something, the same way I'd known it when I first met him; my gut told me so. I knew this but I wasn't going to play his patsy again. "Well, this time I won't lose any sleep thinking about it," I said. "Go drink yourself silly."

"I'm through with all that. Gonna get my act together."

"Famous last words of every drunk everywhere. But why tell me? What do I care?"

I heard him get up. I opened my eyes. He was standing at the doorway looking back at me. "You're a hard son of a bitch, Janeway."

"Yep. Screw me once, I remember it forever. I don't turn the other cheek, Rick."

"What if I told you . . . ?"

I sat up on the bed. "Tell me what?"

"Everything you want to know."

"That would be great, but how do you know what I want and how could I believe you?"

"I'm counting on you to know the truth when you hear it. Or I give you this money back and you owe me nothing."

20

He came back into the room and sat on the chair. His eyes were steady now and his voice was clear. He didn't mention the money again, just sat with his hat in his hands and looked at me across the small space between us. "You tell me," he said. "What do you want to know?"

"Probably all the stuff you can't tell me."

"Try me."

I tried him on an easy one. "How well did you actually know her?"

"About as well as you can know anybody," he said, and I felt my heart pick up. *If only that were true,* I thought.

He twisted the hat in his lap. "You want to know what kind of woman she was?"

."Sure. That'll do for a start."

"She was the sweetest, loveliest, most wonderful girl . . . she didn't have a mean bone in her body." He coughed. "Jesus Christ, I loved her. Still do."

His eyes were focused on nothing now; he looked like he had gone far away to another place and another time. He stared at the wall and his voice became a soft monotone. "I can't believe she's been gone all these years."

I didn't move. I barely breathed, just watched his face and his eyes. He said, "No matter what you think you know about love, Janeway, you can forget it. When I was very young I thought I knew what love was. I knew nothing. I had no idea. She was the love of my life. There's never been an hour of any day when I haven't thought of her. I would have died for her, but I couldn't do that. Instead she was the one who died. She died and left us all."

He covered his face with his left hand. "I've never been the same; never cared much about anything since then. The night she died I got drunk for the first time, and my only really sober moments since then have been when I had to get up to work or when I was tapped and had no money to spend on liquor."

There had always been a sadness about her, he said. "I don't think she ever drew a truly happy breath after her father died."

She was her daddy's girl: first, last, always. When old Ritchey died she looked to another old man for what she had lost, but Geiger was a different kettle of fish. Her father had been her window to the world. He had taken her on the grand tour of Europe when she was thirteen; he wanted her to have everything, *except,* apparently, boyfriends. He sent her to private girls' schools, threw lavish parties on her birthday, encouraged her to invite friends her own age . . . but then the party was over and she was his baby again. The friends winnowed down and disappeared. She was smothered all her life, first by the father who adored her, then by another old man who possessed her. Her father had tried to protect her and only made her insecure and dependent. It doesn't matter how much money you've got if you don't believe in yourself.

"I was her childhood friend long before she ever thought of having a life on the racetrack." He leaned back in his chair. "I can close my eyes and see her just as she was then." He didn't move then for a long time. His breathing became shallow and then seemed to stop. I leaned forward and put my hand on his arm. "Rick?"

His eyes flicked open. "My name is Richard Lawrence."

Candice thought he had a storybook name. Like Lawrence of Arabia, she said, but what she always called him was Ricky. Just a jump away from Tricky Dicky, I thought.

"I never told anybody about her, she was my secret, and she was the only one who ever called me that."

Rikki-Tikki-Tavi, she called him.

"My father worked in Wall Street," he said. "My mother was an elegant lady who belonged to clubs and society. Was . . . is . . . I have no idea now whether they are alive or dead. At twenty-two I was going to study medicine, and I had two older brothers and a younger sister. Later, when Candice died, I went straight to hell. And when everything in life goes bad, the racetrack is a perfect place to lose yourself."

He and Candice had a secret friendship in New York State, where they both grew up. Her father would go almost daily into the city on business, and Rick — *Rikki-Tikki-Tavi* — would meet Candice there in the woods. "Mr. Ritchey had an estate that sprawled across two hundred acres, about forty miles from the city. He had a driver and a butler and a stable. Not racehorses, not then: polo ponies, hunters, show horses. He was always interested in a fine horse, and if he saw one he liked, he bought it.

"We lived down the road, about half a mile

342

from their gate. One day I saw her picking flowers just inside the gate. She was watched by an old Negro woman who went with her everywhere.

"I spoke to her through the gate. I loved her right away, from the first minute of that first day. You can see what a sloppy romantic I was. Still am. The difference then was, I went around with my head in the clouds. I idealized everything. I haven't done that in a while.

"We talked for five minutes before the old woman came over and chased me away. But after that I looked for her every day. I would walk the half-mile and then up the road to the gate. Sometimes the old woman was there, sometimes not. When I started school I kept hoping I'd see Candice again, and I did, and we talked, but then she was sent away to a girls' academy about eighty miles away. That didn't matter: When I was twelve I would get out on the road two or three times a month and thumb my way there and back. It wasn't until much later, when we were seventeen, that we were able to steal moments and then hours away from her father and take long walks in the woods."

He blinked and looked at me. "You probably don't believe a word of this."

"I'm sorry, did I give you that impression?"

"It's not you, it's me. My own words suddenly started sticking in my throat when I realized what a drippy old fart I've become."

"Hey, stuff happens over the years."

"Ain't that the damn truth. Stuff happens and a lot of it happened to me. I thought if you knew where I came from it would be easier to swallow. But maybe belief just isn't to be had."

"I wouldn't say that. Not at all."

"It's still no excuse for beating a dead horse, so to speak. If I was doing that . . ."

". . . keep doing it," I said.

He laughed and I found, to my very great surprise, that I liked him.

He took a deep breath.

Said, "You're easier to talk to than I thought you'd be."

"That's because I'm interested now."

"Well, there isn't much more. Then you can ask whatever you want and I'll try to answer. But this is a long reach back through an alcoholic haze. At times I almost believe I can reach out and touch her . . . I can recall every moment like it was yesterday."

He said, "I'm going on the wagon. I've said it before, but this time I swear . . . I swear."

But that wasn't what I wanted to hear, he said. About Candice . . . and what he knew . . .

They never had what could be called a love affair; he was always terrified of touching her and spoiling what they did have. It was idyllic. They were best friends always, so she did have another friend her age. *Rikki-Tikki-Tavi.*

"Mr. Ritchey believed that boys only wanted one thing from a girl. *'If he finds out about you, he'll send me away,'* she said.

"But I would never touch her. Even if I could, I couldn't."

There came a time when he knew he could. "But I didn't."

She was a grown woman. "But I had to use restraint."

Still they would meet quietly: he would come to her; wherever she was he would get there and they would walk and talk of things far away. "Those were the best years, the only years. Everything before then was childhood nonsense, everything afterward . . .

"There was nothing afterward."

He coughed. "How can I tell you about her father?"

Picture a man who loved his only child so much that he became terrified of everything most people would call the best things in life. "I know he never meant to lock her away from the world . . . he *had* to, like he was compelled to hold her close and never let her be touched by anything or anybody. This affected her in a real and profound way. She became extremely dependent. In time, I was her only friend, and nobody knew about us.

"I was so sure we would eventually marry, and I was determined I would never touch her until then. Today that sounds silly, but that's how I was. I would rise up and save her from that insular world old Ritchey had consigned her to. But then he died suddenly and she married Geiger. I had a funny reaction to that, I almost expected it. *It's okay, he's just another old man,* I thought. *Let him have her for a year or two; this too will pass.* But it didn't pass. Who would ever think that old bastard would outlive her?"

"And when she married Geiger, you followed them."

"As far as I could. To the racetrack at least, and I saw her there, and sometimes we talked, and in time *this* became my life. I moved west from New York to Bay Meadows and Golden Gate and the fairs, wherever he went, I could always get some kind of half-assed walking job to tide me over. And I

346

waited for him to die, and he never did."

"What about her mother?"

"Candice never knew her. She died years ago."

I waited but he seemed to have run out of steam, so I prompted him.

"Did you know about her peanut allergy?"

"You couldn't know her and not know that."

"Which may have been another reason for Ritchey to have his paranoia."

"It scared the hell out of him, with good reason."

"Do you think she just got careless?"

"Not a chance. She was way smarter than that."

"Then what?"

"Maybe she killed herself."

"Do you believe that?"

"I know she was very unhappy after her dad died. She once told me, 'I never should've got married.' But if you're asking for my opinion, no, she wouldn't do that."

"Then what did happen?"

He shrugged. "Some awful mistake . . ."

"Or somebody did it to her."

He gave a mighty shudder and sat shivering for most of a minute. "Nobody could do that," he said. "Who the hell would do such a thing?"

"We don't know who was around her then. At least I don't."

"I mean, why would *any*body . . ."

"Don't think of it that way. Think of motives and see if a face pops up."

He furrowed his brow, then shook his head. "I can't imagine any motives."

I ran the list of murder motives through my mind. "There aren't that many. Jealousy, revenge, money, a threat to somebody . . ." I stared into his eyes and said, "Books."

His eyes opened wide. "Man, that's just crazy. I mean, fuckin' *books?*"

"Same as money, except it's peculiar to certain people. And got a lot more sex appeal."

"Books," he said, shaking his head.

"Surely you knew about her books."

"Well, yeah. I know she had some nice stuff . . ."

"What an unwashed schlemiel might consider a real fortune."

"An unwashed schlemiel." He smiled wryly. "That would be me."

"Somebody who truly coveted her books." I thought about the most extreme cases of bibliomania. "There's only one thing wrong with that idea. Most of the books are still there."

"Still where?"

"Back in Idaho. There are some significant missing titles there."

"You mean somebody took them?"

"Looks like it."

"Jesus," he said.

"Does any of this make sense to you? I mean, why would a thief take certain titles and leave other, more valuable, titles right in plain sight on the same shelf?"

He shook his head.

"It's like he didn't know what he was after. Not even enough to cherry-pick 'em."

"And you think this, whoever he was . . . k-k . . . oh Christ, you think he *killed* her?"

I shrugged. "It may be weak but it's the best motive I've come up with."

He shook his head in disbelief. Said nothing for several moments. Then slowly his eyes came up to meet mine. "Where do you come into this?"

"Her daughter has asked me to find out about her."

"Her daughter," he said numbly.

"Sharon." I nodded. "Do you want to meet her?"

He looked horrified. "Jeez, I don't know. Oh, man, I don't think so."

"Maybe she can help you put away some ghosts."

"Or maybe not. Might just make things worse."

"Well, you've got time to think on it. She's not going anywhere."

His eyes were open wide now. "Jesus," he said. "After Candice married Geiger, we never saw each other much at all. Except in the stable area . . . in the distance sometimes I'd see her and she'd wave. Like I was any old friend."

I leaned up and tried to encourage him with a hand gesture.

"It was hard for her to get away, but she did come to see me a few times when Geiger went off from the barn for an afternoon. Just to talk, like the old days."

"What did you talk about?"

"Nothing. Everything. All the storybook stuff we had always talked about. But it was different then. I knew she wasn't happy."

"Did you ever ask her?"

"Oh sure. And one day she got teary and said, 'I've really made a mess of things, Ricky. I never should've . . .' "

"What?"

"I don't know. Can't remember. Maybe she never finished what she was saying."

"Then guess. What do you think she'd say?"

"She never should've married Geiger."

"What might you have said to that?"

"What I did say. I told her what a great girl she was; how she didn't have to stay with anybody if he made her unhappy." He looked as if another thought had come to him. "Geiger was a rigid taskmaster, almost from day one. He had to run everything. If you want to know why his sons turned out like they did, it was old man Geiger. Acorns don't fall far from the old tree after all. You had to know him; he was just a dominant man. Even with all her money Candice couldn't stand up to him. Once they married she was his and after a while I knew she'd never leave him."

Then he said, "Sometimes I thought of killing him."

"Seriously?"

"No, but I thought of it. She needed to be set free again."

"Maybe someone killed *her* in a rage. Did you ever think of that?" I looked at him keenly, but he only shook his head, and then, a long moment later, said, "Man, I can't see that."

But maybe he did see it. "There was a guy who hung around her here for a while."

"What guy? . . . You mean a fortune-hunter type?"

"I never knew who he was or what he

wanted. I saw him a few times from a distance."

"Saw him how? When? Under what circumstances?"

"Jesus, I don't know. I can't remember."

"Was he a racetracker?"

He shook his head. "I remember every little thing about her, but I haven't given him more than a passing thought in years."

"This might be important. Was it maybe Sandy Standish?"

"No. I know Sandy and this wasn't him." He leaned over and looked down at his feet. "I guess I'm not much help after all."

"Don't write yourself off too soon." I leaned forward and looked at him seriously. "Did you ever hear her refer to anybody as the Mad Hatter?"

"No. Doesn't sound like one of her whimsical names, does it? Sounds dark . . . crazy."

"If you remember it, I'd like to know. It may be important."

"Right now I'm getting a helluva headache. Just want to lie down somewhere."

I took the hundred out of my wallet. "No," he said. "You don't owe me anything."

I stuck it in his shirt pocket as he hurried out. I hoped he wouldn't drink it away. But he did.

21

This time he went to a new place where I couldn't easily find him. It took me most of the night, tramping along San Pablo, asking questions, chasing a will-o'-the-wisp, but I got a few leads and went quickly from one bar to another. I found him sometime after midnight, bleary-eyed in a dive down toward Oakland. This was long and thankless work, but I pulled him out of there, and got him in my car, and finally got him back to the racetrack. I left him in his tack room, went back to my own, and two hours later I was up and walking.

Sandy came in at five, Ms. Patterson materialized out of some ether-like fog; we walked half the stable, sent the rest to the track, and by nine-thirty I was finished.

I walked over to Cappy Wilson's barn. He was an old man with stooped shoulders, thin white hair, pale gray eyes, and gray stubble on his chin.

"Rick around?"

"He's sleepin'. If you want him, take him on out of here. I got no more use for him."

I followed him up the shedrow. At the tack room he turned and said, "You his friend?"

"I guess you could say that."

"Look, I don't want to fire him, but I can't put up with this shit."

"No," I said, but I didn't go away.

He looked at me with sad eyes and said, "What does he want from me? I already gave him more chances than anybody on the racetrack. This is a tough business, son. I gotta have people I can count on."

"Sure you do," I said. "It's just that I think he's trying now. I know last night was bad, but how about one more chance? I'll pay his salary for two weeks; it won't cost you anything."

"Now why the hell would you do that?"

"Because he's at the end of his rope. And maybe I just think he's worth saving."

He stood there shaking his head. "By God, you're crazier than he is."

"That's a strong possibility, Mr. Wilson."

"Call me Cap. But don't try to pay me anything, I'll give him one more chance on my own. But I'm gonna make it clear to him; another slip and his ass is gone for good."

"Thanks, Cap."

I called Sharon and left her a message, recapping the news.

Called Erin's room number downtown but no one answered. Left a message that I would get back with her tonight.

Walked through the stable area and talked to people. Today no one I met remembered Candice or the old man except in general terms that didn't add anything to what I already knew. I was beginning to see the end of the trail. Same old faces: nobody new, nobody interesting, nobody who cared. I had covered a lot of ground in two days.

I was eating a late lunch in the kitchen when some racetrackers I knew came in, three old-timers I had talked to yesterday. One nodded vaguely my way and I raised my coffee cup. He looked like he wanted to say something but I didn't push him and I didn't rush away. They got some food and sat one table over. "Hey," the one finally said. "You ever find out what you wanted about them Geigers?"

"A little but it's slow work. You remember something?"

"Not much."

I waited but he didn't seem inclined to go into it. They ate and talked about horses long dead, about lost times and mythic stretch drives and faraway races. *Ghost riders in the sky.* They looked at each other and watched life slipping away, and after a while they began to leave. But the one lingered and I felt his eyes, and that hunch kept growing. There was something I had missed, some fact or impression perhaps hidden for years. Again I asked him if he remembered anything new; again he said not much and smiled. I put my wallet on the table and said, "I don't want to insult you, friend . . ."

"Hey, I don't get insulted. Knock yourself out."

"Twenty-five bucks no matter what it is. More if it helps."

"How much more?"

"We'll have to see about that."

He smiled easily. "There was a rumor goin' around about Geiger's wife. Didn't want to say nuthin' yesterday, but then I thought, hell . . ."

"What about her?"

"She was kinda his own last hoo-rah, if you know what I mean."

"Really? I always heard he was a slick old cocksman."

"Them's the worst kind, when the old pencil runs out of lead. The guys that used to be red-hot papas but ain't so red hot anymore."

He moved over to my table. "When Geiger was young he'd take on anything. Guys used to say, *Lock up your mares, boys, old Geiger's in town.* Then his motor just stopped, if you know what I mean."

"Like many aging men."

"Don't look at me when you say that, son, I can still do a night's work between the sheets. But everybody my age can't, and some a helluva lot younger. It hits some of 'em pretty hard, and Geiger was one of 'em that got hit hardest. But he wanted something to show people, and she was it. She was something special."

"Did you know Geiger had a daughter with Candice?"

"That's what I heard. I guess somebody must have."

"How'd you know all this?"

"Couple of women of our mutual acquaintance, old drinking pals of mine, bed pals with Geiger."

"So when did all this talk begin?"

"Oh, at least a year or two before he brought Ms. Candice around."

We lingered over our coffee and I gave him a fifty.

I walked over to Cappy's shedrow and found Rick up, mucking a stall. He was still green around the gills and he didn't want to talk, especially to me. But I stood there looking over his shoulder until he began to squirm.

"Go away," he said. "You don't need to say anything, I know I screwed up."

"I try not to say the obvious. Sometimes I make it, sometimes I don't."

"I don't know why but Cappy's giving me one more chance."

"Maybe because he's a good guy. Now you pay him back by making the most of it. You don't get many extra chances in life."

"I know, I know, even low in life. Where the *hell* am I gonna go if I lose this job? I'll be out on the street. I'll be in the gutter."

"Don't lose it, Rick."

"Cappy wants me to make it, but he can't be stupid about it. I understand where he's coming from."

"Then hold that thought. You got any money left?"

"Nothing from the hundred, some from the other day — eighty dollars maybe."

"Give it to me if you want, I'll hold it for you."

He surprised me by digging it out right there. "Ninety-two bucks. More than I thought."

"Better keep some for food."

He kept out a sawbuck, then changed his

"I know. I do hate to leave you, but there's a desperation in his face that's hard to forget."

"Stay with him, then. Hold his hand. You'll have plenty of time later to hold mine."

A moment passed. Neither of us wanted to let go.

"What would you do if you were me?"

"Shake things up," she said. "Be decisive. Be the old Janeway. Let whoever he is think we know much more than we do and then be a moving target."

I didn't like the "we" business and of course she knew that. "I don't mean to be one more problem for you, Cliff," she said, "but I'm not going back to Denver until you can come too."

I went over to Cappy's shedrow to pick up Rick. We walked up between the barns toward the kitchen. "I guess I'm leaving next week for Santa Anita."

"I've never been to Santa Anita. All the years I've been out here and I've done nothing but the northern tracks and the fairs."

"You hang tough with Cappy, Rick, he's a good man."

"Yeah, I know. He's probably the only person anywhere who cares if I live or die."

He looked up. "Him and maybe you."

"Hey, that's a start."

We staked out a table in the kitchen and began to eat. He asked if I'd be coming back and I said I'd try.

"You won't, though. I got a feeling this is it."

"This is what, Rick?"

"Just one more case of somebody drifting away."

"It won't be. I promise I'll be back."

Back in the tack room we sat up talking until his words slurred and became repetitive. I stayed with him until he was sound asleep. I turned off his lights and left him there, but the images of his lost life and the feeling of his quiet desperation followed me back to my own shedrow.

In the morning I hit the tow ring and walked horses for five hours with only one short break for coffee. I was feeling good: No aches, no pains, as normal as a madman ever gets. I decided that this afternoon I would go for a run if I could find a stretch of trail or a gym. I needed about five miles to work the kinks out and I still had a few things to do here. I wanted to make at least one more walk through the stable area in case I had missed somebody, and I had to talk to Sandy and see where we stood. He hadn't spoken to me since Barbara pushed him into a corner but I knew he didn't like it much.

They watched from the rail as North Hills breezed half a mile, and afterward Barbara sat in the shedrow while I cooled her horse out. No one approached her: even Bob, who apparently would be her lady's ginney, was cutting her some wide slack. She was a formidable figure with her jacket drawn up around her cheeks and her eagle eyes watching. This morning I kept my distance as well: I didn't try to draw her into any innocuous chatter like last time, and for a while she gave no sign that she even remembered who I was. Sandy stayed occupied at the track while Obie brought his horses up one after another. They huddled at the gap and I could imagine the last-minute advice going back and forth between them. Sandy might well be uneasy about leaving his horses with anyone, but he had made the decision and that was that.

I didn't want to let him get away again, so at one point I said, "Could I talk to you before you leave?" But Barbara was up and coming toward us, and the moment was lost. "I'll catch you later," he said, and almost in the same breath, Barbara said, "What's the story, Cliff?"

"Of course he's coming with us," Sandy said lightly. "Right, Cliff?"

She looked at me and I said, "Of course I am."

"Of course you are," she said, and we all laughed.

Barbara left around eleven and Sandy motioned me to follow him. We walked along the road toward the edge of the stable area and he sat down under a tree. I sat on the grass facing him and said, "First of all, I want to apologize for hemming you in like that. I know you're not thrilled about this."

"It's not your fault. But yeah, I almost quit her there on the spot, before I even got started."

"I'm glad you didn't."

"Barbara's a good woman, but apparently we still have certain things to get straight between us. And I need to do it now, before I move body and soul four hundred miles south."

"You need her to know that you intend to hire the hands yourself."

"Among other things."

"I could go with another stable if I'm causing you any grief."

"Have you had an offer?"

"Bax Geiger offered me a job if I need one."

"That'll be an education on many fronts." He said this sarcastically, pointedly so. "Is he going south too?"

"Looks like it."

"What'd you tell him?"

"Nothing yet. He knows I'm working for you. But even without Bax, I think I can get a job now. I don't need much, nothing really. The main thing is to get on someone's list and get my license stamped so I'll have access to the racetrack."

"So just that quick you've become a racetracker," he said with a trace of amusement. "You don't need any of us anymore."

"It doesn't take long, does it? But it's been good having a situation like this one, where I'm free to come and go. And I want to thank you for that, and I'm sorry if I've caused you problems."

"Then let's leave it this way," he said. "You stay with me, at least till you get settled at Santa Anita. You know Barbara likes you, and the thing about walking hots is the freedom it gives you."

We sat in the cool breeze a while longer, making civilized and irrelevant talk about the upcoming race meet, rich people with fine horses, all the things he had shown no inclination to discuss earlier with any of us. "Barbara's an unusual owner," he said.

"She's been doing this for so many years she actually does know horses better than a lot of trainers."

"Does that make it easier or harder to work for her?"

"Good question. We'll have to see."

"Still, I know it's got to be clear who the trainer is, who makes the decisions."

"I never would have taken it if she hadn't agreed to that. Even then it wasn't easy. Always been my own boss, always ran my own stable. But she's got some killer horses; a man would be out of his mind to let them get past him."

"That filly sure is a nice one."

"She's just one of 'em. Barbara's got a colt that's also undefeated, just about to turn three, might go all the way this spring."

All the way to Louisville, he said.

We're not running for peanuts anymore, Toto.

Peanuts, I thought.

"Life is strange. Barbara could have her pick of trainers but somehow she wants me."

He didn't say anything else for a few moments. Then: "I hope you will stick around, Cliff. I need people I can trust to tell me things."

Now he trusts me. Now he wants me here. How quickly the worm turns.

"I know you're a greenhorn," he said, "but I've been thinking about it, and I think your judgment is sound. That'll carry you a long way. The other stuff you can pick up, but judgment's not something you can learn."

"Just don't forget the real reason I'm here."

"I'm not forgetting anything. But it occurred to me yesterday how much I'm gonna miss Obie when we head south. He's been my other eyes and ears for a long time."

"I can't be Obie, Sandy. Even if I could . . ."

"I *know* that," he said with a touch of his old testiness. Then, softly: "I know that. I don't expect you to be Obie. But if it wouldn't crimp your style too much, maybe you could keep your eyes open and let me know if you see anything unusual."

I didn't ask what he expected me to see. He cleared his throat and said, "Do you even know what you're hunting for? Do you have any idea?"

"I know exactly what I'm hunting for," I said. "I just don't know who yet."

"What, then?"

"I'm hunting a vicious killer, Sandy."

A sober moment passed. "A fellow who bashed Cameron Geiger's brains in and tried to do the same to me," I said. "And there may be other things for him to answer to."

"Any idea how long it might take you to find him?"

"If I knew that I'd already have him, wouldn't I?"

He nodded as if that slightly abrasive comment made perfect sense and we sat there a few minutes saying nothing. At some point I said, "The stakes are too high not to find him."

"When you do find him, what'll you do about it?"

"Whatever I have to do."

"Well," he said, breaking another silence, "let's walk back. I'm meeting Barbara for lunch. We'll get some things ironed out."

We got up and headed back into the stable area together. I could hear the announcer calling the horses for the first race. Off to my right the procession began, the horses being led around the track toward the saddling paddock by the grandstand. It brought the warm afternoon to life. But Sandy poked along, as if he still had things to say before we got swallowed up in the crowd, and didn't know how. Once or twice I had to stop and wait for him. Whatever it was, he never got to it. We turned into his row and I saw people I knew, either by names or faces, and I thought no, it doesn't take long to be absorbed into this life when you live and breathe it.

Now, for example, there was suddenly a man I knew in the next barn. I had to blink to be sure, but in that brief moment he looked at me furiously out of the dark, without wavering. It was Junior. He backed around the shedrow and hustled down the other side.

I sat in the chair outside my tack room and watched the horses coming and going. I watched the people leading them and the ginneys in the barn across the way. I watched two birds fluttering and the muck truck scooping out the manure bin. And so I saw the day grow older.

I heard the call of the first race and I knew the horses were charging up the backstretch. Other than that, the stable area looked deserted.

Junior didn't return.

Sandy was gone two hours.

Barbara was with him when he returned. She smiled affably and said, "Hiya, Cliff," but Sandy only nodded as they went by. We had nothing going that afternoon, so Sandy had chosen today to make his announcement. "An early dinner, boys, on me, in a real restaurant," he said, I thought a bit smugly. Whatever had happened at lunch, he looked pleased about it. And so, just after feeding and hot showers, we all piled into three cars and drove to a restaurant called Tigris, specializing in foods of the Middle East. Barbara had raved about it and hoped we'd like it, though I suspected none of the racetrackers had ever had anything like what they were about to eat. Barbara had them seat us in a small private room, where we were set up at an oblong table. The food began coming: excellent, I thought, wishing Erin could be here. The boys ate cautiously at first, then with greater appetite, and Barbara watched us eat with growing satisfaction. But there was an air of unease at the table, a feeling of something too long in the wind finally coming to pass.

Dessert. Coffee. Uneasy laughter.

I paid the first compliment to them both, toasting them with a glass of white wine. "This is really superb, Barbara. Just great, Sandy."

The others quickly said you bet, right you are, hear-hear, wowie.

At last Sandy got to the point. He stood at the head of the table and said, "This won't come as a surprise to any of you, but I'm going to train some horses for Barbara down south this winter. Obie will be in charge of my own stable, and I know you-all will work as diligently for him as you have for me."

Barbara smiled broadly and said nothing.

"Bob and Cliff will go with us." Sandy looked at me rather than Bob and said, "I'd like you to go down ahead of us and check us in; bed down a dozen stalls and get us ready. We'll be along shortly." I asked when he'd want us to leave and he said, "Tomorrow morning."

This was annoying but I'd have to work with it. A strange evening, I thought as we left the restaurant, a strange situation, but that, I was learning, was life on the racetrack. If the man said to be ready at dawn, you got ready. It was assumed you were free when you signed on, and many lived out their lives that way. Some of them saw the outside world only when they had to move between race meets.

One last bit of business at Golden Gate: That night I hunted Rick down and gave him his money back. He was upset at the news. "I thought we'd be together for a while," he said. He looked hurt, betrayed if I had to put a name to it. "You're never coming back," he said, and there was something heartbreaking in his face and in his voice. "I promise, Rick. You just keep your chin up and stick with Cappy, I'll get back here as soon as I can and we'll decide what to do next." I clutched his hand and told it all to him again, but suddenly I knew that I was just another in a long line of his personal disasters, and finally there was nothing to do but to walk away. I took that picture of him with me as I looked back down the dark shedrow and waved.

I called Erin from the phone booth, a short call. I told her to turn in her rental car and be ready to leave at daybreak. But I had a hard time sleeping that night: The vision of Rick stayed with me.

22

Bob and I were out at five o'clock, just before dawn. He put our two folding Army cots in my trunk, along with our bags and some blankets, and I drove us down the freeway into town. I told him we had a passenger and Erin was waiting for us in the hotel lobby. She stashed her bag in the trunk, crawled into the backseat, and we were off.

"Erin, Bob: Bob, Erin," I said, and they shook hands across the seat.

"So where did Janeway find you?" Bob said.

"Won me in a poker game in Reno. I do laundry and other occasional jobs."

They got on famously from the first few minutes.

We were taking the fast inland route, east to Interstate 5, south across the great plain, over the Grapevine to Los Angeles, then east again through Glendale and Pasadena to Arcadia. "Old-time ginneys say this trip used to take all day," Bob told us. Now we would do it in less than five hours, plenty of time for gregarious strangers to become chummy. An hour out of Golden Gate, Erin and Bob were old friends. They joshed each other and there was an air of easy camaraderie that we all found contagious. But there was also a cautious threshold still uncrossed. We were somewhere in the middle of the state when I stepped gingerly over it.

"So how long've you been with Sandy, Bob?"

"Four years next month."

"He seems to be a good guy to work for."

"Yeah, you can learn a lot from him . . . if that's what you mean."

"So how'd you guys meet?"

"I was passing through, had no idea of doing anything with horses, and a guy I met knew a guy, you know how that goes. Next day there I was, muckin' out stalls at Golden Gate."

"And found it such fascinating work you've never looked back."

"Something like that. Of course there's more to it than just mucking and shoveling, as you know. I'm looking to buy my own horses, somewhere down the road."

"That's what I heard. Got one picked out yet?"

"Only about a dozen times is all. The trick is to get the right horse for the right money."

"And then have a lot of luck."

"Yeah, there's that. But I'm still young and patient. That's the other thing you've got to have. Patience." He smiled and took his own stab in the dark. "Why do you ask, kemo sabe?"

"I was just wondering if there'd be any honest work here for Erin."

"Now there's an idea." Erin leaned over Bob's shoulder. "Cliff wants to get me off the streets and out of hotel rooms, and that would probably do it."

Tentatively, he asked, "What do you do besides follow Cliff around the country?"

"That's about it. He runs a white slavery racket."

Bob laughed politely and said, "There's almost always room for somebody when you move into a new race meet. We'll have to ask Sandy."

"I would be a very raw somebody," Erin said. "I don't even know which end of a horse the hay goes in and which end you muck up after."

"Sandy will actually like that. It means he can show you how he wants things done and he won't have to pay you much to start. Maybe you could do what Cliff does, walk hots." He looked at me as if he couldn't make up his mind what to say next; then he said it anyway. "Cliff's not around half the time, he works strange hours, so if you're looking for something to keep from going stir-crazy, that might be it. I hope you're not scared of horses."

"She's not scared of anything," I said.

Erin reached over and gave my ear a playful twist. "So, Robert. Do you think he'd hire me?"

"Hey, I'm just a working stiff myself. But maybe we can figure something out for you by the time we get to the racetrack."

I asked him what he thought of Sandy's arrangement with Barbara.

"It's a pretty unusual deal," he said. "Great break for Obie."

"Barbara sure seems like a sport," I prompted.

He took five seconds to respond to that; then he said, "Yeah, I'd say so."

"I could cut a steak on that edge in your voice."

"She is a sport," he said, quickly now. "Why, did you hear otherwise?"

"Tell you the truth, I haven't heard anything about her."

"You will. But yeah, she plays it pretty close to the vest unless she likes you. She does like you, Cliff, so stay on her good side."

A long minute passed. "Sounds like she keeps everybody on a short leash," I said.

"What*ever* makes you say that?" he said with a smile.

"Suddenly I've got a hunch Sandy's gonna have a helluva time getting the space he needs to work with these horses his way."

"Just remember, I didn't say that." Another stretch of time passed. Surprisingly, he said, "But I guess I'd be lying if I said I didn't have some of those same thoughts myself."

"Why would that be?" I said in an innocent voice.

Then, like a shaded window briefly opened on a lighted room, he said, "Barbara can be short when you rub her wrong. She fired one crew just like that." He snapped his fingers five times. "Trainer, ginneys, bug boy, everybody."

"Obie said the trainer was incompetent."

"I'm talking about the one she had before that, who was not incompetent, but it was the same kinda deal anyway. One day you think you're doing great, the next day you're all out on your butt." He grinned. "Butts."

"That would make for an uneasy shed-row."

"If you're Sandy, it probably does. Me, I can always go back to rubbing his horses, so I should be fine. Let me give you a tip, old buddy. Stay way the hell over on her good side. Talk nicely about her horses, and when she's in one of those quiet moods, give her plenty of space, don't say anything. And don't ever cross Charlie. Her husband."

"What's he got to do with it, he's never around."

"But when he is around he's always watching. He's got eyes like a hawk, hell, he *is* her eyes. I heard he's the one who had that first trainer axed. Some silly thing somebody said got his back up."

"All I've ever seen him do is get out of her car and go off by himself. I've never even heard the man speak."

"Don't worry, he speaks plenty when he has to. Last month he was just full of opinions, you couldn't pay him to shut up. And Barbara listens is what I heard."

We arrived in Arcadia three hours later. The racetrack was beautiful in the warm noonday sunshine: the seafoam-green grandstand stretched out beyond an enormous empty parking lot, giving the illusion that racing was alive and well everywhere. I knew how the rise of easy gambling had taken its toll on this colorful old way of life. Centennial, Longacres, Ak-Sar-Ben; these were just a few of the casualties on the roster of lost racetracks around the country, but Santa Anita looked well and eternal. There was a man in the stable gate, though racing wouldn't begin here for three weeks. Bob showed his license and said we were with Sandy Standish, and we all got in without a hitch. The stable area looked half-empty. We had been assigned to Barn 107, over in a far corner near a thick hedge that overlooked Baldwin Avenue. Sandy had called ahead and had a full bin of straw and hay delivered, and we set to work, bedding our stalls and getting ready for the horses. I brought up the straw and cut the bales open with a knife; Bob and Erin spread the stuff around with pitchforks, about eight inches deep, and slowly it began to look and smell like a living shedrow.

This went quickly and we finished before three o'clock. We set up folding chairs in the shedrow, and Bob went out and got us another Army cot and some more blankets. "Looks like we're in business," I said, and we sat in the yellow afternoon sun with the eerie quiet everywhere around us.

At some point I asked, "Will I get us in

trouble if I jog around the racetrack?"

"Give it a shot," Bob said. "If anybody stops you, we'll say we never saw you before."

"Before what?"

"Before I saw you hopping that horse over in Barn 98."

I ran five brisk laps. My feet made solid thumping sounds on the fast track, which echoed flatly as I came past the enormous empty grandstand. I looked up at the thousands of vacant seats and felt strangely like I'd made a right turn and had come to the place I needed to be. No rhyme or reason: it just felt right. Sometimes you do things like that.

Bob and Erin stood at the rail and watched me go past. Bob cupped his hands over his face and shouted down the track. *"It's Janeway by two lengths, Cliffie J. is second by a length and one half, Brokedown Ginney is third, and moving up fast on the inside is Lop-Eared Hossman! And now with only a sixteenth of a mile to go, the crowd goes wild. It's Don't Gotta Prayer passing everything on the outside!"* I heard them laughing as I went past, I pulled up a quarter-mile east and doubled over. I gave them a gesture, not quite obscene, not quite decent, and I walked past the stands cooling out. I skirted the jockeys' room, the paddock, and walking ring, went past the statues of Seabiscuit and Georgie Woolf, turned and came slowly back to the rail where they still waited.

We took showers in the rustic bathrooms and congregated in the shedrow as night fell over the San Gabriel Mountains.

23

We left everything where it was and went looking for a place to eat. There was a restaurant called Henry's, just across the parking lot near East Huntington and Colorado, and we staked out a table for three and had a good dinner. We took our time and laughed away an hour, had a walk through downtown Arcadia, and got back to the racetrack before nine-thirty. Tonight there was no urgency to get to bed: no horses to feed and muck at dawn, so we had a rare occurrence for a racetrack crew, a day off. I knew the routine now. Racetrackers work seven days a week: Christmas, New Year's, the Fourth of July, they were all just workdays; the horses were always there to eat and poop, to be watered and brushed and taken care of. We still had no idea when Sandy might roll in: could be any time between later today and the end of the week, but we were tied to the spot; we had to be here whenever he arrived, so there was no time for sightseeing. We sat in the cool shedrow for another hour; then Bob retired to one of the tack rooms and soon turned his light off. Erin came past my chair and squeezed my shoulder.

"You look like a man with his thinking cap on."

"I'm always thinking, Erin, I'm a pondering fool. But it's like any case; the more I think the murkier it gets . . . until suddenly if I'm lucky I get a brainstorm that leads somewhere."

"So what is the fool pondering tonight?"

"All of it. Who killed Cameron and why? Who cracked my head open and tried to turn me into French toast? Is this about the books, or does it go deeper, farther back to Candice and her time? Or is it all related somehow?"

She had no answers either, so we sat close for a time and were satisfied to hold hands. At some point she went into the end tack room and closed the door. I sat alone, still awake, still restless, gearing myself up for a long night.

I had a hunch, not the first time that had happened. I'll never know why: maybe something about a cop's intuition when a situation gets ready to pop. I had been right enough times over the years to listen when that voice started. But another hour passed and nothing happened. I was tired after all, and soon I nodded my head and fell asleep on the chair.

When I opened my eyes I knew I had slept deeply for three hours. I knew it was early morning. There was no sound or light from either tack room, but I was sure that some noise, a sharp rap, an object knocked over, *something,* had caused me to open my eyes.

Within seconds I was fully awake. I heard it again, a faint clink followed by footsteps somewhere out in the black shedrow. I was well hidden, still sitting in the pitch blackness near the hay bin, where no light got in from any side. This was not like a stable area during a racing season, which could also be dark at midnight. This was more like an alien world with ghostly shadow barns all around it and no life anywhere. *The City of the Horse-people:* My stupid thought of the day, but it wouldn't let go. I had come alive in a world where intelligent horse-people ruled, and I was under their thumb. My second stupid thought — horses don't have thumbs — but somewhere, I knew, were real people with real feet and thumbs. They were not from this part of the stable area, and yet someone was walking. Somewhere. I heard the crunch of a foot wearing a real shoe, not the clop of a horseshoe. I still couldn't see him, and for a time I couldn't hear him either. Then, a sound: just a step, around the corner. A *foot*step. He was in this barn on the opposite shedrow. Drill a hole straight through the stall from where I sat and you'd knock him over. I felt my heartbeat pick up. During the season I wouldn't think twice about it; I'd be accustomed to ginneys getting in at all hours, but now, at whatever hour this was, a footstep stood out like a Chandler first edition in a section of Goodwill dreck.

I didn't move.

I thought it was two o'clock, maybe three. Suddenly I had a bad feeling about it and I sat frozen in my chair. He was still directly opposite me, moving slowly down toward the tack rooms on the end.

At last I got out of the chair. Stepped into the shedrow. I made no sound as I walked. Fresh in my mind was the vision of Cameron Geiger, draped over a river branch with his head blown open, not to mention my own brush with death at the hands of the same crazy man. I moved one short step at a time, keeping up with him as much as I could: a step then wait; step then wait; stop, listen, move again, wait. I could see the dim outline of the end of the next barn, lit up by a faint beam of reflected moonlight. Now I heard nothing. No more walking, no sound. I had a sinking feeling I had lost him. He was important, he was somebody real, and I had spooked him. I thought he had probably turned and hightailed it back up the shedrow, but I resisted the temptation to hurry. I eased past the empty stalls to the end and peered around the corner.

Nothing.

Still as glass.

The night brittle, cool, fragile as black crystal.

I moved slowly with my back to the wall. I was standing three feet from Erin's tack room, straight across from her door, with the moon bouncing off the manure bin my only light.

I took a step. Another.

Quiet now.

I held my breath.

Peeked around the opposite corner . . .

. . . and there he was.

The shadow man stood ten feet away.

I flinched. He had a gun, and the gun went off in my face.

I was a dead man. I could feel the burn, I thought, like cayenne pepper, like sandblast, like kindling doused with gasoline and touched by fire.

I had been shot several times in my life and each time felt worse than the last. *They're catching up with you, baby,* I had thought at some point. *This time you really are dead meat.*

But I didn't feel dead. Except for the sandblast effect, I hadn't been hit. I recoiled and tripped, falling back in the shedrow. My head was still there, I had enough brains to spin as I hit the ground, and I rolled away from him toward the tack room door. He rose up at the corner and fired again. I felt it rip through my shirt at the collar. I kicked the door, kicked off from the wall, and rolled back at him. He shot twice and missed both times as I twisted myself under his feet. I heard the door jerk open and Erin yelling my name. I shouted at her to get back, stay inside. That had as much effect as it always did. I saw her shadow bolt past and collide with his. She had him by the hair and was jerking him across the shed-row: they were in and out of the moonlight for less time than it takes to tell it, and the two of them spun crazily into the first stall. I charged in after them. He fired another round and I heard the pin click on an empty chamber. Erin must have smacked him: The collision had a distinctive jab-in-the-chops sound. I heard him grunt and saw him go twisting out of the stall, a pale figure like a fleeting ghost. He rammed into something, which turned out to be one of the posts holding up the roof; then he fell in the puddle of water under the spigot. I rolled toward him and got my legs tangled with Erin's as she leaped out of the stall. She stumbled and fell as he leaped up and took off down the black shedrow, running like a deer.

By the time I got up and moving he was in the tow ring, crossing into the next barn. I stumbled across on this end and saw him briefly, running full-tilt along the fence at Baldwin Avenue. *I'll get him now,* I thought: *There's no way he can get out of here.* Then, just that quickly, I lost him.

I heard footsteps coming fast: Bob, running up and past. "Where's Erin?" I said.

I trotted down the shedrow and crossed into the next barn. I went across the tow ring. Didn't dare call out, didn't dare not call.

"Erin!"

No answer.

"Erin!"

Nothing but the sound of the breeze.

I hurried to the barn across the way.

"Erin!"

Down a dark shedrow: across another tow ring into another shedrow. The tack room doors hung open, revealing the small, bare quarters, empty now in the moonlight.

"Erin!"

"Shh."

I stopped moving.

"I'm over here," she whispered.

I groped my way through the dark. She was standing just inside a stall, breathing heavily. I eased inside and put an arm over her shoulder. She was trembling and yet she had chased a crazy man down a dark shedrow alone.

"Where'd he go?"

"Don't know . . . not sure."

"Maybe he's gone."

"Uh-uh." She squeezed my hand. *No, he's here. Don't move.*

"I'm going after him."

"No!" I heard her take a breath. "That's what he wants. He's still got the gun."

I moved my foot. We stood, watched, waited, and time passed. At least fifteen minutes.

"Erin," I said: "We can't keep standing here."

"No." She egged me on with her hands and followed me gingerly out into the shedrow.

Nothing. Nobody.

"He's gone," I said, but she still didn't believe it.

We walked around a few barns and headed back to 107, looking over our shoulders.

Just a prowler, the cops said: Most likely someone who'd gotten past the gate and shouldn't be here. A prowler with a gun for effect, they said. Most people who had a gun waved in their faces would come across with their cash. Unless it wasn't cash he'd been after, I said.

I told them what had happened up at Golden Gate. What had happened to Cameron and to me. They listened then and they asked more questions. I told them about Candice, that I had been hired by her daughter in Idaho to find out the truth about her death. Bob sat through all this without saying much, but suddenly now he had been pulled into it and we all knew it.

The cops covered the stable area, talking with everyone they found. They made a list of people stabled here who had arrived early. Bob knew a few of the trainers and some of the ginneys on the list, but nobody with any reason to shanghai us.

They talked to the overnight stable-gate guard, who swore he had been awake the whole time and nobody had come in without a license. The guard always kept the gate closed during the late hours, so anyone coming in would have to stop and state his business.

They would talk to the front office about putting an extra guard on. And it would probably make the newspaper. The *Times* guy was aggressive, he had heard the radio call and was already asking questions. "Lots of shootings in L.A.," Erin said. "Surely he can't cover them all."

But Santa Anita was not Watts. Erin and I sat in the shedrow that morning. Sometimes we just sat; sometimes we talked.

"You were damned magnificent," I told her.

She smiled wanly. "I didn't feel so magnificent. In fact, I haven't felt like my old fearless self since last year."

"Don't remind me."

Last year we had both come much too close to cashing it all in.

"I've made a startling discovery, old man. I'm not quite ready to die yet."

"Good thing to learn."

"When you mess with bad people you never know. I do know that since last year I'm not as easy as I was. A feeling of real mortality has crept into my head."

"Maybe you should get out of here. Fly off to Denver, get lost."

"Do I look like someone who'd cut and run out on you?"

"I didn't say that."

"You were thinking it."

"It's not polite to tell a buddy what he's thinking."

"No, but . . ." She took a deep breath. "No."

"I'm starting to think this flake may follow us now no matter where we go. Somehow we've become a threat to him, more than just a couple of yahoos looking in dark corners. And there's another thing. He's already killed one fellow — never mind that Cameron was a fairly worthless fellow, somebody ought to do something about it."

"And that would be you."

"You see anybody else applying for the job?"

She sighed loudly.

"And then there's Candice, Erin. Somebody should do something about Candice."

24

During the night Sandy had left a message at the stable gate. Barbara was ill with flu and that had delayed them for a day or two. They were now looking to arrive day after tomorrow, or at least by the end of the week. Till then we were on our own.

We sat in the racetrack kitchen, which had opened for breakfast, and we talked it over. Bob was restless now: His mood leapfrogged between darkness and daylight. "I don't know whether we should hang together or split up," he said in a down moment, but in the brilliant new day he would put on more confident airs. "I don't think this is going to happen again," he said, but then he asked nervously what I thought. "I don't know, Bob," I said: "On the face of it there's no reason to think you're in any danger, but you might give this some thought. Whatever's in the wind may already be there, so unless you're getting sick of my company, and I wouldn't blame you for that, it might be smart to either get far away or stay close till Sandy gets here." There was no work to do till then anyway, so I thought I'd drift around and ask some questions. This way I could use the time to our own advantage, keep moving and maybe make the day pass quicker. Bob liked this suggestion, and right after breakfast we wandered through the stable area and he and Erin stood chatting nearby while I asked the same questions about Geiger, his sons, Candice, and the old days.

This was an obvious time-killer. Geiger had never raced here to my knowledge, but soon we found some old horsemen who remembered him from their own days long ago up north. "I knew him on the fair circuit," one old trainer said. "I was just starting out then and I had me a booming stable of four head. I raced at Santa Rosa, Vallejo, Sacramento, places like that in the fifties and sixties, and I ran into Geiger and his missus out in Omaha a couple of times as well. The first year I met him I thought he was a little distant, but he warmed up after that. He often had his young wife with him, sometimes not but she came out fairly often. A real looker she was, and more than that, she was a charmer. I think he liked to show her off."

Another old man chimed into the same conversation. "Wasn't likely you'd forget her if you ever met her even once. That lucky old bastard Geiger; I can still see her sittin' in the shedrow with him, sayin' nothing while he had opinions about everything. I heard some people say she was snooty, but I never put any stock in that. If you made contact with her eyes, what you saw was a tragic figure. If you said something to her as simple as good morning, miss, why hell, she'd light right up and talk your ear off. She'd talk about the weather, the newspapers, anything to keep you there so she wouldn't be alone again. That was my impression, anyway. She was lonely as hell, that's the feeling I had." Bob considered this a breakthrough, but what had we actually learned? We already knew that some people had found Candice unforgettable, that she was vivid in some old memories even years after the most superficial contact. After a while I was only going through the motions and that was how, when a vital lead dropped in my face, I almost missed it.

"I saw a woman I know in the kitchen," Bob said that afternoon. While I talked to a trainer who faintly remembered Geiger and had never met Candice, Bob had walked over to the kitchen on a coffee run. I gave him a grunt and he said no more about it for several minutes. On the face of it this was going to be just another horny race-tracker story, but Bob was too thoughtful to be swapping trash. We were walking past the kitchen when I looked at him and he had that enigmatic face he sometimes got, the half-smile that disappeared if you blinked twice.

"Okay, Bobby, what's going on?"

"Nothing. I was just telling you about this woman I met in the kitchen but you didn't seem to be interested so I let it drop. Want to go inside and sit?"

We went inside and sat at a corner table.

"So what gives?"

"That lady who poured us the coffee . . ."

I saw a gray-haired woman at the register and in that moment I knew that something had happened and it was more than just another horny racetracker story.

"Her name's Martha," Bob said. "For want of anything better to do, she's been knocking around racetracks all her life. I might even call her a racetrack junkie. Being such a gregarious fellow, I used to chat with her once in a while. She's made the rounds for years, Northern California, the fairs, she was at Golden Gate last year. So this morning I asked her about Geiger, and what do you think? She was at Bay Meadows when Geiger was racing there, just before and after he met his leading lady. She's done everything on racetracks from walking hots to slinging hash in the kitchen."

She had walked hots regularly for Geiger, long ago.

"She remembers them both very well. Amazing coincidence. What are the chances we'd run into somebody like that in a racetrack kitchen four hundred miles away?"

"Pretty good if I'd asked the right people."

I looked at him just in time to see the smile vanish.

"It's a small world, Cliff." His smile flashed again. "You gotta keep your eyes open."

Right from the start she had a way about her, a demeanor that had smart written all over it. "Sometimes I wonder if I've wasted my life," she said. "I know I coulda been somebody. Like Brando said, I coulda been a *contender.*"

All in all though, she had enjoyed her run. "I've done all right, but I was seldom willing to work that hard. You get out of life what you put into it, right? And I've had my fun. The racetracker's life was always a good one. Oh, the things we did."

Women weren't allowed on the racetracks at night in those days. "But I was adventurous and got ginneys to sneak me past the guard in the trunk of a car. All this other stuff, like working in the kitchen, this is what I had to do to make ends meet."

She wanted to be a writer. "I never wrote like a woman. Faulkner was my hero."

"I've got a friend who would fight you to the death over a statement like that."

"And I'd tell her she's too busy being defensive. Even with the good ones like Willa Cather there's a difference in the voice. That's all I'm saying, a woman just writes differently than a man."

Like a lot of wannabe writers, she went through terrific bursts of writing and then let it slide, sometimes for months. "I once wrote forty thousand words in a weekend."

Long ago and far away: She had been at Arlington Park then.

"When I was young I wrote everything: journals, fiction, poetry; I published some of it, too. I did an article for *Collier's* way back when, and my God, for a week I was *rich*. I wrote for horse magazines — *Turf* and *Sport Digest* when it was going, articles for *The Blood Horse,* and for a while I was a stringer for the *Thoroughbred Record.* You probably never even heard of those rags. I love publication day but I hate all the sweat that goes before it. What I really like is being out on some racetrack. If I'm gonna sweat, give me a pitchfork, not a typewriter. So I'll work in the kitchen for a while but as soon as a real horseman comes in and offers me something I'm out of there."

They all knew her, all the old-time trainers. A job would come along. It always did.

We were sitting in a restaurant in downtown Arcadia, waiting for our menus. I had left Erin and Bob in the shedrow and come alone. Sometimes it works better that way.

Her name was Martha Blackwell, she had written as M. J. Black, and her face just radiated character. It was deeply etched with the lines of living, and her smile was quick and wide and genuine. "So you want to know about the Geigers," she said.

She knew them all: the old man, Bax, Damon. "And I knew Cameron, the old son of a bitch."

"You heard he was killed?"

"Everybody knows that by now. I shouldn't speak ill of the dead, but I'm not politically correct and that man was a bastard."

"Well, he died a bastard's death."

"Yeah." Just a twinge of regret now: "What

a way to go."

"And you knew Candice," I said.

"Sure I knew her."

"I'm trying to find out how she died."

"Somebody fed her peanuts," she said without blinking an eye.

"Got any idea who?"

She listed her head to starboard and said, "Somebody who knew where and what she ate. That coulda been any number of people."

"Want to give me a list?"

"You thought about the old man?"

"Sure, but why would he do that?"

"Just wondering how far you've actually thought about it. People who marry aren't always in love with each other. Or if they are, they don't always stay that way."

"Even so, they don't kill each other without a reason."

"He might've had two billion reasons."

"He already had her money."

"Unless he was on the verge of losing it. She was pretty generous in the beginning, but I think his act lost its charm as they went along."

"What was she going to do," I asked, "leave him and take the money with her?"

"I can see where he might have thought that."

"No offense, but do you know all this or are you guessing?"

"The shedrow was my home, Mr. Janeway, at least during the daytime. I overheard things. I wasn't a sneak, but . . ."

"Sometimes people say things."

"And there are places, adjacent stalls for instance: stalls in an opposite shedrow. You've seen what the walls are like; you're doing your work and suddenly you hear voices."

I doubted this. Unlikely, I thought, that Geiger and Candice would discuss their intimate affairs in a stable area with ginneys all around. Then she said, "I worked with them one summer at the farm up near Frisco. You didn't have to be eavesdropping to overhear things there."

"What did you hear?"

"Everything." She looked at me as if she expected me to understand. "When I was young I wanted to write about it. I wanted desperately to write their story. That's why I wrote everything down at the time it happened."

As revelations go, that was a stunner.

"I was planning to write a book," she said. "Been promising myself that for years."

"A book about Geiger?"

She shook her head. "Not chapter and

verse, no. Who cares about the real Geiger anymore? He was well known in his time on the racetrack, but to the average Joe today he's a nobody. Besides, there's too much trouble when you write about real people. Geiger's dead now, I could have my way with him, but there are too many people important to his story who aren't dead."

"Then where does that leave you?"

"I thought I'd use them in a novel." She took a deep breath. "That's the best way to get at someone who's real, use him in fiction. But hell, it looks like I'm no fiction writer and it probably doesn't matter. If I was really gonna write it, I'd have done that by now, wouldn't you think?"

"I don't know, Martha. Occasionally something happens, the sleeping giant wakes up."

"You trying to talk me into something?" She laughed lightly and we ordered our food.

"Just making a point. Whatever you tell me can be off the record."

"What's the point of that? How could you use it?"

"I'll do the best I can to keep it between you and me. But in the end you're right, I'm trying to find a killer."

"I always liked Candice," she said softly.

"What a classy broad."

I looked at her straight-on. The time was suddenly ripe.

"So who do you think killed her?"

"I don't think," she said. "I know who it was."

She still didn't give me a name, not yet. We were in that early feeling-out stage and she was trying to decide about me. We went to her place, a small upstairs apartment on the edge of Arcadia. There she unwrapped half a dozen logbooks, found the one she wanted, and told me to knock myself out while she boiled some coffee. I turned the yellowing pages and read her small neat words. She had been in her late teens that first year, the year of Candice. "I was younger than she was but in the ways of the racetrack I was her mentor," she said from the kitchenette. "Geiger taught her zilch. Keep 'em ignorant might have been his motto."

I heard her clatter a room away. "Imagine, with all her money and looks she could've done anything, and she wrapped her life up in this old man. She wanted so badly to please him; that was her whole gig in a nutshell. She wanted him to be happy with her."

But he wasn't. He couldn't be because, as time went on and his old age settled in, what made him unhappy couldn't be fixed by any woman.

One day she overheard them talking: just a snatch of conversation in the empty shed-row when he was at the farm. She wrote it down that night, verbatim she said. She rummaged, and dug out the notebook.

Across the years Candice said, *This doesn't matter.*

Doesn't matter to you. But it can be damned devastating to a man.

We won't let it be. We just won't let it.

Easy for you to say. Look, I don't want to talk about this.

I love you anyway; you know that. And it's only a small part of life.

It's a helluva big part of a man's life. Just the fact that it doesn't matter at all to you matters like hell to me. I don't want to talk about it.

Don't worry, then; it's fine.

No, it's not fine. It's not fine, goddammit, it is *not fine.*

Then let's go to the doctor.

No way any goddam pill-pusher's gonna fondle me.

From the stove Martha said it didn't take a Rhodes scholar to figure that out.

"She never wanted a lover," I said. "She only wanted her daddy back."

"There are women who don't care at all about the physical lovemaking. I was like that, and it took me a while to understand it. And maybe I did listen a little more than I should have. I was just interested. People were my stock-in-trade. You understand that."

"Sure."

By the second year everything had changed. "I came in late," Martha said: "caught up with them at Pleasanton, in the middle of a short race meet. He was still doing the fairs: Jesus, he didn't have to do that small-time stuff anymore, and maybe that was his trouble; he didn't have to do anything then. My own opinion is, Geiger was one of those guys who needed to work. He needed to *have* to work, you understand what I'm saying? He couldn't exist on busywork, what he did had to be real, and it had to make a difference to him that he had to do it. And that's what was wrong. With her money she had given him the freedom to do anything, and what he did was nothing at all: he didn't have to turn a lick anymore for as long as he lived. He worked anyway, every day during that time, and he still won races. But for me, that was a great summer out on the farm. I mucked stalls and stared at the sky. Candice had her little girl with her then, cute little kid with pigtails."

"Was it just the three of you?"

"There was an old black woman they hired, a nanny I guess you'd call her. But she had to leave for some reason and I helped with the kid for a month or so. And Candice made a friend from the next farm over. I've forgotten her name."

"Gail."

"Yeah, that's it. I took care of the kid when they went walking."

"Were there ever any guys around?"

"Just one."

"Did you know who he was?"

"No idea. He came to visit once or twice and they went walking up through the glen."

"But it wasn't Sandy Standish?"

"No. I know Sandy and this wasn't him."

"Did you get a good look at this guy?"

"He only came those few times while I was there. But yeah, I saw him. I was gathering firewood one day and they came out of the woods not fifty yards away. And I had great young eyes then."

"Did they see you?"

"Oh yeah. I looked right into his face."

"What are your chances of remembering

him after all this time?"

"I don't need to. I wrote a description of him that same day."

She looked at me and smiled. "I'm a writer, I still do that. Tonight I'll probably write a hundred words on you."

I stared at the floor and took a deep breath. "Do you by any chance still have that description?"

"I've got everything. I'm a packrat. I'll find it and make you a copy."

"Thank you." I made a note. "Did you ever see them again after that?"

She shook her head.

"What about Candice? She ever say anything?"

"No, I think she was too embarrassed."

"How often was Geiger there? Did he come to the farm often?"

"I couldn't tell you that. He came near the end of that summer for about three weeks. He arrived suddenly; I remember that. She was surprised and flustered when he showed up out of the blue. She had somebody coming to see her."

"Same guy, or do you know that?"

"Same guy, same car. But they got lucky, Geiger was tired after his trip and he took a nap. She went out on the road and headed the guy off at the gate. I could just see that car through the trees, and them talking for just a minute. Then he left."

"You remember what kind of car it was?"

"Pale green. If you're asking me the make and year, no."

I wrote down "pale green car" anyway, though it had probably been gone for years. "So what did Geiger do while he was there?"

"Lazed around. Then packed 'em all up and took 'em off to Idaho. I went up to San Fran, got myself a rubbing job. Same old, same old."

"How was Geiger with the child while they were there?"

"I thought he was distant. But then they had some racing people out, an end-of-summer bash, and he really came out of his shell for that. He bounced her on his knee and laughed and tried to get her to talk. You know, the doting-dad routine. But I always thought it was an act."

"Why was that?"

"Because as soon as it was over he went straight back to his old ways. Distant. Brooding. It was like the kid had that one window into his life and that was it. Like he was showing her off for his friends. Before and afterward she didn't exist."

"Like maybe he was trying to prove something?"

"Maybe he was."

I made a few cryptic notes. "Did you have any more to say with Candice?"

"We had a couple of conversations, just before they left. She was asking me if I had ever worked with any great horses; I think she was trying to get him to go to the yearling sale at Keeneland and buy some expensive horses, but he didn't seem to care by then. If you want my opinion, I think he did care. He cared desperately but was afraid to put his ass on the line. I didn't realize this then, but I've thought about it since and I'd bet I'm right. He was afraid to fail, especially at that stage of his life. Here was this guy who knew everything about bad-legged gimpy horses, and I think he was afraid to buy himself a real racehorse. He thought there'd be a spotlight on him then, and that's the last thing he wanted. What if it broke down? What if it ran badly, for any of those weird reasons? What if, what if, what if — you can drive yourself crazy with stuff like that." She shook her head. "But damn, I think he was a great trainer. He coulda been a *real* contender."

"And instead he retired himself," I said.

"Yep, and that was his undoing. He was one of those guys who should never retire. Guys like Geiger need to die in the saddle."

So he let Junior run things and he just watched and got old. "I was long gone by then," she said. "I was working for other trainers, but I'd see them at one race meet or another, and I always tried to pass the time with Candice."

We leaned over a scarred and rickety coffee table and she poured coffee I didn't need. I still hadn't pushed her about Candice's death, but it was there in the air between us and I knew we'd circle our wagons and get back to it. "You said you were her mentor. Can you elaborate on that?"

"At first she wanted to know everything, but not because she wanted to know it: it was because of him, because it would give her a leg up into his life. She didn't know that racing was already becoming his past life; she had made it that way with her money. Look, I'm not pretending that I was her great confidante, but once in a while there'd be a look or a sigh, sometimes a word or two, a question that told more than it asked . . . occasionally a whole conversation."

"Did you ever ask her any of this?"

"Oh no. No, no, no, no. Today I might, but back then she was like some porcelain goddess and I was way too young and insecure to butt in." She laughed. "But I knew my horses, she didn't, and so she asked and I told her things."

"Like what?"

"What horses were about, and the men who raced 'em. How they're trained and made fit. What she had bought into when she married him. That's what she was really asking. So over that year we became friendly. We were never bosom buddies or anything like that, but often in the morning she'd come out to the barn where I slept and we'd talk. And over time I got the drift of things. I knew he was losing interest in racing, in just about everything that had mattered to him. Now I know he had nothing else going for him, or so he thought, and she was bright enough to realize that."

"He was losing it."

"Slipping slowly into the Sargasso Sea. Not that I'm any gifted analyst; it was just obvious. Candice understood this before I did, I was kidding myself if I thought she didn't, and he knew it too. He had started this long slide and he couldn't do anything to pull himself out of it. That's what happens to some men who have lived long and well on their own terms. I read that somewhere and now I believe it. They get old and nothing much matters anymore."

She leaned over the table. "There's nothing more destructive at any age than getting everything you ever wanted handed to you on a platter."

I sipped my coffee. She smiled. I put down my cup and made the smallest possible hand gesture. "So who killed her, Martha?"

She gave me a now-or-never look. "I've been living with this forever. I never told anybody, but it's been on my mind every day all these years."

Suddenly she said, "Look, I said I'd fish out that description for you, but don't waste your time. It wasn't that guy who killed Candice. It was Baxter. Bax killed Candice."

25

"He's crazy," she said. "If you're looking for reasons, what else do you need to know? If you spend any time at all with Baxter, you will understand one thing about him. He's a bona-fide fruitcake, a true loony bird. He belongs in a corner of some nuthouse cutting out paper dolls. Let me tell you something."

She tried valiantly to pour us another top-off, but this time I stopped her by putting my body in harm's way. She sat and suddenly she was off again.

"There was a story that got started about Bax. Seems he was convinced somebody was trying to sabotage him by messing with his horses' feed. So Bax begins testing it by eating it himself. He gets into a bale of pure locoweed and eats it all with blueberries and nonfat milk, and he's been like this ever since. They found him doing a polka at midnight with all his fillies and mares. I'm not making this up. Somebody may be, but it's not me. They say when Bax was young the Army wanted to give him a Section Eight, but he was so far beyond that, they didn't have numbers that high. The scary thing to me is, you never can tell what a guy like that will do. He'll be just fine for a day, a week, two months, two years. Then he begins to slip and the cracks appear. They get wider and he starts babbling, talking but making no sense at all. Bax has a persecution complex as wide as the Mississippi River. Ask anybody who's ever worked for him. They all love him to death at first. He's so easy, he knows his horses, and he leaves you alone if you take good care of them, but then he'll slip off the edge and start howling at the moon."

He wasn't like Junior, she said. "Junior was just a case of bad temper. That's all he ever was, a blowhard letting off steam. Mad because life hadn't gone his way. But mad as in angry, not nuts."

Baxter was the real McCoy. "It's frightening how normal he can be: normal and bonkers almost in the same breath, depending on how something strikes him. It's not always something you can see, either. Haven't you heard yet about Bax and his ways?"

She had worked for him one whole summer: had even gone with his crew to Hot Springs. "At first I thought I was going to love working for this guy, but one day during a rainstorm he went haywire. He had a horse that was favored to win going away, except for one thing. The horse absolutely would not run on an off-track, and guess what? God made it rain that day. God made it rain, the odds dropped off, and his horse ran way up the racetrack. Hell, he's probably still running, back there in Arkansas. Bax should have scratched him the minute the rain started that morning, but no, for some reason known to nobody else, he got it in his head he needed to win *that* race, no matter what, so he let him run and got what he asked for. Horse runs dead last. Say what you want about Junior, he never would've done that. Hold him back, let him win another day, that was Junior. Bax is the greatest example I know, how you can be cunning and crazy all at once."

So the morning after the mud debacle she had found him in his horse's stall, standing in that inky darkness with the most wicked-looking butcher knife she had ever seen. The light from the shedrow gleamed off the blade, the only light anywhere in the world that morning. The rain was still falling and

Bax was talking to his horse like they were blood adversaries, enemies older than time. "Make no mistake, asshole, I can kill you whenever I want to," she heard Bax say, somewhere out in the ink: "I can put this blade right through your neck and nobody will do a thing about it."

A horse is nothing more than a piece of property, Bax said. "So if I tell you to run in the mud you goddam better run your bloody guts out in the fuckin' mud, you hear that?"

Son of a bitch, he said, more times than she could count.

"What have you got to do in your whole fat-ass worthless life? Stand here, eat, sleep, shit, work fifteen goddam minutes a week, and twice a month I ask you to run me a horse race."

It was almost like that poor horse could understand him, she said. Long after dawn he was jittery, upset. "You think Junior would do that to a horse?"

No, I didn't think even Junior would do that.

"Horses pick up vibes. Maybe they don't know English, maybe they can't do long division and diagram sentences, but the good ones are nobody's fool. And I think they know hate when it comes straight at 'em like that."

She fluttered her hands in a gesture of pure nerves. "So try this," she said, and her voice quaked. "Then he says, I could put you where I put Candice, just remember that if you're ever tempted to screw me around."

The air in her place felt suddenly cold. I looked in her eyes again and she was very serious and credible. There are people who are believable with crazy facts and she was one of them. I nodded my belief and I could see her taking heart from that.

"I couldn't work for him after that," she said. "But the damndest thing happened. I was afraid to quit. Suddenly it was like he'd been talking to *me*, not the horse. Like he'd been talking to me all along, it was all some kind of warning. I would see him staring at me in the shedrow and there was something about him that made me flat-out afraid, and in that moment I believed he knew I'd been there, I had heard his craziness. I believed it then and I still do. So I worked through the meet and after a month I faded away. I told Bax my best friend was sick in Tuscaloosa or some silly place, and I left the state for a while. Screw it; life's too short as it is.

"That was years ago and he still looks at me funny. He'll stare at me clear across the kitchen. I try to smile and be pleasant, but hey, I've even given that up. Now I get busy real fast. He knows, and he knows that I know. Just this morning he came into the kitchen and said, 'Hey, Martha, how's your friend in Tuscaloosa?' We've never said a word about it in all these years. I almost dropped dead there on the floor."

She shivered, recalling it. "I can't live like this. He's got me looking over my shoulder, everywhere I go."

Her fists were tight on the table. "You don't have to take my word for anything. I can give you a whole list of ginneys who worked for him, a list as long as my arm. Most of 'em stay just long enough to cash their first few paychecks; then they're out of there. He's only got three or four regulars he can count on, two women and a guy who've been with him a while. And now I'm thinking I may leave here too. Maybe I'll go someplace where the racing's good and there's not much chance of running into people."

We looked at each other in the dim light of her apartment. I felt as if my understanding of the case was beginning to focus and become clearer. But there was still too much out of synch; there were pieces that didn't fit with the others. Why this was I couldn't yet figure, but I was going to find out. I gave it the full thirty seconds, all I could allow with Martha looking in my face. Either she was lying, and I couldn't imagine why, or Bax had long ago confessed a murder to a racehorse in the middle of the night. Either Bax was crazy or maybe we all were. Either this was one case or two. Either it was about the books, random murders, or everything was linked so tightly it couldn't yet be pried apart. For me it had started as a quest to find some missing books, soon there was a murdered man who was also the main suspect in the book thefts, and now we had a crazy man; the bastard had come much too close and wasn't about to stop now, and I feared for everyone: Erin, Bob, and especially this woman sitting beside me. Maybe it isn't anything we know, I thought; maybe it's just what he *thinks* we know.

"Martha," I said softly, "I need to ask you a favor."

Warily she said, "It won't cost you anything to ask."

"This is a big one."

26

Sharon was dozing in her kitchen when I called. I explained what I needed and why, she said she'd wire us some money, and I began laying the groundwork for a hit-and-run operation. I would hit, Martha would run, and hopefully I'd get Bob and Erin out of here as well.

I called Golden Gate and left a message for Sandy. We needed to talk, ASAP.

I rented Martha a motel room across town, out near the airport. She had a big box, her logbooks and notes, and this was all she needed to take from the old place. We shipped it to Idaho, leaving her with only the small suitcase to carry.

Now came the hard part. I picked up the money Sharon had wired me and drove back to the racetrack in the fading afternoon. Erin was watching my approach with wary eyes, as if she knew exactly what was in the wind. Bob came to the open tack-room door and slouched there waiting. I sat in the empty chair and cleared my throat.

"This is not a good sign," Erin said. "When he clears his throat, bad things are happening."

"So how was Martha?" Bob said.

"Very good. I owe you one."

"You want to tell us about it?" Erin said.

"Not particularly."

She looked at Bob and rolled her eyes. "He wants us out of here."

Bob brought out a third chair and sat facing us. "Be serious," he said.

"He is serious," she said.

"She knows me way too well, Bobby. And I know her."

"You want us to leave when?"

"As soon as possible. Tomorrow morning would be good if we could arrange things that soon. At least by tomorrow."

He shook his head: half dismay, half disbelief.

"It may just be for a few days. A week or two at the outside."

"Give me one good reason and I will leave," Erin said.

"I'm setting a trap for this bird."

"And you're afraid we'll get in the way and mess it all up."

"You each make me more vulnerable, not

423

less. And you can double that four times over for both of you."

I waited through the deadliest silence.

"I don't want to go," she said.

Bob just looked at us. "What the *hell* did Martha tell you?"

"I'd rather not say just yet. In fact, neither of you may be in any danger at all. It might just be me he wants. Probably is. But I'd rather have you somewhere far away."

Erin sighed loudly. "And just like that I have ceased being an asset."

"You will never stop being an asset. But do this for me, please. Look at it as a short vacation. I promise you'll be back before you know it."

" 'Please' is the key word, Bobby. I know he's serious when he goes polite on me."

Erin and I walked up to the racetrack alone. At the rail I put my arm over her shoulder.

"I don't want to go," she said.

"I know you don't."

"I will never forgive myself if something happens and I'm not here to take care of you."

"You do that so well, too."

"Damn, I hate this."

"Help me with Bob, will you? He doesn't want to go either."

"I'll persuade Bob, if this is really what you want. If it's truly necessary."

A moment later she said, "So is it? Necessary?"

"I don't know. That's the crazy part, I just don't know."

"Is this really what you want?"

"No. But I've got to ask you to do it anyway."

"I'll do it, then, under vigorous protest."

"Thank you."

In the morning I found Baxter over in Barn 136. His three ginneys were still unpacking saddles and bridles and other odds and ends. Bax sat in his shedrow, watching a blacksmith shoe one of his horses. I stood behind his chair and said nothing as the file husked a hoof into shape and the lightweight shoes were nailed in place.

"Hi, Bax."

"Janeway. So what, you come over to get that job I offered you?"

"As a matter of fact I did want to talk to you about helping out till Sandy gets here. I'm going stir crazy over there."

"So talk."

He was less friendly today: Maybe it was just his time of the month, one of those mood swings Martha had told me about.

"What about it?" I said: "You need help or not?"

"I always need help. Hard to get good hands these days. Are you a good hand?"

"I've got a strong back and a weak mind, and I don't tire easily."

He warmed up a notch and laughed. "Hey, you're hired. You rub 'em too, or just walk?"

"I've got a little to learn about rubbing 'em yet, but I'll pick it up fast."

"Good. Anybody can walk, but I've always got a need for another ginney. Just get into it, use your head, and ask Rigger or Ruthie if you've got any questions. If you run into anything you can't handle, see me." He stretched out his long legs and said, "When can you start?"

"Right now on a temporary basis."

"Come to work full time and I'll pay you two-fifty a month for each head. Start with three; if I like what you do I'll give you four. I pay on the first and fifteenth every month."

"How about we leave it temporary for now? Hey, this is a freebie, Bax, you won't owe me anything," and suddenly he brightened. "You wanna work under them conditions, damn right I need the help."

His head ginney was a middle-aged guy named Rigger Boyles. He wasn't friendly or hostile, just all business. I soon learned that he had a nickname, Rigger Mortis.

"You gonna sleep in the tack room?"

"No, I'm just filling in and I've got a room."

"Let me know if you change your mind."

I walked back to Sandy's. The shedrow was quiet, almost tomblike in the late morning. Bob was sitting in the sun, watching the action in the tow ring, but absently, with his mind far away. A young woman brought a black colt out from the opposite barn and blended into the walking circle. Business was picking up. Another stable had moved into our barn on the far end and we heard another was coming that afternoon across the way. I sat in the shedrow beside Bob and we talked. He asked where Martha was and I shrugged, implying I didn't know. "Looks like she quit her job at the kitchen," he said.

"That's how it goes. Nothing lasts forever."

"Nope. Not many career opportunities over there. But she didn't give 'em any notice."

"That happens, too."

"Unlike Martha, though."

Meaningless small talk: a time killer. At last I said, "Bob, you might consider following Martha's example and getting the hell out of here."

"Is that what she did?"

"Looks like it."

"Get out and do what?"

"A little vacation is all."

"How am I supposed to pay for all this?"

"Not to worry. There's money coming from your guardian angel."

"Jesus. Just go, just like that? I might as well tell Sandy where to stick his job."

"I'll try to cover you with Sandy when he gets here."

"Crap," he said under his breath.

"Yeah, I know."

"Why, for Christ's sake? Make me understand why and I'll go."

"I can't make you understand what I don't quite understand myself. But I've got a deal for you. Something you can't refuse."

"Oh wow. Do I keep both hands in my pockets while you tell me? Or just bend over now?"

"This is ranch work, Bob, it's a piece of cake. Same kinda stuff you're doing now, only better money. Fine working conditions, happy people, good pay, needy horses. That's how I was sold on it. I think it can be fixed with Sandy for you to be gone till we see how the wind blows. But starting now, I'm going to be busy elsewhere."

I could see the worry in his eyes. "I hear Erin's going with me."

I nodded.

"She's a good gal, Erin."

"Yes she is."

"You're a lucky bastard."

"Don't I know it."

I dug deep for something else to say. "This is the right thing, Bob. Just don't tell anybody."

"Who would I tell?"

I clapped him on the shoulder. "This too will pass, Bobby."

That afternoon I got them booked on a connecting flight to Idaho. I handed Bob a roll of money and sent them off in a cab with no time to spare.

I called Martha from a bar near the racetrack and asked how it was going. Her nerves had worn thin.

"I left him a message at the stable gate," she said. "Told him I'd call him there at four o'clock."

"And he was there then?"

"Oh, you bet he was."

"What was his reaction?"

"I couldn't tell at first from his voice." I heard her take a deep shivery breath. "I knew he was uptight when he found out it was me," she said. "More so when I told him what I wanted."

"I'll bet he was. Was he shocked?"

"I think I'd describe him that way. Shocked numb in fact."

"So what did he say?"

"He denied everything, but then I got angry and there was a quieter time when he just talked about the old days."

"Did that strike you as weird?"

"This whole goddam thing strikes me as weird. But I know what you mean. Here I've just accused him of murder and he slips into this quiet soliloquy, a reverie. The guard finally told him he'd have to stop tying up the phone."

"Did you get a tape?"

"Yeah, I've done lots of interviews, I know how to do this. It came out fine."

"I'll hear it later. But for now, what did he say? Exactly, Martha — as close as you can remember it."

She paused a moment, then said, "He couldn't believe I would say something like that. It's not true, he said, over and over, but conversationally, not at all angry like you'd expect. I mean, what would you do if some dame called and told you something like that? You'd hang up, right? Not him. He says, Look, we've known each other way too long to let stuff like that be said, as if we were ever bosom buddies, as if I was betraying him and throwing his long, warm friendship back in his face. He comes at me with this hurt on his sleeve till I wanted to ask him for a barf bag. People don't trust each other anymore, he said. I told him there are good reasons for that, but he rambled on, remembering the days when it was just him and Damon and the old man. He remembered the first day I ever worked a race meet, years ago at Tanforan, how I walked horses for the stable across from him. He remembered things I had long forgotten, the colors of the silks, for God's sake: what colors my first trainer had, and I remembered them too as he talked about them. He said how pretty I was, how different everything is now. The life, the horses, everything: It's a whole new ball of wax. I almost felt hypnotized listening to him, his memories are so *vivid,* so real, and to anybody who worked here then, they're true."

On the TV behind the bar the news bozo had passed off to the weather gal. Denver, Idaho, or Southern California, they all look alike: sweeping hair, perfect teeth, drowning the viewer in plastic. *Back to you, guys.*

"What happened next?"

"More of the same. I let it go on for a while, then I cut him off at the knees."

"What'd you say?"

"I know you didn't want me to get into this yet, but I had to say it. Had to. Damn, I thought I was about to explode. So I said come on, Bax, let's knock off the bullshit, I know you killed Candice. I didn't have to fake the anger. When I think of Candice and I think of that idiot doing that to her, I can't help it, I just get livid." Her voice trembled. "And I've got to tell you, he frightens me."

"Easy, Martha, it's all right. Just stay put, you'll be fine, you'll be out of there tomorrow. So you told him you knew about Candice. Then what?"

"Talked about maybe meeting him."

"Umm-hmm. How'd that go?"

"It was easy. He's the one who brought it up. It sounded so natural; all I had to do was play my role. We really need to talk this out, he said. We can't have you go off believing this stuff, much less spreading it around. Like yeah, I would believe such a thing and still meet him alone somewhere. He must think I'm the one who's nuts."

"Is that what he suggested, that you meet him alone?"

"He certainly implied that. Someplace, you know, where we could hash it out, and he could convince me — his words — that he was okay."

The moment settled and I pondered it. There seemed to be nothing else to say: Just meet Baxter at the time and the place. "Where?"

"Restaurant called Larson's, downtown Inglewood, away from the racetrack but public, you know, with people around. I told him that's the only way I'd even consider it."

"And he believed this?"

"I don't know. It sounded okay at the time, but the whole conversation was almost surreal."

"When is this meeting supposed to take place?"

"Tomorrow evening after work, around six o'clock."

We didn't say anything then for almost a minute. I was running the whole screwy scenario through my head and apparently she was doing the same.

"What are you going to do?" she said.

"Play it by ear."

"Go there and meet him."

"At least go there. Watch and see what he does."

"Are you going to confront him?"

"I'll see how he acts when you don't show.

Then, maybe."

She said, "Maybe I should show."

I waited for the punch line.

"If you were there too, I wouldn't worry," she said. "Just don't let us out of your sight."

"Not even for a moment, Martha." I took in a breath. "Are you sure you want to do this?"

"I think I should be there, look him in the eye, see what kind of lies he comes up with."

If I ever had a doubt about her, it was gone now. She shivered and I could hear the flutter in Arcadia. "I'm . . ."

"What?"

"Nothing. You'll really think I'm nuts."

"Let me in on it, Martha, we'll be nuts together."

"It's just that when he was talking, there was suddenly something so touching about him. His voice quivered like a little boy about to cry. At that point he almost made me believe him."

I wanted to tell her that this might only be the classic ways and means of a psychopath: one of the countless variants in the craziness of the human animal. I wanted to say there are eight million stories in the Naked City and this may be one of them: at least she'd be old enough to remember that line. I wanted to ask if these were the antics of a harmless screwball or the methods of a vicious killer feeding his own bloodlust. Somebody was certainly killing people: Maybe the local news guy would figure it out *in depth* after the fact, but I thought the odds were against him; I wouldn't bet on him finding the bathroom in the three minutes he called depth on TV. "What are you thinking?" Martha said across town, and I had no easy answer. I could give her my old standard, "I don't think, I just react," and sure, it's a funny line but even I get tired of it. Hard to believe, but there are actually times when I become annoyed with my own bullshit. Unless you're on TV, there are no easy answers. There never are, out here where the real people live and die.

27

An hour before the dawn I was sitting in the shedrow, surrounded by nothing but the void. There hadn't been much sleep in my immediate past. My chair was propped back against the threshold of the open tack-room door, where I had been sitting for a while now, slowly waking up. In the dark I could almost picture the ghosts of the great horses that had run here — Swaps, Round Table, Citation — and I looked off across the tow ring at the barn across the way. The time was four-thirty by the clock in my head, and sure enough, almost at that second, the ginneys began stirring down the row and I heard hungry horses nickering in the distance. Lights began to appear two barns away, then in my own shedrow at the far end. But where I sat only the darkness remained, deeply black.

So was this the day of Baxter? Obviously I didn't know how this would all end but I was primed, I believed something would happen, and I sat still until the first trickles of light began spreading across the mountain range and down along the backstretch rail. I let my chair drop softly, got up, stretched, and headed over to the kitchen for some coffee.

The place was buzzing with horsemen: trainers, exercise boys, ginneys, hot walkers, and jockeys. About one face in three was a woman's. And then there was me. It didn't take long to get established in the closed environment of a racetrack and already I knew some of them, if not by name, at least by their faces. I nodded to people as I took my coffee and sat for a moment, sipping it. All around me the hum of voices wafted, the rustle of the *Daily Racing Form* and the occasional *Los Angeles Times:* all around was laughter, coughing, the blowing of noses, the soft murmur of serious discourse. Another day, and money was here to be made and lost.

I heard him coming. Amazing how fast an old cop can pick things out in a collage of common sounds. I played him cool, keeping my eyes down studiously on my *Form.*

He sat without being invited. Slowly I raised my eyes and with my gentlest, pleasantest smile on, I said, "Hi, Bax."

His face was deadpan, and for the moment I didn't know whether he'd try to be palsy or call me outside and haul my ashes. "I had a phone call from Martha," he said. "You wouldn't know anything about that?"

"Martha who?"

"The woman . . ."

". . . who works in here, oh yeah," I said as if in very sudden enlightenment. But I left the question open to see where he'd take it.

"She's gone. You know anything about this?"

"About what? What would I know?"

"That's what I'm asking you."

"Hell, I don't know anything, Bax. Sounds like you're pissed about something."

"I might be," he said, "especially if I found out certain things."

"I might be too, if I were you. Any number of things tend to piss me off these days."

He stared at me until I said, "Anybody at this table got any idea what the hell we're talking about?"

"Nobody's here but you and me, pilgrim."

Pilgrim. I smiled and he blinked at me. "Well," I said, "I'm afraid I can't offer you much enlightenment this early in the morning."

"Bullshit." He smiled at me when he said

that but the smile was a little late coming.

I kept playing dumb with the slightly raised eyebrow.

"Where's she gone?" he said.

"Martha? I have no idea."

He shook his head. "Where is she, Janeway?"

"I'm sorry, did I stutter? I don't know."

"You know, all right," he said, and I looked at him steadily. "You know," he said again.

I shook my head.

"Where's that other ginney who was with you?"

"He's gone too."

"Gone where?"

"I don't know. Maybe he ran off to a desert island with Martha. Come on, Bax, what's going on here?"

"I'm trying to decide something."

"Lay it on me, I'll see what I can do with it."

"I already told it to you, I want to know where Martha is."

"That I can't help you with."

I waited calmly but he seemed to have second thoughts. "I want to know why you came to me asking for work," he said. "Now of all times."

"You offered me a job, as I recall, and

now's as good as any other time. Sandy's been pretty testy. Kinda like you're being now, all of a sudden." I leveled him with a look and said, "I've never worked well for a man who goes off if the moon doesn't come up right."

"Like me, you mean?"

"I never said that. I haven't worked day one for you yet, I don't know how you are."

"Sounds like you're already giving notice and you haven't even got the job yet."

"I'm trying to answer your questions is all. You're the one who started this line of talk."

A slow smile played around the edge of his mouth, but his face remained tight.

"Look, Bax, if you've got second thoughts . . ."

"No, I was just wondering about Martha."

"Martha and me, you mean. Why would you even think about that?"

"You two have been seen together, talking. Then the woman called and jacked me up and I'd like to know what you know about her."

"Nothing."

"That's it then, nothing?"

"Not a damn thing. I know she writes, she's interested in books, and so am I. I met her in the kitchen and we've had two or three talks about writers. She likes William Faulkner and I wanted to know somebody who can explain him to me."

"William Faulkner," he said dumbly. "That's what you're telling me this is about? William Fuckin' Faulkner."

"That's it."

He looked at me like some alien life-form and I said, "He's not easy to read, Faulkner. You ever tried reading him?"

"Not today."

"Take a look at him and you'll see what I mean."

He shook his head. "I don't know why anybody'd read shit like that."

I watched him walk away, oblivious to the people around him. An old man loudly invited him to join a table of fellows like himself but he went on by without even a nod at their existence. Someone at their table chuckled softly as he went out into the rosy morning. I lingered just long enough to finish my coffee, then I headed over to Bax's shedrow.

Horsemen and horses were suddenly everywhere. Racing would begin in less than three weeks and the place was filling up. Bax had gone to the track and I decided to play it as if this morning's conversation had never happened. Let him run me off with the chain end of a lead shank if that's what he wanted. I asked Rigger Boyles where I should start and he said, "Hold that horse when Bax brings him back and then we'll find you something." Bax returned in five minutes. He didn't run me off, he just handed me the horse while his ginney gave him a bath. We covered him with a blanket and I started him around the tow ring. This went on for a while: I walked hots until Bax said, "You want to get your feet wet, you can get that gray horse ready for the track. See if you can figure out which end his ass is fastened to."

That was it: He was giving me a baptism by fire and I had no idea what to do next. I stood in the stall for a minute trying to work it out. The horse needed a bridle. Okay, what kind of bridle? D-bit, ring-bit, what? I leaned over the webbing and asked the ginney in the next stall if she had ever rubbed this horse. "Yeah, he's a bit pissy," she said. "Catch him wrong and he bites." That told me something at least: I put him in a D-bit and brushed out his mane. "Wake up, pissy one," I said, and the horse nuzzled me and let me drape an arm over his neck. *Hey, I like this guy,* I thought. So what if he did have his pissy moments, he hadn't had them with me yet.

Bax returned and I led the gray out into the shedrow. Bax looked at the bridle and said nothing about it, so I must have passed the first test. He saddled his horse and gave his boy, who was actually a girl, a leg up; then they headed along the road to the track. I began drawing a bucket of steaming water and got ready for their return.

I washed the horse with a sopping wet sponge and scraped him off. I walked him too, and so the morning went.

Bax left without a word. His guy Rigger and I hung out with one of his two girl ginneys until Rigger left.

"Except for Rigger, Bax seems to prefer women pretty much across the board," I said.

"Yeah, we're easier to work with, we're gentler with the horses, and we don't tend to have troubles like drinking and carousing."

Her name was Ruth: she was in her late twenties and had been with Bax two years.

"How's he to work for?"

"He's always been good to me. I think he gets a bum rap from others."

"Maybe I'll be workin' for him," I said; "but it does seem like I got off on the wrong foot."

"Don't worry about it. He might seem like

he's out of joint, but then he'll be fine tomorrow."

"Why does he get a bum rap from the others?"

"I don't know, maybe because he's different."

"Because he's not exactly Mr. Warm, perhaps?"

"He's got his moments. Really, he's an okay guy. But he makes some people uneasy."

"Why do you suppose that is?"

"I'll tell you what, I don't spend a lot of time thinking about it."

"I can understand that. Life's too busy. You know his brothers?"

"Can't know Bax without you know Damon. Personally, between the two of them, I'll take Bax every time."

"What about Cameron?"

"He's dead. You must've heard."

"I heard he was murdered."

"Yep. Only half the state for suspects."

"A real sweetheart I take it."

"*Oh* yeah. What's the saying? Cameron was so crooked he had to screw his pants on."

We laughed together. "Look," I said, "I don't want to pry too much . . .."

"Funny how I was just thinking that my-self."

"It's just that I've already got a job . . ."

"And you don't want to go from bad to worse."

"Smart gal."

"Who you working for now?"

"Sandy Standish."

"Hey, that's a class outfit. And the word is he's gonna train Barbara Patterson's horses. Why would you quit there?"

"No aspersions on Sandy. We just don't see eye-to-eye on everything."

"You're not gonna see eye-to-eye on everything with any of these guys. If that's what you're lookin' for, good luck."

"I hear you."

"You gotta remember who's the boss and who's the hand."

"That's what I needed, Ruth. Somebody to remind me of that."

28

I had a note at the stable gate from Sandy: a two-liner that simply said Barbara was better but still not well and he hoped they'd be here in a few days. I lay on my cot and slept over the noon hour. At two-thirty I called Idaho and Erin answered the phone. "Sharon's gone to town to get something for her horse's eye," she said. "Looks like you're stuck with me."

She had been pondering the wisdom of not going directly home. "I feel like a fifth wheel out here. On the other hand, I'm uneasy at the prospect of not being here. Does that make sense?"

"Yeah, it does. If you get too restless, Sharon will give you a pitchfork."

"That's the other thing. If I went back to Denver now I'd just get into some legal case. It would be much more difficult to get away again if I had to."

Louie and Rosemary were great people,

she said. She hadn't spent much time yet with Lillian or Billy. "Did you know Billy thinks you're great? I'll try to straighten him out."

She thought Bob was already in love with Sharon.

When we hung up I felt a sense of deepening isolation, as if I had cast myself adrift with no idea where I was or how long I might be here.

I asked around and quickly found a high-quality electronics dealer in this part of town. I told the man what I needed, the best, smallest tape-and-wire setup I could get. Cost was no object. People rise to the occasion when you speak those four words, and I paid lots of Sharon's cash and left with a miniature system absolutely guaranteed to record the suspect without losing a breath or a cussword. I could stand far up the block and hear them talk.

Back in my tack room I played around with the wire — pushed its buttons, got comfortable with it. Bax returned after a late lunch. I saw him walking in the distance with Damon, who must have arrived within the last twenty-four hours. They walked over toward the kitchen together, heads down, Damon apparently doing most of the talking. I saw them come back about forty minutes later with a third man, a guy who looked like Junior. This time they crossed into a shedrow two barns down and I only saw them for an instant, but that cowboy hat of Junior's was the giveaway.

I headed over to Bax's shedrow again. Bax hadn't chased me away yet: I still had afternoon chores. The daily grind. I mucked my stalls and brushed my horses starting with the gray, who forgot his sweet disposition of the morning and tried to take off my right arm. Treacherous prick, I said under my breath, but I fondled his ears and soon we were uneasy friends again. I passed time with Ruth and the other ginney, whose amazing name was Dulciana Hammermeister. Her nickname was Dulcie and that was what she went by.

"She's a pussycat," Ruth said.

Bax arrived. He seemed surprised to see me there but didn't say so. I hauled my muck sack out to the bin. I now seemed to have four head, one of which needed his legs wrapped. "The secret is to get his bandages tight enough but not too tight," Ruth said. She took me by the hand and showed me by touch. "Start your wrap like this, away from the tendon."

I did him up and undid him, several times until I got the feel of it.

"He's often sore, poor guy," Ruth said. "Ice helps."

"How do you use it?"

"Bax stands him in ice for two hours before a race. How do you feel about that?"

The idea didn't thrill me. I wondered what a horse does if he's breaking down and can't even feel his legs. But for now I said, "Hey, Mr. Bax be da boss-man."

"You got it, Mr. Bones. Two of yours get their ankles brushed with oil and Kendall's. It's a mix Bax makes up; he keeps it in a plastic jug in the tack room. I'll show you how it's done."

She said the horses got a hot mash for supper. "I'll show you how to cook it."

Bax sat at the end of the shedrow, watched us work, and said not a word.

He left suddenly before the work was done. Ruth and Dulcie settled into a spirited card game with some visiting ginney guys from Barn 64 and I got out of there. Time was wasting.

It was a long drive in traffic over to Martha's motel. She gave me a spontaneous hug and I spent the next half hour showing her how to use the little device I had bought. We went over it several times so there'd be no slipups; then we headed out to Larson's

Restaurant in my car.

I was still almost an hour early, which was fine. I wanted to case the joint and pick my best place for a stakeout. I was counting on my ability to see without being seen; I had been good at that back in Denver in my days before books, and I figured I had a pretty fair chance even when the perp knew what I looked like. But there was always the possibility I'd be seen no matter how good I thought I was, and then I'd have to improvise. Get in his face was always a plan. Make him forget about the others by turning myself into a tower of menace.

The restaurant was a pleasant surprise. The layout was just what the doctor ordered. Lots of light, plenty of vacant tables in the hour before the rush might begin. There was an old-fashioned drugstore across the street, complete with a soda fountain. The drugstore was as crowded as the restaurant was empty: lots of kids hanging out after school, eating ice cream floats and drinking cherry smashes. I put Martha at the fountain, on the last unoccupied stool near the end. I got her a *Times,* more newspaper than the average burglar and all the accomplices in Southern California could hide behind. She could easily see into the restaurant over the top edge of the day's leading rape story: She could see the whole room wherever Bax might choose to sit.

"Go when the time seems right," I said to her. "Don't worry, I'll be close."

I went into the place next door and did some mindless browsing. Good thing I was diligent: Baxter also was early, arriving just a few minutes later. He looked around the dining room and finally picked his table, facing the outer door. The minutes stretched on: a waitress brought him some munchies, which he barely touched. However, he gulped his coffee and called for more. Nervous Bax, I thought: uneasy Bax. I wondered what he'd do or say when we finally did come face-to-face without all the camouflage, and I wondered when that might be. I wasn't quite ready to mess with his day yet.

At quarter past six he called the waitress and asked her something. He'd be describing Martha now, wondering if any message had been left for him. Almost in the same second the waitress shook her head, but he kept her there through another long exchange. The waitress was beginning to look annoyed when Bax gave up and settled back for the duration.

We waited. Some dinner trade was beginning to trickle in and the staff was looking at Bax in annoyance. He sat in oblivion through all of this. He looked like a dime-store dummy or maybe a model for a funeral home. He seemed damned determined not to leave and then, suddenly, he erupted. He slammed his hand down with what must have been the velocity of a gunshot. Everybody in the place jumped half out of their chairs and the waitresses all froze where they were standing near the kitchen. From there I could see the face of the waitress: uneasy, uncertain, trying to be pleasant in a difficult situation.

Bax ordered more coffee and the waitress brought it. She asked a question and he shook his head. No dinner, he was saying: just the coffee. She walked away, looking over her shoulder.

It was some time later when I realized I was standing in a thrift store. I turned my head and stared at a wall of books twenty feet away. The usual crap, I could see from there, the sign said ALL BOOKS 75 CENTS. I forced myself to look across at Bax again, but the books kept drawing me back. Instinctively my eyes bumped along the spines and darted across the street again to Bax. I saw a shelf of detective fiction, probably all donated by the same guy. Book club stuff: I could tell it without ever touching a book or opening a cover. After you've been in the business a while and felt ten thousand of these goddam things, you just know. That's also how you make mistakes, by assuming you know more than you do. I looked across at Bax, a study in scary eccentricity. The waitress was keeping her distance: If he wanted a refill, let him send up a flare and she'd bring him one posthaste. I looked at the books, dropping my eyes down a shelf and skimming along a row of mixed-bag fiction and nonfiction: trade editions, mostly thicker and taller than their book club counterparts, but you can never be sure from a distance. Damn, I wanted to rifle that shelf. How long could it take and where the hell would Bax go anyway? I could do it in half a minute, just long enough to touch them and feel the paper, just long enough to lose him. Talk about half-assed incompetence, how about a detective who loses both a killer and a witness while he's groping through things like *The Slim Man's Girdle Book,* looking for something that had never been there in the first place. Even Peter Sellers wouldn't do that. Well, maybe he would but there wasn't any salvation in that thought. It didn't matter, I shouldn't care: it was all dreck anyway. I looked across the street but Bax hadn't moved. No sign yet of

Martha: I hoped she was only waiting for the perfect moment and not getting cold feet. I gave the bookshelf a final gander and there, twenty feet away, was a copy of *The Long Lavender Look* by John D. MacDonald, Lippincott, very scarce in its first hardback edition. Maybe this was, maybe it wasn't: It sure looked pretty good from here. Visions of five hundred bucks danced in my head, and that's when Bax chose to get up and leave. I saw Martha come past my window and hurry down the street behind him. I looked back brokenhearted and left the book there.

She turned on her wire. "Are you with me, Cliff?" she said, but I had no way of answering. I was with her though as she followed Bax through the streets to a parking lot. "Sorry," I heard her say. "I should have gone after him sooner but my feet wouldn't seem to function."

Yes, she was clearly nervous: her breath came quickly and shivery. "I'm okay now," she said. "I'll be fine."

I watched her from a doorway. She approached him softly as he fumbled for his keys.

"Hey, Bax."

What happened next was even stranger

than what we had just been through. Bax said, "Jesus *Christ,* Martha!" and whipped around and sagged against his car. "Goddammit, don't you know better than to walk up on a man that way?" I was standing not fifty yards away; I could reach them in less than ten seconds if I had to. I heard Martha say, "So what do you want, Bax?" and there was a moment of quiet when Bax said nothing at all. I had almost given up on him: The dark thought crossed my mind that my pricey little gizmo had malfunctioned in some way, but no, I could hear him breathe. He had a cold. Martha said, "Talk to me, Baxter" and what followed was five minutes of screwy dialogue.

"You talk to me, Martha. You goin' away somewhere?"

"What difference does that make?"

"I was hoping, you know . . ."

"Hoping what?"

"We could get all this behind us. Become, you know, friends."

Martha said, "What are you doing, Bax, asking me for a date?" and I thought, *Damn, she's good.*

"That wouldn't be the strangest thing that's ever happened," Bax said.

"It sure would to me. First that you would

ask, second that you'd even think I might go."

"Hey, you're here, aren't you?"

"I've got to admit, I am curious."

"About what?"

She laughed. "About what? You've gotta be kidding."

"Oh, loosen up for Christ's sake. Let's go back to that restaurant and have some dinner and get this straightened out."

"Why don't you straighten me out right here and now?"

"You really want to talk this out in a parking lot?"

Another pause. Then she said, "Come here. Come closer where I can see your eyes, and tell me you didn't kill Candice."

Oh, wow, she is good.

"I have no idea where you're getting this," Baxter said.

"One of your horses told me."

"That's what you said. You know if you repeat that, people will think it's you who's crazy."

"Just say it again."

"Say *what?*"

"Say you'll put that horse in the ground, same place you put Candice."

He whispered something, so softly that even my equipment couldn't pick it up.

"I've never been much good at lipreading," she said. "Say it so I can hear you."

He laughed. "I don't know what you're talking about."

"You're lying. You should treat your horses better than that, Bax, they'll run better for you."

"You're saying I said this to a horse?" He blew his nose and it sounded like Krakatoa erupting. "You really need some professional help, Martha. That's all I came out here to tell you. You're sick."

"That's funny coming from you. Look at you, you're losing it even as we speak."

Suddenly his tone got angrier. "How the hell did you come charging into my life, anyway? Who have you told about this?"

"You think I'd tell you that?"

"You told Janeway for one. I know you did."

"Who's Janeway?"

"Oh, don't give me that shit. How the hell do you expect to have a conversation if you're just gonna stonewall me?"

"Look, all I want from you is this. Just admit what you said, that morning in the barn. Just admit it, Bax."

"I don't know what you're talking about."

"Then we seem to have run out of things to say."

"That would be your choice, not mine."

I heard him get in his car and slam the door. Heard the window go down.

"I've always carried a torch for you, Martha. Bet you didn't know that."

"Actually I could tell, with those endearing looks you've been giving me across the kitchen."

He made a kissing sound and I heard his motor start. "Last chance at the big time, Martha. Going . . . going . . ."

"What do you want from me?" she said, but he drove out of the lot and left rubber on the street.

Martha exploded in my ear. "Shit! Did you hear that?"

I watched Bax's taillights grow small and disappear up the freeway ramp.

"I wanted him to at least admit what he said. I needed to have him do that."

At last I walked into the lot and met her there. "Did you hear what he said? When he whispered to me, could you hear it?"

I shook my head and she looked upset, on the verge of tears.

"Don't worry about it," I said. "This wasn't a total bust by any means."

"Wasn't any smoking gun either."

"You did fine."

"That bastard," she said. "Oh God, I hate that man."

I drove her to the airport, gave her some money, and waited with her, watching till her flight boarded and the plane pulled back from the gate. She was off to Idaho, where, for the moment at least, there was safety in numbers.

29

Bax and I now slipped into a game of cat-and-mouse. This was not planned: It just evolved from events that had led us down that path. I lay in my tack room before dawn and stared up into dark corners, coming slowly awake. I thought I'd heard someone at my door. I got up and opened it. Nobody there. I looked down the long shedrow and stood in the dark doorway. I stood there for a long time and nothing moved, no one came, no more bumps went bump in the night, and in normal times I wouldn't have given it another thought. Just the remnants of a dream. I had no plan beyond this morning; nothing beyond the course I had set, to play it by ear. I would show up in Bax's barn this morning and see what happened: I'd rattle his cage if the chance came up and see where that might lead. I sat on the bed and worked the cobwebs out of my eyes, dressed in the dark, opened my door, and there he was, standing in the empty shed-row not thirty yards away. He didn't move and for a moment neither did I. He was wearing black clothes: a black windbreaker, black hat, dark pants; he might have been the invisible man if I hadn't had great eyes and been watching for him anyway. I would be watching for him everywhere now, every minute, every step I took.

"Bax," I said pleasantly.

He came forward slowly, one step at a time.

"So where's Martha gone?"

"Didn't we go through this yesterday?"

"Oh yeah, I forgot. You said you didn't know."

"But you didn't believe that."

"Still don't, but what the hell. I just wanted to tell her I'm sorry about last night. Maybe you can tell her when you see her."

"No reason for me to see her."

"Yeah, right. So what're you up to this morning?"

"Thought I'd come over and rub your horses. Isn't that the routine?"

He laughed dryly. "I knew you'd say that. How'd I know you'd say that?"

"Great minds think alike."

"That must be it. You decided what you're gonna do when Sandy gets here?"

"He's got first dibs on me. I'm gonna miss your gals, though. Even Rigger has his moments."

"I'm sure he does, if anybody can ever figure out when he's having one. Anyway, you be sure to come over and see us."

I smiled in the dark.

"You're actually becoming a pretty good hand, Janeway. Next thing you know I'll have to pay you."

"Well, there is that."

"I'll bet you're having so much fun, you'd keep right on working for nothing."

"Only a fool would do that, Bax."

"And you ain't no fool, are you, pal?"

He came closer. I still couldn't see his face: The morning was black as hell in the dark places under the shedrow roof. He took a breath and said, "This is nice but I gotta get movin'. See you over there then."

He turned away but stopped when I said his name.

"Now what's on your mind?"

"I'll be happy to work my shift. I'll be on time, I'll do my stuff, I appreciate the chance to learn it, actually. Ruth is a great gal and a fine teacher. But, Bax . . ."

He turned back and looked at me, looked toward me actually, for I was as much in the shadows as he was. "What's on your mind now, cowboy?"

"Don't come up on my tack room in the night like that."

"Why, pilgrim, did I scare you?"

"Just don't do it."

"You musta been talkin' to Martha, Cliff. Next thing you know she'll have you believing all kinds of bad stuff."

"It's not a good idea, Bax. Not good to sneak around like that."

"I wasn't aware I'd been sneaking. Thought I'd just come over and say hi to start the day, but I will certainly watch that in the future. I'd appreciate it, though, if you'd take a little more respectful tone. Remember who the boss is."

"Over there you're the boss. This is my own turf over here."

"Thanks for straightening that out, pilgrim. Got any other tips for a fella who can't seem to do anything right?"

"Can't think of any right now. See you in a few minutes."

Over in Bax's barn, Ruth and Dulcie were up and at it. I heard the coffeepot perking as I knocked on the open tack-room door. "Want an egg sandwich?" Ruth said.

"Sure. Two with their eyes closed."

"Mayonnaise?"

"You bet."

She plopped two more eggs onto her hot-plate. The three of us sat around for a few minutes, eating our shedrow sandwiches and sipping our coffee until Rigger got there. The morning opened like a glorious picture book, the sun streaked down the mountain range in the east as the work began. I rolled under the webbing and began tending my first horse: the mucking, the hauling, the dumping; all the glamour stuff that started each day. Suddenly I felt a grip on my shoulder as I came back into the shedrow from the muck bin; I turned quickly and there was Bax, grinning in my face. "Hey, Janeway," he said in his cool voice, almost melodic. "Glad you're still with us, buddy. I just knew you were gonna be a good one." Then he disappeared into his morning, out to the track with Rigger. He worked straight through and we all worked with him, at his pace. He left us as usual as soon as the work was done, saying nothing more to anyone.

I went downtown and checked that thrift store the moment it opened, but of course my MacDonald was gone. I touched the inch-wide gap where it had been and I swear it felt warm.

30

The craziness stretched across the day. I found three dead mice in my shedrow, at the door of my tack room. One had a string tied around its neck. I remembered Bax had claimed to be appalled by death, a guy who would never touch a dead mouse, but I had only his word for that. Maybe he had been yanking my chain then, maybe he was the exact opposite. At noon I was called to the stable gate for a telephone message. I expected something from Sandy, but when I called the number it rang at a local funeral home.

When I returned to Bax's barn he asked how I was doing. "I want you to be happy here, Janeway," he said. "By God, I'm going to steal you away from Sandy."

"Oh, Bax, I am delirious with joy," I said, and he roared laughter all the way down the shedrow. In the distance I heard him saying, "Hey, Ruthie, Dulcie, let me tell you what that goddam Janeway said . . ."

It wasn't that funny, Bax. But I heard the girls laughing anyway.

He hung around all day. I heard Dulcie and Ruth talking when he made a coffee run up to the kitchen. Ruth was puzzled and a little annoyed. "What's going on with Bax?" she said. "He's acting keyed-up and weird as hell today." Dulcie laughed and said maybe this was the beginning of one of his mood swings. "Well, I hope not," Ruth said. "This job is tough enough without having him breathing down my neck in the off-hours." She was rubbing six, which I had discovered was truly a helluva workload, and with all that she was normally a tireless and cheerful worker. We did a light mucking at noon: Bax returned in half an hour, walked along the shedrow, and looked in on each of his horses. A few minutes later Damon and Junior arrived. I was in my gray's stall brushing out his mane and I heard Junior first, talking to one of the girls. "How'd you like to rub two more?" he said, and the two of them laughed at the joke. "These are two damn great ginneys you got here, Bax," Junior said, but he got nothing for his trouble.

This is the kind of man Baxter Geiger was. He was spacey, that was already obvious. I didn't know what he had, maybe a textbook case of attention deficit disorder, maybe something much worse than that, but today he was clearly unclear. He would focus intently to the exclusion of everything else around him, then he'd snap back in an instant, refocus on his original point, and become annoyed with everyone around him who had missed some vital piece of it. At the moment he looked alternately spacey and riveted to what was happening. He had told Junior nothing about my being there, and didn't until the moment when we all met face-to-face. He passed my stall and quietly said, "Come on out here," and I followed him up the shedrow to the tack room at the end. "Hey, boys," he said loudly, "here's a friend of yours," and Junior stepped out and stopped in his tracks.

"The hell you doin' here?"

I smiled and said, "Same old stuff, Junior. Muckin' and haulin'."

Junior looked at Bax. "You know who this is?"

"Junior, I know who everybody is," Bax said.

Damon came to the door. "What's this?" he said, beginning to bristle.

"Do I answer that, Bax, or do you?" I said.

"Oh hell, you do it."

"I am a man of many faces," I said, deadpan. "I'm the guy who will rub your horses, I will muck your stalls, and all for free. I am also the guy who's looking for a killer, and if that happens to be you, Damon, I will hang you so far out to dry your ass will have two new cracks in it."

Bax laughed like mad: he doubled over and slapped his knees with both hands.

"That's it, you're out of here," Damon said. "We don't need this shit."

"I think you're forgetting whose shedrow this is," Bax said, still laughing. "I'm the one over here who gets to decide just what shit we need or do not need."

"I said get rid of him," Damon said, and Bax's smile did a slow fade.

"I mean it, Bax," Damon said. "He's in here under false pretenses. If I report him you know they'll deep-six his ass out of here."

"And if you do that," Bax said, "I'll pull *our* horses out of this here race meet, and you boys can pack both of *your* asses back to Idaho."

"Don't you threaten me," Damon said.

"That's not a threat, asshole, that's a promise."

"You can't do anything without going

through God and the executor all over again."

"Don't push it, Damon," Junior said.

"I'm not taking orders from you either," Damon said.

"Oh *yes,* you are," Bax said. "You're so used to having everything your way, but it ain't gonna be like that this time. You're taking orders from every damn body, and if I want Janeway, you'd better not mess him over."

"Yeah," I said. Couldn't help myself, then almost died laughing with Bax, who was doubled over again, convulsed. From a distance the girls were watching and struggling not to laugh as well.

"You crazy prick," Damon said, and he stalked out.

Bax sagged to the ground laughing. He pointed at me and yelled, *"Yeah!"*

I gave him a hand up, but then he yelled *"Yeah!"* and it all began again.

He yelled across the shedrow. "Did you hear that, Ruthie? Yeah! Goddam, I like you, Janeway! Where the hell did the attitude come from?"

"It comes easy when you've got nothing to lose."

That night Bax came down late, around ten

o'clock. Ruth was strumming a guitar and singing softly in a high, lovely voice. Suddenly there was Bax, standing in the tow ring like a statue. But when you looked at him it was impossible to say how long he had been there: It might not have been suddenly at all. Ruth stopped playing and almost dropped her guitar. "Jesus, Bax!"

Bax came into the shedrow. Gone was the hilarity of the afternoon: Now he was somber, almost angry-looking. "Take a walk with me, Janeway."

We walked out toward the darkened racetrack.

"We sure put that bastard Damon in his place today," he said. "That was great."

But he wasn't laughing now. The happy hour was in the distant past.

We walked a few steps, then he said, "I still want to know what you're cookin' up with Martha. And where the hell is she?"

"I believe she's out of touch."

"The hell does that mean, out of touch?"

"I think it means she doesn't want to talk to you anymore."

"She's nuts. You know what she told me? You got any idea what she thinks?"

"Why don't you tell me?"

"Goddam woman says I killed Candice. She thinks I blew my own brother's brains out. But of course you knew that, I'm sure she's already told you."

"So did you? Kill Candice?"

"Hell no! Jesus, you got a nerve asking me something like that with a straight face."

"You know where she'd get that idea?"

"I know exactly where she got it."

"Want to share it with an interested party?"

"She overheard me talking screwy to one of my horses years ago."

"What'd you say?"

"That horse refused to run in the mud. I said I oughta put the son of a bitch in the ground. Said I'd put him where I put Candice."

"And you don't see why that would bother her?"

"Look, it was just me being me. I don't treat my horses like that, I was putting on a show for Martha. Can't you understand that?"

"It wasn't funny, Bax."

"Well, that's too damn bad, that's how I am sometime. She was a screwy bitch and I wanted to rattle her cage. But then she wouldn't let it go, she kept looking at me like I was some kind of monster, and after a while it was almost a game, seeing how long it could go on."

He took a deep breath. "Now I'm getting real tired of it. So listen, Janeway, and maybe some things will clear themselves up. I did put Candice in the ground. I was one of her pallbearers, for Christ's sake. Now what do you want to make out of that? Tell Martha that when you see her. Tell her I won't kill her."

Then he smiled in the moonlight and said, "Not today, anyway."

We looked at each other for a quiet minute.

"How could I?" he said. "I don't know where she is."

31

Sometimes awareness comes slowly in a murder case; sometimes it rises up suddenly and knocks you flat. Sometimes you get an idea and you go with that; sometimes you're actually right. One of the biggest burdens on a working cop comes when he knows something in his gut and then must get the proof and do it by the rules. I didn't have that problem anymore, but the guesswork was the same. If you're wrong you do what I told Sharon many days ago, you drop back and punt. However it happens, the idea is the thing while it's hot, and it changes the complexion of everything. I hadn't had many moments of awareness in the Candice case: I had been too busy getting myself into the racetrack, staying there, surviving two attempts on my own life, and talking with old railbirds who remembered the days of Geiger. The key was finding out who had been close enough to tamper with her food and angry enough to do it. Awareness came slowly the next morning, almost before I was awake. I must have been running things through my mind in my sleep, because I woke up strongly believing two or three things that I had only held as possibles or probables before.

Baxter was crazy. His lunacy wasn't an act.

He was probably certifiable.

But he hadn't done it.

His explanation of what had happened seemed crazily consistent in the early morning. If I was right about that, Martha would be heartbroken.

I began to narrow it down in other ways. If not Bax, who? Somebody who had been much closer than the brothers, someone who was Candice's little secret: a fling almost unknown in her lifetime but a man known now, perhaps in a completely different context.

Somebody who's right under your stupid eyes, Janeway.

Maybe not her first real fling, but certainly her last.

A bookman, not a horseman.

But he had killed Candice for some personal reason, unrelated to books, and then, being the book freak he was, he had begun to plunder her library.

He had been getting Cameron to lift them when Cameron had access to the house. He himself had certainly been in that book room but never alone, not often enough or long enough to steal them on his own, or to do much more than remember certain titles and where they were. But he was a bookman, able to vividly remember and burn into his mind a few cherry things in a sea of things that might be far greater, able to reconstruct an accurate but scattered list of items to get.

Why leave the one when there's something of greater value right there on the same shelf? That question rang again in my head and now I came up with two possible answers: Either he had been sucking up information so quickly he was almost drunk with it and hoped to hell he could remember it later — or he was truly a freaky, bizarre collector, after certain things because they had deep personal significance, probably from his childhood.

In either case he needed a cheap replacement for every book he had Cameron take — early printings, reprints with some age on them — that would look like real items to a casual browser.

He hadn't sold any of them publicly.

These were memorable, unforgettable, once-in-a-lifetime items, but neither Erin's checks nor my own had turned up any of Candice's books in bookstores anywhere. It was hardly a perfect check we had run, but if they had been sold to a dealer, even years ago, wasn't there at least a fair chance we'd have heard something?

Why had he killed her? Murder is a drastic act, almost guaranteed to alter your outlook. Killing Candice pushed him on that road to madness.

Maybe she saw the madness there and she intended to leave him.

Not because of the books at all.

He didn't kill her for her books.

He couldn't have, because her death removed him from what little access he'd had.

The books were only what started it.

Sometimes an ordinary man turns psychotic by degrees. The first time he kills, the consequences are deep, profound, and on some people they have a spiraling effect. Time passes — in this case years. His crime works on him around the clock. He sees Candice everywhere. The bookwoman haunts his dreams and maybe his waking life as well.

By now he may believe he is out of danger,

he'll never be caught, but the deed itself remains a crushing burden. If I really wanted to fantasize, I could picture a tortured man having conversations with Candice in his mind.

Suddenly he is threatened and the motive changes from greed to survival. He becomes frantic as he imagines his world unraveling.

Cameron threatens him. He kills Cameron.

I threaten him. He tries to kill me.

Tries again in a pitch-dark shedrow.

Whoever he is, he's got a lot to lose now.

The Mad Hatter, I thought without rhyme or reason.

There are people who would say catching him would be the best thing I could do for him. That's what he really wants, those people would say.

Uh-uh, I thought in the darkness. To him, getting caught is unthinkable. Now he'll kill anybody, everybody, to avoid that.

And whoever he is, he's not Bax.

"We've got a new horse for you," Ruth said. "Bax bought her yesterday from a trainer over in Barn 18. We had to get another stall, but we can pick her up this morning."

The trainer's name was Bowden: the horse was Miss Fritzi. "I'll bed her stall if you want to go pick her up," Ruth said.

I walked over with a lead shank and retrieved Miss Fritzi. I liked her right away. She had a personality like Pompeii Ruler's: easygoing, curious, affectionate. She was a brown filly, three years old with a white blaze on her head and two white feet. "Hey, sweetie," I said to her, and I led her back through the stable area. Ruth had her new home ready when we arrived.

"Sandy's here. He just came looking for you."

I told them it had been nice and thanked them for the experience.

"Come over and see us in the evenings if you want to," Dulcie said.

"I'll teach you how to play the guitar," Ruth said. "You can teach me how to sing."

We laughed and I hugged them.

Sandy had arrived at one-thirty with two fully loaded rigs, and I pitched in with the unloading. They had brought three ginneys from Barbara's farm, and we started the horses around the tow ring to give them some movement after their long, confining truck trip. A quick walk for each: Now there was much work to do and no time to talk about what to do later. Sandy asked where Bob was and I told him only that he had to go away and I would explain when we had more time. That made him unhappy but Sandy was born to be unhappy and I didn't care. I wasn't about to tell him where Bob was, now or later.

For two hours we were all engaged with busywork: unloading tack, setting up the room that would be used as Sandy's office, staking out the rooms where we'd each sleep, bringing in the rollaway beds and the tables and chairs. There was no time yet even for meeting the crew. Sandy went looking for two more hands, a hot walker and another ginney, and he returned with the ginney, a sour-looking superior bastard who I guessed wouldn't be with us long. We put up a canvas cover on the front of the shedrow, which would keep our horses cool during the hot part of the day and keep our business private all the time. The canvas was done up with Barbara's colors, red and white, and a logo with her initials in big letters. By feeding time we had transformed my dead shedrow into a place bustling with life. I felt better already.

Barbara drove up at four in her year-old Cadillac. She parked at the end of the barn and walked along looking at her horses. We had fifteen head counting the filly Sandy had brought down from his own stable for Bob to rub. "I'll take her in Bob's place if you want," I said. "You could hold his job open till we see what's what." I could see he was frustrated and annoyed but Sandy was born frustrated, and annoyance was his copilot. We would have some things to discuss after we got up and running: maybe later tonight. We did have a tense, caustic conversation in his office.

"So you're rubbing horses now? Where'd you learn that?"

"I did a few for Bax before you got here, when I had nothing else to do."

He didn't like that either. You get so you can tell with a guy, and I hadn't done much that was right in Sandy's eyes since I'd joined him at Golden Gate. He had gone from cold to lukewarm but now he was cold again, and I still had no illusions that I was becoming his main man. "I like new people to learn things my way," he said. I told him I could still learn it his way, but at least for now I knew a cooler from a muck sack; for the moment I could take up some slack and rub four in a pinch. Later I'd tell him not to forget why I was really here. *So fire me, Sandy,* I thought: *I'll have another job with Baxter or somebody else by tomorrow morning.* I watched him walk away and I thought, *There goes a puzzlement, a helluva strange and moody guy.*

I did up some horses: three ankles that Sandy wanted to brush with some solution and leave wrapped overnight. He came along and made me do it again, his way. He came around again and checked my progress, nodded curtly, and moved on, but if there was any difference between what he showed me and what I had learned from Ruth, I couldn't see it. I did it his way. Good judgment prevented me from breaking into the Sinatra song in full voice, there in my stall. Barbara walked up behind me and said, "Hey, Cliff, you're doing great," and in the same moment I saw a shadow pass in the shedrow behind her. I looked up in time to see her husband go by. Charlie. Our eyes met for less than two seconds: Then he turned away and left us there.

If I didn't know better, he'd be a candidate.

Hell, I *didn't* know better.

Strange fellow. Another puzzlement. He talks but he doesn't talk. Never heard him speak. Why is that? What the hell's wrong with him? Apparently he talks to others, not to me. *Maybe it's a case of hate at first sight.*

I decided to get right up in his face and say hi the next time I saw him. But he disappeared and I lost him in the crush of work. I didn't see Barbara leave at all; I just knew at some point that she had.

Now I focused on Charlie. He was the right age and he sure did seem like a cracked prism, a term that happened to fit him perfectly. I didn't know why but I thought it did. I didn't know where the hell he was going when he ran off like that, or what he did, why he was here, or what his business was. Maybe he was a high-class bookie selling insider stuff to some gambling syndicate. All I really knew was that he disappeared immediately whenever they arrived. Barbara always had to go hunt him down when she was ready to leave and she laughed about it good-naturedly, but I could see she was annoyed. On this particular day I heard her shout, "Charlie! Charlie, goddammit, where the hell is that man?" and one of her ginneys told her he had seen Charlie hurrying down the shedrow in the barn across the way. That had been two hours ago, time enough for Charlie to burrow into Fort Knox, steal the national gold supply, round up a herd of horses, and apply for Martha's old job in the racetrack kitchen.

I called Idaho after we got set up and I talked to Erin. "Everything's fine up here," she said. "We're all getting along famously in your absence. How's your madman doing?"

I told her Bax was still a suspect but had been downgraded to lukewarm.

"So where does that leave you?"

"Scrounging for a new leading man. How about you, really? How's your mental health?"

"I may go back to Denver after all."

"Mucking stalls isn't quite your cup of tea after all."

"It's been good, grand actually, a real break from my daily grind, and I love Sharon. But somebody's got to make some money."

I sensed growing discontent and I told her so. "What's up?" I said into the silence.

"I think we have some things to discuss."

"Issues."

She said nothing for a moment, but I had sensed as much. She had never been quite the same since we'd had that other brush with madness over in Paradise. She had come so *damned* near death and that kind of experience will change a person's mindset. She still had buckets of nerve, but things were not working out quite as we had envisioned that first night when she came into my bookstore. "This is probably not something we want to do on the phone," she said. "But we do need to talk."

"Give me a hint, so my subconscious can be working on it till I see you again."

"Oh, it's the same old stuff. We made some big and glorious plans for our life together in books. I still think it would be a great life, except for one tiny thing. You don't really want it. It took me a while to understand that."

I didn't know what to say, probably because I was afraid she was right.

"I'm changing you, Cliff, not the other way around. You're becoming tentative, not the charge-into-hell, damn-the-torpedoes, full-speed-ahead rover boy you were when we met."

Funny: I had had that thought myself.

"What you really want is to be a cop again," she said.

"Well, you don't have to worry about that. It'll never happen."

"Oh my dear, it *has* happened. You're never going to be a bookman in that upper tier; you don't have it in you. You want to be a cop; you're still a cop at heart. Correct me if I'm wrong, break in at any time with challenges or interrogatories; beg to differ to your heart's content. But then be honest with yourself."

The longest silence in the universe followed this defining statement. "Damn, Erin, this sounds like you're giving me the old heave-ho."

"I'm not." She sighed. "Really, I'm not. But I am asking you to take another look at it."

"Okay, that didn't take long. Now what?"

"Don't be a wise guy."

"Hey, wasn't it you who pushed me this way? Yes, I believe that was you. Something about me becoming the book cop."

"I only want you to do what you want. If I know nothing else about you, I do know this — you will never be content just running a bookstore on East Colfax, and you don't want anything higher than that from the book world. It's really not you who's changing, it's me. I guess two crazy people in a row will have that effect."

"Come on, Erin, they're not all going to be crazy."

"If there's a madman anywhere you will leave no stone unturned in your effort to find him. And suddenly, for some strange and maybe unknowable reason, that world is losing its charm for me."

"So what do you want me to do?"

"Nothing now. Just think about it, and don't get yourself killed out there."

The second-longest silence now stretched

between us.

"I might change my thinking if you'd let me come back and help you," she said.

But no, that wasn't an option. No way.

32

Nightfall, and another duel of words with Sandy. He was there through the feeding hour: He supervised the cooking of the evening mash for the horses and stayed around to see how they ate up. I left him alone for most of this time but I was always there as well — always in sight, always an irritant, always waiting. At seven o'clock he said good night and walked away, but I followed him out to his car and caught him just as he opened the door.

"Hey, Sandy. Got a minute?"

"No, I don't. It's been a long day."

"What can you tell me about Ms. Patterson's husband?"

"Charlie? Nothing, why?"

"I'm just finding him a little strange is all."

"What the hell's that supposed to mean?"

"It doesn't mean anything, Sandy. Not yet."

"What's *that* supposed to mean? Listen, I

don't want you bothering him. Either of them, is that clear? I don't need to tell you, she is very important to me in the scheme of things."

"Who is he, Sandy? How long have they been together?"

"You're not listening to me, Janeway. That's a bad habit you've got."

"It tends to happen when I encounter resistance without reason."

"I don't need any reasons. This is my stable and I am ordering you here and now, you leave Charlie alone."

"Is Patterson his last name?"

"It's *her* name, for Christ's sake. She's like a lot of rich women, she goes by her own name."

"What's his?"

"I don't know. What the hell are you looking for?"

"I told you that the first day I met you. It hasn't changed since then."

"You are going to cost me plenty if you keep on this way. I can't believe you're actually thinking of talking to Charlie about all this foolishness."

"It's not foolishness and I am going to talk to him."

"The hell you are. You can get your stuff together and get out of here right now."

"I can do that. But I'm still going to talk to him."

"I wish to Christ I'd never met you," he said. "You've been nothing but trouble."

"I'm sorry, Sandy, I truly am. But these things go where they go."

"You're not sorry about anything; you don't give a damn what happens to me. You don't care about anything and you're willing to embarrass everybody with this crazy business."

"I'd rather not do that, but if I have to . . ."

I think that was the moment when he finally realized he had never had the upper hand with me. He couldn't order me to behave; he couldn't tell me to get lost or do anything. I saw his jaw tremble and I understood then how desperately he wanted Barbara's horses and what he'd suffer to keep them. He would never be the boss: She was. He was only her latest in a long line of trainers and he'd be gone too; the first time he said or did something she found offensive he'd be out of here. And Barbara blew with the wind, there was no telling what might offend her. I was her pet of the month: Fire me and explain that to Barbara. I didn't know this for a fact but tonight I'd put money on it.

"Don't do this," he said, and my
went up.

He said, "What the hell have I ev
to you?" and it went up again.

I made a gentle hunkering-down g
If we were old pals that's what we'
hunker down in the shedrow, go out
beer, talk it over. But Sandy had never
a palsy guy. I said, "I don't want to h
you, Sandy, and I'll do my damnedest
to, but right now I need some answers ar
you're not helping me much."

"I don't know what you want from me."

"Tell me about Charlie."

"I don't know anything about Charlie.
He's her husband, that's all. I don't ask
personal stuff like that, and I have no idea
what you're getting at."

"How long have they been together?"

"How the hell do I know that?" The old
anger flashed but he covered it quickly.
"Forever," he said.

I waited for some kind of elaboration but
it was a long time coming.

"What are you thinking, Charlie's a
gigolo? Charlie's somebody who just
popped up and latched onto the rich
woman, is that what you think? And what
difference would that make anyway? It's

none of my business and it sure isn't any of yours."

"What does forever mean?"

"It means a helluva long time. I first met Barbara fifteen years ago. He was with her then, so it must've been true love."

"Was it fifteen years ago or longer?"

"I don't know, I didn't keep a stopwatch on him. What are you asking me?"

"If Charlie might have known Candice when he married Barbara."

"Stop doing this, Janeway. You are messing me up royally here."

"Was Charlie always weird?"

"What's weird? Hell, I never thought of him as weird."

"Come on, Sandy, the guy's a spook. If that man's not weird, we don't know the meaning of the word."

"He never was like that, take my word for it."

"Until when?"

"Until you came along."

33

I felt my heartbeat in the middle of the night and finally I had to admit it. Erin was right. This was what I had missed like crazy and would never get in kind from the book trade. The life-and-death rush. The slow, steady building of a case. The questioning, the tightening noose, the hot nights in the box downtown. Dueling with the professional badass, the frightened stonewaller, the killer with the sweet face. You get a hunch and you ask your questions until the hunch gets stronger, hardens, becomes a fact, and the perp cracks. I thought of Billy back at Sharon's farm — eager Billy, full of wide-eyed energy, pumped-up and wanting to be a cop. But I had not told him the whole truth, had I? I missed it so much more than I'd told him, far more than he would ever know.

So Barbara Patterson's man Charlie was now officially weird in my mental casebook.

Another fact: I had shaken him up without as much as a hello or a watch-where-you're-going-stupid passing between us. I didn't yet have Charlie's book connection but I knew in my heart it was there. As sure as God made apples, Charlie whatever-his-name-was was a bookman, not a horseman. I could see him in my mind, perusing a shelf of books, browsing in a bookstore, maybe my bookstore, reaching for the rarity, devouring Candice's books with his eyes, with his hands. I hadn't yet spoken to the man but I tasted blood. I couldn't hear him but I could see him, always in the book world.

The day dawned windy and gray. I was out with the crew, mucking my stalls, doing my chores, waiting for Sandy to come and do whatever he had to do. Waiting for Barbara and Charlie. This morning they were all later than usual. The sky was getting white over the mountains when we started walking the walkers, using Sandy's work chart for guidance, and Sandy arrived ten minutes later. He shuffled into the shedrow and passed just a few feet away, apparently without seeing me. He called for a red gelding named Fireball, one of mine as it turned out, and I led the horse into the shedrow and held him while Sandy put on the saddle and bridle. Still nothing. He looked right past me as he gave his boy a leg up; then they headed up toward the track. Nothing was said when they came back, either. The hot walker held the horse while I washed and scraped him and draped him with a cooler, and the business of the morning went on.

Barbara appeared suddenly, so late I had almost given her up for the day. No sign of Charlie yet, and in fact he didn't come at all. The morning faded away, Barbara sat in her director's chair while Sandy finished up on the track. I went about my work, watching them as closely as I could while trying to seem disinterested. They talked occasionally; Sandy said something and Barbara laughed politely and that was all. They went up to the kitchen at eleven and left together in the early afternoon.

Finally I began meeting the crew. I shook hands with the ginneys and the hot walker and then with the exercise boy, who was also hanging around watching. "Nice people," I said just for something to say, but it opened him up and led me into something else.

"How long you been working for Barbara?"

"Three years come summer."

"I sure like her," I said easily. "She seems

easy to work for."

"As long as you do your work and take care of her horses, Barbara'll love you to death."

"Can't ask for more than that. What about Charlie?"

"What about him?"

"I guess what I'm really asking is, how much authority does he have around here?"

"He make you nervous, does he?"

"A little. He never seems to have anything to say, so I just wondered."

"Well, here's a word to the wise between us girls. He's got plenty to say, and he's not shy about saying it. She's the boss but he's got her ear full time, so don't get on his bad side."

"So how do you not do that?"

"Don't say anything to him at all unless he speaks to you first. Answer his questions but don't volunteer much more than that. If there's a problem, refer him to Sandy."

"You know anything about him?"

"Nope. I don't ask and you shouldn't either. Just do your work."

The subject of Charlie came up one more time. During the afternoon feeding I overheard some talk in the shedrow. Sandy was consulting a man I had never seen, a vet, I gathered from their conversation. One of

Barbara's horses had a history of sore knees. The horse had been on butazolidin up at the farm, his ginney said, and the vet was offering his advice. Sandy said, "I want to talk to Barbara first and get a more detailed history. She's taking her husband to the airport tonight, but she'll be here in the morning. Can you come back?"

The vet could come back tomorrow. More to the point, Charlie was gone.

Where had he gone?

Anywhere, I thought, to get away from me.

But why would he do that when I'm such a cuddly, lovable bastard?

Now there was nothing much to do till Charlie came back and no telling when that might be. In fact Charlie might not come back at all, so that night I thought the hell with it and I had my way with the crew. I wasn't worried now about offending people with my nosiness, I just went ahead and got as nosy as I needed to be. The exercise boy wasn't staying on the racetrack: he had a young wife and a small apartment in Arcadia, so my questions at least hit fresh ears. The ginneys with one exception were like employees everywhere: Gossip was a way of life with them. I tried to back into things with topics of benign interest. I asked about

Barbara's farm and learned that it was a hundred-acre spread up north. They all worked up there and came down to the races whenever Barbara did. They all seemed to like her. She had gone through a number of trainers, that was true, but except for one crew she fired long ago, with her hands she was easy. I thought of Candice's dad with his place in New York and I commented how nice it must be to have money, hoping that one thing would lead to another. The one older guy stood apart and regarded us with a disgusted look. "She's got a right to demand things of her trainer," he did say at one point. "She's paying him plenty, so she's damn well got a right. Look, let's knock off the bullshit, okay?"

But bullshit unleashed can be hard to contain, and slowly it crept back into the talk. I was glad when the old guy left us and retired to his own tack room, gladder yet that it was way down at the end of the shed-row. Now I asked about Charlie. Just in the spirit of getting stuff right, I said; just because I didn't want to get off on the wrong foot. Now a different Charlie seemed to emerge. One man thought he was a nonentity. He talked a lot; he schmoozed with the ginneys and occasionally when they won one he was the dispenser of tips. He

loved to sit on the Cadillac and gab while
he handed out those big bills: more than
Sandy's tips at Golden Gate, these were
fifty-dollar bills, and the general feeling was,
they didn't give a damn about money,
Barbara and Charlie: they lived for the moment and always had. It was hard to get off
on the wrong foot with Charlie. But make
no mistake, in her shedrow Barbara was the
man. She had her own trainer's license; did
I know that? No, I did not. She wasn't
interested in actually training the horses
herself, but on some tracks even owners
were not allowed backside without their
trainer along and she had no patience with
that.

I kept it going. I was asking as a greenhorn, and they all wanted to dispense
knowledge.

"Charlie's a great guy, you know," one of
them said.

"How so?" I asked with keen interest.

"He just loves to throw money around. If
you ever get a chance to help him, Jesus, do
it. He tips like a wild-eyed son of a bitch."

"Help him do what?"

"Move his books," the guy said, and I felt
my heart turn over one more time.

"What books?"

"Oh hell." The guy rolled his eyes. "Just

bring a strong back."

"Charlie's got more books than the freakin' Glendale Public Library," another said.

"He's not kidding," said the first guy. "When it comes to books, Charlie's an animal."

"He's got three houses, all full of goddam books."

"At least three. You've never seen anything like it in your life."

"Books stacked up from floor to ceiling. He's got 'em in fifty-gallon barrels, piled on top of each other to the rafters."

"Books up the kazoo."

"I asked him one time if he'd read them all and he just looked at me like I was the crazy one. But he gave me three hundred that day, just for doing the donkey work. So don't say anything bad about Charlie, not to me."

I laughed with them and talked some more, and at some point I worked things around to Charlie again: Charlie and his books.

"Did any of you notice what kind of books these were?"

"Hell no, who cares?"

But the other guy said, "I'll tell you one

thing, there ain't nothing special about 'em."

"They're not pretty books," I said.

"Not so you can tell it. Textbooks, crummy old storybooks, everything under the sun except comic books."

"Anything you can put between hard covers," the first guy said.

That night I knew I'd have a hard time sleeping. I walked out to the telephone and called Erin. They were all sitting around in Sharon's living room: Bob, Louie, Rosemary, Lillian, Sharon, Martha, and Billy. Laughing and talking. Swapping old war stories. "What's up?" Erin said in my ear. I told her things were looking up. "Today I think I found my bibliomaniac."

34

But now where had he gone? I had a sinking feeling that I had seen the last of Charlie: He had a make on me, he knew I had
one on him, and he had taken flight. *There's
a reason why he's acting this way and I'm a
dummy for not seeing it,* I thought. Never
mind his guilt or innocence: there's another
reason, something he can't hide forever.
Maybe he thought I had seen him — that
was a strong possibility. Somehow in the
black shedrow I'd had a chance to see his
face. I missed it but he doesn't know that
so he's gone now. Where would he go and
how could I find out? Back to Barbara's
farm would be my first guess, but no sure
thing. Where else would be anybody's guess.

Only Barbara knew for sure, so I would
have to ask Barbara.

I took a deep breath. I was about to louse
up Sandy's world and I knew it, but if Charlie was my cracked prism the stakes were

501

too high to pussyfoot around with him.

The workday began. This morning Barbara arrived first. I had seen her often
enough to know she was not a morning
person, so I didn't attach any significance
to her mood. She walked glassy-eyed along
the shedrow, not speaking to any of us. She
did beg a cup of java from the ginneys and
she sat in her chair apart from everyone,
sipping it from a Styrofoam cup. *This was
the time,* I thought. I actually took a step in
her direction, but then Sandy arrived and it
wasn't the time at all. I had to feel my way
with both of them.

I went mindlessly through my chores,
mucking my stalls, leading my horses out
for Sandy to saddle. Now the ramifications
rose up from nowhere. What would the most
likely result be of breaking it on her suddenly, without warning? Would she be
angry, amused, defensive, or wary, and what
would she do about it? I didn't know her
well enough, I had no idea what her personal relationship was with Charlie so I
couldn't say, but I didn't think she'd be
amused. Whatever I did, I had to figure the
result was going to be permanent. I might
well lose my access to the racetrack, so I
had to make this shot count. But win or
lose, I had to make a move.

I made it that morning.

"Hey, Barbara."

She blinked as if she'd never seen me before that moment. She squinted at me in the sunlight, and in that first few seconds I couldn't tell what her reaction would be. I had followed her and caught her at her apartment, in a swanky-looking building not far from the track, but far enough, unless Sandy also put in an appearance.

"Cliff," she said, smiling pleasantly. "What on earth are you doing here?"

"I was wondering if we could talk for a few minutes."

Now she was wary, understandably so. The smile faded and she said, "Look, if it's a job-related thing, you really ought to go through Sandy."

"It's not. It's personal."

I saw in her eyes the jumble of questions. What the hell could we have to talk about? What kind of personal discussion could even a lucky stablehand have with her? How did I know where she lived? My status with her was suddenly shaky.

"I don't think so," she said and the air got frigid. "Talk to Sandy."

"I can't. He doesn't know about this."

"And I do?" She looked at me closer now

— took a step my way and said, "I don't like the sound of this."

Wait till I spring it on you, I thought: *see how you like it then.* In that moment I looked for inspiration and there was none: I was flying by the seat of my pants. I said, "It's about Charlie and his books," and she almost smiled again. "All right, come inside," she said, and we stepped into her world, her home away from home.

It was a very nice world, an elegant apartment with a big-screen TV and what looked to be an expensive sound system, a bow window that looked over a garden, and a well-stocked liquor cabinet. She gestured to a chair and I sat while she put on a kettle of water. "You want some tea?" she said, and I couldn't think of anything I wanted less than that barf-inducing substitute for coffee but I said, "Love some," and I prepared to gag it down. We waited while she put the stuff out to steep. "This is really a special tea, hard to get over here," she said. "I hope you'll like it." I lied like sixty and said I was sure I would, and in fact the tea surprised me by being drinkable and almost good. We settled in our chairs and she said, "Okay, what's it all about?"

Before I could tell her, she said, "I'm sure you know Sandy will be very unhappy if he hears about this."

Not as unhappy as he's going to be later, I thought. "I should've seen him first."

"You probably should've. But I won't tell him, if you've got a good reason for coming around behind his back."

"I'm a book dealer in my other life," I said.

"How interesting. And now a light begins to dawn. So where do you have your other life and what are you doing here?"

"I got burned out. Hey, that happens even in something as fascinating as the book world."

"Oh, I can understand that."

"When I was a kid I loved horses. Read the *Black Stallion* books, got hooked."

"I did too," she said. "I was never the same after that."

"That's how I got on the racetrack."

"And then you heard about Charlie."

I nodded. "All I wanted to do after that was talk to Charlie about his books."

"I'm sure he'd love to show 'em to you. But I don't think they're for sale."

"I just wanted to see them, and I didn't know if Charlie was coming back."

"And you couldn't stand the thought of all those books just lying out there."

"No," I said.

"Well, I don't think he's coming back. Not

for a while, anyway."

"I heard he has several houses full of books."

She said, "Hmm"; then, after a long pause, "I have the feeling I should fire the whole bunch of you. Don't you know it's not polite to talk about your employer?"

"Hey, don't let me get the others in trouble. This is all my doing."

"I'll bet it is."

We looked at each other and in that moment she was an enigma, impossible to read. "I guess I can't help myself," I said. "I'm a bibliophile, just like Charlie."

"Oh God, not another one. What is it with these ratty goddam books that turns respectable men into . . . what would you say? How would you describe yourselves?"

"I don't know how to. I probably shouldn't have bothered you."

Then the smile was back. "Actually, I think Charlie would rather enjoy talking to you. He comes racing with me but his heart's never been in it. He's never really happy unless he's mucking around in a new stash of old books."

I nodded.

"This makes perfect sense to you, does it?"

"Yeah," I said simply, in a very small voice.

"You're not a book *dealer* at all, are you? You're like Charlie: You buy them but never sell them."

I shrugged pathetically and played that role. Now she'd either kick me out or open up.

She smiled and said, "Want some more tea?" and I took heart from that.

"Yeah, it's great."

She poured; I sipped. She said, "I've been trying to understand that man for years, and now look, you're another one. You come to me like this, knowing your job may be on the line, and all for a peek at my husband's books."

"What can I say?"

"You can start by admitting that you people are freaking nutso."

I gave her my best self-deprecating look.

"I wish I could understand why you do it: What there is about a bunch of silly books that makes your nuts bark?"

I laughed: It was a funny, unexpected line. "I don't know," I said, "but I'd sure love to talk to Charlie."

"I'll bet you would but he's out of touch now. Maybe when he comes back he'll see you. Do you think that'll do any good?"

"I don't know. What are you trying to do?"

"Put some sanity into the man, for God's

sake. But what good will you do, you're as crazy over these books as he is." She breathed deeply, a sigh of vast frustration. "Well, you're here now, you're the first one of these book freaks I've ever known other than Charlie. Are there many like you around?"

I shook my head.

"Damn, I hope not. Where does this come from? What causes it?"

"I don't know."

"I was hoping you could make me understand it, because in more than fifteen years with him I still don't get it. He's driving me crazy, you know. If we ever do split up, it'll be over these damned books. So you tell me, Cliff, what makes you guys tick? Just make me understand that and I promise I will make it well worth your time."

I finished off the tea.

"You can't, can you?" she said. "You're as crazy as he is."

She stirred on the couch. "I think you're gonna have to find work elsewhere."

I nodded, sadly I hoped.

"I liked you, Cliff, I really did. But now it would be a major-league distraction to have you around my shedrow."

"Maybe I could just work for Charlie," I said. "Just part time, here and there, you know, when he needs the help."

"Jesus, listen to yourself. I can't believe I thought you were so normal, and here you are spouting the same crazy stuff I've heard for years." She shook her head. "Nutso."

"I could help him."

"Or screw him up even more than he is now."

"I wouldn't charge him anything."

"You wouldn't charge him — Jesus, Mary, and Joseph, listen to you!" She rubbed her temples, tired of it all. "How could you help, by moving his books around? By telling him how great he is? How do you think that would help him? You'd just feed into everything that's wrong with him."

"When will he be back?"

She made a sad laughing sound, as if the world had suddenly become too much for her.

"Barbara? When can I see him?"

"Who the hell knows? He's gone away on one of his so-called book-buying trips. He said he was going to Seattle, but he doesn't even tell the truth about that now. I found out anyway, I saw his airline tickets. I dug through his underwear for the damn things, I rooted around through his dresser to find out, and that's what he's got me doing now, that's what he's turning me into."

She said "Seattle" again, with deep anger. "Seattle, my ass," she said. "He's not going to any damned Seattle, he's going to Idaho."

35

My flight from Salt Lake was two hours late and I got into Idaho Falls in the very early hours of the morning. I had a rental waiting at the airport: I shifted my bag into the trunk and checked to make sure everything was where it was supposed to be: my heart, my gut, my gun. Then I headed out on the road to the farm. I had declared the gun and sent it through with my luggage. Still there was red tape; still there were questions. Then there had been the long night in the air and now I was tired: not exactly the ideal circumstances to face a killer, but you do with what you're dealt in this business and I imagined I'd be wide awake when the moment came. I wasn't sure yet what moment was coming or when: All I really knew was that Charlie was on his way and so was I.

I pictured them all sitting up in the dark: Louie cradling the shotgun, Billy with his

.22, Bob somewhere nearby, and the ladies — Lillian, Sharon, Rosemary, Erin, and Martha — sitting together in the black corner of the room. On the face of it they had him seriously outnumbered, but he'd be running on high octane, he'd be frantic, he had killed and they had not, and they'd be nervous. I had to be careful not to get myself shot by friendly fire on my approach in the dark.

I had called the cops in Idaho. They had sent a pair of uniforms out to the farm and had warned Sharon that Charlie might be on his way. They were there for two hours but they couldn't do much more until he actually showed up. There were no outstanding warrants against this man; so far it was all fear of the unknown. Even if he did come to the farm he'd have to break some law before they could detain him. Their advice was to get out until they could all figure which way the wind was blowing.

"They don't understand why I can't go," Sharon said. "I've got horses to take care of. I can't just walk off and leave 'em here."

I talked to her twice en route — first from the L.A. airport and again from Salt Lake.

"I'm not leaving," she said again.

She said it had gone around the room like that.

"I'm not leavin' either," Louie said.

"I'm not going," Billy said.

"Well, I ain't goin' if you ain't," Rosemary said.

And so it went. Even Bob and Martha had decided to ride it out, whatever happened. At some point Erin had told them all that they had more than the horses to worry about. Charlie was a book freak. If he got desperate enough and angry enough he might torch the houses to get at the books. If he believed he was lost, they had to be prepared for anything.

They didn't want to take that seriously but I thought it was a real possibility. I knew a bit about bibliomania, and in the most extreme cases a biblioperp is like unhinged freaks everywhere: irrational, driven, super-focused on his goal, whatever that is.

We arranged a signal so they'd know it was me coming up on them: I'd hold my headlights steady on the front window and quickly flash my brights three times.

All was calm in Idaho. The world seemed peaceful on the brink of the new day, and that was all I knew for sure as I drove out to the farm.

The voice on the radio said today was December 10: only two weeks left till Christmas. The date rang a bell that had nothing to do with shopping or St. Nick, but I couldn't remember in my tired state what it was. This will all be history in a little while, I told myself: and yet I couldn't shake the feeling that I had taken a wrong turn somewhere. What a depressing thought: that I had leaped blindly into the friendly skies and the killer was still somewhere in California.

Or somewhere else.

The morning was black and clear with a bit of snow on the ground. Traffic was sparse.

I got to the farm at four forty-five.

I stopped at the fork in the road. Nothing doing back at the main house.

I pushed on to Sharon's. It was just as dark there but I expected that. I flashed my lights and all was well. The door opened and Louie stood framed there with his shotgun.

I parked out of sight behind the house and went inside.

Hugs and handshakes all around. Louie watched the road; Billy watched the back; and the rest of us sat at a roaring fireplace while the sun came up and pushed our demons away.

Now came the moments of self-doubt.

514

"What if he doesn't come?" Sharon said.

"Then I'll have to find out where he is."

"What if it turns out he's still in California?"

"We'll cross that bridge when we come to it."

"Would you go out there again?"

"If I have to. We'll see."

"I'm going outside," she said. "I've got chores."

"Give it another half hour. Let it get good and light, then I'll send Louie out with you."

The cops called. Just checking in, they said.

Sharon and Louie went out and did the chores. I couldn't go, couldn't take a chance he might see me before I saw him, but I sat at the window watching, just beyond the curtain, my gun on the cushion beside me. Erin and Rosemary got our breakfast casseroles ready. The timing was perfect: The food came out of the oven just as we got washed up and ready to eat it.

The day dragged. The cops called at ten and again at two. I talked to them at two.

"They don't think he's coming," Sharon said.

"Doesn't sound like it from the tone of the one guy. But they're good cops, they don't want to take any chances."

I talked to Bob. He was still taking a doubtful approach, but I could see the tension in his face. "Something's gonna happen, isn't it?" he said, and I told him yeah, maybe. "I think so," I said. I talked to Martha and told her again that she had done fine back at the racetrack. She shook her head and said, "I let him off the hook." She didn't believe me when I told her Bax hadn't done it. "Somehow he's pulled the wool over your eyes," she said. "He's good at that, he's like a magician." I talked to Louie and told him I was glad he was there, and I said the same to Billy later. "Just be careful with that gun, Billy," I said, and immediately regretted the preachy tone.

At some point Erin and I found time to talk. She sat beside me in the window well and said, "Why don't you get some sleep? I'll watch."

"I was dead tired a few hours ago. Now I'm wide awake."

"Just close your eyes. Lean on my shoulder. Sleep will come."

I did and sleep did come, but only for twenty minutes. I awoke with a jerk at three-thirty.

"It's okay," Erin said, putting a hand on my arm, but I was suddenly nervous in the pale afternoon.

"I can't believe we're doing this again," she said. "Not after the last time."

I had nothing to say to that. After a while she said, "You know sooner or later your luck will run out."

"Is that what you think it is, luck?"

"Oh, don't get your maleness all upset, I know how good you are. But do you think you're always going to be stronger, faster, smarter than the other guy?"

"I always have been."

"How many times did you get shot?" She sighed, knowing the answer. "Your back looks like a piece of the moon."

"I promise I won't get shot again. Not more than once or twice, anyway."

"All it takes is one. One who's better, luckier, or more devious. What's that old cowboy saying? Never was a horse that couldn't be rode, never was a man who couldn't be throwed."

"So what do you want me to do, walk out and leave them all here?"

"No, of course not. I'm just talking to hear my own voice, but that doesn't help, does it?"

"It does if you're trying to be annoying."

Eventually she got to her point. "I said I'd never do this; now here I am. Second-guessing you. Acting like a schoolgirl."

"That'll happen when you almost die trying."

Again I was impatient with her. What's your point, I wanted to say, but then she told me. "I don't want to do this anymore, Cliff. I want us to be normal."

"I've never been normal."

"I know you think you're playing that for laughs but it's not funny."

"What's funny is that you'd think I think that."

I wanted to say, What are the odds? What are the chances that we'd ever get another case like this? But what were the odds of a second one? If you play the odds often enough, you lose. It would be hard for her to believe at this moment, but not all or even a few bibliomaniacs become psychopaths. "So what do you want to do, bag it?" I said. "Call it a day, you and me?"

"Oh no. Oh God, no! It hurts me that you would even say that."

Then she said, after a long pause, "Is that what you want?"

"I want to be a cop again."

There it was, the one thing she couldn't tolerate.

"I love the book trade. But I still want to be a cop."

There it was, out in the open at last.

■ ■ ■ ■

The phone rang. Sharon answered in the kitchen.

"It's your friend Carroll Shaw from the Blakely Library," she said. "I forgot I've got an appointment with him. Made it weeks ago."

Suddenly the date crystallized and I remembered. "What'd you tell him?"

"This is not a good time. But he came all this way, what could I do?"

"When's he coming out?"

"He's downtown now. I told him to come on. Sooner the better, right?"

I rubbed my aching head. "You know this could take days. I'd love to meet him after all these years, it would be great to compare notes over your books, but this could take a long time. Damn, he should've called to confirm."

"I'll let him have a quick look and then tell him he'll have to come back. I'll fly him back at my expense."

"A quick look could take three days. He's a bibliographer, Sharon; he'll want to take extensive notes and shoot pictures. But give him a very quick look, for now. That's more than fair under the circumstances. We don't want him in the way when Charlie gets here."

I was fidgety as I waited for Carroll to arrive. I thought I had handled this case badly from the start. As a backstretch schmuck I had been much too tentative. Erin was right: I was suffocating under other people's rules and procedures. I had been too afraid of violating some kind of racetrack rule and getting kicked out, so I hadn't asked the right questions soon enough. I'd certainly have tumbled to Charlie much quicker, and once you have a guy in your sights you can always pry out the truth. Well, I knew the truth now, didn't I? Now to prove it, get us all out of here alive, and wing it with Erin back to Denver.

But things are never that simple.

Carroll arrived just before dusk. I saw him pull into the yard, his rental sporting a custom library plate, BLAKELY4, under his windshield. He was wearing a snazzy gray suit and a snap-brim gray hat. I was surprised at his dandylike appearance: Somehow I had always pictured him as a kind of roughneck like myself. Maybe that's why it had always been so easy to deal with him by phone: We talked the same language without the expensive shell of the Blakely

Library separating us. Now he was here and he walked quickly to the door, disappearing under the overhang. A few seconds later I heard him knock.

Sharon opened the door. I tucked my gun under the window cushions and started down to the front to finally meet him. I heard him come into the hall, his voice a room away. Then I saw him from a distance and I stopped in my tracks. There was something disturbingly familiar about him, and a fleeting impossible thought ran through my head. I stood still, looking through that hall into the front room.

"It's good to meet you at last," he said.

I knew that voice so well. So what was wrong with him?

Then he took off his hat and I could see his face.

Charlie's face.

I heard Erin come in. "Hi, Mr. Shaw," she said.

"Erin, what a pleasant surprise. I didn't know you'd be here."

It was Charlie, talking clearly now in Carroll Shaw's voice. Charlie, stripped of his weirdness, stripped all the way down to the weirdest part of him. Charlie the killer.

"I'm afraid I have some disappointing news for you," Sharon was saying. "Something else has just come up. I would normally never do this, but in this case it can't be helped."

"That is disappointing. I hope whatever it is, it's not serious."

"I'd call this fairly serious."

"Anything I can help with?"

"I doubt it, but thanks for asking."

"This is totally my fault," Charlie said. "I really should have called earlier. Do I at least get a little peek, or do you not have even that much time?"

Carroll, the soul of etiquette. Charlie, the considerate killer.

"I can give you a look," Sharon said. "How much can you do in one early evening?"

"Not nearly enough, if what Cliff tells me is true. But I'll take what I can get."

I didn't move — didn't want to attract his attention by even a breath or a bump.

"Well, then," Sharon said. "Do you want to go down now?"

They were coming my way. I stepped back against the wall. Only a shadow here to hide in: no nooks or crannies, no convenient wall of books. I stepped back, knowing it was neither deep enough nor dark enough; it was just what I had. I held myself still as death, knowing that could never be still enough, and then they came through the narrow passage and he was just a few feet away. He saw me first as a bad vision, a dream perhaps that had dogged him across the country and was now here to rise up and bugger him. If I had yelled *boo* at the top of my voice I think he might have passed out from fright. Unfortunately I didn't do that: I waited for him to make the connection himself. This took only a few seconds on the long end.

"Janeway," he said in a watery little-boy voice. "Jesus, what are you doing here?"

Sharon had stopped and waited for him at the end of the hall. He wavered. His eyes rolled back in his head. Softly, I said, "What do you think, Charlie? I hope we can . . ."

I never got to tell him what I was hoping. He screamed a long, mindless curse and brought out a small pearl-handled .32 and waved it in my face. But there was Billy, stepping out of the back room, forcing Charlie to retreat half a dozen steps away. Billy, forcing himself between us with my gun in his hand: Billy, in a textbook police stance, holding the gun out with both hands, yelling, "Freeze, motherfucker!" at the top of his lungs. But Charlie raised the gun and Billy shot him. He spun crazily and fell; his gun flew up and clattered violently off the ceiling, and Billy moved through the room, picked it up with a piece of cloth, and directed everybody to stay where they were. "I'd do what he says," I told Rosemary. "Right now he's in charge."

I looked in Billy's eyes and said, "Right now he's the man."

Then, when he was ready to give it up, I took my gun from his trembling fingers, hugged him tight, and told him I would always owe him for saving my ass.

36

The bullet had shattered his shoulder and blown a fist-sized chunk out of his back. For a while it was touch and go, but for an even longer time I knew only what the Idaho Falls cops released to the press.

The motive apparently was greed. Long ago, when he had access to the house, Cameron had begun lifting the books and selling them to Charlie. This all escalated to murder when Cameron wanted more money and threatened him. But as theories went, this had some holes in it. Erin and I groped our way through it on the flight back to get my car in L.A., and we were still talking it over with mixed results on the long drive to Colorado.

I tried to keep up with the case from Denver. Sharon sent me all the newspaper accounts and I did some research on my own. One of the arcane nicknames for Carroll, I discovered, is Charlie, and soon I was able to follow Candice's logic to Lewis Carroll, creator of the Mad Hatter.

I began writing a journal of the case, which I would deliver to Sharon when I had all my facts in order. Some of it was still speculation. I did know Barbara had helped him get into the Blakely and had shepherded his rapid advance. She had used her money and her position on the board in hopes he'd find real books a sane alternative to the crazy stuff he had hoarded for years.

Charlie had thrived in the Blakely and had soon become its rising star. This much had come out in the press. He had rare and wonderful books to donate, and a few of them still had the enigmatic Candice bookplate. He saw the library's collection as his. I can see him now, walking at night through that dark mausoleum of treasure, holding the key, glorying in his new acquisitions, gloating over what he had.

At the same time he went crazily on, hoarding thousands of junk books as Charlie, sucking them up by the tens of thousands, stashing them in houses, then in warehouses, until Barbara was driven almost crazy by his obsession. She thought she knew what he was up to, but storage lockers and duffel bags are still being found, stuffed with Charlie's books. The count will run into millions.

An ironic postscript: One day Sharon called me. "Junior wants me to ask you if you'll still do the appraisal on HR's books?"

I laughed out loud. "I'd rather have lung cancer than go back to work for Junior."

"Still, the estate's got to be settled. The appraisal's got to be done by someone we trust. This time I can make them pay you well."

"I don't think so, Sharon. I'll send him some names."

More than two months after he was shot, Charlie spoke his first words. Once they began the words gushed out of him.

"He wants to see you," said the man on the telephone.

I had to go, I still had a job unfinished. The Blakely was eager to cooperate: They offered to pick up my tab, however long it took to put things straight, but Sharon said no. "You work for me."

This wasn't the library's fault, she said. They were victims too.

Yeah, I thought. Victims like any library that's blinded by treasure and too willing to acquire it without getting all the provenance, all the proof of where it had been.

I left Denver in March, prepared to stay a month: more if I had to.

First I had to see Charlie. He held the answers to Sharon's books and until I talked to him I would never really know this case. By then I had read all the classic texts on bibliomania: If there are experts on such a bizarre topic, I suppose I was becoming one.

Still I had no real handle on extreme cases like Charlie. Maybe nobody does. Some people believe there is a mysterious current at work between a bibliomaniac and his stash of books, as if having them gives him an almost mystical connection to all the knowledge they contain. This empowers him: he absorbs it through his pores and into his heart and bones. He believes this without conscious thought, but the feeling builds as his books grow in number and depth. It feeds his spirit and makes him connect with untold thousands of scholars and writers he will never read.

They had Charlie in California by then, so I drove up to the hospital where he was being held. They showed me into a room where he sat in plain white clothes behind a wire screen. He sat up straight when I came in.

"Cliff!" he boomed.

As if we were old buddies. As if nothing

had happened.

We stood looking at each other a room apart, and I knew this was a man who would kill me in a heartbeat. I greeted him coolly. "Charlie," I said. He recoiled from the name as if I had slapped him. "Carroll's my name," he said. "You of all people should know that."

I pulled up a chair near the cage and we sat talking.

"Barbara's leaving me," he said.

Why did that not surprise me?

"Whatever happens, I'll have to go it alone."

What did he want from me? But I knew even then.

"Turns out she's just like all of them," he said. "In the end she's a taker."

"Is that what Candice was?"

"No!" He recoiled from the question, shriveling behind the wire cage and growing smaller for a moment. "Candice was the sweetest girl. Goddammit, you know better than that."

I shrugged an apology.

"I'm sure you've heard from others how wonderful Candice was."

I nodded.

"A finer woman never drew a breath of air."

"Then why did you do it?"

He shook his head vigorously and re-treated from the question. "Candice was a superb woman. I never would have hurt her. She was a lady."

She was the great love of his life. She was all he could think about from the first time he saw her. This went on for quite a while and his voice settled into a soft droning. An hour later I said, "Carroll," and he nodded. "I know," he said. "I know, I know."

We sat through several quiet minutes. Then he said, "I've got a deal for you. Something you can't refuse."

I put both hands in my pockets, a gesture that was lost on him.

"I've got a deal," he said again.

I nodded and he got to it in time, in his own way.

In exchange for certain favors, he would answer my questions. But I had to be will-ing to understand his side of it. I had to listen with an open mind.

I had conditions of my own. "I want a list, every book you ever got from Cameron, anything that might even remotely be con-nected to Candice."

That would be easy, he said: He remem-bered them all in detail, he knew each title intimately, and he had them all stored in one place in the library's new acquisitions room. I knew it would not be quite that simple: Many other books would have to be examined, but his list would be an essential starting point. And this is how, late that first afternoon, we began to talk.

I stayed there two days. And at night I studied his list and reconstructed what he'd said in my notebook. There was a sameness to it, a gush of words that amounted to a few important facts, the rest justification, babble, and occasionally the crazy hope that I would still be his bookscout when he got back to work at the library. "You always were my best pair of eyes, Cliff."

I tried to smile. Didn't quite make it.

"For what it's worth, you were the only one I could count on to buy me a book and I knew sight unseen that it would be a beauty."

"Trust goes a long way in this business, Carroll."

I was looking in his eyes when I said that, but he looked away.

"We'll do it again, you watch and see if we won't," he said. "When I get out of this goddam hole, we'll be the greatest team since Batman and what's-his-face."

"Robin," I said.

"Yeah." He laughed and finally, in that moment, Charlie fused into Carroll.

"You know I never meant to hurt anybody."

"Yeah, I know that."

That night I wrote his words in Sharon's journal. A short entry: two pages of dialogue.

You know I never meant to hurt anybody. Especially not Candice.

I loved her.

Why couldn't she understand that? All I ever wanted was for her to let me love her.

But as time went on, I could see I was losing her. What had started in such joy had become frightening to both of us. Maybe sometimes I did become too possessive but I was always afraid she would leave me. She was afraid as well, but of what?

Me? How could she be afraid of me? I only wanted what was best for her, always.

Always.

At least now she's beyond all that hurt. I gave her that. I set her free. Wherever she is, you can bet she's thanking me.

She was never happy.

Never.

Candice was born with a broken heart.

I could have helped her, but she said she was leaving me. On that last day I ground the

532

peanuts into a pulpy mush and worked it care-fully into her cereal. She was helpless after one bite.

I sat beside her and held her hand, and watched her die.

Then I cried. Don't suppose you'll under-stand that but I loved her. It's important that you understand how much I loved her. And she loved me too; I know she did. But she was mixed up. All her life she was tortured and confused.

Now you know what I did and why I did it. Don't forget your promise. Don't betray me.

She's better off, that's why I did it. I did it for her.

Because I loved her.

She's better off.

She's better . . .

. . . better . . . happier . . .

She is so much happier now.

I was at the Blakely four days. It's easy when you have a list and the books are all in one place, but I took my time and looked through the entire library anyway.

When I was satisfied I drove out to Golden Gate, where the spring season was going strong. I looked up Cappy Wilson and we had coffee in the kitchen.

Rick had died one morning in February.

"He just never got up," Cappy said. "The poor bastard never got out to work. What a sad way to end a sad life."

I felt deeply diminished by this news. "You did what you could for him, Cap," I said, but I knew how he felt.

Rick's spirit followed me across the desert.

I stopped in Idaho on the long trip home. Sharon was sitting on her porch half asleep when I pulled into the yard. I shut the car door and her eyes fluttered open; she smiled and began stirring on her chair.

She was alone. Martha had stayed with her three weeks and had reluctantly left for racetracks in Florida, where there wasn't much chance of running into people. "She doesn't ever want to see Baxter again after calling him a killer."

Bob and Louie had gone to Montana to pick up some sick horses. "I think Bob wants to stay here," Sharon said. "At least for a while."

"You're an easier boss than Sandy."

"Sandy turned out strange, didn't he?" she said. "He still hasn't called me."

"He's not going to, now."

"So what do you think? Is he my father?"

"There's no way to tell if he won't cooperate."

"The hell with him," she said, suddenly

534

angry. "He knows where I'm at."

A moment later: "I'm never gonna hear from him, am I?"

I shrugged. *Probably not.*

Sandy had returned to Golden Gate. He had run eight of Barbara's horses in Santa Anita stakes races and had done no better than one fading fourth-place finish. But the final blow had come when he entered his own horse in a $50,000 claimer and had won pulling up by twelve lengths. Barbara fired him loudly that same afternoon.

Sharon took this news with quiet amusement. "Junior and Damon aren't setting the world on fire either," she said. "Five starts, zilch to show."

"Time wounds all heels," I said and she laughed sadly.

"Here's a question for you," she said later. "What am I gonna do with Bob?"

"I don't know, Sharon. What do you want to do?"

"He's a good hand. Works hard. Likes it here." She closed her eyes and tilted her head back at the blue Idaho sky. "He's in love with me. A girl can tell."

"So where does that lead?"

"Not where he wants it to. He's way too young."

"He's not that young."

"How old do you think?"

"As a guess . . . mid-twenties maybe."

"Oh God," she said.

"Play it as it goes, Sharon. Be loose and see what happens. Since you asked."

I asked how Billy was doing.

"Fairly well, I think," she said. "One of these days he may show up on your doorstep."

"I can handle that. I've still got a few friends in the Denver cops and I'd like him to meet them. It's no slam-dunk, you still have to take the tests and do better than the other guys. That's life in the city."

She leaned over. "I'll bet you were a helluva cop, Janeway."

"I was pretty good," I said modestly. "But let's face it, this wasn't my greatest moment. This time I was way too slow on the uptake."

"You were quick enough when the chips were down."

"Thanks to Billy I'm here to tell about it."

She had a package for me. "Don't open it now. Wait till you get home and just accept it with my love and gratitude."

She brushed off my objections. "Accept it with grace or I swear I'll give it to Goodwill."

I thought there was a hint in that.

"Looks like books. Feels like books." I sniffed at the wrapping. "Smells like books."

"Just a few old things. Some second copies I had lying around."

I helped her with the chores, and that night I stashed my stuff in the tack room over the barn. We went to the Sandpiper for dinner and afterward she came over and we sat in the open loft and looked out over the road and talked.

She asked about Erin.

"I don't know what's going to happen," I said. "Right now there's something pretty deep that's dividing us."

"You're a magnet for killers. She doesn't like that."

"Yeah. It's hard to believe but she's lost her taste for it."

"Give this some serious thought, Cliff. She's a good woman."

"She's a very good woman. I just can't give her what she wants anymore."

"Your wants change when you reach a certain age, you need some peace and quiet. That's where Erin is now. She wants stability. At the same time, you are what you are. If you get too lonely, you can come up here and stay with me."

I slept alone in the tack room and struck out for Denver the next day. It was an all-day drive and I got home after dark. That night I opened Sharon's box and was floored at what she had given me. Inside was a note. *I may send you something else from time to time if you promise to keep happy. Love and thanks from Idaho.*

And that night, unable to sleep, I went out and drove the streets of Denver. It was a windy, rainy night along East Colfax. I went to my store and began working on my promise to Charlie. The next day I sent out a case of books. Junk fiction. Dupes. Second copies I had lying around. Third copies, fifth copies, old books, stuff that had been in the store forever — stuff I would never sell, but the beginning of an exciting new stash for Charlie.

The perfect gift for a bibliofreak.

ABOUT THE AUTHOR

John Dunning is the author of four previous novels in the Cliff Janeway series: *Booked to Die, The Bookman's Wake* — a *New York Times* Notable Book of 1995 — *The Bookman's Promise,* and most recently *The Sign of the Book.* An expert on rare and collectible books, he owned the Old Algonquin Bookstore in Denver for many years, and now does his bookselling online. He is also an expert on American radio history and the author of a novel, *Two O'Clock, Eastern Wartime,* about the radio world, as well as a nonfiction book, *On the Air: The Encyclopedia of Old-Time Radio.* He was for many years host of the weekly Denver radio show *Old Time Radio.* In the 1960s he worked as a ginney on the California racing circuit, at Bay Meadows, the state fair in Sacramento, and at Golden Gate Field and Santa Anita. John Dunning lives in Denver, Colorado.